Advance Praise for

NEVER WHISTLE AT NIGHT

"The combination of folklore and the travails of contemporary life is potent. Hard-edged and dread-inducing, *Never Whistle at Night* showcases major horror talent."   —Laird Barron, author of *The Wind Began to Howl*

"I've increasingly come to suspect that the best work in contemporary horror is being written by Indigenous writers, and *Never Whistle at Night* makes me certain of this. Consisting of more than two dozen stories by turns fierce and strange—sometimes about storytelling, sometimes political, sometimes just very, very unsettling—this is a deeply satisfying anthology."

—Brian Evenson, author of *The Glassy, Burning Floor of Hell*

"An extensive collection of Indigenous stories ranging from the humorous to the terrifying, this anthology is a must-read for everyone. Your new favorite author is absolutely in this book."

—Amina Akhtar, author of *Kismet*

"Melodious, haunting, and visceral, *Never Whistle at Night* enchants from the very start with fiery confidence and merciless ghosts. These are stories that dig their fingers inside you and carve something truly special. An absolute must-read."

—Hailey Piper, Bram Stoker Award–winning author of *Queen of Teeth*

NEVER WHISTLE AT NIGHT

NEVER WHISTLE AT NIGHT

AN INDIGENOUS DARK FICTION ANTHOLOGY

EDITED BY

SHANE HAWK & THEODORE C. VAN ALST JR.

VINTAGE BOOKS

A DIVISION OF PENGUIN RANDOM HOUSE LLC

NEW YORK

A VINTAGE BOOKS ORIGINAL 2023

Library of Congress Cataloging-in-Publication Data
Title: Never whistle at night : an Indigenous dark fiction anthology /
edited by Shane Hawk, Theodore C. Van Alst Jr.
Related Names: Hawk, Shane, editor. | Van Alst, Theodore C., [date] editor.
Description: First edition. | New York : Vintage Books, 2023.
Identifiers: LCCN 2023000271
Subjects: LCSH: Paranormal fiction—Indigenous authors. |
GSAFD: Paranormal fiction. | Short stories.
LC record available at https://lccn.loc.gov/2023000271

Vintage Books Trade Paperback ISBN: 978-0-593-46846-3
eBook ISBN: 978-0-593-46847-0

Book design by Christopher Zucker

vintagebooks.com

Printed in the United States of America
10 9 8 7 6

For Auntie Cheryl.
We miss you dearly. And to her
boys, Stohn and Landon. Love you.

—SHANE HAWK

For Amie, Emily, and Blue

—TED VAN ALST JR.

CONTENTS

FOREWORD

STEPHEN GRAHAM JONES

I can't deliver this as well as Joseph M. Marshall III did once upon a talk I went to—he's got that delivery that makes you *listen*—but I can rough it out, anyway: someone's driving an empty road . . . let's say this is the Dakotas. The Great Plains. All that grass, the land rolling up and down real slow. It's night, too—it's always night in these kinds of stories.

I forget the setup, but not the final image: These four dudes on horses, booking it from here to there. Say, blasting out of this copse of trees, diving for a coulee or something a couple hundred yards across the way, their chests to their horses' backs because you're less of a target that way. And this line between here and there, it takes them right through the edge of this driver's headlights.

"What?" I imagine this driver saying—I think Marshall was relaying a story he'd heard, not one he was in—and kind of letting their foot off the gas, so they can coast a bit, maybe convince themselves they're not seeing what they're pretty certainly seeing: four riders in traditional getup, on painted horses, going somewhere urgent at late thirty at night.

I'd probably take my foot off the accelerator as well, and lean forward shaking my head no, that this isn't really happening, that this can't be happening, or if it is, this has to be a joke, or some *Scooby-Doo* situation, or some kind of night shoot for a film.

The way Marshall told it, though, which I'm guessing is the way it was told to him, was that it most definitely was happening.

These riders were booking through that darkness, looking to duck into another.

Then, when it got to be time for them to cross the road this car was making its way down—and this was the part I, leaned forward in my auditorium seat to soak every bit of this in, was worried about, since horseshoes on blacktop can be ice skates, especially at speed—instead of thundering up and over, these horses, and their riders, they slipped *through* the road, and then . . .

Okay, I don't remember the rest.

My guess is that those riders got where they were going, blipped away, and maybe the driver, or Marshall, for us, was able to cast them as players in this or that thing that happened a century and more ago, and knit it back to now.

Cool, great, wonderful.

What stories like this do for us is make the world just a smidge bigger, yes? We now have to expand the borders of the real, to allow for, say, two timelines to simultaneously exist. No, not just exist, but *intersect*.

To make that a horror story, though? To make it horror, then I think one of those riders needs to look back at the driver in that car, which would mean this is going a touch further than just "intersection." There's recognition, now. You, the driver, have been seen, and, who knows, maybe that means you're officially an interloper now, and that's when stories start to get complicated, and good.

So, to keep on with the horror version of this, the driver coasts past, audibly locks all four doors of their car, and then accelerates into the safe-safe night—only for a painted horse and rider to suddenly be standing in the road before them. Or maybe that driver, leaning down to dial a late-night show in on the AM, catches a shape in their rearview mirror: that painted rider is in their *back seat* now.

At which point we have to decide whether this driver's Native or not, yeah? If not, then, no, you don't want to see someone in traditional getup suddenly, and wrongly, in your back seat. Because you know some justice is probably coming for you. There's not a lot of room to swing a war club in the tight confines of a car. But I bet there's enough room.

If the driver *is* Native, though, then maybe this is a team-up? Maybe this is the origin story of the comic book drama about to spool out for fifty issues: you and this warrior from back-when, settling some certain scores.

That's not horror, though. That's fantasy.

No, for the horror version of this where the driver's Native, I think what they need to see in the rearview mirror when they look, it's not a shape they don't recognize in the back seat, it's the paint on their own face that they can't account for. Generally speaking, Indians are pretty nervous about possession narratives, since those are more or less stories about a body being colonized, which we know a thing or two about, but . . . the way to twist that, it's to make the entity possessing you *itself* Native, yeah?

This can put a protagonist in a good bind, and then the story can go horror, as it's easy to be all "down with the invaders," "out with the settlers," "fighting terrorism since 1492," but it's different when some of them are your friends, and family, and you're coming to out of breath, standing over a body in a living room, the walls painted with blood.

Maybe I'll write that—with all due thanks to Joseph M. Marshall III, of course.

Really, though?

Could be his story's already horror, yeah? Sure, the way he told it was more . . . it was more about how there's more to the night, and the land, than we generally acknowledge. Which is to say: when we feel his story in the base of our jaw, in the hollow of our chest, in the sway of our back, then the world clicks that smidge wider, to allow more stuff to be going on.

Or, rather—and I get this more from his delivery, that evening— actually the world's this big and *bigger*, we just have to have the right eyes to see. Which is pretty Philip K. Dick, really, and sort of Lovecraft, too: there's more here than we thought, and, now that we've gotten a glimpse of that, there's no going back to the way it was.

Compelling stuff; Joseph M. Marshall III's a good speaker, a good storyteller. Good enough that, come one in the morning the evening he told that story to us all, at a table way in the corner of an emptied-out hotel lobby, me and some other people are still talking, doing that thing Indians tend to do when it gets dark: whispering scary stories to each other, stories I won't repeat here because . . . like the title of this book says, you don't *invite* bad stuff, right?

But . . . let's say there was more than one bigfoot story that night, maybe some little people stuff secondhand, but, mostly, the stories were all doing that thing Indian stories tend to do, that Marshall's had done as well: end inconclusively. Which isn't any kind of failure. It's more like a handoff: "Here, this is yours now, it lives in your head, and it'll keep going, and growing, sending tentacles out into your life."

Thanks, man. Just what I wanted.

But?

It's kind of what we all want, really.

And, sure, the anthropologists and social scientists and literary critics can all shrug and say maybe we like stories that function like that because they mean our story—the story of us in what's for the moment called America—hasn't quite processed all the way through yet, hasn't completed. Things can happen. This place can be ours again. Why not.

I'll buy that, no problem. Makes sense.

But what feels like an even better explanation for why we tend to like our stories to end like that, with bleeding over, bleeding across, haunting *us*, it's that it feels kind of fake and wrong and all too American to throw up walls between what's real and what's maybe not real. So, telling ourselves stories about the world being bigger than we thought, big enough for bigfoot and little people, that's really kind of saying to the so-called settlers that, hey, yeah, so you took all that land you could see. But what about all this other territory you don't even *know* about, man?

Or, really: Why you don't come over here into the dark with us, *into* that other land? We can show you a thing or two, maybe. About the way things really are. And about the way they should be. The way they can be. The way they will be again.

I can't wait.

Part of me's still sitting at that table in that hotel lobby, I mean. And, I say all of us sitting there, scaring ourselves with stories, were Native, but, at some point in it all, I clearly remember someone going back through Joseph M. Marshall III's story piece by piece, and then someone—maybe not Native?—calling foul, asking us to slow down, slow down.

Their objection was that the story made no sense, because why didn't those riders' horses clamber up onto the blacktop, spark across? First, it would have been more dramatic, and, second, it would have meant they were corporeal, not just smoke and light and wishful thinking.

Kind of as one, I recall, with, like, a single set of quotation marks, we all explained that the reason those horses didn't do that was that, a hundred-plus years ago, that roadbed wasn't there. Of course. The horses not going up with the blacktop wasn't a mistake in the story, it's the thing that makes the story *real*, it's the fantastic element that serves as proof—all we needed, anyway.

But?

That roadbed in Joseph M. Marshall III's story didn't necessarily just have to be absent in the nineteenth century, either.

Those riders gliding through it might not be born yet.

There's scary stuff in stories, sure, there's stuff that keeps you up at night, there's stuff that makes you watch the darkness you're driving through that much closer.

But there's hope, too.

Just—some nights you have to wade through a lot of blood to get there.

So, for these next 392 pages, let these twenty-six writers take you by the hand, lead you into the darkness at the heart of—let me put some quotation marks around it—"America."

Just, don't look back at your footprints.

Best to not look back at all, really.

STEPHEN GRAHAM JONES

Boulder, Colorado

December 26, 2021

NEVER
WHISTLE
AT NIGHT

KUSHTUKA

MATHILDA ZELLER

"You don't have to love him, just make his baby," Mama said, hanging the fleshy swath of salmon to dry. "It might have colored eyes, you know, maybe blue eyes. He'll pay you to keep quiet about it."

Mama had always been Machiavellian, but this was next level. Not even the old ladies who gossiped about her would have guessed she'd try to pull something like this. I shuddered and slid my knife up the side of another salmon, severing a long fillet of red flesh and silver scales. The cold, wet flesh reminded me of Hank Ferryman's lips, which he constantly licked while talking to us village girls. His hands were wide and stubby, his cheeks were pocked and ruddy, and his breath smelled like a caribou carcass that had been left in the sun for a week.

"He's rich," Mama reminded me unnecessarily, "and I'm sure he wouldn't be wanting his wife back in Kansas knowing he's got a kid up here. The money could really help, you know."

"He's probably got kids all over the Kobuk Valley," I muttered, "and I don't want to make anyone's baby."

Except maybe Pana's, but even then, that's not happening until after I finish college. Which costs money. That we don't have. Which is why this conversation is happening in the first place.

I brought down my knife too quickly through the filet and caught the side of my thumb. Blood blossomed along the cut and I brought it reflexively to my mouth, the taste of my blood mingling with the fish's.

Mama sucked her teeth. "Stupid girl! Go inside and clean that up. You're getting blood everywhere."

The cut stung, but it was a way out of this conversation and away from Mama. I jogged back to the house, pressing my jacket sleeve around the cut, which extended from the tip of my thumb down the side of my palm. Not wanting to take the pressure off it, I kicked the door with my toe.

It was Pana, not my aana, who opened it. My heart fluttered a little, despite having known him my whole life.

"What are you doing here?"

He grinned that perfect grin, complete with deep set dimples and one eyetooth missing. "Having tea with your aana."

"Why?" Not that I minded, but he was supposed to be on shift in the mines.

"There was an accident down at the mines. Frankie and Aqlaq and a couple of the white guys too. You know, the ones visiting from Kansas."

"Which white guys?" Maybe one was Hank Ferryman. Maybe Mama would leave me alone then.

"Jim and Bob. They all survived, but they're in really rough shape. Had to be flown to Fairbanks."

"Oh." My heart sank a little. "How did they get hurt?"

Pana's face darkened. "Maybe you should come inside."

Aana waited on the overstuffed chintz sofa, her dark eyes smiling at me from their nests of deep wrinkles. She was aged but ageless. I swear she hasn't changed since I was four years old.

"It was Sedna," Aana said by way of greeting, "she's the mistress of the underworld, and they're mining into her domain."

Pana shook his head. "The foreman said it was a bear, or maybe some wolves."

"A bear or maybe some wolves?" Aana repeated, cackling. "He didn't even see what happened, he is throwing guesses into the dark."

I sat down next to Pana. "Sedna is mythology, Aana—"

"Sedna is angry," Aana interrupted. "They're coming uninvited, and taking what's ours. They don't belong here, in our land, in our beds—" She clenched her jaw tight, swallowing hard. "—But Sedna is gracious enough to give warning. She only tore their guts out. A wolf or bear would have stayed to eat the guts. They wouldn't be alive in the hospital right now if it weren't for Her grace."

I turned to Pana, my own innards tightening. "Their guts were torn out?"

Pana nodded. "Torn up across the abdomen. Torn up everywhere, in fact."

I raised a skeptical eyebrow. "And they're saying it was wolves?"

Pana shifted defensively. "If they weren't saying it was wolves, you know who they'd be accusing."

Us. All of us. I nodded my head.

"What did you do to your hand?" Aana said, reaching for me with one hand and smacking Pana's knee with the other. "Pana, why didn't you see she's hurt? Go get the bandages."

Pana jumped up to get them. He didn't need to ask where; he knew my house as well as I did.

As soon as he was out of the room, Aana leaned toward me. "He wants to marry you, you know."

I sighed. "I know." Pana had been saved last year by a visiting preacher and was now determined to marry me before I moved in. Common-law marriage was what basically everyone else did, but not Pana, no. He wanted to go to a little white chapel and promise God he'd love me first.

"Your grandfather married me first," Aana reminded me, smiling.

"I know," I repeated. I'd heard the story a million times, how he'd waited and saved till he could take Grandma and Eddie, her baby from a visiting schoolteacher, all the way out to Fairbanks for a marriage and adoption. He'd wanted to do it properly, he said. She thought it was stupid at the time, but it had grown to be a major point of pride with her.

I wasn't sure I saw the point—it was a lot of money, but Pana cared about doing it that way, and I cared about him.

Pana returned with the first aid kits and pulled my hand into his lap, gingerly unwrapping it from the jacket sleeve.

"I'm taking Hank Ferryman's boy hunting this weekend," he said, pouring some iodine onto a bit of gauze. "Hank says he wants him toughened up out there on the tundra."

I rolled my eyes. Pana and his crew would do no such thing— not if they wanted repeat business. They would take the kid out there, make him feel like a big, tough hunter while doing all the actual work of packing things, unpacking things, and hauling things, and he would have stories to take back to his buddies in Kansas. It was about the kid's ego, and the dad's too.

"I'm sure he'll shoot the biggest caribou known to man," I said, "with razor sharp teeth."

Pana grinned. "By the time he gets back to Kansas it'll have turned into a polar bear."

"That he killed with his bare hands," added Aana, her face splitting into a wide grin, revealing teeth worn down by years of leatherworking. "Like this—" Her hands made violent strangling motions. Pana and I melted into a fit of giggles, as if we were both ten instead of nearly twenty.

Pana finished my hand and I stood reluctantly. Here—with him, with my aana—this was my heart's home. Outside that door lay wolves and bears, and Hank Ferryman and Mama.

When I returned to Mama, she was smiling.

"You have a job this weekend."

"A job?"

"With Hank Ferryman. He's having a party at his lodge. He needs hired help. You know, cooking, cleaning."

A curdling feeling gathered around my ears. "Why don't you go work for him?" It was a stupid question that we both knew the answer to. Mama rolled her eyes.

"I already told him you'd go. You're going."

"No."

"No?" Mama's hand tightened on the knife she was holding. I did my best not to look down at it. My heart trilled like it was trying to beat for three people.

"I don't want to."

To my surprise, Mama's grip loosened on the knife and she shrugged. "Maybe I'll send Esther, then."

My mouth went dry. Esther was my fifteen-year-old sister. My sweet, compliant sister. Mama wouldn't. She couldn't. As I stared at her, though, I knew she would.

"I'll go." I picked up my ulu and rocked it across the salmon, chopping its head.

"That's what I thought," Mama replied.

Some days, I hate her.

———

"The Land of the Midnight Sun," bellowed Hank Ferryman, punching my shoulder playfully, "more like the Land of the Six P.M. Bedtime."

Was he always this loud or was the closeness of the truck amplifying his voice? He chortled at his own joke.

"Tapeesa. Hey, Tappy," I cringed at the improvised nickname. "Tell me a Native story."

I shook my head. "That's a bad idea." The sun had set an hour ago and we were bumping over the half-frozen ground in the dark, with nothing but the truck's headlights standing between us and the darkness. Snow had begun to fall, thick and fast. Alone with someone like him, in the darkness like this, seemed like the worst possible place to bring up the stories that could catch the attention of a spirit.

"It's a swell idea! Hank Ferryman doesn't make bad ideas! Don't forget, I hired you for the evening."

The last sentence fell like lead between us. He hired me to cook and clean for his party, not tell him stories. I wasn't hired to do whatever he felt like doing. My hands curled into fists. Still, maybe it would shut him up.

"Fine. Fine." I wracked my brain, but in the darkness, I could think of nothing bright and benign. "There was once a girl named Sedna. Her father threw her over the edge of his fishing boat. She tried to save herself by catching on to the edge of the boat, but he brought a knife down onto her fingers and cut them all off. They became the first seals, walruses, whales. She became the goddess of the Underworld."

Hank waved his hand impatiently. "I already know about Sedna. I got your buddy Pana to tell me about her. Tell me something new."

I pulled my coat tighter around me. "There are kushtuka. They appear to us, taking on the appearances of those we love. They try to get us to go with them."

"To go with them where?"

I pulled my coat even tighter, suddenly feeling cold. "I don't know."

Hank was quiet for a blessed minute. Then he let out a guttural snort that blossomed into full-blown laughter. "You call that a ghost story, missy? Your ghost stories are as bad as your watermelons up here."

"We don't have watermelons up here."

"Damn straight you don't. I can tell you some ghost stories from Kansas that'd put hair on your chest. In fact—"

My head slammed into the dashboard as Hank floored the brake, sending us into a fishtail. When the car finally stopped, he sat, his chest heaving as he stared out at the road ahead of us.

A figure stood before us in the headlights, cloaked in heavy furs. Black hair tumbled down in wild rivulets to her elbows. She pushed back the ruff of her parka. She was me. Or would have been, were it not for the pupils that covered the whole of her eyes, and the hideous, obscenely wide grin that distorted the lower half of her face.

Hank let out a small scream and floored the gas, ramming straight into her. A thunder roll of sickening thuds juddered through me as she tumbled up and over the hood of the truck.

I looked behind us but saw nothing in the taillights as Hank continued to pick up speed, his breathing ragged and shallow. He muttered to himself thickly for a moment before looking over at me with a little nervous laugh. "Some deer you got out here, huh?"

I stared. "That wasn't a deer."

"Don't be stupid," Hank scoffed, "I saw it with my own two eyes. You saw it with yours. It was a deer, plain as the nose on my face."

A gentle tapping noise sounded on the glass behind me. I shuddered, unable to turn around.

"I think there's something in the bed of the truck."

Hank's hands tightened on the steering wheel. "No there isn't."

Tap. Tap. Tap.

"Don't you hear that?" I felt those eyes on the back of my head. Those eyes, all sea-black pupil, wide and hungry.

"All I hear is you trying to amp me up. Wasn't enough to tell me your ghost stories, you want to spook me now."

Tap. Tap. Tap.

His body stiffened at the noise. "Stop it. Tapeesa. It's not funny at all."

"It's not me." Surely he could see both my hands, silent in my lap.

He huffed impatiently, but didn't say anything else. The tapping stopped. He relaxed, laughed a little.

"You really had me going for a minute there."

I didn't reply. There was no point.

By the time we reached his lodge, an oversize monstrosity on the edge of a lake, he was back to cracking bad jokes and resting his hand on my knee, removing it when I batted him off, only to drop it there again a second later.

"You'll love this place. I can't believe I haven't taken you out here yet. I had everything flown in from Anchorage, it's all custom. Top of the line." He was grinning like a kid. I hated his familiarity, as if I were a friend who hadn't gotten around to visiting, instead of a village girl whose mother he'd leveraged to drag me out here.

He slipped out of his side of the truck, swinging his keys and whistling. I sat on the passenger's side, my dread growing in the stillness.

Tap. Tap. Tap.

I turned this time, and saw her. She was me, this kushtuka with inky black eyes and black hair, billowing and wild. When our eyes met, her face split again into that freakishly wide grin that nearly reached her ears and revealed pointed molars. Meat-eating molars. Flesh-ripping molars.

Hank's voice registered from somewhere in front of the truck. "Aren't you coming, Tapeesa?"

I opened my mouth and closed it again, unable to bring myself to make a sound.

The kushtuka tapped the back window of the truck once more with a long, black fingernail and disappeared.

I tore my eyes from the back window to see him trundling over to my door. "You're one of these fussy, old-fashioned girls, aren't you? You want a big strong man to open the door for you, is that it?" He chuckled to himself and opened my door.

I climbed out, scared to take my eyes off the truck bed, as if doing so would make the kushtuka materialize again and leap on us, ripping at us with those pointed teeth.

The lodge was massive, with vaulted ceilings and mounted animal heads everywhere. Above the fireplace hung two spears, crossed over each other like they were European swords or something. But they weren't European. They were Inuit. I recognized the carvings on them, the worn leather bindings that secured the pointed stone ends.

"Those spears—"

"Artifacts. They're incredible, aren't they? Genuine ancient artifacts, you know."

"They're my grandfather's."

Hank Ferryman's smile stayed frozen on his face. After a pregnant pause, he laughed. "You're mistaken. There are so many spears out there like these."

"I recognize the carving."

"They're nothing; Indigenous motifs that have been carved a thousand times over."

The back of my neck felt tight—beyond cringing. "If they're not his, where did you get them?"

Hank shrugged, as if I'd asked a stupid question. "My secretary found them for me."

"Found them?" Stole them, more likely. From my widowed aana.

"Found them, bought them, it doesn't matter. You're here to work. There's the kitchen—" He pointed to a corner of the lodge sectioned off by granite countertops. "My secretary was here earlier—they've dropped off recipes and groceries for tonight's dinner."

I stalked over to the kitchen and grabbed the ulu that was sitting on a wooden holder on the counter. Hank bounded over and snatched it from my hands.

"That's an *artifact*. It's for *decoration*."

I looked down at the ulu in his hands. It was newly sharpened. The baleen handle was worn, polished to a bright shine from all the times it had been gripped. I wondered whose aana he stole this from. "It's a tool. For cutting."

Hank rolled his eyes. "You are basically white. Your dad's dad was white, your mother is white. You should be able to understand that modern knives are better." He pointed to the block of knives on the counter. "Carbon steel. Flown in from Japan. Top of the line. Try them, honey, I promise you'll never go back to an ulu."

If he saw I was shaking with rage, he didn't show it. I strode to the knife block and drew out the largest one, grabbing a cutting board and a bag of potatoes before I could give in to my urge to run him through with it.

"See, now? Isn't that fabulous?" Hank Ferryman pumped a fist as if he had just taught me to fish and I'd caught one. He didn't wait for a reply before continuing, "I gotta take a piss. Make sure the champagne is in the fridge, will you? No one likes it warm."

I made dinner. Other men showed up and ate, made passes at me, laughed and talked to Hank. I passed the hours in a deep fuzzy rage, forcing myself through the motions of arranging canapés on a plate, pulling a roast from the oven, slicing it up on a serving tray. I couldn't bring myself to fake smile at them. There was something outside the house that was clearly murderous and looked just like me. There was something inside me that was clearly murderous and felt nothing like me.

Someone popped the cork off the champagne bottle and I jumped, letting out a small scream. The room exploded with laughter and Hank grinned at me, pushing a champagne glass over the counter toward me. "You clearly need to loosen up."

I pushed it back toward him and left for the bathroom. I needed to be somewhere, anywhere, away from these people.

I locked the bathroom door and pulled myself onto the counter, leaning my head back against the mirror. It was colder here, a welcome relief from the heat in the main area. I breathed deep, sizing up my options, wondering if I could get the police to look into how Hank got my grandfather's spears, if they would actually care at all. Probably not.

A heavy dragging sound slid along the hall outside the bathroom. I looked down, watching a shadow pass along the crack under the door. The air filled with the thick smell of old fish. The shadow paused. I pressed my lips together, hardly daring to breathe.

After an eternity, the shadow continued on, past the bathroom door and down the hall. I slipped off the counter and stood in front of the door.

The murmur of laughter and conversation went silent.

Hank Ferryman's voice broke the silence. "Tapeesa, I told you to leave the artifacts *alone*." His voice should have sounded plaintive, but it didn't. It trembled.

A scream tore through the air, followed by a trampling of feet, breaking of glasses. More screams. I sat on the counter, my mouth growing dry. Someone was running up the hall toward me. The handle to the bathroom door rattled, followed by pounding that made the whole door vibrate. "Let me in!"

THUD.

The heavy crack of a skull on the floor preceded a wet, tearing sound. Something dark seeped under the bathroom door, and it wasn't until the smell hit me that I fully registered what it was: blood.

Primal growls turned into satisfied chewing and smacking noises. I pressed my back against the bathroom mirror, drawing my knees to my chest. My heart thudded in my ears and my breathing sounded too loud. It, that kushtuka, would hear me. It, that creature, would find me. My blood would join with the blood on the floor.

After what felt like an eternity, a rustling of furs and padding of feet told me it was leaving. I heard the front door banging open, the sound of feet on gravel walking away.

I couldn't stay here. It could come back. It would come back. I needed to get home, to my aana and her shotgun. Would a shotgun work against a kushtuka? Surely it would—if it weren't flesh and blood itself, it wouldn't be able to do . . . whatever it just did.

I dropped to the floor as silently as I could, holding my breath while I turned the doorknob.

I had seen a lot of blood in my life. I had gutted fish and caribou, slaughtered ducks and sliced up eels. But that was orderly, deliberate, purposeful. This—this was not that.

Bloody footprints covered the floor. Blood spatters and smears graced the walls. There weren't men here, there were *pieces* of men. *Entrails* of men. I took a step forward and my foot grazed something wet. I looked down; it was an eye, bloodshot across the sclera. It rolled, revealing a blue iris, as blue as Hank's.

I fell into a squat, hugging my knees, pressing my toes down to stop myself from falling into the mess. I didn't want to touch the ground. I didn't want to touch anything. I pressed my shoulders between my knees and vomited.

Outside, Hank's sled dogs started barking, working up into a panic. I looked around. I had to get out of here. Hank's keys had been in his pocket, but now—I could barely bring myself to cast my eyes around the room again—this was a search I couldn't undertake.

The dogs. The dogs could take me home, and away from that thing, whatever that thing was.

I grabbed my grandfather's spear off the wall, the ulu off the counter, and stepped lightly out onto the gravel. New snow was starting to fall, dusting the gravel and recoating the already fallen snow in the yard. I pressed my back to the log exterior and side-stepped toward the barn where the huskies were. Their barking had died down and now they were all panting and whimpering anxiously.

I stepped into the shadowy barn, straining my eyes against the darkness. If she was in here, they'd know, wouldn't they? If she was still there, they'd still be barking. But they weren't. They were just whimpering and staring at me. Still, my scalp prickled. She'd be coming back. Something deep inside me knew it.

I grabbed their harness and began hooking them up as quickly as I could, praying that the snow was deep enough, that the dogs would know where to go, that I wouldn't fall off. I'd driven a sled a few times before, but I wasn't good at it. Not by a long shot.

Something shuffled in the dark. The dogs' whining intensified. My hands shook as they buckled the last clasp and I jumped onto the runners. Something shuffled again, and the rancid fish smell filled the air.

She was here.

"Go," I hissed to the dogs. "Mush!"

The dogs whimpered, looking around anxiously.

I tried to whistle at them, but my mouth was too dry.

Something bit into my arm, sharp and cold.

I screamed, and the dogs took off like a shot. I snatched the handle with one hand and slapped the kushtuka with the other. Her nails dug into my flesh and searing cold shot through me. I raised the arm she was gripping and bit down hard on her hand. A scream echoed across the tundra as she fell back, and we gained speed. I looked over my shoulder and saw her in the moonlight, a dark spidery figure loping toward us across the white snow.

I shook the reins, urging the dogs to go faster. The sound of her awkward lope and heavy breathing grew louder.

We swerved through scrub brush. She bounded over it.

She was gaining on us.

BLAM.

A shot rang out across the hills. BLAM. It was a shotgun.

Who on earth was shooting their gun at this time of night?

BLAM.

I prayed the bullet would miss us, that it would find my kushtuka.

BLAM.

We had come to the river and the dogs swerved to run parallel to it. The kushtuka cut the corner, closing the distance between us. I could feel her breath on the back of my head, smell the blood and fetid flesh.

BLAM.

The smell subsided. I looked back behind me, and she was on the ground, inert. The dogs slowed to a walk and my knees buckled with relief.

BLAM.

Why were they still shooting? The kushtuka was dead.

Someone grabbed me, throwing a hand over my mouth and another around my waist, tackling me to the ground.

"Don't. Say. A. Word." It was Pana. "Buck—Hank's boy—has absolutely lost his mind."

I nodded. We crawled behind a rock and sat stock-still, muffling our breathing with our coat sleeves.

Footsteps grated across the stones on the riverbank. "I got one, two, three, three little Indians all for me," Buck sang. I ignored Pana's whispered protests and peeked around the boulder to see Hank Ferryman's son nudge the inert kushtuka with the barrel of his rifle.

"You're an ugly one, aren't you?" he muttered.

The kushtuka shifted.

Buck nudged the kushtuka with the butt of his rifle. "Are you dead, or do I need to blast you again?" He spoke as if he were offering a complimentary turndown service at a fancy hotel, rather than threatening mortal violence.

The kushtuka made a quiet whimpering sound.

"Or better, perhaps, with my own bare hands."

He dropped to his knees and put his hands around the kushtuka's throat. It made a strangled sound, writhing against his tightening grip.

A knot twisted in my stomach. I should have been relieved to see the kushtuka go, but in that moment, she looked at me.

She looked like me.

Somehow, she was me.

Buck squeezed harder and she kicked and flailed, her foot connecting with the butt of the gun, sending it skittering toward me across the snow. Ignoring Pana's protests, I lunged forward, grabbing it and bringing it level, jamming the butt into my shoulder.

"Stop." My voice didn't sound like mine. It sounded desperate, primeval, superhuman.

My finger went to the trigger. My voice trembled when I spoke. "You're killing her. Stop."

I fired a warning above his head and he froze, then slowly stood, hands above his head, turning to fix me with a grin as ugly and unsettling as the kushtuka's.

"Those devil Natives thought they could abandon me," he said through his manic grin, "They were wrong. They were all wrong. I showed them."

Pana stood up now, turning a flashlight on Buck. His blond hair and pale face, his expensive thermal coat and snow pants, they were all spattered in blood.

My finger went back to the trigger. He wouldn't be missed; his father was already dead. If he lived, he'd kill and kill again. He'd kill my people. He'd kill Pana.

I leveled the gun at him and took aim. Warm, gentle hands covered my hands, and I heard Pana's voice in my ear.

"Please don't. He isn't worth what we'll pay for this."

The tightness welling up into my chest broke into a sob. I lowered the gun. This was it, how we all ended. Defeated by their brutality, and a world that would choose them and forget about us.

Buck screamed. There was a spear in him. The kushtuka on the ground held the spear, grinning widely.

I was on the ground, holding the spear. I was holding it, with my own hands, as Buck's blood trickled down and warmed them.

I let it go, scrambling to my feet as he fell. There were bruises around my neck, my throat hurt when I breathed. Where was the kushtuka, where was Pana?

Buck fell onto his back, the spear sticking straight up out of him. Pana lowered the rifle, tears streaming down his face.

"I thought he was going to kill you."

"The kushtuka—"

"Buck went on a rampage. Both elders who came hunting with us are dead."

"There was a kushtuka—the kushtuka killed him. She was right here. She looked just like me—"

Pana opened his mouth to protest, then looked down at Buck. He took a deep breath.

"You know what, Tapeesa? I think you were right. I think there was a kushtuka."

I pulled my hands into the thick furs I was wearing. They were beautifully made. The trim was black with little red flowers and green leaves trailing along the edge. They were handmade. *Artifacts*, even.

"I thought I saw that hanging in Hank Ferryman's lodge," Pana said. "It looks just like one my aana made once."

I walked to the sled, my legs shaking. "Let's take it back to her then, okay?"

Pana nodded, tossing one last glance over his shoulder at Buck. His freshly dead body smelled good, so good, I was sure the wolves would find him soon. I swallowed the saliva gathering in my mouth.

"Come on, Pana. I think I have your aana's ulu on that dogsled. She'll be wanting it back."

Pana paused, then nodded, taking my arm. "Thanks, Tapeesa."

I smiled. "You, my dear, are most certainly welcome."

Mathilda Zeller is the first generation of her family to grow up outside the Kobuk River Valley but feels strongly about preserving and carrying on the stories from that region. She lives in New England with her husband and six children.

WHITE HILLS

REBECCA ROANHORSE

White Hills is everything Marissa ever wanted, right down to the welcome sign by the community mail drop reminding everyone of the HOA rules. Some people don't like HOAs, but Marissa loves them. They keep the houses looking nice and the people uniform, and isn't that one of the reasons she and Andrew chose to move here?

Well, that and its proximity to her in-laws.

And of course, the private golf course that Andrew spends most weekends on, and the no-children-allowed pool where she promised to meet her new friend Candy for drinks. (Only Candy never texted her back even though she sent a dozen *Hey Girl* texts with funny emojis, and even one pretty serious *RU OK?*)

Marissa pushes the uncomfortable thought of Candy's ghosting out of her mind and focuses on the positive as she pulls her BMW through the gate, tossing a wave to the security guard, admiring the way the afternoon sun catches on her new wedding ring, and then turning away as if he doesn't matter. But of course, it matters. What good are her accomplishments if there is no one there to bear witness?

Marissa has many accomplishments. Her body, for one. Tucked and toned and filled to perfection by the best professional surgeons, trainers, and estheticians Houston has to offer. Hair bleached to a stunning shade of summer. Hours spent on her social media accounts as a budding beauty influencer.

Some people think marrying well is not an accomplishment, but they never grew up poor outside Chillicothe, Texas. Never slept four siblings to a queen size in an old two-bedroom house owned by their meemaw, never had to wear hand-me-downs to class or the same stupid pink blouse three years in a row for school pictures.

The memories fluster Marissa, and she adjusts her Gucci sunglasses as she clamps down on any emotion that might dare to ruin her perfect eyeliner. She tosses an expertly bleached lock of hair over her shoulder and gives the Bimmer some gas.

It's the baby, she thinks. Pregnancy makes women emotional. All the baby IG influencers say so.

She presses a freshly manicured hand to her newly bumping belly and smiles.

She hasn't told Andrew yet.

He's a good man, a really good man. But he's at a crucial crossroads in his career, and it's very important that the company see that he's CEO material. Part of that is a willingness to travel and work weekends and well, live and breathe the company. There's just no room for a child.

She understands.

But some men, well, some men don't think they want a baby until they see that little wrinkled face and those teeny feet and they smell that distinct newborn smell, and then it all comes together.

Andrew will come together, Marissa's sure of it.

As long as it's a boy. She read that most women have boys first, anyway. It's nature's way of ensuring the man will stick around. She likes that, that nature has her own mind about things.

She pulls into their circular driveway, and now, looking up at their home, tears do come. Four bedrooms and three and a half baths at almost five thousand square feet. European white oak floors, Gaggenau appliances in the kitchen, separate his and hers walk-in closets.

Marissa was wrong when she said White Hills was all she ever wanted.

It is more. It is the dream.

All 4,914 square feet of their house is silent when Marissa walks in, her bright pink Manolo Blahniks tapping across the marble entry. The model furniture, even the fancy appliances she loves: it is all as pristine as the day they moved in, mostly because Andrew is always working and Marissa doesn't make much of an impression on anything, even a house.

But that will change when the baby comes!

She can almost hear the toddler giggles, the pitpat of tiny shoes, the harried voice of the nanny.

Soon, baby, she thinks, and touches her hand to her belly. Wonders how best to work her angles for Instagram once she starts to show.

Her iPhone dings with a text.

She eagerly digs through her Birkin and pulls out her phone.

It's from Andrew: *Meeting some fellas to watch the game at the club. Be home late. Don't wait up.*

Marissa's heart flutters, and her stomach drops.

She had planned to tell Andrew about the baby tonight. Was counting on it. But now, she's staring down another night alone,

one she can't even mitigate with a bottle of Chardonnay (the baby, after all!).

Unless . . .

Marissa squares her shoulders. This is an opportunity, not a setback, and if there's anything life has taught Marissa it is that when God closes a door, he opens a window. She turns on her toe and marches right back to the car. She doesn't bother to wave at the guard on her way out (it's much more important to be seen arriving than leaving) and heads to the club.

She's mostly sure that Andrew loves surprises.

Dark mahogany and cigar smoke greet her as she makes her way from the tasteful lobby to one of four bars at the White Hills Country Club. The six-figure membership fee was a housewarming gift from her in-laws.

Her favorite part of the club is the upstairs patio bar modeled in a Mediterranean style, the place where she met her new friend Candy, just last week. Candy was four hours into an afternoon of day drinking when the two women exchanged lipstick compliments over the bathroom vanity. Candy asked Marissa to join her, and Marissa would have never said yes except Andrew was off talking to the golf pro, and it had been two hours of Marissa sitting on an overstuffed chair waiting, her thighs sticking to the leather below her Lacoste skirt. So, when Candy slurred an invitation, Marissa accepted. Candy was tall and thin and although her roots were dark, she had that California girl aura about her. Or was it Florida?

That's it, she thinks to herself. Candy's gone back to Florida. Only don't they have cell service in Florida? Again, a bad feeling threatens, and Marissa quickly buries it.

She skips past the stairs that lead to boozed-out Tuscan fantasies and almost best friends. She follows the sound of football instead.

Marissa hesitates just inside the sports bar, momentarily blinded by the darkness. Small flatscreens cast illumination against the walls, and she's flustered by what the limited light reveals.

Heads. Mounted on the wall are heads. Deer, elk, even a water buffalo. And is that a wildebeest? Marissa thought those existed only in Disney movies.

"Ball on the Washington twenty-yard line and it's fourth and inches. The Texans are going for it."

The words of the TV sports announcer barely register, but the groans of the dozen or so men into their high-end lagers and low-balls of liquor are the sounds of disappointment.

She recognizes Andrew's voice among them, a half shout at the quarterback to DO SOMETHING, and beelines to the barstool where her husband sits, a drink in hand. She touches his shoulder, and the smile he started with sours around the edges.

What a surprise and *did you get my voice mail* slur from his lips. He doesn't say *what are you doing here*, but Marissa feels her violation, his contained outrage.

She drops her hand. Steps back from his unhappiness.

She almost has second thoughts.

But Marissa believes in maintaining a girlboss attitude which doesn't allow for second guessing.

She lifts her chin and confirms that yes, yes, she got his message to stay home and not wait up, but can't a wife miss her husband and besides, she has some news.

Another groan from the crowd as their chosen football team blows it, and the guy next to Andrew, a heavier gray-haired business suit, curses crudely under his breath.

Marissa stands just to the side of Andrew's stool, hoping he'll offer her his seat. She makes a light comment about being on her feet all day (although she spent most of the day sitting in front of her laptop or in the manicurist's chair).

Andrew doesn't budge, but gray-haired suit slides over to make room for her. She accepts gratefully, giddy to be welcomed into this masculine domain. Only then does she notice the other women in the room are waitstaff in low-cut blouses. She wonders if the wives of the club know about this place and decides they must. It's all kind of exciting, anyway. Men being men.

Andrew's absorbed in the game again, a hand now absently resting above her knee. Her confidence soars. She loves the weight of his fingers, the press of his wedding ring against her thigh. She's never been into sports, but she finds herself watching the TV anyway.

Another lost opportunity by the team, and the man next to her, the one that gave her his seat, jokes, "The team's been trash since they changed their name. Goddamn social justice warriors ruin everything."

Marissa doesn't follow sports, but she knows what he's talking about. She's seen people complaining about "The Chop" on Tik-Tok, read an article about Indian mascots in *Vogue*. She raises her voice so everyone can hear. It's a declaration.

"I'm part Native American, and those mascots have never bothered me."

She realizes her mistake immediately.

She doesn't need to look to know that the gray-haired suit is staring at her, disgust curling his lips. She tries to laugh it off, backing toward the safety of her husband, but Andrew's eyes are wide, mouth hanging open, face red.

"I was kidding," she ventures. "I'm not really—"

"Let's go." Andrew's hand that had rested so nicely on her leg is now pulling her roughly to her feet and dragging her out of the room, that ode to masculine violence with its animal heads and football games.

She trips, her heel catching on some unseen divot in the silk rug. She stumbles, feels the sharp pain in her ankle and knows she's going to fall.

"The baby!" She shouts it, unthinking.

Women lose pregnancies like this. Women fall and something breaks inside them and then there's clotting and blood and and and . . .

She catches herself before she hits the floor. All that Pilates has given her a strong core and good reflexes.

Everyone's staring now. Andrew most of all.

She wants to rewind. This was not the way, not how she wanted to announce it.

But there's no going back. Only forward.

She straightens, ignoring the pain in her ankle. Touches a hand protectively to her midsection.

"I don't want to hurt the baby."

Later, in bed, Andrew simmers. It's a silent kind of rage, and something Marissa can usually fix with a well-timed application of oral sex, but now Andrew's spurned her advances and instead, he simmers.

Until he bursts.

"Why did you say that?" The words are a plaint, not anger, after all, but a soft kind of sadness.

"Say what?" She's rubbing La Mer cream on her hands, her legs tucked under Italian sheets.

"The part-Indian thing."

"I thought it might help."

"Is it true?"

Marissa hesitates. She has family stories, old pictures of browner-skinned ancestors. In high school, she joined the Native American Club.

Before she can answer, her phone dings. A text. It's very late for anyone to text her.

"Who was it?"

She sets the phone down, feeling much better than she did moments ago. "Your mother. She texted to congratulate us on the baby. How did she know so fast? Someone at the club must have told her."

She thinks of the bartender, the waitress in the low-cut top, gray-haired suit.

She expects Andrew to smile back, but he only sighs, heavy and disconsolate, the sound of wind through bare branches. He leans over and kisses her on the forehead. It's a lingering kind of kiss. It almost feels like a goodbye.

"What's done is done," he says.

She doesn't understand what he means so she chooses to ignore it. "She's coming over tomorrow. We're going to go to brunch, and then to a baby specialist she knows."

Andrew sighs, his blue eyes immeasurably sad. "I thought you were French."

What a strange thing to say, but before she can ask more, Andrew's turned out the lights.

Marissa tucks herself down into the sheets and pulls the Frette comforter up to her neck to stop the sudden shivers.

Elayne, that's Marissa's mother-in-law, is thirty minutes early. Her knock is crisp and precise, much like the woman herself. Elayne smells of Joy Baccarat and her Chanel suit is flawless. Pale silver hair gathers at her neck in a chic chignon. It would be crude to say Elayne looks like a million bucks because, surely, she looks like two million.

Marissa isn't ready. Hasn't had her decaf latte yet or finished drawing in her eyebrows. Without them she looks perpetually surprised, the top half of her face somehow missing altogether despite careful contouring around her nose and forehead.

Plus, she's wearing sweats—rag & bone cashmere, but Elayne eyes her hoodie like it's from the local mall. She taps her Rolex and reminds Marissa she pulled some strings to get her into this specialist today. The least her daughter-in-law could do is be ready to go.

"Marissa," Elayne says once they're in Elayne's Tesla and Marissa is suitably draped in Burberry silk georgette and linen, "is that an ethnic name?" Elayne drives an electric. Not because she supports environmental causes, but because she owns stock in the company and once went on a yacht cruise with one of the Musk cousins. It's quite a concession, she tells people at parties, since her family comes from oil money.

"Hebrew, I think."

The Botox-smoothed corners of Elayne's mouth turn down.

"Or Latin."

They don't speak again until they arrive at the specialist's office downtown, although Marissa tries to engage her mother-in-law in conversation at least twice. Once about the traffic and then about Andrew's golf handicap. Both are equally prosaic fails, and by the time they pull off the freeway, Marissa is desperate to get out of the car.

The Houston skyscraper is a glass palace, an ode to a time when oil barons ruled this corner of the world. The weather has turned heavy, the promise of rain coming in off the gulf.

On the elevator ride up, Marissa stares at the dwindling skyline. Thinks of Chillicothe where the buildings never got higher than three stories, and the diner in College Station where she met Andrew after an Aggies football game. She told him she was a student there and that her parents had died, and she was living with an aunt. That last one was true, but she knew there was no way he was going to ask her out if she told the truth.

Sometimes lying is bad, but sometimes it's the only way to survive.

The nurses are all business smiles as they shuttle Marissa into a posh exam room. She can't fault the pale cream and stone décor in here. It reminds her of the spa at the St. Regis.

"I don't need to have a pelvic exam, do I?" she asks an attractive brunette woman with lips the color of sugar-free cranberry juice.

"Open wide."

The nurse swabs her mouth, says the specialist will be in to see her soon. She sits on the exam table, fully dressed, feet swinging off the end. Most doctor's offices have educational posters on the wall. Emergency numbers to call for mental health issues. She even had one doctor, a feminist-minded lady from India, who had a poster of how to do your own vaginal exam. She never went back to that one.

Here, there are drawings in frames, captured behind glass. Medical drawings. They look ancient, or at least old, like they belong in a museum, not this swank doctor's office.

Marissa hops off the exam table and moves closer. She sees now the drawings are diagrams. Human heads being measured and annotated, their features grossly exaggerated.

She can't quite read the cursive words, the unfamiliar numbers.

It reminds her of the sports club last night and her whole body shivers with a deep primal revulsion she doesn't quite understand. Part of her wants to look closer, comprehend what she's seeing, but another part of her wants to get as far away from the drawings as she can.

The knob on the door turns.

She covers her mouth to keep a scream in.

It's Elayne.

She's holding a smoothie. She eyes Marissa standing there with her hand over her mouth and her eyes wide. She waits for her to shuffle back over to the examination table and sit.

She offers the smoothie to Marissa, which Marissa sniffs but doesn't accept.

"What's in this?" she asks.

Elayne, who is not used to being questioned, raises an eyebrow.

Marissa, who is not used to questioning, rushes her words. "It's just, I'm allergic to strawberries. All kinds, even the local kind, and the organic ones at Whole Foods. And I don't want, well, I have to be careful what I drink these days." She looks meaningfully down at her belly.

Elayne proffers the smoothie, again, and this time Marissa takes it. Sips delicately from the metal straw, and that seems to placate Elayne. The drink does taste faintly of strawberries, but she's afraid to counter Elayne.

"The whole thing." Elayne's smile is brittle. "For the baby."

Marissa feels the hair on her neck rise. She wishes she hadn't come now, had begged off with a headache or morning sickness.

She sucks on the straw, the only sound in the room an embarrassingly loud, wet slurping, until the smoothie is mostly gone. Elayne gestures for her to finish it all, so she upends the glass and lets the last bit slush out across her lips.

She hands the empty glass back, her stomach feeling queasy.

She's pretty sure there were strawberries in there, and now she's worried about having a reaction. Last time, her throat swelled and hives broke out. She's worried, but at least she's in a doctor's office.

At least she thinks this is a doctor's office.

Elayne never actually said, did she?

Elayne sets the glass on the table beside her and roams to the window. The view is spectacular. The freeway glitters below.

"I'm not even mad," Elayne says, her gaze fixed on something in the distance. "Perhaps I should be. I mean, you lied to Andrew. To us. But then, I admire a bit of gold-digging ingenuity. I'm still not sure how you convinced Andrew to elope."

Now she turns, and Marissa feels small under her scrutiny.

"But 'part Native American'? I'm sorry. We can't abide that. And in a grandchild of mine? Well, do we know how dark the baby might be? How *savage* they might be?"

"But I'm white." Marissa holds out her pale arm as supporting evidence.

"Well, we certainly thought so. And there are white people who claim to be Indian all the time. I mean, old family stories, an enterprising relative who married an Indian for land rights. And I hear the Indians themselves say that kinship matters more than blood and isn't that quaint. I'm sure that's why they have blood quantum rules and ancestor rolls."

Marissa has no idea what blood quantum is. It sounds very technical, like dog breeding.

Elayne continues. "I hoped it was all a mistake, I truly did. But we checked."

Marissa remembers the mouth swab the nurse took. She thinks of the drawings on the wall.

"People say 'mutt' like a badge of honor," Elayne says. "What has the world come to when you can't be proud to be purebred?"

Marissa feels the first cramp just as Elayne trails off. She can't keep the small gasp of pain in, and as the next cramp rolls over her, her breath comes out in a moan. Elayne watches, silent.

"Oh!" Marissa clutches her belly.

"You're bleeding." Elayne's words are an observation. Her cool blue eyes track the spread of blood across Marissa's white pants.

Marissa bends over double, panic starting to clog her brain. Focus, she tells herself. This can't be happening, this can't be happening, positive thoughts, manifest the life you want.

"I'll get . . . someone." And Elayne is gone.

The floor is cool when Marissa lies her head down against it, although she can't remember falling. She wonders where the nurse is, where the doctor is, where Elayne is. The smoothie glass sits watching, her sole witness. That, and the heads in the drawings, dissected into brain size and nose and eye fold.

Another cramp rips through her. She screams. Begs. Tries to get to her feet and ends up skidding in the mess of blood and . . . oh god.

The baby.

She vomits up bits of strawberry.

She thinks this is the worst of it, that this was somehow her fault, that this is all a mistake. She reminds herself that everything happens for a reason. Only she can't quite think of the reason for this.

Her lies, of course. And her outburst. And maybe she wasn't grateful enough in her gratitude journal. She babbles all this to Andrew as he drives her home from the specialist. She's wearing a borrowed skirt and underwear stuffed with the thick absorbent pads they give women after they've given birth, but there's not going to be a birth in Marissa's future.

She closes her eyes and lets the roll of the freeway distract her.

And the thing is, she begins to realize, Andrew knew. He knew when he left for work early, knew when Marissa prattled on about brunch with her mother-in-law and stroller shopping. Knew because he came to pick her up and had towels covering the passenger's seat and didn't even act surprised or say he was sorry.

She tries to ask him about it, but all he says is "I told you I didn't want kids."

"No, you didn't! You just said not now, not . . ."

She trails off at his look of pity, the way his lips press together as if she's embarrassing herself.

They pass through the gate of White Hills, around their circular driveway. She doesn't notice the guard on duty, forgets to read the HOA sign. Andrew helps her through the door, across the European oak floors and into the bathroom. She takes a very long bath that afterward she won't remember taking. She swallows down the Trazodone she keeps in the medicine cabinet. She curls up in her Italian sheets.

"I'm sorry," Andrew says.

She turns toward the wall.

"Mother will be here in the morning."

Marissa wants to scream WHAT FOR? She never wants to see Elayne again, never wants to be weighed and found wanting. And the worst part of all, the worst part is that she still cares what Elayne thinks. Wants to apologize, or explain, or claim innocence.

If she comes over tomorrow, you will have another chance to please her, Marissa thinks. And the shame of the thought burns through her like a lightning fire.

Marissa closes her eyes and doesn't answer.

Andrew's quiet so long that Marissa rolls over to face him, but he's not standing by the door anymore. He's gone. To the club or to sleep on the sofa or maybe even to a business meeting.

When she finally sleeps, all her dreams are of Indians.

———

Elayne arrives early again, but this time, Marissa's ready. She won't make that mistake again. She's freshly showered and styled, eyebrows perfect, pantsuit Balenciaga. She's made Earl Grey steamers and egg bites, and she's put them all out on the kitchen island.

She recites her mantras under her breath, the ones she posted this morning on her Instagram stories. And most of all she smiles like nothing ever happened.

But she can't quite unclench her hand from the edge of the kitchen counter.

Elayne slithers into the kitchen, once-overs the tea and tiny omelets, once-overs Marissa.

Marissa asks if she slept well, makes some banal comments about her own sleep. (Slept like a baby almost passes through her lips, but mercifully she stops herself.)

Elayne watches. Knows a performance for her benefit when she sees it. Says, "We're not quite done, you know."

Marissa holds onto her smile with all she has.

"There's the matter of your little bit of Indian blood. I would think a finger should do."

Marissa doesn't understand.

"Well, people say, 'part Native American,' but really, dear, what part? Your left side? Your right? And how can we get rid of that? But I have a compromise."

She reaches across the island and slides the chef's knife from the block. Places it between them.

"The pinkie should do. Cut that off, and we'll call it purged."

Marissa laughs because who wouldn't laugh in the face of a monster.

But the monster doesn't laugh back.

"I can take all this away, you know."

Marissa feels a tiny moment of triumph. "We didn't sign a prenup."

"I've already started the annulment paperwork."

"You bitch!" That comes out of Marissa's mouth before she can stop herself.

Elayne's sigh is an indulgence. "You're upset about the fetus, but honestly, what was that? A month? Two months? Barely a dream. You're young and fertile. If that's what you want, go have a half-breed baby with someone else. Just not here, and not with my son."

"But—"

"I'm offering you a way out if that's what you want. But look around you. The house, the car, the clothes on your back. It comes at a cost. You don't simply roll in here with your mixed-race blood and think you deserve all this permanently, do you?"

"Andrew—"

"—won't stop me, but I can take him, too." Her lips purse. "We both know you were a fling, but clever girl that you are, you convinced him to elope. But it won't last. The novelty will wear off, or you'll claim to have a headache one too many times, or open your silly mouth in front of his friends like you did at the club, and he'll want nothing more to do with you." Her smile is tight. "Men must sow their wild oats, but we won't be harvesting, dear. No, you're a passing interest, which I will tolerate for Andrew's sake, as long as you"—she points a finger at the blade between them—"know your place."

This is a test. Marissa understands now. And she sees that her pathetic breakfast and her trendy clothing was little more than an amateur's gambit. Here is the master setting out the knife. Here is when Marissa must decide what she truly wants, and what she is willing to do to get it.

"I think we can tear up those annulment papers, too. Come to a reasonable alimony agreement when the time comes."

Marissa stares at the pink polish on her perfect nails. She spies a chip she hadn't noticed before.

Elayne's sneering lips move, form a single word that seals her fate.

"Chillicothe."

Marissa looks up.

She slides off her shiny new wedding ring. Her manicured fingers wrap around the knife's handle.

Everything for a reason. A door, a window. 100% girlboss.

No going back. Only forward.

She smiles at Elayne, and this time she means it.

"I want White Hills."

Elayne nods.

Marissa brings down the knife.

Rebecca Roanhorse (Pueblo descent) is a *New York Times* bestselling and Hugo, Nebula, and Locus award-winning author. She has published multiple award-winning short stories and novels, including two in the Sixth World series, *Star Wars: Resistance Reborn*, *Race to the Sun* for the Rick Riordan imprint, and and two in the epic fantasy Between Earth and Sky trilogy: *Black Sun* and *Fevered Star*, with the final book, *Mirrored Heavens*, forthcoming in 2024. She has also written for Marvel Comics and for television and has had projects optioned by Amazon Studios, Netflix, and AMC Studios. She lives in Northern New Mexico with her husband, daughter, and pup.

NAVAJOS DON'T WEAR ELK TEETH

CONLEY LYONS

The first sign of trouble came when I walked outside and saw my homemade pride flag snarled up over its crossbar. Staked in pale coarse sand at the end of the driveway, just beside the mailbox, it was my way of announcing I was here for the season; it smelled like the cedar sachets Grandma put in her sock drawer and flapped cheerfully in the breeze coming off the ocean. Today, the flag was twisted up around the crossbar and knotted around the pole, as if some red-cheeked, lemon-mouthed tourist strolled by on a dawn walk and decided they didn't like "the gay agenda" staring them in the face.

Fuck that shit. I jogged down the stairs in my bare feet, careful to avoid the step with the jagged edge, and padded across scratchy gnarled grass to the mailbox.

It took thirty seconds to unknot the flag—a faded panel of pastel scraps my grandma had stitched together maybe ten years ago, right after I'd come out—and loop it back over the crossbar. After I finished, I walked back to the steps to rinse the dust and grit from my feet, wondering which one of our neighbors could be so damn petty.

When I turned on the hose, cold water soothed down both calves and pooled around my heels, blooming dark on dry, rough concrete. That was when I heard movement out on the road. Up walked a string bean–looking guy whose lean, defined stomach was pale as a slice of fatback. His blond hair was swept back from his angular face, like a rakish gangster in some silent film. He wore a blue T-shirt slung over one pink shoulder, well-fitting swim trunks, and no shoes. Coming back from the beach.

He raised a hand in greeting before I could pretend not to see him. "Looks like your water pressure is way better than mine. You put in new plumbing or something?"

"No." I pointed the hose away from my shorts so I didn't flash him a semi. Water splattered past my hands and onto the pea gravel around the spigot. "Hot out, huh?"

"Hotter now." String Bean huffed out a laugh. "Especially when I see a beautiful guy like you."

Sweat glinted in the soft pale hair along his arms and legs and in the gentle crease of his lower belly. I couldn't stop staring. My heartbeat thumped low and insistent at the base of my throat, making me stupid and quiet.

"I'm Cam," he said finally, and walked up, extending a hand. "Staying over on Third Street through the long weekend. Cousins gave me their timeshare."

I took it. "Joe. Here for the summer."

Bleach-white teeth flashed in the noon sun when he smiled at me, and when he let go of my hand, he reached out and plucked the hose from my fingers. Still watching me out of the corner of his eye, he held the hose up over his neck, letting cool rivulets patter softly down his bare chest and settle in the waistband of his swim shorts—which were growing tighter and more see-through by the second.

A hot bolt of desire coursed through my middle. I wondered

how the hell he'd learned to show off like that. I wanted to see it again.

Cam lingered under the spray for a few more seconds before handing the hose back to me. "Better rinse off before we go in."

Sunrise Beach was a sand-bleached island town right off the Intracoastal Waterway: quaint enough to have a soda-and-snack shop on Main—with nowhere else to eat on the island—but notable enough to boast multimillion-dollar oceanfront homes. It was the type of place everyone's grandparents liked because it was cheap, simple, and a half day's drive from home. A certain kind of millennial still loved it because it made their Insta reels look like a sherbet-colored Magnolia showroom.

I knew most of the families on our street, of course. It was hard to be standoffish considering we were the first brown folks to own a house on the island. After the war, my grandpa didn't want to go back to New York; building skyscrapers wasn't his thing, and he didn't have many ties to Saint Regis. He stayed here, since his basic training had been nearby. Saved up money from various jobs to go to night school, became a certified public accountant, and ended up landing at a community bank. Became the first Indian in the Carolinas to sit on an executive financial board, not to mention the first to make anywhere near that Beaver Cleaver kind of money. He and my grandma had always dreamed about retiring at the beach, so I couldn't be mad that they'd actually gotten to do it. Now that the house was mine, I'd been cleaning it out, little by little, over the past three months.

Cam laughed when I told him all this, like hearing about my rise to homeownership was a great story. "What a big shot. Coming out to your beach house for the summer."

"It's all right." I tried to act casual. All it did was make me paranoid that the smile would drop from my face. I missed my grandma's rosemary tea boiling on the stove, and the way she'd hum "Coat of Many Colors" while standing next to the coatrack. "This is the first year I've come here alone."

"Huh. You don't look like a dude who'd be out here by himself."

"Who the hell was I supposed to bring?" His comment made me bristle like a kicked dog. "I've done plenty of solo trips. Studied abroad by myself in college. I hiked the fucking A.T."

"Geez, keep your damn shirt on, Joey." Cam's laconic drawl was at odds with the playful wink he gave me before he wandered into the kitchen. "Or don't. I like a man with a smart mouth."

"Look." I sighed, torn between wanting to rip Cam's shorts down his fish-belly legs and wanting him to leave me the hell alone. "I'm not in the mood for company right now. Mind if we pick this up later?"

"Oh, come on, Joe." From the creaking in the kitchen, it sounded like Cam was opening up a couple of cabinets. I stood there gawping like a speared tuna while he rummaged through them. "Can't a thirsty guy just grab a bottle of water?"

The backs of my hands tingled hot with sudden nerves. "Seriously, dude. I've got a lot to do."

"Suit yourself." Cam returned from the kitchen, holding a water bottle and eating from a bag of salt-and-pepper chips. "If you want to do lame chores all day, then at least come meet me tonight. You owe me that much."

You had to admire his persistence, I guess. Not like any other available men were beating down my door, even during tourist season, when the island was full of third wheels and single brothers-in-law dragged along on the family vacation. Most of my Grindr dates weren't this enthusiastic about meeting in real life. "I don't know."

Cam only smirked, watching me from the doorway like I'd tossed off a witty one-liner. "You'll have fun. I promise."

We met up again around eight thirty, when the blood-orange sun
had disappeared behind dark lapping waves and a wild corn-silk
moon lay bright in the sky. Because there wasn't much else to do
on the island, we walked to the mailbox.

Everybody knew about the mailbox. We used to watch that '90s
movie in school whenever a teacher called out sick and forgot to
leave a lesson plan for the sub, because it was set in our hometown.
A lonely man and woman start writing love letters to each other,
communicating only through the mailbox, and in the end they
find out they're next-door neighbors. They get married eventually,
but keep the separate houses for some reason, and write to each
other every day until the guy dies of old age or cancer or something. Terrible ending. I never understood why anyone in love
would want to keep each other at arm's length.

"Apparently the porn version of it was called *Bosom Buddies*."
Cam leaned down to whisper this in my ear, jostling me out of
my thoughts.

I shivered when his breath fogged warm against my neck but
pushed him away by reflex, watching with a surge of glee as he
stumbled sideways into a thatch of tall grass. "Like that old show?"

"No, they got it out of a girl's book. *Amy of Seven Gables* or
some shit."

"Why would they name a porno after a girl's book?"

"Who else is gonna walk out here to look at a rusty mailbox?"
Cam pushed hair from his face. "Actual men?"

I gestured between us with one hand, giving him my best don't-
be-stupid glare. "Dude."

"Not you, fairy tale. I mean straight men. You know? Torqued
out from the gym, hunting on Saturdays, church on Sundays
kinda guys."

"Who's gay now?" I drawled, snickering when Cam looked annoyed. "Come on. You totally have a type."

"Yeah, but it ain't that."

I wasn't sure what he meant but didn't press him for details. We were within sight of the mailbox now. Dinged sandblasted metal had rubbed off most of the paint, but its monochrome flag letters were as clear as ever, reflecting checkerboard pools in the dark line of the rising tide: BOSOM FRIENDS.

"So what is?" I asked.

Cam laughed, low in his throat, like he'd expected the question. "If I told you, you probably wouldn't give me the time of day afterward."

"Technically, it's nighttime," I pointed out, not wanting to state the obvious. *Tell me. I want to know.*

He motioned me forward without another word, hooking a thumb around a long chain under his shirt. Threaded on the end was a small ivory bead, no bigger than my pinky nail. Maybe it wasn't a bead; although the top had an oval roundness, like the curve of a waning moon, the bottom was jagged like a stair step or the legs of a kid's plastic chair. Like it was supposed to fit up against something.

"Elk tooth," Cam murmured, his words clouding and fizzing in the small space between us. "From my last guy."

He sounded like he was seventy years old, talking about a nice girl from homeroom who he took to the junior prom. But the bright insistent burst in my gut, a warning flare against saying something stupid, made me rethink the impulse to joke. Instead, I chewed the side of my cheek, weighing how soft muscle rippled harmlessly against the ridges of my back molars.

"He was Navajo," Cam continued. "Out New Mexico way. Before I left for my next post, he gave it to me for safekeeping. The eye teeth are good luck, you know."

"Didn't know that was a Navajo thing."

In this light, and because our faces were so close together, Cam's bared teeth gleamed brighter than the one hanging around his neck.

"Got a whole collection back at the house." Each word warmed the shell of my ear. "Shark. Fox. Mountain lion. Maybe if you're good, I'll show 'em to you."

I was afraid he was going to say something too serious, or that he might try to kiss me, and to avoid it, I dropped to my knees in the sand. Cam's hand tangled roughly in the top of my shaggy hair as I pressed my mouth to the inside of his thigh.

We were quick, but it wasn't romantic. Cam held me by the ears, thrusting into my mouth with fast, messy jerks, stopping only when tears leaked from my eyes and my throat fluttered wildly. Then he'd pull off, leaving me gasping for breath, my fingers digging into the back of his cargo shorts. I couldn't hear anything he was saying; every time I surfaced to catch my breath, black spots danced in front of my eyes, and my vision dipped like the waterline. That spot was down by the waves, accompanied by a distant voice. That one was up by the grass, blobbing a winking trail from the shoreline to the surf and back. Near, far, nowhere—oh, god, I was gonna pass out.

Cam yanked my hair in two fists, thrusting forward with a grunt; I had to stifle the reflexive gasp caught in my throat to keep from choking when he finished. He didn't move for a long time. I'm not sure how long, but every second ticked by like an eternity. My eyes burned, my hands shook, and my body ached for breath—a beached whale on the shore of someone else's pleasure. Finally, just when I felt my vision dimming around the edges, he withdrew, letting me sink to the sand.

I coughed like a tuberculosis patient, gasping and wheezing

for at least a minute with my fists digging into the cold and wet, before turning back to him.

What was that for? I wanted to ask. *Why was that good for you?* But he probably wouldn't answer the question. He watched me fumble around on my hands and knees, a lazy smirk on his face, pale cock still hanging out of his shorts.

"Use my leg" was all he said.

I thought about refusing, or getting up and trying to salvage my pride with a dramatic exit. Instead, I crawled over and wrapped both arms around his quad, letting my thighs bracket his lean calf. When he didn't say anything, I began to move.

The next morning, I woke up to silverware clattering in the kitchen. Before I could haul my ass out of bed or untangle my legs from the sheets, in strode Cam, grinning at me like we hadn't gone our separate ways after we got back from the mailbox. He was wearing a pair of dark basketball shorts and no shirt and had a smear of peanut butter sticking to the side of his palm.

"God, you look good belly down."

I scoffed, even though it was hard to get a full breath, staring over one shoulder. "What are you doing here?"

"Come on." I watched the fine lines on his face carve jagged grooves into his forehead and around his eyes. "Can't a guy come over to say good morning anymore?"

"How'd you get in?"

"Side door. Picked the lock." With a pleased laugh, Cam slid across the backs of my legs, pinning me to the bed with his weight. He palmed my quads through the sheets, and then turned, so he was lying on top of me. "Didn't you miss me?"

"You should've told me you were coming over," I said, trying to ignore the way his hand was sliding between my body and the mattress. "Cam. I'm not kidding."

You can't walk around here like you own the damn place. You can't break into my family's house.

"Shut up, Joey," he breathed, low and fond, and put his free hand over my mouth. His fingers curled around the edge of my jaw like trailing vines, warm and weighty. My heartbeat pulsed rabbit-fast in my throat when I realized he wasn't going to move them away.

He was rougher that time: pinning me to the bed with his full weight as he speared me like a gutted fish, one palm clapped across my mouth and the other twisting painfully at my belly. He spat on his cock, a pitiful attempt at slicking up, and pistoned his hips in fast deep thrusts until he came inside me, collapsing onto my back. When he finally let me up, I limped gingerly into the hall bathroom—half-hard, aching, and chafed raw but trying not to show it—and he belly laughed, like seeing me wince was the funniest thing in the world. That was the first time I thought I was in trouble.

It's hard to explain why I didn't kick Cam out after that. We'd only hooked up for a few days. By normal standards, I didn't owe him anything beyond a polite brush-off and a snack for the road, if I was feeling generous. But every time I thought I should end it, or thought about the rest of the summer stretching out in front of me, long and lonely, he'd manage to knock me out of my rut. Being with him wasn't all bad, either. When he was on and at his best, he could command an entire room's attention, turning heads to him like flowers bending to the midday sun. He'd charm waitresses and delight strangers with jokes and never falter—never worry that someone hated him or consider how much space he took up in a room.

I wasn't like that. I'd never been good at boosting anyone's confidence, mine included. One time, down in the workshop when I was about eight or nine, I'd asked my grandpa what he thought our best qualities were: us grandkids, that is. I even let him talk about Abby first, since she was his favorite.

"Real bulldog," Grandpa said without hesitation, mouth twisting in approval. "Hard worker." And it was true; anyone who saw my sister knew she didn't take any shit. By the time she was a sophomore, she was first in her class, on homecoming court, and in as many clubs as she could fit into a five-day week. This was before the accident, of course.

"Okay. What about me?"

"Ah, my Joe-Joe. You're tenderhearted."

"I am *not*," I insisted, although I was sure it wasn't an insult. "Grandpa!"

"It's all right," he said, waving through my irritation like he was brushing aside a gnat cloud; I watched his hand burnish the air under the pull-chain light bulb. "Not every dog in the pack can fight."

Disappointment clenched my chest like an unseen fist, squeezing until the pressure made the words burst from my mouth. "What if I want to?"

He gave me a sharp look, as quick as if he were figuring someone's taxes. Up went one eyebrow, a fearsome dark squiggle in the valley of his face. "You want to?"

"I can do it," I swore, edging up on my tiptoes, bouncing with excitement. "I promise."

"All right." He motioned me away from the table saw, using one work-booted foot to shuffle my light-up cartoon sneakers into position. "Make an *L* with your feet. Put your weight on your back leg."

I focused all my energy on staying still while he arranged me into the right shape: feet shoulder-width apart, knees bent, back straight, chest turned slightly to the right, head forward. After a minute, he urged my hands up.

"Make a fist," he told me, closing my limp fingers into a loose circle. "Don't stick your thumb inside, or you'll break it. Tuck it behind your first finger. And don't lead with the knuckle, either."

He walked around me in a half circle, approving, as I struggled not to let my arms drop to my sides.

"Okay." Twitching up the legs of his jeans, he knelt down about a foot away from me, and stretched out a hand, palm out, until it hovered within the center of my vision. "Aim for the center of my palm."

Fear twisted in my stomach like a bad meal. "I have to hit you?"

"It'll be fine," Grandpa assured me. "Won't hurt a bit."

"Maybe we can practice on the seat cushion," I hedged, coming out of my fighting stance as my back leg wobbled and folded in like a rusty chair.

"No. You're gonna tap my hand, right here." Grandpa thumped me in the chest with two fingers so I'd straighten up. "Come on. Let's see it."

His hand trembled a little midair; I worried that even striking it with two fingers might make the shakes worse.

"But what if I—?"

"Come on, now."

My arms were sore from holding them up for so long. "Maybe we could just—"

Grandpa's easy humor melted away, replaced by a hard, flinty expression I'd never seen before. "Damn it, Joseph, you want to fight, then shut up and hit me!"

Startled, I flinched back and lost my footing. The back of my head thunked against some plywood, my eyes filled, and I started to cry in thin, reedy gulps.

My grandpa's face showed every minute of his age when I finally looked at him, but he didn't yell at me or tell me I was stupid, just moved forward on his knees, cupping the back of my head in one gnarled hand before showing me his clean palm. "Hey, you're okay. No blood."

"I'm sorry," I choked out. "I didn't want to hurt you."

He was quiet as he brushed sawdust off my shoulders and straightened my shirt. When he cleared his throat and lifted my chin so he could look at me, all he said was "If you ever do fight, Joe-Joe, don't think about hurting or not hurting. Fling sand in their eyes, twist their nuts, take them down at the knees. Just stay calm, and don't let yourself get cornered."

"Why not?"

Grandpa gave a sharp, ugly laugh. "'Cause if you're cornered, you're desperate. And desperate men do things they might regret down the road."

After the first couple of weeks, the tooth collection made its way into the house. A slash of sour fury fizzed in my stomach the first time Cam showed it to me. I knew I was supposed to be impressed, and made all the right noises, but watching him dote over it made me want to pick up a hammer and smash that wooden box into pieces. He treated that fucking thing better than me, wiping specks of nonexistent dust from the lacquered lid at least once a day.

Once a week, he'd take out pale yellow, seaweed-brown, and basalt-black teeth to polish them with a microfiber cloth before placing them back into the velvet-lined box. He'd talk to them gently, lovingly, as if they were long-lost friends. Hell, he'd even named most of them: Marlon. Pinkie. Brie. Terminator. Underneath that varnished lid, he'd tucked a scrawled list on lined yellow paper, featuring their names, locations, and dates.

I sent a picture of the open box to my childhood friend Billy
Jack, a Lumbee bartender who used to live a few towns inland. We
ran track together in high school but didn't talk often. He'd send
me grainy unfocused pictures of the family every now and again;
they'd moved to Manteo so he could pick up more private gigs.
Since I had little to send back except funeral news, I sent him a
picture of the tooth collection, half-open on a polishing day, trying
to make it sound funny:

> new dude collects animal teeth. even keeps a navajo elk
> tooth around his neck. weird, right?

All I got back was a raised-eyebrow emoji and the cryptic:

> bro your white boi hookups just keep getting creepier and
> creepier
> pretty sure those are human teeth in the back, too

Rolling my eyes, I typed out a quick reply:

> relax, he prolly just kept his childhood molars or smth

Three dots appeared, then vanished.

> no kid has gums that big, dude.
> i'm gonna ask one of my regulars whos a dentist, see if he
> can back me up
> if i'm right you should make like an elder, sage your
> whole damn house to get rid of the bad medicine

only bad medicine you know is bon jovi, I wrote back, but quickly
pocketed my phone when I heard Cam's voice nearby.

"Who the hell are you smiling at?" he asked as I looked up. "You're not back here coming on to some other dude, are you?"

I would have laughed, but the dark flush in his face and the snarl curling his lip told me it was a bad idea.

"No," I said, offering a stiff smile. "Just checking my email."

Cam didn't say anything at first. Then, he came closer, looming over me until I had to walk backward to keep from being knocked over. Only when my back hit the wood-paneled wall did he stop, flash a wolfish grin, and rap my pocketed phone with his knuckles—same way idiots in the locker room acted in tenth grade, if they were about to towel-whip you in the nards.

"What?" I asked him. The sudden shift in mood made my head spin. What the hell was he trying to do? "Cam, why are you laughing?"

"Ah, Joey." Cam bared his teeth in another smile. "I know you. Probably on the 'gram, trying to see who complimented your shirtless pic."

I had posted a selfie there yesterday. Wasn't that sexy, just a regular candid snap Cam had taken while I was walking back to the blanket. Had gotten a couple of emoji-laden comments from friends, and that was all. I didn't even tell him I'd posted it. I didn't even know he'd seen it.

Cam leaned down like he was going to kiss my neck. Instead, his breath fogged against my ear. "Just remember, baby. Nobody gets to look at you but me."

Sometimes, Cam would stop what he was doing to stare at me, searching my face the way someone else might study a museum painting. He'd watch me go through whatever I was doing, unblinking, and then offer up some bald comment:

"I should tie you to this chair so you can't ever leave."

"One day, I'll have you all to myself."

"You gonna think about me when you die, Joey?"

That one made me startle. "What, like on my deathbed? Jesus."

"Sure." He made a pleased noise. "Say you're ninety years old, telling the rest home about all the hot dudes you banged in your twenties. Promise you'll remember me?"

"How could I forget?" The huffed laugh slipped out before I could stop it. "The guy who choked me on the beach with his dick and picked the lock on my door the morning after. Wasn't sure if he was gonna kiss me or kill me. That's romance, baby."

Cam blinked at me as if I'd made some passing comment about the weather, but his flat, uninterested look widened into a snakish smile. "Better than. 'Cause it's forever."

Cam had basically moved in by Labor Day weekend, although none of his stuff had made it into the house except the fucking tooth collection. Selfishly, I was glad about that; it meant I didn't have to trip over his Xbox controllers or a duffel full of old T-shirts every time I walked around my bedroom.

What I hated more than anything was how he'd begun to move my stuff around. First it was boxes or bags of old clothes getting shuffled from the living room and down to the workshop, which was annoying but made sense. Then he started picking knick-knacks up at random, proclaiming he'd toss them out: a soap dish my grandma bought in the mountains, a bronze ship my grandpa put in the tiny window of the hall bathroom so it could sail along the clouds. But Cam's least favorite thing in my house was the brown-and-white ceramic crock that sat in the middle of the kitchen counter. With a dark lip and interior, but a pale glaze outside, it featured line drawings of the Three Sisters—corn, beans, and squash—on the front in faint brown strokes. Looking at it made me imagine how many generations of flour- and oil-spotted hands had picked it up. It was the one thing my grandpa kept from his home in Saint Regis. Cam took every opportunity he had to let me know how much he hated it.

"That thing is so fucking ugly," he told me on Monday afternoon. I'd just washed a week's worth of dishes and was wiping down the vinyl with diluted bleach water.

"No, it isn't," I answered sharply, and scrubbed a little harder at a dark smudge with the sponge. Filmy gray foam bubbled up below my fingers, and a damp spot pressed its way into my hoodie pocket, where I'd slung a couple of dry rubber gloves. "It's an antique. Handmade."

"It's some bullshit seventies grocery store reject, Joey. There's not even a lid. What the hell is it even good for?"

"I don't know," I snapped, pushing the sponge across the countertop with as much force as I could manage. It flew out of my hand and bumped against the side of the crock, bouncing harmlessly off to one side.

"Uh-oh," Cam mocked, picking up the crock by the lip with one hand. "Better let me hold this before you break the damn thing. I sure hope I don't drop it . . ."

He stumbled back and forth across the linoleum, stretching his mouth into an exaggerated rictus as he tipped the crock from side to side, letting it slip from his fingers inch by inch before catching the base of it in his other hand.

As I watched him pretend to slip and fall with my family's crock clenched in one hand, any last bit of attraction to him fell out of my head. I no longer saw him as Cam, the hot summer stranger, or Cam, the mysterious dude with the tooth collection. I just saw a jackass who thought it was funny to toy with things I treasured—who liked turning everything about me and my family's house into a joke. And I was fucking tired of it.

Ignoring his slapstick act, I walked into the living room, scanning the tables for the one thing he gave a damn about. When I spotted that pale wooden box tucked carefully by a set of keys, I snatched it up.

Cam's laugh, distant and raucous, still echoed through the house. "Whoooooa, I'm dropping the shit-colored jug, Joey!"

"Fine!" I called back.

I'm not sure what I meant to do next—if I would rush back to the kitchen with a fake act of my own, or crow that I could act like an idiot, too, and watch the color drain from Cam's face as I held that ugly pale box over the garbage disposal.

A series of shrill pings in a row caught my attention instead: it was my phone, chirping over and over like I'd been caught on a holiday group text. Frowning, I walked over and glanced at the screen; I had three missed calls, two voice mails, and at least a dozen texts, all from Billy Jack.

I couldn't tell which message had come in first, but the text that caught my eye was in all caps:

> THEY'RE DUCKING HUMAN TEETH, DUDE
> 4 ON THE FAR RIGHT AND THE FRIST 2 IN
> BOTTOM LEFT OF PIC
> CARLTON SAYS 2ND AND 3RD MOLARS
> MAYBE—3RD ARE WISDOM TEETH
> NOONE HAS WISDOM TEETH LAYING
> AROUND IN BOXES
> THIS DUDE IS BAD DUCKING NEWS

A dark canyon had cracked open inside me, replacing every useless feeling in my body with the insistent press to *move*, quick and quiet. I placed my phone on the table and walked carefully toward the back door, still wearing my hoodie, no shoes, and with Cam's tooth collection tucked under my arm.

As I walked out, leaving the door ajar, the canyon filled me with a single purpose: go to the pier. You know the pier better than anyone.

I went, still walking, because running would have drawn too much attention. I ignored the line of idling cars that sat waiting to get onto the bridge crossing the Intracoastal Waterway. I ignored the distant sounds of people packing up houses and cars and plastic-wheeled beach carts. I floated past the road and down the boardwalk until the ground under my feet was pale shifting sand and the dark choppy gray of the Atlantic opened up in front of me.

Automatically, I hooked a right off the boardwalk, heading directly under the pier. High tide was coming in. On any other weekend, the thin stroke of shade beside the long columns of wood pilings would have been dotted with weary, sunburned beachgoers trying to get out of the heat for a few minutes. Today it was quiet except for the static buzz of the waves.

A twinge at the base of my skull, sudden as the strike of a match, made me turn around—and there, slightly out of breath as he jogged up to me, was Cam, squinting against the light, though it was overcast.

The sprawling canyon inside my body made me brave. I dug my toes into the hard, spongy sand. "You saw my phone."

"Joey," he answered, still smiling that same toothy grin, "I don't want to hurt you. I promise."

He took two slow steps my way, but something was wrong; he wasn't moving the way he normally did, and there was a weird lump jutting out from his windbreaker sleeve.

So I threw the wooden box straight at his face, savoring the horror that rippled over his features as he batted it up toward the rocky shore. Enamel bits sprayed out along the cratered sand, but Cam didn't go after them, and I didn't have time to course correct.

When I barreled into him, the force of the blow drove us both into a damp, algae-covered piling; reeling from the impact, I barely had time to suck in a breath before Cam was surging forward with both fists. He punched me twice in the gut, sending a sharp shock scorching down my middle.

Groaning, sputtering blood, I doubled over, but instead of trying to haul myself up into a fighting stance, I flung my aching body down into the sand, knee-first, welcoming the cold lap of the tide against my lower legs. Slinging a handful of wet silt up into Cam's eyes, I swung my right leg forward and around, catching him just behind his left knee and forcing his feet out from under him.

He went down with a yelp, arms pinwheeling as he sailed backward. A long streak of silver flew out of his jacket and landed back on the rocks with a metallic thunk. I didn't stop to see what it was, just stumbled forward into the surf, slamming my fists into his mouth and temples as hard as I could. Pain knifed down my knuckles, but it didn't stop me; I hit him again and again until I couldn't tell whether the thick blood dripping down my nose and mouth was mine or his—until Cam wasn't struggling anymore.

Only then, my split hands cramped and shaking, did I stumble off him and back up to the rocks—past the lacquered box, lying half-open by a dark column, past the partially buried teeth jutting up from the tide pools at odd angles. From here, they looked like any other seashells. I fumbled around the boulders at the base of the pier before I found what Cam had hidden up his sleeve: glimmering in the low light, sticking out from the seam of a few smaller rocks.

An old pair of needle-nose pliers.

Conley Lyons is an Indigenous writer of Comanche, German, and Irish descent. Raised in North Carolina's Blue Ridge Mountains, she currently lives in Charlotte, North Carolina. She has a BA in English literature and creative writing from Elon University and an MFA from the Institute of American Indian Arts. She was also an inaugural Natalie Diaz Fellow for Jack Jones Literary Arts. Her writing can be found in *them* and *Bitch Planet: Triple Feature*.

WINGLESS

MARCIE R. RENDON

I watched Punk carefully pull one wing off the fly, then the second. The fly joined five other wingless creatures walking around the wooden picnic table as Punk unscrewed the top of the mason jar and quickly pulled another fly from the twenty or so buzzing around in there. The July heat baked down on us. Punk's sun-darkened skin looked bluish in the creases of his arm and on the back of his neck. Mine a reddish brown. Punk was always relegated to outdoor work while I was confined inside doing mundane chores. Rarely were we allowed in the same space at the same time. Today was different.

At ten, I was two years younger than Punk. I marveled at his lightning reflexes—the quickness with which he grabbed a fly out of the jar, and how he gently held the fly immobile between the thumb and the pointer finger of his left hand while he used the same fingers of the opposite hand to remove the wings without killing it. He looked at me and grinned as he pulled a wing off, his brown eyes turned black with excitement.

Today had started out like any other summer day. Wake at sunrise. Roll out of bed. My bed was in the attic. Bare wooden rafters with spiderwebs in the dark corners. Steaming hot. Punk's bed was on the screened-in porch attached to the northern side of the house. Out there, the nighttime chill never wears off until around 9:00 a.m.

I guess he captured his supply of flies as they suction-walked across the wire mesh screen of the porch. Because it is my job to houseclean, I also know he has a jar of black crickets and grasshoppers under his bed. I know what he did to them. At that time, I didn't know why he had a small jar of human hair hidden at the very back of the bottom drawer of his dresser.

When I woke up, I headed downstairs to help start the farm breakfast. Eggs and bacon. A cast iron skillet full of diced potatoes left over from last night's meal. This morning I was quick, and lucky. I only got head-slapped once for breaking the yolk on an egg as I cracked it into the frying pan. Later, I was slapped across the face with a slimy wet dishrag for failing to get all the bacon grease off a plate when washing the dishes. Depending on the foster mother's mood, some mornings could become an all-out brawl.

The beatings ranged from slaps to the face to body-damaging attacks with any hefty object in her reach. I have a movie-type memory of hiding under the kitchen table with her screaming like a maniac, "Get the hell out from under there!" All the while she was bent down, swinging a cast iron frying pan as hard as she could, aiming for any part of my body. Thank God I am small and quick enough to scoot into tight spaces. With one rageful swing, she cracked the table leg. At that exact moment, Punk walked into the kitchen.

"You stupid, cowlike bitch." He was grinning while he said it. The same grin he had on his face as he calmly pulled wings off flies here at the wooden picnic table. She whipped around, cast iron frying pan midair. I can still see the jiggling of her underarm fat and hear her scream as she tore after him.

I can hear his laughter as he ran, the screen door slamming behind him. She pushed through it and chased him around the gravel driveway out front. I peeked from behind the kitchen curtain as I watched him dart back and forth, getting within a foot of her swinging arm, then dashing away. She screamed, "Stop running, get over here!" He laughed, head thrown back as he ran, lifting his knees high like a cartoon character on TV, always just out of reach. She finally gave up, doubled over, breathing heavily, hands grasping her side, and the cast iron frying pan dropped on the ground. Punk continued to taunt her by skipping to the barn, grinning over his shoulder in her direction.

That night, with the attic window open, hoping for a small breeze, I heard soft thuds, like the sound of hay bales being tossed around. I went to the window to try and figure out what the sound was. The tightening in my gut and the rapid beating of my heart told me whatever was going on wasn't good.

Punk didn't come for breakfast the next morning. I was told to stay inside and clean the house from top to bottom. I didn't see him for three more days. When he finally did appear, he gave me a wink with the one eye that wasn't black and blue. He grinned even though he limped to the table, winced when he sat down, and used only his right arm while eating. When I got a chance to sneak outside and talk to him behind the barn, where he was tossing chicken feed, I begged him to tell me what happened. He refused. He couldn't move his left arm for a good week or more, and through his thin shirt I could see what looked like a bone pushing against the skin between his neck and shoulder.

The next couple of weeks were heavy with silence. When the foster parents walked, their heavy feet echoed on hardwood floors inside the house. Outside, dust puffed up on the roadway as they walked from the house to the barn or the garage. Pale green and yellow moths moved softly through the air. Airplanes flew silently overhead, leaving contrails in long white streaks across the blue sky.

Mealtimes were silent. Everyone avoided eye contact. "Please pass the potatoes," "please pass the gravy" followed by the mandatory "thank you" were the only words exchanged. It was understood that Punk and I couldn't leave the table until whatever food we were served was gone. Parsnips made Punk gag. With every bite, he would jump up, run from the table, and throw up outside. Each time, the foster mother would spoon another pile of the ugly vegetables onto his plate. She took delight in serving parsnips every other night.

After a constant stream of parsnips being served, with Punk throwing up at each meal, Punk arrived one night at the supper table and groaned slightly when he saw it was parsnips again. My stomach clenched, but when the vegetables were plopped on his plate, he shook his head slightly, grinned and said, "Thank you." I side-eye watched him stuff his mouth full, then wash it all down with big gulps of milk. He winked at me. Took another big mouthful and gulped more milk. The parsnips were gone. Punk moved on to eating mashed potatoes and a pork chop. The foster mother angrily scraped her fork across her dinner plate as she shoved her own food into her mouth.

It was during that time of silence and tiptoeing around that Punk shared a secret with me. We were at Sunday service, sitting next to each other on the hard wooden pew of the Lutheran Church. I was drawing butterflies in a small notebook. Punk was competing with the church choir on who could sing loudest. The foster mother got red in the face and reached over her husband's lap and squeezed Punk's thigh until her knuckles turned white.

I watched him close his eyes and bear the pain. He didn't flinch or move his leg. He continued to sing, "*Rock of ages, cleft for me*"—holding the *me* longer than the choir and then breaking into a long, off-key *ee* at the end of the stanza. Some big kids sitting in the back pew got the giggles. The foster mother used her fingers to flick Punk in the face. The song ended, and the minister began to preach. The foster mother folded her hands in her lap, lips scrunched and eyes squinted. I could almost hear her thinking, *Wait until we get home,* as the minister preached forgiveness.

Punk nudged me with his elbow. When I looked, he opened his suit coat and took something out of the inside pocket. At first, I couldn't see what it was. Then he put it in my hand. I knew enough to very carefully—sneakily, in fact—open my hand to see what he had given me.

It was a tiny doll made of straw. It had human hair and wore a tiny scrap of fabric I recognized as cloth from one of the foster mother's dresses. One of her best dresses. I felt my eyes widen. I quickly closed my hand over the doll and handed it back to him.

He grinned. His eyes shone. He opened his suit coat again and pulled a sewing pin out of the pocket. Barely opening his hand, he stabbed the pin into the straw doll. After a few swift pokes, he put the pin and the doll back into the pocket of his suit coat. He reached over and took my writing pad with hand-drawn butterflies flitting around flowers and wrote in tiny letters, *voodoo doll.* I leaned slightly forward to look at the foster mother, wondering if she was in pain. She glared at me, and I quickly sat back.

Back at the farm, Punk was told he wouldn't eat for the rest of the week or until he repented for his sin of embarrassing the family at church with his "ridiculous singing." He was sent out to feed the chickens and move hay bales around in the upper loft while we sat down for Sunday dinner. It was hard for me to eat. Afterward, while cleaning the table, I hid a biscuit and a piece of chicken in my pocket. After washing and drying the dishes, I went outside to find Punk.

He was throwing a pocketknife into a human target drawn in mud on the far side of the barn, out of sight from the house. I gave him the food. Before he ate, he showed me how to throw the knife. When he threw it, it stuck in the wood. When I threw, it landed in the dirt. He said, "Don't worry. It just takes practice."

By Thursday of that week, I begged him to repent. I didn't want him to starve to death. He laughed and said, "Raw eggs are the new health food."

On Friday, we were told to get out to the garage. It was time to butcher chickens. I had been with this foster family since school let out for the summer, and I had no idea how this job was done. Punk seemed eager to get to work. Sharp knives were lined on the planks of the wooden tables that were set up. Plastic buckets were on the ground next to wire crates with live chickens clucking loudly.

I watched as the foster father got a fire going in a steel barrel and placed a metal washtub filled with water over the flames. Once the water was boiling, he grabbed a chicken from its cage, stretched its neck over a large log, and chopped its head off with a quick swing of a small axe. He threw the head in one plastic bucket and the chicken on the ground. The chicken, headless, took off running across the yard. "Get it," the foster mother yelled at Punk.

Punk chased the flopping bird as blood squirted in all directions. When he brought the chicken back, the foster mother, holding it by its yellow, clawed feet, dunked the still-flopping, headless bird into the boiling water. After a couple of minutes, she pulled the steaming, stinky, wet feathered mass out of the water, slapped it on the wooden table, and showed me how to strip the feathers off the dead bird. I choked back vomit.

When the birds were stripped naked, she used a cleaver to cut the chicken open between its legs. She reached inside and pulled the guts out and dropped them into a plastic bucket at her feet. It became an assembly line of chop, flop, chase, boil, pluck, and gut. I was afraid to throw up and just kept plucking feathers. Punk began singing, off-key of course, *"Great big gobs of greasy, grimy gopher guts, marinated monkey . . ."*

As the word *nuts* flew out of his mouth, the foster mother, hands covered in chicken-gut slime, karate chopped him right across his neck. He didn't make a sound as he collapsed to the ground. I thought he was dead.

She kicked him. Yelled, "Get up, you lazy bastard."

Her husband quickly stepped between them. "You knocked him out," he said. He leaned over Punk. "Hey, kid. Get up. Come on, get up." He gave Punk a shake.

Punk moaned.

"I thought he was dead. Maybe his shoulder's broke," I heard myself squeak.

"Nah, he just got the wind knocked out of him," the man said. He pulled Punk up. Set him shakily on his feet. Even as darkly tanned as Punk was, he looked like a ghost. The foster father walked him to the porch. I watched through the screen as Punk was flopped down on his bed.

The man came back. "I told him to catch his breath and then get back out here," he said as he pulled another chicken out of the wire cage and chopped off its head.

It became my job both to chase the flopping, headless chickens *and* to pluck the soggy feathers off them.

I can't tell you exactly how or why it happened. I know I saw red. I still thought I might throw up. Then I thought I might pass out. In my mind, I saw Punk stabbing pins into his straw doll.

The foster mother was using one hand to hold a leg away from the bird's body so she could reach in with her other hand to pull out the guts. The cleaver she had been using to split open the chicken lay on the table beside her. I picked up the cleaver and, quickly, using both arms and all my strength, I chopped off the hand that was inside the chicken.

I remember sitting at the picnic table with Punk as he pulled wings off flies. Maybe her scream brought him running from the porch. I'm still not sure how we ended up sitting at the picnic table together. I know there was an ambulance. I know some neighboring farmers showed up. I heard someone say the social worker was coming to get Punk. I remember Punk's grin and the wink he gave me when I was placed in the police car. The last thing I saw was his thumbs-up wave as they took me away.

Marcie R. Rendon is an enrolled member of the White Earth Nation and an author, playwright, poet, and freelance writer. As a community arts activist, Rendon supports other Native artists/writers/creators to pursue their art.

She is the award-winning author of a fresh new murder-mystery series that features protagonist Cash Blackbear, and she has an extensive body of fiction and nonfiction works.

The creative mind behind Raving Native Theater, Rendon has also curated community-created performances such as *Art Is . . . Creative Native Resilience*, featuring three Anishinaabe performance artists, which premiered on TPT (Twin Cities Public Television) in June 2019.

Rendon received the McKnight Distinguished Artist of the Year Award 2020 and was recognized as a "50 Over 50 Changemaker" by AARP Minnesota and Pollen in 2018. Rendon and Diego Vazquez received a 2017 Loft Spoken Word Immersion Fellowship for their work with women incarcerated in county jails.

QUANTUM

NICK MEDINA

"Mother fuck," Amber Cloud said, studying the certificate in her left hand, then the one in her right. Both bore the same header:

**UNITED STATES
DEPARTMENT OF THE INTERIOR**
BUREAU OF INDIAN AFFAIRS

"Didn't I tell you it'd turn out this way?" Dave Blackburn said. He pulled her down on the sofa next to him and wrapped an arm around her. Lips pecking her temple, his eyes strained to read what the certificates said.

On her left:

This is to certify that:
<u>*Samuel Joseph Scott*</u>
born <u>*2/17/21*</u> is ⅛ degree Indian blood

On her right:

> This is to certify that:
> _Grayson Joshua Blackburn_
> born _12/28/21_ is ⁵⁄₁₆ degree Indian blood

"I know Sammy was as much a mistake as Gray, but didn't your mama ever tell you not to get your kicks off the rez? To keep the bloodlines pure."

Amber backhanded Dave's chest. "They were surprises, not mistakes. And no. My mom told me to marry a rich white man who could afford to move my ass out of here."

"What are you doing with me then?"

"Shut up, Dave." Amber pushed his arm from her shoulders and took to her feet, pacing in front of the TV. "How do I get Sammy on the tribal roll?" She eyed the meager fraction on Sammy's certificate as if she could will it up to one quarter.

"You don't."

"You know what this means . . ."

"It means Sammy's gonna be pissed on his twenty-first birthday."

"It means Gray will have opportunities that Sammy won't."

"Kinda funny, isn't it . . ." Dave said.

Amber scowled at him.

"Not funny," he said. "Ironic is what I meant. It's usually the firstborn who benefits most. You know, the heir and the spare."

Amber's mind cycled through the disparities her unintended boys might face, one of them entitled to money from the tribe's casino, the other out of luck. Gray would afford the university of his choice. Sammy would settle for community college or a trade. Gray would buy a house and land. Sammy would bust his ass to afford rent. Gray would see the world. Sammy would see the same work route day in and day out. Gray would be Native. Sammy would be something else.

"Nothin' you can do about it," Dave said.

Sammy fussed in the boys' bedroom as though upset about the news.

Amber stood between the cribs, Sammy on her left, Grayson on her right. Both boys favored her tawny skin, her dark brown eyes, her raven hair. But only one was like her and Dave.

"You put that there?" she whispered to Dave, standing in the doorway.

"It's the same one my ma hung over my cradle when I was a kid."

Amber's fingertips played over the spiderweb-like netting of the dream catcher dangling above Grayson's crib. She wondered if she should get one for Sammy, to protect him from evil in the night.

"Do you think it'd even work for him?" she asked Dave, her eyes on her oldest child, curiously curled in his crib, his nose near his toes.

"Why wouldn't it? Because he's a mutt?"

"Don't say that."

"We're all mutts," Dave said. "Just not as much as him."

Sammy stirred. His body uncurled, and he pulled himself into a standing position using the balusters of the crib. He smiled at his mother, drool dripping down either side of his mouth, and reached for her over the railing. Amber stepped in his direction, subconsciously hating his smile because it belonged to his father, the white boy who hadn't enough money to move her off the rez, let alone pay for Pampers.

Mutt, she thought, thinking Dave might be right. Maybe

Sammy was a mistake, just like hooking up with his father. She rushed to Gray when he suddenly whimpered in his sleep.

The per capita checks arrived. $1,159 each. More would come next month. And the month after that. The statement for Grayson's trust fund arrived as well, his money already earning interest in the account he wouldn't be able to access until he turned twenty-one.

"That's yours," Amber said, speaking in soft, high tones to the baby balanced on her knee. Gray grasped a corner of the bank statement with an uncoordinated, slobbery fist. He shook the paper, wetting it, tearing it. Amber giggled. "My little Indian." She nuzzled his fuzzy head as Sammy crawled across the floor at her feet.

"Daddy!" she said to Gray upon hearing a truck door slam outside.

Beaming, Amber held her check up in one hand, the sealed envelope containing Dave's in the other, as her man came bursting through the door.

"Big John LaBarge is dead," Dave announced.

Sammy crawled up beside his mother. One of his dimpled hands battered her bare foot.

Amber's smile faded. "No, he's not," she said to Dave, refusing to believe. Big John had been ancient when she was born. She'd thought he'd be ancient forever, the last of the tribe's old-school Indians.

"Word's getting around," Dave said. "I just heard the news over at the Black Bear."

Squeezing his mother's leg, Sammy pulled himself to his feet and pinched the knee opposite his baby brother.

"Down," Amber said, wincing. Her palm against his forehead, she pushed Sammy back onto the floor. "What were you doing at the Black Bear?"

"Having a drink with the boys." Dave plucked his envelope from her hand. "Told 'em I'd be back."

"You'd better not blow it all on booze."

"Who made you my mother?" He grabbed a fresh pack of cigarettes from the carton on the counter and crammed it into his back pocket.

"What about Big John?" Amber said.

"What about him?"

She shrugged. "It'll be weird without him around."

"Maybe it'll mean more money for the rest of us." Dave tore open his envelope, letting it fall once he had his check in his hand.

"Maybe," Amber said.

Dave kissed the check, then bent and kissed Amber on the head. Sammy climbed up her leg again.

"I'll be home late," Dave said on his way out the door.

"I said get down," Amber snapped, knocking Sammy to the floor.

"Aren't they adorable?" Amber pulled the pair of moccasins, each no bigger than the size of her palm, from the box on the coffee table. "Handmade by Mink Oshoge. She crafts the cutest damn things."

Dave swung Grayson high into the air, making the baby squeal. "What'd those run you?"

"Don't worry about it. They're worth it." She shook the little leather shoes, making their tassels shake and their shiny glass beads rattle. "Anything for my little Indian."

"You know he's going to outgrow them in a month. The kid grows like a weed. He's already almost as big as your mistake."

"Huh?"

Dave jerked his head toward the corner where Sammy lay on his side, needing a new diaper, atop an old sweatshirt and other dirty laundry. His arms and legs straight out before him, they looked extra long compared to his narrow body, sunken around the waist and sheer around the ribs.

Amber returned her attention to the moccasins. Her face lit up. "He can wear them to the funeral. For Big John. He was more Indian than all of us."

"Hate to break it to you, babe, but Big John's not gonna care."

"So? Everyone else will. I can't wait for them to see."

Dave swung Grayson again, then planted him on the couch beside his mother. She blew a raspberry at the child, making him laugh some more, then slipped the moccasins onto his chubby feet.

"I knew he'd like them," Amber said.

Gray rolled onto his back, toes in the air, and reached for the beads attached to his new shoes.

"Perfect for when he starts to walk," Amber said. "Soft. Flexible. I wanna film him when he takes his first steps."

"You haven't filmed the kid enough?" Dave stuck a cigarette between his lips and grabbed a lighter from the coffee table.

Amber picked up her phone and scrolled through the videos she'd shot of Gray. Dozens of them. "I don't wanna miss a moment." She turned the camera on the boy. "This little Indian just got his first pair of moccasins," she said, narrating. "One day he'll be chairman of the tribe."

In the corner, Sammy stirred, his left leg scratching the itch on his side.

Dave picked the narrow piece of wood with strings strung through it up off the table. "The string game!" he said. "Haven't seen one of these since I was a kid."

Amber snatched it from him and dangled it over Grayson's

head. The child, planted in his high chair, giggled and swatted at the strings. "I want him to be raised in the ways of the tribe. All the old traditions. The old-fashioned toys. I want him to know his roots." She gave in and let Gray grab the stick from her. One end went straight into his mouth.

"He's a little young for it, don't you think?"

"It's in his blood." She shrugged.

Dave took his usual seat at the table, one hand holding a cigarette over an ashtray, the other making sure Grayson wouldn't hurt himself. Amber turned to the boiling pot of pasta on the stove. She heaved it to the sink to pour the water out.

"I've been thinking about Big John," she said, steam billowing in her face, fogging her sight. "It doesn't seem right to just let him go."

"What do you mean?"

"He must be at least three-quarters. Maybe more."

Dave's face frazzled. "I don't understand."

"His quantum."

"Yeah?"

"It's high."

"So?" Dave questioned.

"Just seems like a loss to the tribe."

"Big John's a big loss." Dave wouldn't argue with that.

Amber set the pot back on the stovetop, her back to Dave. "He was special," she said. "We'll never see the likes of him again."

"Did you even really know him? I mean, when's the last time you saw Big John?"

Amber shrugged again. "It's just a shame, is all I'm saying." She scooped a large spoonful of the plain macaroni elbows from the pot and turned toward the high chair. Her sight still a bit hazy from the steam, she saw something scoot across the kitchen floor, from the corner to the table, where it vanished from sight.

"Yeah, well, what can you do?" Dave took a long drag and

blew the smoke at the ceiling. "You know what they say about balance . . . that the Creator grants us the gift of choosing our parents before we're born so that they'll help us find balance within ourselves, ultimately allowing us to decide how we're born and how we'll die."

Amber, pondering the question Dave just posed, having heard little of what he said after that, flicked the noodles from the spoon onto the tray attached to Grayson's high chair. Gray dropped the string game to the floor, his hands groping for the macaroni instead.

"I guess death's as important as birth," Dave said.

"Maybe," Amber muttered. "I just worry about what will become of the tribe. You know, in time? When the blood runs out."

Sammy crawled out from under the table. Not on his hands and knees, but on his fingers and toes, his vertebral column stretching his skin. He sat beneath his brother's chair and clamped the string game between his teeth.

"It's up to us to make sure the blood lines don't run too thin. Remember what my mom said?"

"Only Netflix and chill on the rez. Got it," Amber said.

Done shoving noodles into his mouth, Gray fussed to get out of the chair. Dave hoisted him and carried him out of the room, leaving Amber to clean up the mess. She brushed the cold and soggy remnants from the tray into her hand. Sammy whimpered. Amber tossed him the scraps. They spattered on the floor.

Amber pushed Grayson along in his buggy, Sammy keeping pace behind them. She parked the stroller beside a picnic bench and lifted the boy out of it.

"Swing time," she said, carrying Gray into the park. Happy

babble spilled from his mouth as she secured him in the baby swing. She'd just given him a push when she spotted Claudia Wolf, her old friend from high school, coming down the path, practically being pulled along by the terrier mix affixed to the leash in her hand.

"Claudia!" Amber waved, beckoning her over.

Claudia's face lit up. The dog yipped and made a beeline for Sammy, scratching in the sand to the left of the swings. "How've you been, girl?" Claudia said. "Last I heard, my mom told me you were about ready to pop. This must be your little angel." She smiled at Grayson, stroking one of his fleshy cheeks.

"He's my little Indian," Amber said. "A total doll." Her gaze traveled from the dog, still yipping at Sam, to Claudia's free hand, now resting on her belly. "Are you . . . ?" she asked.

Claudia's smile widened, showing off gums. "Sixteen weeks," she said.

"That's great! You know what this means, don't you?"

"What?"

"Playdates!" Amber said.

Claudia laughed. "Of course. We need to catch up. What's it been, two years since we've seen each other?"

"Yeah, since you left the rez."

"I'm back now," Claudia said. "Probably for good."

"Is it . . . ?" Amber asked, eyeing Claudia's belly.

"A girl," she said.

"I mean the father. Is he at least one-quarter?"

Claudia's expression puzzled.

"The bloodline," Amber said. "Will your baby be on the tribal roll?"

The dog leapt and yanked the leash, forcing Claudia to grasp it with two hands. "Oh, the roll . . . yeah, she'll be . . ." Claudia's eyes flickered. She looked lost for a moment.

"Everything all right?" Amber asked, pushing Gray again.

"Can you?" She offered Amber the leash and Amber took it. "It's just my blood sugar," Claudia explained. "It's a bit harder to regulate now that I'm . . ." She motioned to her baby bump.

"Oh right," Amber said, remembering that Claudia had been allowed to eat fruit snacks in class and that she'd periodically injected herself with insulin.

Claudia retreated to the picnic bench, where she unzipped a little kit that she pulled from the bag on her shoulder. She filled a syringe, then lifted the side of her shirt and stuck the needle into the lateral part of her abdomen. Done, she capped the syringe and zipped it up inside the kit, which she left with her bag on the bench.

"You've heard about Big John?" she asked, returning to the swings.

Amber nodded, eyes still on Claudia's kit. "The funeral's tomorrow. We'll be there."

Claudia took the leash back and gave it a yank. "That one yours?" she asked, jerking her chin at Sam, yipping like the terrier, rolling around with it in the sand.

"Sam!" Amber clapped her hands, giving Claudia a sympathetic smile.

"Could use a trim, couldn't he?" Claudia said of his matted appearance.

He could use more than that, Amber thought. "Grayson's getting his first cut before the funeral," she said. "Is there a custom for that?"

Claudia shrugged.

"I'll ask Dave."

"Maybe we'll see you there," Claudia said.

"I'll look for you."

Claudia pulled the terrier mix toward the picnic table, Sam growling with discontent. She picked up her bag and the kit and started on her way. "Great seeing you," she called over her shoulder.

Amber waved, her heart giving a kick when Claudia's kit, which Claudia had clumsily tried to shove into her bag, fell to the ground. Amber crept to the table and picked the kit up. Before calling to her old friend, she eased the zipper back and took the syringe out. Pocketing it, she cried, "Claudia! You dropped this."

Mourners wearing button-up shirts, black dresses, dark slacks, and knit blouses stood outside the chapel, puffs of smoke dissipating overhead. A flask went around. It was empty before Dave and Amber, Grayson in her arms, got out of the car and crossed the lot.

"Would you look at him?" Mary Kingfisher said, clutching her chest. Her eyes bounced from Gray's sunny smile to the moccasins on his feet. "He's absolutely precious."

"He looks like my dad, doesn't he?" Amber said, cheery with pride. "A little like Big John, too."

"He's definitely related."

"Number 1223 on the roll."

"Good for him," Mary said.

"Have you been inside?" Amber asked.

Mary nodded, her joyful expression wiped from her face. "Go say your goodbye."

Dave pulled open the chapel door, and Amber took a step inside, only to quickly retreat. She glanced down at the sad sight sitting on the curb, wide eyes searching for attention from someone, anyone.

"Can you keep an eye on him?" she asked Mary. "I shouldn't bring him inside."

"Of course," Mary said, her demeanor turning even more dour when she glanced down at the curb. "He seems . . . well-behaved."

Amber stiffened, her fingers wrapping tight around the strap of the bag hanging from her shoulder. "I'll make it quick."

Dim and cool on the inside, the chapel stretched out before Amber and Dave. A few dozen people sat in the seats facing the casket up front. A handful of others milled about, squinting at photos of Big John, dabbing their eyes, blowing their noses. The faint sounds of flute music floated on the air. It reminded Amber of autumn days when she was a kid, back when Big John would sit on his porch and play, making music that predated them all.

From the rear of the chapel, it was impossible to tell that it was Big John in the casket. It could have been anyone with any color of skin. Struggling to swallow, Amber scanned the seats. She didn't see her parents or Claudia, just a bunch of the elders marking the passage of a dear friend.

Amber passed Gray to Dave. Reaching for his mother, Grayson let out a shout, which seemed to grow louder as it echoed through the chapel rather than rapidly fading into oblivion.

"Take him outside if he gets too fussy," Amber said to Dave.

"Do you want me to come with you?" he asked as she started down the aisle toward the casket on the stand.

Amber shook her head. "Take him to the elders. I'm sure they'd love to see him . . . the next generation."

Dave slipped away, and Amber resumed the lonely journey. The right side of her mouth turned up in a smile when she heard the happy reactions to Gray's appearance, all the sighs and *aww*s. She hoped they'd see the tribal resemblance when looking at him. She hoped they'd see Big John.

Amber stood before the casket and looked down at the man she thought would always be around. His flesh was only a shade or two lighter than she remembered, his long hair whiter than ever.

"Big John," she whispered, one hand landing on top of his, clasped over his chest, heavy and cold. Through his thin, old skin she could feel his knuckles, his bones, his veins. She knew she ought to say a prayer, to wish him well on his voyage from this realm to the next, but the words wouldn't come. All she could think about was how valuable he was.

Glancing over her shoulder, Amber saw that the elders were still engrossed in Gray, giggling so hard that he gasped for every breath. Her hand, cold now too, rose from Big John's and slipped into the bag dangling at her side. Her fingers curled.

Eyes on the biggest, bluest vein on the back of Big John's hand, she quickly pulled the syringe from her purse and stuck the needle into his skin.

"Miss?"

Amber startled, stifling a yelp. Her hands went to her mouth. The syringe sagged, the needle still stuck in Big John's flesh.

"You shouldn't be doing that."

Amber turned to find a man with pale skin standing beside her. Dressed in black and white, his hair was combed in a meticulous part. He reached for the syringe and gently removed it.

"I just . . ." Amber said.

"Just what?" the man asked.

"I don't want it to go to waste."

He raised his eyebrows at her.

"His blood," she said. "It's valuable. There'll never be another drop like it."

"I'm sorry," he said, "but it's already gone."

Amber's face puzzled.

"He's been embalmed," the man explained. "It's a common practice. We drain the blood to preserve the body."

"What do you do with it?"

"We dispose of it."

"You just throw it away?"

Lips tight, he nodded. "What were you going to do with it?"

"I just thought . . ." She looked over her shoulder again, toward the door this time, standing between her and the mistake she wanted to fix. "Big John was more Indian than the rest of us."

The man offered a halfhearted smile. "I suppose it was the blood that made him that way."

Amber lay next to Dave in the dark, half-asleep while Grayson fussed on the bed between them.

"He looked good," Dave said, tired, groggy.

"Huh?"

"Big John."

"Oh . . . yeah . . ." Amber thought about what the funeral director had said, thought about the empty syringe. "What are we really?" she asked.

"What do you mean?"

"Is it our blood that makes us who we are?"

Dave was quiet long enough to make her think he'd drifted to sleep. "Sounds like some philosophy shit," he eventually said.

"Yeah . . . what do we know?"

She closed her eyes and rubbed Gray's back. Once he'd quieted, soft squeaks—whimpers—floated in from outside. Amber lifted her head from the pillow, straining to hear.

"Do you hear that?" she whispered to Dave.

Silence ensued. "Hear what?" he grunted.

The whimpering persisted. Scratching sounds came from the front of the house.

"That," Amber said. "Do you hear that?"

Dave snored.

"Hey!" She shook him, sitting up in bed. "Did you leave the dog out?"

He grunted again.

Amber hopped from bed and crept into the hall, where she stalled. Poking her head back into the bedroom, she said, "Do we even have a dog?"

Dave rolled onto his side. "We have something," he said.

Amber followed the whimpers to the front door. Something was scratching on the other side, aching to get in. Amber pushed the curtains aside in the nearest window. She saw shadows, darkness, and hair. The something whimpered again, and Amber felt it this time, deep inside.

"My god," she gasped, opening the door.

The something wasn't a dog or anything she recognized, though she knew its name. Clawed fingers and toes carrying its long and withered body, covered with a combination of bleeding bald spots and hair tangled with clods of dirt and worse, it crept inside and collapsed on the floor. Crud-crusted eyes looked up at her as it labored to breathe, drawing arduous breaths through the shrinking holes in its muzzle.

Repulsed by the sight of it and its smell, Amber slowly squatted and pulled the thing toward her. It whimpered and whined, getting blood on her fingers. She could feel its bones through its gauzy flesh, fragile and fine.

Still thinking about what the funeral director had said, Amber picked it up and carried it through the house, to the boys' bedroom, where she placed it in its crib.

"Sammy," she said.

Knowing now that the *something* could grow into anything, she took the dream catcher from over Gray's crib and hung it above Sammy's head.

A Chicago, Illinois, native, **Nick Medina** has gone in search of Resurrection Mary, the "Italian Bride," the "Devil Baby," and other Windy City ghosts. An enthusiast of local and Native lore, his recent novel *Sisters of the Lost Nation* features several supernatural myths and legends. A graduate of DePaul University, Nick has degrees in organizational and multicultural communication and has worked as a college instructor. Connect with him on nickmedina.net, Instagram (@nickmedinawrites), and Twitter (@MedinaNick).

HUNGER

PHOENIX BOUDREAU

It is always hungry. In the time Before the Other People came, the original People's stories about it had given it its own form. The People wouldn't dare to say its name in the dark; they whispered its stories to one another and their reverent fear sustained it. The People had called it a spirit of evil, but it has only ever been hungry. The modern People have forgotten; Other People came and erased its stories, tried to pretend it didn't exist. But it has always been here and always will be. It is as inevitable as the Land itself. The People forget, but it does not.

It is gaunt, starving. More than starving: ravenous. Without its own form, the hunger becomes its form. No physical body, no limbs to cram People into its gaping, slavering maw. No high-pitched, crying voice that sounded so like a People child to use in the dark, frozen nights to lure a meal to it. No tongue to taste the flesh and blood of its victims. No stinking breath to make the People freeze in fear, knowing they looked at their own death. And no stomach to be filled. When it had its own form, it could *almost* feel, for a moment, that it could be satisfied. That the hunger would go and it could be at peace.

Still, hunger consumed it, and the small, whispering voice it could use to lure the Empty People remained. Empty People were of all people; they came from every place, every land. It could eat them, but they were not as satisfying. The Empty People were missing something inside, but they still had a use. If it whispered long enough at them, one would let it in. And then, through them, it could eat.

And so in the concrete and steel forest that covered the Land, disconnecting the People from their own home, it hunts. Nothing more than a shadow. Nothing more than a dark thought. Nothing more than a voice that says *let me in so we can both be fed.*

It has always been a liar.

Starving, it finds a group of Empty People. They are the ugly, pallid Other People whose language is harsh and jagged. The Other People are disgusting, foul, but sometimes they are Empty and it has to eat. It listens to them, six young men who think they are invincible. Nobody thinks that word, but there is a feeling in their thoughts, a taste, that is arrogance. The surety that *they* are above everyone else. That their actions will have no consequences, whatever they do. People with that flavor to their thoughts are easier to convince.

Of course, it has been one long desolation, one long hungry season since the Other People came and took the land and the language and the very lives of the People. A hungry season even for it. That never happened in the time Before. It had never starved then. Always hungry, yes. Always needing. Always *almost*. But since the Other People came, it has been ravening. Not now, though. It will possess one of these Empty young men, and it will feast.

These men all live in one house. They are what they call *frat brothers*, something like the warrior friendships of the People from before. But these men do not wage war. These men do not defend their people. These men do not hunt for food. They attend a *university* where they share ideas and learn to be the best Other People they can be. Their dreams are filled with a greed almost as endless as its own hunger.

It whispers. It whispers and tastes the thoughts of these Empty young men. It pushes itself into the edges of their dreams. It insinuates itself in the dark corners of their desires. Waiting. Begging. Hungry. *Hungry.* And one night, a party . . .

Their guard is down. One of the young men's thoughts are hazy with alcohol and drugs, and his own dark hunger seeps into his mind. This is all it needs. While the Empty young man thinks of violent sexual conquest, it slithers into his consciousness. Then expands itself until it is everywhere in the man's body. Its vision becomes clearer, hunger sharper. It breathes with the young man's lungs, tasting all those present with each inhalation. There are so many of them gathered here, so many possibilities. It could eat everyone in this place. It might, then, get close to being satiated.

A jagged grin opens like a wound across its face. The hunt has begun.

And then, like a gift from the Spirit World, there is a People girl coming into the house. She is beautiful in a way the Other People never can be, shining with the history of her People on this land. Her dark hair cascades over her shoulders, reaching halfway down her back. The smell of sage drifts from her and its mouth waters. That scent reminds it of the time Before, of cold prairie winters when it could hunt as freely as it wanted. It remembers the sweet fear of the People when they huddled in their shelters and tried to ward it off.

It watches her through the eyes of the man it possesses. She moves from the living room to the kitchen, greeting people she knows. It watches her take a bottle of beer.

"Hey, Summer!" One of the Other young women calls to her. "I finally started *Reservation Dogs*." The People woman's eyes light up, and she goes to the other.

"Yeah? Did you like it?" she asks, and they are soon deep in conversation about a pack of dogs named Bear, Elora, Cheese, and Willie Jack. Her voice is sweet, with a cadence of her People's language, though she speaks the Other People's discordant one. Her laughter ripples out, and she gestures expansively as she talks.

It has never been so hungry in its whole long existence. It has never wanted a meal more. Its mouth waters. It watches.

She glances at it, standing across the room from her, in the Empty man's body. Her smile tightens a little, eyes narrowing. *Can she see it?* It knows there were once some of the People who could. But it also knows that these modern People don't know the stories like they used to. They have been fractured from their own origins, separated from their language and their beliefs. Ever since the Other People have been on this land, the People have suffered and it itself has hungered more deeply than before.

The woman comes to it. It swallows. The need to devour making its vision hazy.

"Hey Chris," she says, voice casual. It takes a breath.

"Hey," it says. Some of its own voice bleeds through the young man's; surely if she can see it, she will hear that growl and be warned. It is too full of craving for this girl's flesh to be as cautious as it should be. But she doesn't react to its voice, and it sways a little closer to its prey.

"What's good?"

She smiles. It smiles back, searching the man's thoughts for the right response.

"You know, you know," it says. She laughs, taking a drink from her bottle. She lays a hand on its arm, and the contact burns through it. All it wants, all it has ever wanted, is the taste of this girl's blood and fear. To crack her bones between its jaws and suck the sweet marrow clean. To roll her organs on its tongue before it swallows them whole.

It wants, and it wants, and *it wants*.

It puts its hand over hers. She glances up, eyes sharp, and withdraws her hand.

"This party ain't shit," she says, and it hears a small note of fear in her voice. It grins. "I'm gonna go."

"You just got here, how d'you know it ain't shit?"

She gives him another smile, this one thinner.

"Well, you're here, for one," she replies. It laughs, the sound barren as moonlight on snow. She takes a step back. "Uh, okay. I'm gonna . . . circulate. See ya later." She walks away, glancing back at it in confusion. It laughs again. Oh, the beauty of the hunt. The beauty of closing in.

She takes out her phone, sends off a text. It watches her, and she glances uneasily at it now and then. She doesn't talk much to other people now. Pretends to drink her beer. Tries to keep distance between it and herself. Its joy, fueled by her fear, is bright and sharp. The harsh smile is frozen on its face. The man it possesses has his own hunger for her; the images run and run through his head until he's half-crazy. His hands on her bare skin, leaving bruises as he takes what he wants. His mouth on hers so that she cannot cry out or breathe unless he allows it. Her nakedness spread beneath him, braced for his invasion. The man's mouth goes dry at the thought, and its own hunger twists around the man's desire. They are both ravenous for her.

When she steps out of the back door to make a phone call, they follow. They stay just inside, the Empty man talking to someone while it listens to her.

"Hey, cousin. I'm gonna head out. Party's rank. No, I'll be fine, I'll just walk. Oh, shut up, it's a campus in the middle of a city. Worst that's gonna happen, I'll have to listen to some first year white Native Studies student tell me about the impacts of colonialism or some dumb shit. Ehe, ekosi maka." She drops her phone back into her purse and glances over her shoulder. It pretends it is not watching. She steps away from the light of the house and looks up. There is no chance of seeing the stars; too much light pollution. Too much of the Other People on the People's land for her to be able to see.

Still, she smiles. Gets a pack of cigarettes out of her purse and lights up. Walks away from the house, out the back gate and into an alley. It follows her. Its hunger is a delirium now, sweet and euphoric. The Empty man, too, is filled with his own mad desire for her flesh. His lust makes it feel on the edge of strength for the first time in centuries. Once they devour Summer together, it will feel better.

The young woman walks into a wooded park, digging her phone out of her purse to glance at now and then. Stops to write a message. The hungry creature in the Empty man's body slinks in shadows after her, moving through the sparse darkness of the Other People's city. Summer doesn't seem to know she's in danger, and it slavers after her with a silent snarl of need. The girl is all it's ever wanted and if it cannot have her soon, it will become a hungry spirit once again, melting the Empty man's body into nothing with its desire.

Summer turns down a darker path, going deeper into the green space that's part of the city's eco-revitalization project. This little splinter of green is part of a network of parks like it all over the campus, and this is the largest. It feels secluded amid the ugliness of the city, and the hungry creature's confidence rises as it follows its prey.

Drool runs down its chin, pools in the back of its throat. In the cold shadows of the path, it will take the girl. No sodium lights here, no bright, glaring eco-friendly lamps to reveal it to its prey. No: it knows terrain like this. Dark, and smelling of the first decay of autumn. The first chill of winter on the back of the slight breeze stirring bright leaves. The promise of the biting, voracious cold that makes skin ache when exposed. The bleakness of the hungry season, the time when it is the strongest.

Summer stops on the path, and it keeps snaking toward her. She must hear the footsteps. Then again, maybe not: she's looking at her phone. This new generation, so distractible. In the Before time, a girl would not linger alone at night. Not when the days shortened, and the nights grew cold and long. The People then knew what lurked in the cold empty dark. Summer doesn't seem to know, though. She is about to learn.

She steps off the path, and it almost laughs. Moving with uncanny speed, its hands are reaching for her, close enough to feel the heat of her skin.

Then a sharp, high whistle from the trees on one side of the path shatters the silence. Summer stops at the sound. Its eyes narrow and its hands pause; that whistle sounds *human*. But no matter: it will be finished with its meal before whoever is approaching knows what is happening. It will be satisfied and leave the Empty man to deal with the consequences.

"Summer," it growls.

The girl looks up. She is not startled. She *smiles*.

"Hey, Wehtigo. What's good?"

Her fear has dissolved somehow, and it recoils from her as she reaches into her purse. Only now does it recognize that the smell of sage and tobacco on her wasn't an echo-memory of the People

Before. The awful stinking cigarettes of the Other People masked the smell: she has been cleansed in the smoke of the sacred medicines. It hisses.

"Here, got something for you," she says.

She pulls her hand out of her purse. Opens her fist. Sage and tobacco mixed with cedar and sweetgrass assails it. She opens her hand, blows the powdered medicine between them. It jerks back, stumbling. Some of the powder lands on the man's clothes and burns through the cloth, searing the skin beneath.

"What are you doing?" it snarls.

"Fighting you," she answers, grinning.

It gives an enraged scream. It can hear something moving in the trees just off the path, and it turns to look. It can see something, someone, there.

"Hey, big ugly. Ya spooked?" Summer says, and the creature turns back to her. She laughs again, digging again in her purse. A spike of hot fear goes through it. She pulls out a small cedar branch, and it takes another step back. Cedar is a sacred cleansing plant to her People. A spiritual and physical medicine. She reaches out and taps it on the arm with the branch. It shouts in pain.

"I can hurt you," she sing-songs.

It hears the thing from the woods approach, and it whirls around, desperate.

It is only another People girl. This one has short, brightly colored hair. She is wearing jeans, a hoodie, and fringe earrings. Carrying a larger bag than Summer's, with the same scents of medicine wafting from it. The creature screams at her. She blinks, opens her mouth, and screams back. Its own scream is silenced.

"Rain!" Summer scolds. "Stop it!"

"Fuck. Why do they do that?" Rain asks, pulling out two more cedar branches.

Summer shrugs, moving to align herself with the newcomer,

keeping it between the two of them. She digs yet another cedar branch out of her bag, so each of the People girls is holding one in each hand. They reach out, touching the ends of the branches together to create a circle around it.

"Oh! Did you hear *Rez Dogs* is getting another season?"

"Yeah, I did. I'm glad, because shit ended weird between Elora and Bear. I don't want that to be the end of it," Summer says.

It lunges to one side, hoping to escape. Rain flicks her wrist, letting the branch touch its body. Bright pain floods through it, and it's driven to its knees. It tastes cedar on its tongue and gags, falling forward.

"They're nitotem. It's not gonna stay weird. Trust," Rain replies.

The young women move in a circle around it in shuffling side steps. A round dance. Rain shakes powdered cedar, tobacco, sage, and sweetgrass from a pouch cupped in one hand behind the branch, letting it fall as she dances the circle, and it's trapped.

It roars this time, rising out of the Empty man's body. Rain swings a branch, almost hitting it. It shrieks, lunging at her. She drops the branch, stumbling on the circle enough to create an opening. It gives a frosty laugh, and it sees her shiver at the sound.

The taste of her fear cuts through the scent of the sacred medicine. It grins.

"Summer!" she shouts, but the other young woman is already moving. Armed with more powdered cedar and tobacco, she crosses the circle and opens her hand at it. The medicine scorches through it and it shrinks back into the Empty man, grin gone.

"Settle down," Rain commands. "You gotta wait until we're ready."

Summer pulls a small dish, along with more sage bound together, from her bag. She holds the dish in one hand and looks at Rain. It wants to howl. Scream. It cannot remember another time it was consumed by fear. It has been hunted before, of course; the

People could not help trying to free themselves from it. It has been driven out, but it cannot remember ever having been trapped.

"Please," it says. The Empty man's lips move, but its own wintry voice comes out. "I will help you get anything you want. Let me go and I will—" Rain waves a cedar branch to stop it.

"We don't want anything from you," she says. She puts the branches down, reaching for something in her bag. "Leave this man alone. Come out of him."

Summer sings low in her throat, walking the circle again with the smudge bowl in her hands. It whines as the smoke drifts to it. It turns to Rain because she is not speaking the words that will banish it.

"Please let me have this one. And his friends. Then I will go," it begs.

"Liar, liar, pants on fire," Rain replies. She picks up a branch, whatever it is she got out of the bag in her other hand. The Empty man's brain gives it the word *blowtorch*. She uses it to light the cedar, creating thick smoke. She lights another branch, and another, laying them on top of the medicine circle they've already made. The cedar smoke mingles with sage, and it begins to cough. It feels itself come unanchored from the Empty man, the smoke forcing it out. It feels Chris's eyes slip closed and his breathing run shallow as the young women work, and it can't stop it.

Summer moves to him, sage still burning. She passes the bowl over him, murmuring prayers for him in Cree: "Ahaw, Manito nimiykosinan tawiyawitsahotahk. Moyaywak kakicimahhaw awa oskinikiw. Ahaw, ekosi nitwanan."

The spirit can't fight; the smoke fills its mouth before it can speak. And now that it is being forced from the man, its power recedes. Its mouth is dry from the smoke, its eyes burning. It strains to reach for one of the young women, either one, but there is too much good medicine around them. The scent of sage and cedar drives it away. The smoke rises with it caught like a rabbit in a snare, and it cannot even scream its frustration. It drifts into the sky, rising above the city lights and into the night. And then it is dispersed into the cold dark, scattered between stars unseen by those below.

Summer and Rain look at each other, and then down at the man lying in the medicine circle. Summer nudges his foot with hers, putting the smudge bowl down.

"Chris?" she asks. "Hey."

He coughs, sitting up. He blinks and glances around.

"What the hell?" he demands.

Summer shrugs. "You okay?"

He glares at her.

"I don't wanna know what kinda Indian voodoo shit this is," he says, scrambling to his feet. "I don't want you coming to any more of our parties, either."

Summer scowls. "Your parties ain't shit, so that's no skin off my back," she retorts. Rain moves to her side, taking her hand. Bitterness floods through her; they'd just saved his pathetic whiteboy life. He didn't even know what they'd done for him. He'd never know. And if he did find out, he would think it was his due. That she owed him his life. She squeezes Rain's hand to keep from saying more.

"Cousin. Let's go home," Rain murmurs. "He's not worth it." The young women stand together and watch the frat boy turn and stumble-run in the direction of his house.

"They never are," Summer agrees. She tips her head back to look at the stars. She can't see many of them, not when they're obscured by the light pollution. But she knows they're there, older and as inevitable as the Earth itself.

Among those stars, the Wehtigo is already gathering itself back together. The Empty man's lingering bitterness is enough to give it the strength for that much. It is *hungry*, and it will hunt again. Soon.

Phoenix Boudreau is a Cree woman, mother, and writer living in Edmonton, Alberta, Canada. She is previously unpublished but comes from a line of champion storytellers. She has listened to her mother tell her family and tribal lore since she was a kid. She lives with her four children.

TICK TALK

CHERIE DIMALINE

Bilson refused to go by Bill, so people called him Son. People loved it, they felt like they had a claim, some kind of relation. Son pretended not to notice the frequency with which his name got peppered into conversation, real casual like. "Hey, my Son. How's things going there, Son?" He'd really rather not have more relatives. He liked being untethered.

Son grew up in Toronto, which is very cold. And he hated the cold. As soon as he could, he left his mother and their cramped apartment and hitchhiked to Florida. When he was tired of racism and beaches, which so often seemed to coexist, he moved on to Georgia, picking a midsize city to look for whatever he thought existed for him in the heat. But Savannah was too beautiful. It made him feel inadequate, and it was hard to get laid with your confidence lagging. So, he moved on, this time to New Orleans.

"You'll love it. Loose women, loud laughter, and all the beer you can drink for less than a twenty," William, who did go by Bill, told him at the local bar one afternoon. "And there are lots of service jobs if you're willing to deal with nonstop music and titties."

Son was, in fact, willing to deal with just those very things. So, he packed a duffel bag, left a note on the kitchen table for his roommate, and hopped a bus to the Big Easy. He arrived the day after his thirtieth birthday. Two years later, he really wasn't so sure what was so damn easy about it. Maybe the passage of time, because that seemed to have no bearing on plans made here, the city melting into the Gulf like cardboard left out in the rain. Except for the Quarter. That was melting like a wedding cake under an August haze. Intricate and fancy, but really just out to give you plain old diabetes and offering the flies somewhere festive to fuck.

One day, the phone rang too early to be good news. It was early enough that his hangover hadn't quite murdered his buzz, so the conversation felt he'd dreamt it.

"Son?" It was his aunt Beatrice, a large woman with a whispery voice who had just recently discovered marijuana, which became the gateway drug to an obsession with macrame.

"Yeah?"

"Your mother's passed on, I'm afraid."

The next day he was on a bus heading back to Toronto, having left behind his secondhand furniture and a trumpet he never learned to play. (He thought one must play the trumpet if one lived in New Orleans.)

After the small funeral, he told his cousin he was headed home. But then he found himself not quite sure which direction to go.

"Maybe go see your dad. He's getting up there," Frank replied, adding that tone of guilt that is reserved for family members who knew you before puberty. "And he's all alone."

Son did not want to go see his father. That would mean going even farther north into the cold, as if that direction was a straight path away from the sun. But, he had little money, and no ambition left, so the next day he found himself on another bus. This trip was a lot shorter. He barely had time to nap and do the crossword before he'd arrived at a half-assed stop built into a gas station where someone sold homemade butter tarts alongside diesel.

The walk to his father's was also not long, but it took forever, especially as he was in no hurry. He hadn't bothered to call ahead. He wasn't sure his father would have offered him a lift, anyway. The house was set back from the road and surrounded by grass that, by November, had already started to brown and crunch.

His father met him at the door, shrunken in flannel, crooked now like his house, a place he'd inherited and not bothered to change much.

"You're home."

Son didn't know how to answer. It wasn't a question.

"Yup."

They didn't speak again until the coyotes began to howl in the failed fields.

"Night, then."

"Night."

His father turned off the living room light and Son sat in the dark, listening to the creaks of old wood from all around him, haunted by the sounds of hunger calling from the forest.

The house was built on one of the plots given to the half-breeds for their "loyal service" in the War of 1812. Really, it was a way to empty the island handed over to the Americans and tame the wild men known for hunting and canoeing in the new settlement, to slow their quick movements under the weight of property and chores. It almost worked. Son's father, Alexis, a direct descendant of those men, had spent his life in a fishing boat, refusing to till the land meant to break him. Still, he seemed broken enough.

Son had left years ago with his mother when she packed up a matched set of red suitcases and headed for the city. He didn't really have memories from that time. Leaving a father you barely knew didn't really stand out. So when the letters arrived, quick two-line missives signed with the initials "A. D." requesting he come back for the spring hunt or the fall hunt or ice fishing, they were easy to ignore. He didn't even keep them as some sort of souvenir. He'd just thrown them away, sometimes after adding an extra D to the front of the initials in pencil.

That winter passed in a blanket of deep quiet in the dusty house. They drank coffee for breakfast, ate sandwiches for lunch, and something frozen and quick thawed, then fried for dinner. They took turns doing the dishes in the farmhouse sink. When they needed something, Son took his father's pickup into town and got it, hoping he wouldn't run into one of the relatives who'd never left. Mostly, this worked out. Once a man asked him, "Hey, aren't you Alexis's kid?" And he responded, "No," then paid for his cowboy steaks and left.

When spring hit, Alexis started to talk, as if the ice itself had been the reason for his silence.

"S'lot warmer than it used to be this time of year. Could use some meat for the freezer."

"Want me to go to the Foodsaver?" Son was bored, anyway. He was always bored now. Boredom was everywhere, like a color.

"Should go hunt, likely." Alexis said it while looking out the window, wistful, like a man serving time.

"Go, then." Son had grown tired of the man pining by the second week.

The answer was always a sigh.

Son knew the old man was waiting for him to show some enthusiasm, to jump up and declare today was the day they'd go out into the bush. But he just couldn't give it to him. He wasn't even sure why. Maybe for the simple fact that it was all he wanted, and Son was still holding a grudge. When he was a child, the man had refused to buy him a video game console, refused to meet him in the city, had patently refused to be anything other than what he was. No changing him—not for a needy woman or a quiet boy.

Summer was more of an inconvenience than anything. A few people dropped by, older cousins his father's age who wanted black coffee and stayed too long reminiscing. Son thought he might leave then. He'd already gained ten pounds and forgotten what it was to wake up in someone else's bed. But he had no godly idea of where he would go. So he bought two fans for his bedroom and slept long through those hot days. He barely recognized that the heat he had been chasing had curled around the county like a sleepy animal.

Fall brought more talk—as if Alexis were trying to push for more, for something, for anything.

"Deer soon. Lots up at the old cabin, dere. Could set small traps for rabbits. Good slider stew in dat."

His local accent came out the more words he set free. It was cadence more than anything, except *th*s turned to *d*s and sometimes he forgot a word in English and had to use Old French. Son got into the habit of leaving the room mid-story.

The day the old man didn't come downstairs, the day Son found him lying in bed with his hands folded together on his chest like a mausoleum bust, the day he had to call in the ambulance to cart his father's body away—that was the day he finally decided to hunt.

He searched and found everything for the trip in the garage. That's a lie. He knew it'd been there all along. He could have done this at any time, with little extra effort to load the old man into the front seat, pack an extra gun, maybe a few more cans of tuna. The truck's bed was filled with odds and ends—tires, a rusted jack, a bone saw—all covered with a blue tarp. He didn't bother to empty it before adding his own supplies.

The drive to the cabin was about an hour, turning opposite from the routes you'd take if you were headed toward something. The silence was back, deeper than ever. It filled the cab until Son had to open a window and let the wind push it out. He arrived at dusk, pulling into the overgrown drive and turning the engine off. Then he just sat there.

What the fuck was he doing? He hadn't been hunting since he was eleven, the season before his mother told him to get his things and come along, now. The cabin wasn't even familiar, though it was in that way where nothing was a surprise. Nothing called him inside. At least at the house, Alexis had stood in the door, red suspenders faded, black coffee in hand. "You're home." There was no one to tell Son where he was now.

Eventually, he climbed out and went inside.

The cabin was shared between the older cousins and, as they were all men and used to not much, the structure itself was manly and not much. Built on a poured cement platform, it was a single room, barely bigger than the garage. The wood had been left raw for many years, but after the front had to be replaced due to rot, someone had covered it in metal sheets scavenged from cheap garden sheds. The roof was shingled with a crooked pipe chimney bursting out of the corner. Mismatched windows were embedded in the front wall and held with yellow caulking and pink insulation. There was a latch lock on the front to keep the animals out. Nothing to keep humans out, because there was nothing to take. Anyone who would go in was likely related in some way, anyway.

He went in and, not being able to bear the empty hours before dark, fell asleep. When he woke up on the hard couch, there was that moment of orientation. He was waking up someplace new and instead of being confused, a part of his brain he hadn't used in a year stretched. The morning light leaking in the bare windows was thin. It was still early enough to go out. He set water to boil on the camp stove and got ready.

The bush was both different and exactly the same. It had its own language, but even so, it could refuse to speak. When Son first walked into it, it held its breath. He, in turn, shifted his weight as he moved, producing sound that echoed and filled the absence. Bad form, he knew, but he also felt like he needed to prove something, maybe just that he could exist here.

There were no deer, no rabbits, no grouse. Even the squirrels were gone. It felt like being in a gallery meant to resemble a forest and not the forest itself.

"Fuck this," he seethed after crouching for two hours at the base of a maple and seeing nothing but his shadow move. His muscles were aching. His camo pants too tight with new weight. "Who does this on purpose?"

It was just after lunch when he packed it in, whistling his way back to the cabin out of spite. He left the guns and supplies outside the door like badly behaved children, dragged his bones inside, and promptly passed out on the same hard couch. He fell asleep with the gnawing hunger of those who have failed at something important.

This time, when he woke up, something was different.

It was dark now; the afternoon whittled away to evening's

bone. He was very aware that the windows had no curtains. He felt exposed, vulnerable. His clothes were twisted and damp with sweat. He stood and peeled off layers of fleece and denim. The pellet stove had been left on and it was hot in the one-room shack. He suddenly needed to get as much off as he could, as quick as he could.

He was down to his socks and long johns when he saw it. Already as big as a kernel of corn, dark as a blood blister—a tick burrowed in his stomach.

"Oh, fuck me." He felt nauseated. He sat down hard, then sprang back up when sitting made his stomach wrinkle, and he felt the bug's outer shell on a new patch of skin. "Oh, Jesus."

He tried to remember what you had to know about ticks. Well, they spread disease. Also, and most disgustingly, they stuck their entire head in you. You had to remove it without breaking the head off or it might get infected.

"Goddammit," he rushed to the kitchen counter and yanked open the drawer. Tin utensils and loose batteries clattered to the floor. He kicked at them, looking for tweezers. Nothing.

He didn't want to look, but he had to. He couldn't trust his eyes. *Is the tick already growing? That's impossible. Isn't it?* It was the size of a nickel.

"Frigging vampire." He grimaced. Taking a deep breath, Son relaxed his muscles. The shift made the tick move, and he tightened right back up.

There was one room attached to the main area, a small addition made after he'd already left for Toronto—a bathroom with a composting toilet. He went there now.

"Where the hell are the tweezers, old man?" Talking out loud was meant to comfort him, but it added an anxious pitch to the air instead.

He flicked on the overhead light and searched the bathroom

shelves. Iodine, gauze bandages, toenail clippers with a missing spring, no-name aftershave, a roll of scratchy single-ply toilet paper, bandage wrappers, a broken pen, and a half-full bottle of rye. He took the bottle and left.

In the main room, he paced while he drank, not able to sit, not wanting to look at his stomach but unable to stop thinking about it. He was sure he could feel its weight now, like a small limb, a limb with a fat back and sharp claws, with teeth that were sunk into the soft meat of his stomach. He needed to get this thing out of him.

"What else? What else?"

He could cut it out. There were at least three knives in the cabin, one of which was sitting on the wooden coffee table. Just then, the thing wiggled its legs, tickling the skin around the puncture.

"Holy fuck!" Son fell back against the wall. It was bigger than a quarter now! How could it grow so fast? He had to get it out before the monster sucked him dry. He would do it—he would carve the damn thing out.

He took one last generous swig of rye and went for the knife. In his rush, his foot caught on the pile of clothes by the couch and his arms pinwheeled, looking for purchase. Before he hit the ground, his head caught the corner of the coffee table. Everything went dark.

He dreamt of his father. Alexis was standing by the window in his faded red suspenders. Outside, the coyotes were howling.

"Who are they here for?" the old man asked.

"No one," Son answered, but felt a nagging guilt. "They're just here."

"No," the man shook his gray head. "They're here for someone."

Son decided to come clean. "It's you, Dad. You're dead. They're coming for you."

The man let the yellowed curtain drop and turned. "Oh, my

boy. Animals don't come for those who are leaving. They come for those who are forgetting. Now then, who is it?"

It was the owl that woke him.

"Hoo. Hoo," it called.

"I don't know," Son mumbled. "I don't know."

"Hoo. Hoo," it insisted.

The dream faded like smoke. Son's head felt huge and wobbly, like a balloon filled with blood. He had to hold it, to keep it steady, so he began rubbing it with his left hand and opened his eyes, trying to focus. He saw the owl in the window just as it took flight, leaving the moon like a bright eye pressed to the glass. The moon and the bathroom light were the only illumination, so it took Son a minute to figure out the wet on his fingers from his forehead was blood.

"Oh, dammit." He struggled to sit up and felt a deep tug in his guts.

He reached down to rub at the spot, forgetting until his hand hit the smooth, warm curve of the tick's bloated body. It took a moment for him to register this thing, this growth, the size and shape of a lightbulb hot with his own blood, as a tick. He kept his hand on it, feeling down its thorax to where it connected to his stomach, a lock-and-key fit, tight as a drum.

His scream was high and messy, filling the cabin, spilling out into the woods. He kicked his legs, knocking over the folding chair, upending the bucket of pellets that went skittering over the wooden floor. He flailed wildly, hitting himself on the wooden legs of the coffee table, knocking a glass and the knife to the floor. But the movement only made things worse—he could feel the pull of the bug's feed, the pinch of its deep connection. And with so much blood taken, soon, he was barely conscious. Small lights blossomed and burst under his eyelids until, finally, he lay still.

So this was it then. He was going to be killed by a fucking bug?

He covered his face with his hands, rubbing at his eyes, trying to stay awake. When he dropped them, his fingers touched the cold metal of the knife that lay near his leg.

He couldn't remember if you could kill a tick and then dig it out or if you were supposed to kill it after? There was no information in his head, no memories of being told. Why couldn't he remember? He knew he'd had ticks before. Knew it had been in this very cabin. He could kind of recall the hands that pulled the bugs from his young skin—they were his uncle Jimmy's, with nicotine-stained nails, calloused from the lumberyard.

"Are they poison?" he'd asked then. But he couldn't remember a response. Couldn't bring back the voice that would have given him the answer.

"Fuck it." He held his breath and held his breath, forcing his hand on to the slick, hard bug. It was so still that if it weren't for the suction he was sure he could feel, it was like an accessory and not a separate living thing. And somehow, impossibly, it was getting bigger. Now it was like he was spooning a gazing ball, one that was showing him a future he did not want.

He raised the knife and jabbed, any worries about injuring himself with a miss now gone. The blade punctured the shiny shell leaving the blade soaked with his own transfused blood. It turned out to be a bad idea—the thing squirmed and thrashed against him. It was hard to hold still, to not get caught up in its panic.

He would have to carve it out instead of trying to stab it, but it was impossible to keep the blade steady, to cut small and precise, but he had to. The bug was still wiggling, throwing its weight around the root of its neck. Son lowered the knife to his skin, both slick, and cut two small lines up and out from the puncture, hissing like a kettle at boil. He dropped the knife and put both hands around the softball-size monster, pulling with everything he had left, grimacing, teeth grinding, veins tight.

"Get out!"

Skin tearing, grip loosened from injury, the tick's head finally pulled through the opening, slow at first and then all at once. The release happened before Son could stop and the momentum threw the bug across the floor and into the far wall, into the shadows.

"Oh Christ, oh Jesus," he huffed, placing both hands over the hole left in his stomach. He panted, willing the stars to clear from his view, trying to see where the thing had landed.

Breathe. Just breathe. In and out. Slow down, now.

The instructions came in his uncle's voice—he finally remembered. He had to breathe—slow and even—or he wouldn't be okay. He'd freak out and lose consciousness, and then who knows? Was the thing even dead? What if it came back, sinking into the warm hole it had made in his torso?

"Okay, okay. I'm all right," he told himself. "I got this."

He reached over and grabbed up his sweater, pulling it over his head with a grimace, then stuffing his undershirt underneath it, up against the wound. He was light-headed, and every beat of his heart sent new blood gushing into the makeshift bandage. He wanted to puke, to scream, to lie down—all of it. But he had to move. There was no sign of the thing. No sound in the cabin save his own loud breathing. It could be anywhere now. Eyes trained on the darkness by the door, he grasped the knife in a sweaty fist and pulled himself to his feet. There was a moment where he wasn't sure if he could do it. Standing up felt like pushing his head and shoulders into a cloud and he wavered a bit.

"Move. Now," his cousin Mad had told him once; maybe they were freezing? Maybe an ice fishing accident? There were things he needed to remember. "If you stay still, you give up."

Moving like a swimmer, Son paddling his way toward the door, toward the darkness where the bug had landed. He could see a splatter of blood on the wall. He had to fight to keep his lower body moving at the same pace as his upper body or he would end up on his face. He had to drop the knife to grab the doorknob, the other hand still holding his undershirt to the hole in his guts.

Standing now, in the open doorway, everything was so far away—the pickup truck, the trees, the road. The sun was rising, a smudge of bright on the bruised horizon, but even that was distant, irrelevant. Instead, he could smell the cheap coffee and stale air of his father's house.

Son pushed himself toward the truck on unsteady legs. A few wobbly steps across the uneven ground and he banged into the hood. He made his way, hand over hand, down the side of the vehicle, feet dragging and slow. He was thirsty. His breathing was shallow. He was exhausted in the way that happens only when you use new muscles. It took two tries to get the door open and then he threw his body inside. For a moment, he wondered if his father was worried and then he remembered—the empty of the bedroom, the way a person's breath could be recognized only when it was no longer in the room.

"You're gone." He said it aloud into the truck cab. There was no old man sitting at the kitchen table listening to the radio, no one to tell him he'd forgotten to get bread, or to remind him which island was named for his great-grandfather. There was no one waiting for him.

He felt hollow, and it wasn't just from the tick gouge, or the blood loss. He had to fill himself now, to claim all the space left open. And so, hands on the steering wheel, engine on, Son began to laugh. It shook him in a bad way, pushing his gut to leak, his head to throb, but he couldn't stop. He had to gasp at the air he needed. His laughter started to sound like high yips. Outside the truck, the coyotes called from the trees, answering the sound of his hunger.

And from the bed of the truck, a small skittering, a trail of blood, and then the tarp lay still again. Son turned on to the main road and headed for home.

Cherie Dimaline's (Georgian Bay Métis) 2017 book, *The Marrow Thieves*, was declared by *TIME* magazine one of the Best YA Books of All Time, won the Governor General's Award and the prestigious Kirkus Prize for Young Readers, and was named a book of the year on numerous lists, including the New York Public Library and the CBC. Her novel *Empire of Wild* became an instant Canadian bestseller and was named Indigo's Best Book of 2019. Her follow-up YA book, *Hunting by Stars*, was a 2022 American Indian Library Association Honor Book. Her new witchy novel, *VENCO*, debuted at number one on Canadian bestseller lists. Cherie lives in her community and is writing for television and stage.

THE ONES WHO KILLED US

BRANDON HOBSON

We saw the ones who killed us, risen from deep in the cold earth with the mud and the worms, heading north across the town square, where colored stones paved a way to the river with its amber waters known best for being the place where our women disappeared. Didahihi! All across town, we saw the disarray of the soldiers who had fled, their guns left behind, along with three old government wagons that had once arrived in Oklahoma in the company of many other wagons whose journey, many years ago, had been slower than expected but never forgotten by us, our children, or our ancestors. And among these wagons we saw the bones of animals whose bodies had rotted and been eaten by vultures whose smell lingered with the stench of chickens and hens in the barn nearby.

The night was chilly with the early winter, melding in a cool and anechoic manner that led us to a light on the side of the barn, where our missing women had escaped the slaughter from the evil, drunken men who slept with their mouths open, who had stinking breath and pale bellies, which was a story we had been told since

we were young so that we could better understand the disorder
of the ignorant, derisive fools with their violent intentions. We
thought about that story upon entering the barn through which
the wild chickens wandered, pecking and eating the seed the farmers left for them, and we saw one of our missing women's shadow
stretching over bales of hay across the barn and a sick gray horse
named Gray Horse who had been broken by a Cherokee man
named Gary Gray Horse, that poor old thoroughbred now aged
and too sick to gallop even a furlong. Because of the late hour
there was no vet in sight, no doctor or medicine or anyone who
knew what to do to put this horse out of his misery; therefore we
untied Gray Horse and led him steadily out of the barn and back
into the night, where only the ghosts of our missing women could
find him and heal him and where, beyond the town square, up
near the horizon, we saw the soft glow of the white moon over the
endless plains and knew, right then, that we needed to follow the
ones who killed us down to the river because surely our missing
women would appear there.

Atvdasdiha, it doesn't end. In recent years, whenever we saw
the ones who killed us, we knew there was someone trudging
through the river because we could see their eyes in the night like
the fulvous eyes of a wolf, and those who moved closer to the river
could hear the soldier's gasps as he tried to run away, tripping and
falling, and one time a soldier even collapsed in the water and
began shouting for forgiveness— Imagine that, won't you, what
an awful pity that he begged us to have mercy on him, which was
especially dangerous for him because our anger was too strong
to let his pathetic cries persuade us, goddamn it, so we pushed
through branches and brush while birds flew from the dark trees,
hurtling the rocks we found and carrying our fury to strike down
the soldier for what he had stolen and all the horrible things he
had done during the migration, that puckish, bearded bastard,

and then he shot us with his rifle, or rather attempted to shoot us dead, and how exactly was that supposed to work anyway under the circumstances that we were already dead and wandering as risen dust, so we told him the truth: all actions come to face justice in the end. The others hid near Tenkiller in the trees or under the amber water until they floated downriver, far away, and yet they could hear our voices spiraling into the water and speaking to them in the old ways, predictable and strong, even more distinct and familiar, and our presence was known as we imprecated our wild and conspicuous words on them. Ganosgisgi! They had no refuge even in the darkness of the trees or in the water, and without undressing they harbored no illusions about their safety because they could hear our steps on the twigs and rocks like the panting of hungry, angry beasts, craving the revenge of slaughter so that they would look into our squalid stares, their power dissolving, and see our fury before they died.

We led Gray Horse down the hill toward the river, where we saw the ones who killed us gathered around one another, talking in their language and laughing as if they hadn't remembered the previous years when we carried them away, dragging their feet across the ground like a dead animal, yet there they were speaking with the same simplicity they had in the past, unaware or absent of any premonitory feelings about our attacks, which only denoted their own ignorance even more than their physical appearance, for many of them were hirsute and clumpish, mouths open and making noise, and the pale leader's face hung from his skull, which made his strabismic eye rutilant in the night, and we were certain when they saw us they would become fearful as we besieged them, howling. But once they noticed us approaching, they merely raised their arms in a gesture of welcome and invited us down for a time of good merriment and mirth, which surprised all of us, and we stopped with Gray Horse to yell at them, "Ganosgisgi! Didahihi!"

and still, like simple and foolish people, they spoke to one another cheerily in their own language, mouths gaped open, continuing to wave us down as an invitation to join them.

Atvdasdiha, how could they misunderstand our intentions? In recent years, they never failed to recognize us as our cries of vengeance echoed throughout the woods, a big broad wave that swept across them so that they grew fearful and guilty like the dreams of the humiliated men before them, buckled and resistant in their steadfast shame, rapacious and tight-fisted, resigned to utter weariness and regret. Yet here they were now as slothful as any crowned impassive army of men protected by the tranquil shadows of our trees in the night, goddamn it, every one of them grinning like wolves that made us want to fall down and roll around with rage, wondering if this was some sort of mix-up of identities on their part, what the living hell, and from then on we told ourselves we would never let our ancestors know about this failure to inflict fear and vengeance on these people because we already knew shame would be set upon us, especially since this army of inane gredins didn't even carry any ammunition or weapons, at least none we could see from the hill, planning their own fights, so we had to reconvene right there in the moment and examine our mournful realm like a bunch of dotards, goddamn it, focusing on the path that led down to these men so that we could be spontaneous in the drowsy night air, keeping an eye out for leather gun cases or anything else hidden that might be part of their plan to play trickster despite their ignorant appearance, which meant paying close attention to any formulas of puerile solemnity or treaties they tried to make with us even in their own language, just as their predecessors had done, those spiritless ancestors whose illusory consciences evaporated in the wind like smoke. This time would be like the previous years so that their confusion and fear would get the best of them and we could chase them down the river and away from our land, away from Tenkiller, away for good, and by reconvening there on the hill, we ultimately decided we would go ahead and eat with them and play their games until we sensed it would be unsafe, at which point we'd attack—ayostanohvsga!

They continued to wave us down, but we heard the uguku in the trees, which was worrisome since this was surely a call of warning, and yet we chose to ignore it because we refused to believe in the warning of death, indeed a troubling decision on our part because, beloved children, think of your elders who speak of the owl as a dangerous messenger and the tradition of obeyance, won't you, seek not your own pleasure but observe and atvdasdiha and do not disobey because tradition is important, and we were irresponsible not to heed its warning. As we headed toward them, we noticed the hammocks and supplies, crates of fruit and jugs and blankets, but we knew that surely they recognized us, that they felt fear and worry, that once they fed us and gave us drink, they would strike before we could. Nothing was impossible in the crisis of uncertainty even when trying to be deceptive and naive to their intentions, which were extreme and entirely the same as in previous years, and they would need to be on their guard, sharp, resistant to any sudden movements we might make amid camaraderie with strangers who weren't Indigenous and who offered food and drink and music without asking for anything in return, and the closer we got to them the more they welcomed us, shouting out in laughter and raising their jugs like the yampy grues they were, and the louder they became the greater our desire increased to attack without the proviso that we would allow them a chance to talk or say how they killed us and our women at Tenkiller, no sir, there would be no "we are finally deeply forgiving of you for your actions," no "we will not wade through the gentle stream with you like lovers," no "we will not forget about the distinction of class or race or violence against the despotism of years," no peace

or gentle reconciliation, motherfuckers, and no offerings or sudden moments of quiet contemplation and stillness, because this
is about the past, surely the ones who killed us understood this
despite their lack of remorse and lowlife condemnation, despite
their brutal killings and thievery and carrying the dirty innards
of chickens and deer and buffalo from our land, from our land,
from our land.

Atvdasdiha: We decided to resist attacking them for now but
remained on guard to wait for them to strike first, thinking of any
murky reasons slowed by the inclemency of disguised courtesy
to rid even the slightest memory of the past in order to see what
degree any ravages of defenestration we would all reach, the ones
who killed us likely seeing themselves as noble as they stood before
us in their leather boots and spurs and jacket buttons polished
by their spouses whose bodies were only Creator knows where,
and whose agapanthus gardens were the color of the sky after a
long rain, despite the earth they were destroying by leaving our
rotting bodies all over, so when they began to shout hooray for
liberty and justice and hail to the thief, we felt no shame in soon
carrying their bodies to be devoured by the beasts in the woods,
though first we kept our breathing calm and natural and sat with
them and watched as the jubilation began, which was full of music
and hick-filled singing so miserable even Gray Horse snorted, and
while the meat cooked on the fire in front of us, through the
smoke the general called for restoration and unity of all despotism
to be eradicated so that the unburied could take refuge in nearby
structures and make plans for the future of a capitalist society, now
how does that sound, just imagine the general removing his hat
and sipping from his cup and saying that to our faces while liquor
burned his throat, this man whose own plan was to flee into exile
once he dared to escape our vengeance, speaking in false generos-

ity, spitting and murmuring every consolable thing he claimed he knew about the pursuit of liberty and justice since the war, the sigwa, the gayhgogi, and as quickly as he spoke we saw his eyes roll back into his head and he collapsed, lulled by the drink and the music and the crackling fire before us, and we all knew then it was going to be easy: these men were drunk and stupid, careless as they were with the meat cooking over the fire because none of them noticed or seemed to care that the general had fallen over, not even when he managed to crawl toward them on all fours and vomit, or that he shouted in drunkenness that he was the true leader who orchestrated the killing of us and our women at Tenkiller. He lifted a rock from the ground and threw it at them but they kept going on laughing and singing, those diabolical scrotes, because that was the type of people they were, uncaring and selfish, oblivious to the health of others while plotting to project an immense disposition of suffering or torture as they saw fit, convinced they could kill half-asleep, half-dead, docile and inert even, each one his own national emblem of guts and blood, maddened and fearful with their bodies wrapped in the American flag, and now as the general lay there in his own vomit they all took to scrutinizing one another, one by one, as the meat cooked and the liquor swelled their heads.

Nights such as this were not easy. Nights like this, as difficult and harsh as that which confirmed our every motive and certainty that the most threatening enemy will return each year to attempt to attack and haunt us as they did in the past when we were alive and among our loved ones and community at Tenkiller, faced with the startling revelation that their rapacious crimes would affect us for many years and generations without any empathy or confirmation that these nightmarish catastrophes would even be discussed outside the mere listing of historical data; yes, they were

difficult, and don't think we weren't aware of these men's intentions, because one of them approached us and invited us to play
an asinine game that, from what we gathered, involved placing
stones in a quincunx and then rearranging them to see whether
they could be arranged the way they were the first time, a game
they tried to explain in their language by grunting and pointing,
but we decided to watch them play rather than participate, for this
was no digadayosdi, and as they played their game shouting and
jumping around the quincunx where night insects swirled over
wild weeds in the blue light of the full moon. We were as humored
as the fattened armadillos lurking in the shadows, freed from any
fear, intimidation, or threat, so nobody interrupted them as they
played and laughed and howled with their fists raised and mouths
open. We were wrapped in the dismal aura of our implacable bitterness, and anyway, none of the amusement this delivered to us
mattered or changed our minds; see, there wasn't a single power
in this world, nothing, that would make us go back against the
decision we had already made. Nothing. Not the smell of meat
fried in hog fat, or the taste of whiskey on our lips, or the way the
motherfuckers begged us to show them how to play digadayosdi
and then scratched their balding heads, baffled and dumb, confused, strained by their own warm blood like European monarchs
whose catafalques cracked and rotted on the day of burial, whose
human skins revealed the agony of high fever striped scarlet like
the boiled blood of their fathers when they first glanced at us in
high winds and dust out on the plains, or the way they spoke in
calm voices that seemed to appropriate compassion in arduous
ramblings, or the way they celebrated by pointing to the gold spurs
on their boots and stomped while joyful music played by the fire,
even amid fervor in which the general still lay unconscious, or the
way their eyes watered after we demonstrated digadayosdi and they

finally understood how to play it, tapping their hirsute fingers over their hearts in gratitude as if we would lift them over our heads and carry them around the woods to the imagined cheers of crowds, those steatopygous dunces, those sick swine, what sort of public spectacle did they think this was anyway?

This angered us even more as the night grew darker. The ones who killed us shared stories in their strange and confusing language, and we heard the heaviness in their voices and Gray Horse's snorting that rose above even our own suppressed rage like it was carried in a solemn procession to the wide wastelands full of insufferable cold winter winds, and even among the funereal weeds and plush scrogs, the ones who killed us licked the ground and made unusual facial expressions that told us they were starting to feel haunted by the plague we were about to inflict upon them, certainly they could sense it, for we could hear their laughter turn to horror like the crying of pigs on the verge of being slaughtered, the ones who killed us sensing their own fate in the coming hour before the sun would rise, and nobody, not even the rain, could have ever imagined the night would be awakened by what happened next:

Our missing women appeared.

Our missing women emerged from the shadows, one by one, while the general lay unconscious and drunk on the ground, mumbling nonsense, his final words before the stampede that would be carried on through our stories for years and generations to come, while the others carried on in their strange language, the rest of us mere observers as one of the missing women placed little fires around the general so that he would be trapped to burn in his drunkenness and then stepped on until his flesh and bones became ashes. Then the woman hollered, "Dlanusi!" and the flames rose around the general as the air swirled with ashes and insects, and the ones who killed us looked over and saw the blaze around the general, whose face was soft in the tenuous glow of the fire, too drunk and boyish for a fierce struggle to exist among all the dangers of the night while the vultures' carnage and looming shadows and the putrid stench of the gravel roads invaded us like a slow-moving dust storm, like the bloodless hands of drowsy elders touching our faces as they said good night, never knowing whether we would be slaughtered by the white folks who invaded us or threatened to move in and steal our women and land, and sure enough, goddamn it, when the ones who killed us noticed the missing women, they began to move toward us. One of the missing women understood their language and told them in our language that the mountains were formed by a great buzzard who flew across the earth, and suddenly they contemplated us with a kind of melancholy stare through the unforeseeable aims of our silence, because they never fully understood what was about to happen to them, did they, as their clean and warm houses glowed in the night. But their fate was soon visible in the spectral patterns in the rock around Tenkiller, around the river, and around the entire land, their fate so obvious in the ridges of rock and limestone, for each one of them looked horrified at that moment they heard the buzzard story, and we stood and approached them along with our missing women, who showed them their rage, because one should never anger a Native woman or else the consequences will be severe, ask anyone, which was exactly what happened right then: we moved with our missing women to begin the attack on the ones who killed us, and even Gray Horse reared up toward them so that they all screamed when they saw us approaching them.

Atvdasdiha, there were brutal and gruesome deaths. We told our children the story just as we are telling it to you, for the ones who killed us fled like fugitives into the cold water, and we were comforted by watching the river swallow them whole and carry their bodies away, even if it meant we would see them again one day.

Brandon Hobson (Cherokee) is an assistant professor of creative writing at New Mexico State University and also teaches at the Institute of American Indian Arts. His novel *Where the Dead Sit Talking* was a finalist for the National Book Award. His latest novel, *The Removed*, was published in February 2021 and received high acclaim.

SNAKES ARE BORN IN THE DARK

D. H. TRUJILLO

A drop of sweat rolled across Peter's temple and drenched his ear canal. He thumbed it, attempting to push the cold drop of sweat away from his eardrum. He was unsuccessful. The scarce plant life was brittle, the water on their stems having turned to vapor under the relentless sun. This burning hot day gave way for our ancestors to get even.

Peter had no idea why they thought a July hike in the Four Corners was a good idea. The sun was beating down on him, not a spot of shade around to protect him from the burning rays. Grainy dirt was making its way inside his shoes, rubbing against his skin. Red rocks and mesas popped up out of the desert like Whac-a-Mole, disappearing just when they'd reach the shade. The sound of the river called, begging him to cool off in her hands. He had considered stopping and sitting down for a second but, no, that was not a good idea. Not unless he wanted blisters on the back of his legs from the searing heat trapped in the sand.

This was not a place for Peter. His people had been kayaking in Alaska for as long as humans have been on this planet. The cold, that spine-chilling numbness, he could handle. This heat, this blazing, burning, suffocating heat, he could not. He would gladly return to his frozen Alaskan tundra. If he was being honest, Maddie was the only reason they were here. She had called him, asking if he could visit for her graduation. Ever the loving cousin, Peter said yes. Maddie's final request was that he bring her favorite of Peter's uncles, who was the only one to let Maddie try seal meat when they were kids.

"Come on, it should be right around this corner." Maddie's boyfriend, Adam, had the energy of a chihuahua and the bulging alien eyes to match. Peter watched as he took off at a jog, blond hair bobbing along the trail where it curved around a tall flaxen boulder.

A groan fell out of Maddie's dry mouth, "It's so hot, can't we take a break?" She paused, bracing herself on bent knees as she fought to catch her breath.

"No way! It's right here! Come on you guys," Adam shouted back at them, excitement raising his voice. Adam peered at the rock face, his eyes running over the delicately carved figures. There had to be thousands of them: humans, plants, animals, and celestial beings, too.

The sandstone red rock was completely covered in petroglyphs. Pecked or scraped off, the red stone gave way to creamy rust orange beneath. Each drawing illuminated by the stone within. Suns curled around themselves, women had babies, and rams with horns bigger than their heads swam across the rock face. The large mesa blocked the rushing water of the river where it turned from them, leaving them in the space of silence.

Peter rounded the bend as he saw Adam reach up to run his hands across the petroglyphs. "No!" Peter shouted, running to catch him. "Don't touch them!"

Adam startled, looking back at Peter in contempt. "What are you scared of? Some ancient curse or something?"

Maddie laughed along as she reached up to trace her fingers along a humanoid figure depicting a birth. "No." Peter glared at the two of them as they continued touching the designs. "The oil in our skin deteriorates the rock, touching it is destructive. You need to stop."

"This thing is like a thousand years old, I think it will be fine." Adam turned around and started scratching at the edges of a glyph that looked to be a turkey.

Peter stepped between Adam and the rock and shoved his arms away from it. "Stop it. Why are you being so callous?" He was shouting now. "These petroglyphs have survived for so long because strangers weren't coming here and touching them all over. We didn't have this problem until petroglyphs became a tourist spot."

"So what, you want to gatekeep rock art so that only Indians like you can enjoy it?" Adam shoved his finger into Peter's chest again and again, punctuating his words physically. "Maddie is always going on and on about the things her little Indian cousin teaches her. Now you don't want to share?"

"Adam!" Maddie stepped back in shock at his words. "That was uncalled for."

Peter shrugged and stood his ground. "At least we know how to respect them."

Adam attempted to get close to the rock face again but Peter stayed where he was. "Move, dickhead. This doesn't even belong to you, you're some Eskimo or something." Spit flew from his lips but Peter stood his ground.

Staring the smaller man down, Peter ignored the slur that left his thin mouth, "So? All I'm saying is not to touch it, not that you can't look at it."

"Whatever, dude, you're such a fucking hippie." Adam scoffed and pushed his overgrown blond hair behind his ear, eyeing the panel over Peter's shoulder.

"You wouldn't say that if I was touching all over George Washington's portrait or scratching at the *Mona Lisa*." Peter crossed his arms. This was a hill he would gladly die on.

"You're right, because at least those are beautiful and actually worth something. But this? This rock art is so damn ugly anyway. They don't even know how to draw." Adam laughed, pointing at the blocky humanoid figure.

"Adam, stop!" Maddie shouted in embarrassment. "Stop it. You're being so disrespectful right now, what is wrong with you? Peter is my cousin, he's just trying to protect things like this, they're important to him." Stepping back and turning to Peter, she scrubbed her hands over her face. "I'm sorry, Petey, for touching the wall, I didn't know. And I'm sorry my boyfriend is being such an *asshole!*"

Peter shook his head and bumped her shoulder with his. "It's all right, Mads, at least you know now." As he turned back around, he saw Adam scratching his car keys across the petroglyphs. Rock splintered around the jagged metal, red and orange dust blooming around him. "*No!*" Peter screamed and tackled Adam to the ground. Together, they fell into the hard-packed dirt, only narrowly avoiding the spikes of a nearby boxthorn.

Adam shouted as he reared up and punched Peter square across the face. The two struggled in the dirt, moving farther from the mesa. Crouching down, Peter hooked his arms across the back of Adam's knees, tossing his body up and over his head. Adam splashed into the icy San Juan water, his backpack and water bottle flying through the air with him.

"That's enough!" Maddie screeched, stepping onto the riverbank in between the two. "Stop it. The sun is setting soon, and we still have a five-mile hike back to the car. I am not going to listen to the two of you fight for the entire hike." Peter rolled onto his feet while Adam flopped onto the sand soaking wet. "Now get up, and let's go. We need to start heading back now, before the sun sets. We don't even have flashlights." Maddie stomped away from them, muttering grievances under her breath.

Adam lay motionless at the edge of the water while Peter took the frozen water bottle from his pack and pressed it against his swelling eye.

Maddie looked at Peter and rolled her eyes. "You've always been such a hothead."

"Maybe you should choose men that understand the concept of respecting other people and cultures before you call me a hothead." Peter sighed and sat down on a rock behind Maddie while she roused Adam from the ground.

"Racist," he muttered beneath his breath, watching Maddie retreat.

"Come on, Adam." Maddie sighed as he protested, muttering about his wet shoes and the long hike back. "You're wearing Chacos. You'll be dry in five minutes."

Adam gathered his backpack and water bottle, patting down his pockets and the bag with increasing urgency. He began to frantically unzip the pockets and dump the contents out onto the sand. He let out a panicked shout and then stood, staring at Peter menacingly. "What did you do with the car keys?"

"I didn't touch them." Peter rolled his eyes.

Adam bristled. "You're a damn liar."

"Why would I hide the car keys when we all came in the same car together?" Peter stood and stalked toward Adam, a solid-ice water bottle clutched in his fingers. "What purpose would it serve for me to trap us in the desert overnight?"

"Probably to murder us or something." Adam scoffed and stalked over to Maddie.

"Oh totally, I want to kill you and my cousin for no reason and then take a five-mile hike alone, in the dark, to a car that I don't have keys to. Makes total sense."

"Enough. I don't want to hear another word out of *either* of your mouths until we find those keys." Maddie dropped to her knees and started sifting through the sand and dirt. Looking up, she saw Adam and Peter standing, arms crossed, glaring daggers at each other. "If you don't help me look for the keys, I am going to leave both of your asses here overnight."

Peter turned around to scour the ground up near the petroglyph panel while Adam removed his sandals and trudged ankle deep into the river. Peter took a small leather pouch from his pocket and sprinkled some ground corn out on the ground in front of the panel. His uncle had many friends in the Southwest, and they had arrived to plenty of good medicine. Finished with his offering, he opened his eyes and looked up toward the sky. Taking a deep breath, he turned back to his hiking companions.

"Did you guys find anything?" Adam called out.

Peter and Maddie both shook their heads. Adam rubbed his hands over his face in frustration. "This idiot probably lost my keys when he flipped me into the water."

Peter shrugged. "You shouldn't have punched me."

Adam stepped toward him. "You tackled me to the ground over some stupid rock art."

"It's not stupid—"

Peter was cut off by Maddie shouting at them. "I told the both of you to knock it off." She was breathing heavily, a sunburn settling over her shoulders and her eyes filling with tears. "You," she pointed to Peter, "take ten steps that way and sit down and be quiet. And you—" she said, rounding on Adam, stepping toward him and jamming her finger into his chest, "sit on this rock and shut the hell up."

Maddie walked up to the river, took her sneakers and socks off, and sank her feet into the cold water. She let out a deep sigh before reaching down, cupping the water, and pouring it along her back and arms. Stewing separately for a few long minutes, she finally turned and looked back at the two men sulking in the brilliant copper sunset.

"What the hell are we going to do now?" Maddie looked at them, her voice wavering while her eyes held on to unshed tears.

"We're going to have to try and hike back." Peter stood and walked over to her, reaching a hand down to help her stand.

"How the hell are we going to hike five miles in the dark?" Adam grabbed his shoes and strapped them back on to his feet.

"Look." Peter sighed, turning toward Adam. "The river runs all the way down to the parking lot. As long as we keep the river on our left side, we can make it back. Even in the dark."

"Whatever you say, Tonto." Adam spat.

"Don't." Maddie shoved Adam and started walking beside Peter.

The pair walked with purpose, trying in vain to reach the car before complete darkness. Desert darkness was like being blind-folded. Peter couldn't spend the night out here, he might actually lose his mind. Besides, Adam never *shut up*. Peter might be doing the punching this time.

Adam was behind them, complaining about his hurting feet and making Indian jokes while Maddie and Peter tried to ignore him. Peter didn't mind much, it wasn't anything he hadn't heard before, but why was Maddie with this guy? Maddie was one of the most empathetic people Peter had ever known. She kept canned goods in her trunk so she could hand them out to unhoused people, adopted an end-of-life cat from the shelter, and paid for Peter's travel to come visit. What could she be seeing in this racist asshole?

"I don't know what the hell you see in that guy." Peter scoffed, attempting again to tune out Adam's rendition of "Indian Outlaw."

"Me neither," she said, her voice withdrawn, nearly a whisper. Her tears had run dry long before today.

They continued the hike as the sun barreled toward the horizon. Maddie struggled to see the terrain beneath her feet, catching on every loose rock and tumbleweed they passed. Peter reached out and caught her by the arm, holding her tight while she regained her balance.

"It's so dark I can't even see my feet anymore." Her breathing was labored, the sound of shifting sand filled the air while she fumbled in the dark, searching for a tree to sit under.

"I have a lighter, we just need something to light." Peter got down on his knees, looking around through the scarce plants and sand for something to use as a torch. Finding a long, broken branch, he placed it across his lap and began ripping some dry desert brush out of the dirt. He packed it into a strip of fabric he tore from the bottom of his hiking shirt and wrapped it around the tip of the branch.

He could hear Maddie's heavy breathing in front of him and Adam's continued groaning about the bloating in his belly. "Okay, I think this should work." Peter leaned forward and lit the tip of the dry grass sticking out of the fabric wrap. Grabbing the stick from the bottom, he lifted it into the air to see Maddie hunkered beneath the tree, head in her hands. Turning, he looked around for Adam.

Adam was sitting with his legs out in front of him, looking at his suddenly bare feet and wiggling his toes. Laughing, Adam kicked his feet around in the sand, watching it fly over and over again. Maddie crawled toward him and looked around. "Adam, where are your shoes?"

"Who needs shoes at the beach?" Adam laughed and kicked sand toward Maddie. She reared back and wiped at her eyes while Adam laughed. "Come on, a little ocean water never hurt anyone."

"Ocean water?" Maddie and Peter shared a concerned look. "Adam, what do you mean ocean water? The closest ocean is like a thousand miles from here." Maddie frowned as he pulled away.

Adam lay down on his back and lifted his arms and legs slightly off the ground. "If we aren't in the ocean how could I be floating right now?"

Maddie groaned and sat beside Adam. Her feet were too sore to squat. She reached down to undo her sandals and gasped, bile rising in her throat. Peter leaned over at her panicked breath, apprehensively bringing the torch lower, closer to her feet. Acid burned in his chest. Maddie's feet were swollen and covered in angry red boils. Even the bottoms of her feet were afflicted, but they had ruptured and were leaking a thick pungent green fluid down her sandals and into the dirt.

Peter sat up on his knees and leaned over his cousin. The firelight danced across the sickly fluid rolling down her red, blistering skin. Her entire body was covered in these pus-filled wounds. Maddie tried to cover her face with her hands and stopped when she saw the wounds on her palms. Her vision blurred with tears while she sat frozen. Peter fought in vain to shut his open mouth but it was a futile fight.

Maddie's hands were coated on both sides, her entire face burdened by the sores, lips bloody where strings of the pus and blood blended together each time she closed and opened her mouth. Even the normally white skin of her scalp was indiscernible from the oozing green sores.

Peter crawled into the bushes, vomiting from the smell of his cousin's rotting, putrid body. The image of the reddened bumps leaking a thick slippery green goo was burned into his brain, the pus dripping, blood running, and the rancid smell replaying over and over.

Maddie sat hunched over, face between her knees, when she

heard a soft giggle tickle her ear. She gasped in fear and threw herself back beneath her resting tree. Maddie swore she could feel the person's breath on her exposed neck. It sounded like the laugh of a child. She frantically wiped her eyes clean of pus, fighting the cry of pain in touching the throbbing sores. Clear-eyed, mostly, she scanned the empty prairie but the night was cloudy, the moonlight weak, and Peter's torch was too far away to make out anything in front of her.

She could hear scuttling in the bushes as the breeze carried the laughter on the tips of the dry grass. "It's just the wind," she whispered to herself. "Just the wind." She was too scared to turn her back on the barren desert so she crab-walked on her hands and feet back toward Peter. Sand dug into her raw broken skin. She could feel the infection knocking, opening the door, no one was home to stop it.

Peter had managed to rouse Adam into a sitting position but he almost seemed worse. Maddie couldn't quite tell what was different, but *something* wasn't right. Adam was looking directly at her face, and laughing. Laughing harder than she had ever seen him laugh before.

"I didn't know monkeys could talk!" Adam continued his laughter, pushing hard against Peter to try and lie down again. "Tell me, do you really fling your shit?" He stared at Maddie in earnest, eyes wide and questioning. Suddenly, he burst out into laughter again and shouted, "I knew it!"

Peter and Maddie shared a look over his shoulder. What was going on with Adam? Maddie closed her eyes as a wave of nausea cascaded over her. "Do you think he ate something bad?" Peter asked her.

She shook her head. "Adam doesn't even eat seafood. He's way too picky to eat something random from the desert."

Peter looked back at Adam, his eyebrows peaking together in

the center of his face. "I don't know how we are going to be able to hike all the way back with him like this. Plus you, like . . . that." Peter gestured to her whole body, the green ooze starting to crust in the dry air. "Are you in pain?"

She didn't respond, blue eyes unfocused staring out into the darkness.

"Maddie? Did you hear me?"

Maddie's attention snapped back to Peter. "Yes, I'm listening, sorry." Maddie shifted uncomfortably, falling to the side before righting herself with her feet straight out in front of her. The child-like laughter was still torturing her, floating into her ears when the breeze came. "It doesn't hurt that much." She leaned back on her hands, controlling the flinch as the sand joined her bloodstream. "The desert is a little scary at night."

"Uh, Maddie, are you sure he wouldn't eat anything?"

Maddie laughed without opening her eyes, "What, you think he found some peyote or something?"

Peter shook his head, scooting back from Maddie to keep Adam in his sight. "No . . . but if he ate something bad that might be why he's so bloated."

Maddie's eyes snapped open and she sat up, eyes flying to her boyfriend's belly. It was bloated, all right. Distended. Hard. Like he had swallowed a basketball. "What the hell?" Maddie's voice was barely a whisper, her eyes darting across the spectacular swell of his belly.

She reached forward, blood and pus smearing across Adam's white T-shirt as she pushed it up to his chest. "Oh my god! *Peter!*" She screamed into the night, and Peter could hear the tears at the back of her throat.

Forcing himself to lean forward, Peter let his eyes drag over Adam's exposed flesh. His skin was stretched tight, purple roses blooming where his capillaries had begun to burst. Movement stirred under his skin, turning, pushing against the confines of its human cage.

"Uh-oh, the pregnant Indian curse," Adam sang out between his trills of maniacal laughter.

"*What?!*" Maddie yelled, erupting into tears. Hot, heavy tears were running down her face, mixing with the blood and pus still growing across her body. Pus mixed with her tears and fell down her cheeks in thick green ribbons.

"Pregnant? You are insane. This whole thing is insane. We must have all taken something and now we are hallucinating. There is *no way.*"

Peter couldn't believe what he was seeing. Adam was pregnant, *allegedly*, with a currently unknown fetus. Maddie, covered in boils, sobbing, and him, just sitting there, stuck in their nightmare. What the fuck was going on? He could feel a panic attack coming on. Thoughts raced but he remained stuck on just one: *Are they going to die?*

"Peter! Did you put some fucking Indian curse on us?" Maddie screeched at him.

Peter couldn't believe his ears. An eerie calm came over him.

"Are you joking? I know you must be joking with that racist shit, right, Maddie?" His voice was smooth, his eyes narrowed at her. "You are my cousin, *my family*, don't say shit like that to me."

Maddie screamed in response. Peter could see the tightness of her skin around the boils, some parts beginning to split the unaffected areas. "Oh shit" fell out of his mouth as he stared at her.

"Oh shit? Do something, Peter!" Maddie's voice had gone shrill, thin, pleading.

"What the hell do you want me to do? Your boyfriend is having some kind of rapid growing man-baby like that vampire baby from *Twilight* and you want me to do something?! Do I look like a vampire doctor to you?"

"Get it out of him!" Maddie screamed as another contraction ripped across his body. "Fix me! This is all going to scar." Sobs wracked her body as the future weighed down on them, looming a permanent disfigurement.

Adam groaned, curling into a ball as he let out a rigid scream. Uh-oh.

Peter crawled toward Adam, gripping his shoulder to keep him still. Muscles rippled across his thin stretched skin. Rolling under his skin they tensed tightly, pulsing before releasing and rolling again. Peter watched the entire thing happen again. He could *see* Adam having contractions. This whole thing was getting harder and harder to deny.

Peter was going crazy. That was the only explanation.

"Maddie, there's no way this is real. We must all be dreaming somehow. Maybe those granola bars were laced by your wacko white supremacist boyfriend or something. People don't grow entire fetuses in four hours. It's impossible." Peter was grasping at straws. This wasn't possible. There was no way Adam was pregnant and about to give birth to a baby . . . or whatever was inside him.

Adam was screaming again, flipped over onto his back he was wailing into the empty desert sky. He pushed onto his feet, shoulders digging into the dirt, his back arched toward the stars. His stomach reached for the moon, distending as though he had swallowed a stick that was slowly reaching for its branch from inside him.

"What are you doing?!" Peter shouted into the night air, aimed at Adam but meant for himself.

"Peter, you have to help him. Whatever this thing is, it is coming out *right now*." Maddie pointed toward her boyfriend.

Blood was blooming under his belly button. Something pushed again, more blood rushing across his arching stomach. Again and again, Adam's *thing* broke through the layers of thin skin and muscle. He panted and gasped for what felt like hours but they had no idea how much time had passed. It could've been five minutes or five days. Finally, there was a wet sound, blood exploding from Adam's belly. A dark slender figure slithered through the broken flesh and blood and slid down his leg onto the desert sand.

Exhausted, Adam lay in the dirt, eyes closed. Peter couldn't tell if he was breathing.

Maddie looked at Peter, white eyes shining in the black night, "Is that a fucking snake?"

"No. There's no way your boyfriend gave birth to a snake. This isn't possible. What the fuck is happening right now?" Peter leaned closer to the slimy creature, shining the firelight over it. It was tan, almost blending into the dirt save for the bits of blood and human sticking to its scales. "Oh my god, it's a rattlesnake, Maddie."

"How in the hell did a rattlesnake just come out of him?" Maddie's voice was timid, hollow as though she was on the edges of sleep.

"You are asking the wrong person. I still think we're just having a *really* bad trip." Peter was struggling to hold on to reality.

Before Peter or Maddie could react, Adam sat up. His eyes flashed wide, scanning the dirt all around him. He leaned forward and snatched the rattlesnake up by its tail. "Hello, baby." He brought the tail of the snake high above his head, leveling its tiny face with his. "How nice to meet you."

Maddie and Peter couldn't move. What in the hell was happening right now? Maddie was covered in blood and pus, on the verge of losing not just her mind, but consciousness too. "I can't deal with this right now." She closed her eyes and lay back flat on the ground.

Peter whipped his head back and forth between the two. He

had no idea what the fuck to do. Adam was shaking the snake by its tail, singing a song to it, asking it to wake up and "join us." Maybe Adam had placed some kind of white man's curse on them instead. That seemed far more plausible.

"Adam, put the snake down." Peter stood up, trying to encourage Adam to let it go.

"Hush, little baby, don't be a brat, Daddy's going to find you a big fat rat." With that, Adam tucked the unmoving snake into his bloodstained shirt pocket and dove into the bushes. Crouched on his hands and feet, Adam was running around like a dog searching for a bone. Peter could hardly see him, his movements so quick, eluding the light from the torch. Peter was worried he was going to lose sight of him, though the slow current of warmth in the air told him sunrise was looming. Soon, there would be light in this nightmare.

Adam wrestled with the dirt and brush, his face buried in a Mormon tea plant when he suddenly went still. "Adam?" Peter walked slowly closer to him, scared the guy had bled out from the hole in his stomach. Peter continued walking, standing directly over Adam's bush-buried head when Adam snapped to the right, then vaulted up from the bush, a tiny kangaroo rat dangling from his mouth.

Peter's breath left him in a woosh and he jumped backward. He hadn't expected Adam to be able to catch anything. His eyes searched for Maddie, who was fast asleep, her chest rising and falling in a soft rhythm while Peter was panting like he'd just finished a marathon.

"Here you go, little baby," Adam whispered while he dangled the bleeding rat in front of the snake. In the scuffle, Adam had broken the rat's neck in his mouth; fur stuck between his teeth and blood coated the edges of his lips. He rubbed the rat's blood across the snake's small face and its tongue came darting out, slithering through the air in search of a fresh meal.

Adam's fingers were holding on to the feet of the kangaroo rat, too close to the starving newborn. Snapping forward, the snake caught the tips of his fingers along with the rodent, fangs tearing through his skin. Adam didn't seem to feel any pain as the snake ripped away, taking a chunk of his thumb with it. "Good boy," he whispered, letting the snake down to the ground to swallow its meal.

Peter stared at the ground, in shock, as the rattlesnake that had chewed its way out of Adam's belly was now swallowing an entire kangaroo rat. He was starting to think eating the rat was not the weirdest part of this deeply unfortunate night. A golf ball–size bulge worked its way down the snake's body, sticking out like they were in a cartoon.

Maybe they were. Wile E. Coyote had to be around here some-where, right?

Peter shook his head as he looked up at the lightening sky. He put his torch down on the path and smothered it with sand, extinguishing it completely.

"Okay," he started, "we need to get the fuck out of here before anything else happens."

He walked over to Maddie and shook her awake. "Can you walk?"

Maddie groaned and sat up, "Yeah I think so. Not like my feet are covered in open wounds or anything." She opened her eyes, vision obscured by green and yellow pus, strings of it interlacing her upper and lower lashes.

Peter grimaced, holding back his vomit. "Don't remind me. You get up, while I wrangle Adam."

Adam had wandered off, away from the river and deeper into

the desert, watching the rattlesnake slither into a burrow to finish digesting its meal. "Petey, I can't leave now, I need to watch my son finish his breakfast."

"Adam, that's a snake. It is not your son." Peter tugged at his arm.

"Yes it is, he's my baby." Adam crouched down to look lovingly at the snake. Peter wasn't sure how he was even able to see it, the snake burrowed under sand the same color as its scales. "Look at him, he has my blue eyes."

"He sure does." Peter was starting to run out of energy. He hadn't slept, and he was still pretty sure they had gone on a horrible drug-induced trip that lasted all night. "Let's get to the car so we can come bring him some better food. How's that sound?"

"I'll bring him with us." Adam reached down despite Peter's protests and stuffed the snake back into the side pocket on his cargo pants. Peter ripped the remainder of his T-shirt in half, tying it around Adam's open wound. He wasn't sure if the blood had stopped or if the rattlesnake venom had cauterized the opening as it chewed through him. Either way, it needed to be covered from the elements. Peter zipped his jacket up over his now bare skin, the zipper tugging on his few chest hairs.

They finally set off again, finding the trail in the daylight, but their pace was slow, painstakingly slow. Maddie was hobbling, using Peter for support. She was barefoot, refusing to strap shoes over the painful blisters. "We don't even have the car keys, how are we going to get home?"

"I know." Peter sighed in defeat. "But hey, it's early morning now, someone is bound to be coming down this trail soon, so maybe they can help us." Maddie sniffled and nodded her head, clutching Peter's arm a little tighter. The sky finally pinkened, the sun peeking over the eastern horizon.

The three had been meandering down the trail at a snail's pace when Peter finally heard voices. Maddie heard them too and perked up, suddenly able to walk faster. As the people came around the bend, he saw Maddie's dad, two park rangers, and their uncle who had flown down with Peter. He did not look pleased.

"Oh thank god!" Maddie's dad ran forward, gathering her up in his arms despite their stickiness. "What the hell happened to you? Where were you guys? I was worried sick when I got home this morning and your car was missing. I called you all, why didn't you answer?" He was rambling in distress, words dying in his throat when he took note of the dried blood and pus coating his daughter's wounded and badly scarred face, the sand she had laid on earlier coating the entirety of her body.

Peter saw the moment Maddie's dad noticed Adam's wound. The man's face grayed, disgust bobbing up and down in his throat. The muscles of his neck pulled tight, as if he could close his throat and stop the breakfast working its way up his esophagus.

Maddie shook her head in silence. Her eyes were swelling shut with tears and pus, exhaustion overtaking her. "I just want to shower and go to bed. We didn't sleep all night." Maddie's dad wrapped his arm around her viscid shoulder, turning and guiding her back the way he had come. He was looking down at the wounds on her legs and Adam's mangled body, his panic thinly concealed as the two quietly spoke.

The park rangers approached Adam's gooey body, taking gloves out of their packs before reaching out to him. He had been oddly silent since the others had joined them. His mouth was closed, his eyes barely visible beneath the paste of tears and sand coating his lashes, and he stared straight ahead, unblinking. The female ranger gripped Adam's forearm, a scream lurching from her mouth as the snake shot out of his pocket, burying its fangs deep into her arm.

The other ranger grabbed the snake, forcing its jaws open and throwing it like a Frisbee across the open desert as soon as it released its hold on her flesh. Adam screamed in terror, attempting to take off after the snake, but Maddie's dad rushed over, grabbing him by the collar and forcing him to stay with the rangers. The park ranger's hands shook while she wrapped her wound. Peter wondered if the bite had venom when snakes were this young. Was it even truly a snake that bit her?

The other ranger made a call on his satellite phone, asking for an ambulance to meet them at the trailhead. "Come on," he said. "We all need to get the hell out of here as soon as possible. You all need medical treatment."

He turned and ushered everyone in front of him, except Peter and his uncle. The group rushed down the trail, haphazardly dragging Adam with them while he wailed and thrashed in an attempt to get to his snake. *His son,* he screamed.

"Peter," his uncle whispered, looking straight into his eyes. "I thought I told you no more magic."

"It wasn't me," Peter said. "Besides, he committed a federal crime. Some blood and pus is nothing." Peter started off down the trail behind the chaos of the group.

"What the hell happened?" His uncle fell into step beside him. "Did you make that boy give birth to a rattlesnake? The boils on your *cousin*?"

"I told you it wasn't me." Peter rolled his eyes as they continued down the trail. He looked skyward at the white clouds set into the orange sunrise of the Utah desert.

"He disrespected our ancestors." Peter pulled the car keys out of his pocket and unlocked the car doors. "Come on, Uncle, they'll be fine and you know it." He opened the door and climbed in, "Man, I could really use a coffee before we head to the hospital."

His uncle glanced back at the park rangers loading the group into an emergency van to head into town; Adam handcuffed and attempting to kick the rangers, Maddie crying, the ranger's arm turning purple all before the sun had fully risen from the horizon.

"What kind of coffee?"

D. H. Trujillo is a fiction author born in Colorado of Pueblo and Mexican descent. The desert is her happy place and serves as inspiration for many of her works. She holds a bachelor of anthropology from the University of Hawaiʻi and a master of forensic behavioral science from Alliant International University. She currently resides in Baltimore, Maryland, with her husband, two spooky black cats, an elder chihuahua named after jeans, and the plethora of ghosts inhabiting her 1949 home. Her debut romance novel, *Lizards Hold the Sun*, was released under the name Dani Trujillo.

BEFORE I GO

NORRIS BLACK

The view from where Davey Church died was spectacular.

A body, broken and bloodied, lying at the bottom of a rocky gorge. A setting sun lighting the clouds ablaze in a chorus of heavenly color. It was hard to believe one spot was a witness to such disparate visions.

Keira wondered if it looked like this the day Davey fell to his death. If the day his battered corpse was picked apart by coyotes and vultures the sun was shining and the birds sang merry songs. She hoped not. It would feel too much like a sin for such beauty to be a witness to such horror. In her mind it had been a dark day, dismal with glowering clouds spitting frigid rain. She could've found out for sure if she wanted. Could've asked when the police came to her home to notify her of Davey's death. Fallen during a hike, they said. She never thought to ask them what the weather had been.

It didn't matter. From that point on, every day was filled with dark clouds regardless of what the sky looked like. As if a mirror to her mood sudden gusts of wind buffeted the hilltop, screaming in her ears and causing her to stumble slightly as if shoved by invisible frigid hands. She steadied herself and stared out at the rolling vista in front of her.

"Why did you come here? What were you doing?"

The only answer to Keira's question was the keening of the wind through the handful of tall, scraggly pine trees managing to grow at the top of the rocky hill. Gnarled roots, half-exposed to the lashing winds, clung to the rocky ground as if they would be swept away the moment they let their guard down.

She knew how they felt.

Why did you come here? Her words repeated, riding the soft murmur of the wind.

Keira spun around, but there was no one there. An echo perhaps, some strange acoustics at play brought on by the irregular ground and the cold, thin air of late fall in northern Ontario. She shivered, only some of it due to the bite of winter's promise in the breeze.

Keira took one last look over the edge; she thought she could see the spot where he landed. A patch of stony ground a little darker than the rest.

Foolish. It had been a year to the day. The inexorable march of the seasons would have scoured away any lasting marks.

Her jacket pocket buzzed and she took out her phone, sighing when she saw the name of the caller before sliding a thumb across the screen to answer.

"Keira? Are you there?" Even through the static of a poor connection and the howling wind she could hear the slight slurring in the words.

Drunk again, she thought.

"Hey, Dad."

"Keira! Oh thank God, I kept getting your voice mail!"

"Service is pretty spotty around here. I didn't know you were trying to reach me," she lied. She had seen the calls but had been ignoring them.

"Spotty? Where are you? It sounds windy." Silence stretched for a moment. "No! Please tell me you didn't go there!"

The distress in his voice was clear and Keira cursed at herself for answering the phone. "Dad, we talked about this. I'm not going to do anything crazy. I just . . . I just needed to be able to say goodbye."

"Keira? Are you there? I can't hear you. Keira?" The line went silent, the call dropped.

"Probably for the best," she said to herself as she tucked the phone away. It was an argument she had no interest in rehashing. When Dad dug in on something he didn't let go, and he was twice as bad after a few drinks. Something that happened a lot these days.

She shouldered her pack and made the hike down the back side of the hill. The sun had disappeared and night was falling fast. Her campsite came into view just as the final, faint glow, the last memory of day, was swallowed by darkness. A pocket flashlight gave her enough light to crawl into the tent and shed her coat, trading its warmth for that of the heavy sleeping bag she had purchased for this trip.

Pulling out a battered paperback, she settled in for the night. Reading before bed was an old habit, but these days it felt like probing an open wound. Keira longed for the evenings when she could barely make it past a paragraph without Davey scattering her thoughts like startled seagulls with some amusing story from his day or by showing her something he found while scrolling through his phone. Each time he would belatedly realize he had interrupted her reading and apologize only to repeat the whole sequence a few minutes later.

He had always been so eager to share his life with her, and for her to be a part of his. Now his life was gone and hers had withered to dust.

As she read, the whisper of each page turning was a slash across a silence so potent it roared in the darkness.

Keira read by the light of an electric lantern until her eyes began to droop.

"Good night, Davey," she said to no one, clicked off the light, and was carried away on a tide of dreams.

Dreams were followed by nightmares and it was there Davey found her.

It happened in one of those weird in-between states—one foot still in the sea of dreams, the other hovering near the shore of wakefulness but not yet touched down. The tent flap rustled aside and her fiancé, broken and bloody, dragged himself through the opening and into the interior of the snug tent. Keira was frozen, unable to move even an eyelash as Davey slid into the sleeping bag beside her. His flesh was ice-cold and she could feel the jagged ends of broken and protruding bones digging into the exposed flesh of her legs. Split, blue lips pressed against her ear.

"Why did you come here?" A whisper as quiet as death but the words unmistakable just the same.

Keira woke screaming. She flailed in her sleeping bag and flung a hand out, pawing for the light, heart fluttering like a bird caught in a net. With a click the warm yellow glow of the electric lantern filled the space. The tent was empty, save for her.

"Fucking dreams," she said, and then broke down. Big wracking sobs with tears running down her face and snot in her nose. She was an ugly crier, a fact she had always hated and one Davey had teased her about mercilessly.

It wasn't until her heart had settled and the tears were wiped from her eyes that she noticed the unzipped tent flap fluttering in the night breeze and the scratches on the backs of her legs.

Sleep didn't come again that night and the little electric lantern stayed on until the faint light of dawn lit up the red nylon walls of the tent. Daylight had a way of taking the mad thoughts of deep night and placing them in rational context. The open tent flap? She had simply forgotten to zip up the tent when she went to bed. The scratches on her legs? Caused by her own nails in her sleep. All very proper and rational thoughts, but Keira wasn't doing a good job of convincing herself. She ate a cold breakfast before breaking down the tent for the three-mile hike back to the car.

She glanced up the steep, rocky path to the top of the hill. *One last look before I go,* she thought. *One last goodbye.* After today she had no intention of ever returning to this particular stretch of the back end of nowhere.

The morning was typical of autumn in the north and Keira's breath plumed in the frosty air as she approached the summit of the hill.

Reaching the top, her steady steps came to a sudden stop. A huddled form stood on the edge of the precipice with their back to her. Nightmares were still fresh in her mind, and for a brief moment she thought it was Davey waiting for her. But no, who-ever this was was shorter with graying hair bundled into a pair of twin braids and a colorful shawl hanging around her shoulders.

"Good morning," said Keira as she came up beside the woman. "I didn't realize there was anybody else up here." The only travers-able path to the top of the hill ran right past her tent and she hadn't heard anyone passing.

"I like the view in the mornings," replied the unexpected visi-tor as she smiled a greeting. The woman was deeply tanned with a round, soft face that transformed into a nest of wrinkles when she smiled. It reminded Keira of the little apple head dolls her grandmother used to make. "You must be Keira."

"I . . . I'm sorry, have we met?" She struggled to find any recollection of the kindly old woman now standing before her but came up blank.

"I know you love him very much, but you need to let him go. They're not the same after they pass over. Calling them back is only asking for trouble."

It was like a bucket of ice water dumped over her head. The memory of cold flesh pressing against hers, broken lips pressed to her ear. "What?" was all she could say.

The old woman regarded her with sad eyes. "You shouldn't have come here. Your pain is stirring up things better left alone. Go home, child. Remember him, cherish him, but leave him here and live your life."

Keira's vision blurred as tears stung her eyes. Angrily, she scrubbed them away with the sleeve of her coat and when she could see once again she was all alone on the hilltop. The old woman was nowhere in sight.

She sat on that windswept hill for hours, troubling over the words of the mysterious old woman. As the sun reached its apex Keira rose and made the trek back down the path but paused as she reached the space where her campsite had been the night before. She took several steps along the path toward her car before stopping, turning around, and setting about raising her tent again, the only sound the singing of birds and the distant chittering of foraging squirrels.

Night came and Keira lay awake, staring at the walls of her tent. She wasn't sure when she drifted off to sleep; she hadn't intended on it. She came to with a start. At some point in the night the electric lantern had died, leaving only the silvery glow of the full moon filtering through a small screen window above her head.

Slumber was slow to relinquish its hold and so it took a few moments to realize she was being watched. An enormous head poked in through the tent flap, regarding her in silence. An angular face, chalky white skin stretched tight over heavy bone with eyes the color of grave moss and lips that reminded Keira of a pair of blood-bloated leeches. Those lips stretched wide in a smile, revealing white teeth, and the visitor spoke in a husky, feminine voice. "Oh! You're awake! I'm so glad you decided to stay after all. Davey is too. He's been just *chomping* at the bit to get at you and I can see why."

"Davey? Is he here, can I see him?" Keira asked. A rational voice inside her was screaming how this was all wrong, that none of it made sense. But it was a small voice and it was shrinking by the moment.

"Of course, child," came the reply as the strange woman peered around the interior of the tent. "But not here. Come! Follow me!" And the pale face withdrew into the shadows.

Keira scrambled from the tent, not bothering to grab her jacket despite the freezing temperature. Ahead she could see the shadowy silhouette of the woman, nearly lost in the evening gloom as she started up the trail to the top of the hill.

The moon was full but stingy with its light.

Keira hurried after, tripping and falling over rocks hidden in the shadows, cutting her knees and hand on the rugged ground. Each time she fell, she got back up and stumbled onward.

The lady with the pale face waited for her at the crest of the hill. As Keira grew closer she could see the woman was impossibly tall, at least nine feet or more in height. Around her shoulders was a cloak made of crow's wings that enveloped her entire form and dragged on the ground behind her. The tips of the wings appeared wet, like they had been dipped in blood.

"Who are you?" The screaming voice inside Keira pushed itself to the fore to blurt out the question.

"I've had many names, none of which you would recognize. I am the Night Mother. I am the last, wet gasp of a punctured lung.

I am the quiet sound of blood cooling in dead veins. I am the end of all things, and all things that end are my domain." As she spoke, a dozen or more hands appeared around the hem of her ebony cloak, each clawing its way across the ground before being sucked back out of sight only for another to take its place. On the last word, they all pulled back and disappeared as one. "But that's not the question you really want an answer to, is it? Go ahead, ask. I won't bite." Bloated lips spread wide in a smile.

"Can you bring him back to me?"

"There it is." Her delighted laugh sent shivers down Keira's spine. "He called for me at the end, you know. Many of them do. They call out for Mother, and I come running to gather them up and bring them home. By all rights he *is* mine. But you did come all this way, and you did ask so nicely. How could I say no? After all, a mother loves her daughters as much as her sons."

She pulled back her feathered cloak to reveal the darkness of an abyss. The broken corpse of Davey Mason lurched from it and into the silvery light of the full moon. His limbs jutted at obscene angles where bones had shattered and erupted from the skin. His face was lopsided where the side of it had caved in from the impact with a rocky ledge halfway down the hill.

"Why did you come here!"

The anguish in Davey's voice was unmistakable and Keira flinched back, stumbling away from the horror in front of her. Her heel slammed against a large rock and she fell backward with a cry.

Backward, into open air.

In her fright she hadn't realized how close the edge was. The world spun, moon replacing ground replacing moon. The pain when Keira hit the ground was more intense than anything she had felt before. Bones broke and nerves screamed, the world nothing but blood and dirt and pain.

Her mind fled, back through hazy memories with sharp edges,

each slicing red lines through her soul as she passed them. The morning the police knocked on her door to tell her of the death of her fiancé. The soft sigh of her mother's last breath as she succumbed to a long bout with cancer, barely heard over the beeping of the hospital machines crowding the small room. The discovery of the tattered remains of her childhood cat on the highway in front of the house where she grew up, the ridges of tire tread distinct in a rope of flattened pink intestine. Further back, before all the hurt and the pain weighed her down. Back to when the entirety of her world was warm and peaceful.

She felt that warmth embrace her and she smiled a bloodflecked smile.

"There there." A voice, soft and husky in her ear. "Mother will take good care of you. It's all over now."

Norris Black grew up on the Tyendinaga Mohawk Territory, where he would spend hours in the woods fighting off imaginary monsters, armed with nothing but a pointy stick. He's been an award-winning photojournalist, a snake enthusiast, and a keen lover of naps in hammocks and currently works as an IT administrator for a nonprofit agency in the snowy wilds of Canada. When he's not writing about the monsters that shared his childhood, he spends his time learning to speak with machines and taking long walks in dark, spooky woods.

NIGHT IN THE CHRYSALIS

TIFFANY MORRIS

A woman's voice, soft with lullaby, sang its wind-chime strangeness into the dark.

Cece woke with a start.

"Kwe'?" she asked. Wide-awake in the dark, no light came through the bedroom window. "Hello?"

The woman's voice was coming from another room. Cece fumbled for her phone and saw the time: 11:45 p.m. Still early. She wished that daylight was shuffling closer.

She turned to the flashlight on her phone and found her battery-powered lantern. She clicked it on, its yellow brightness a little stronger than her phone's dim light, and stepped out into the dark hall.

"Is someone there? I already called the cops," she lied. She wandered, shaking, to the room across the hall. The cold brass knob turned with no effort. A rustling sound scurried over the floor. She shone her lantern there.

Eyes were watching her in the dark but she could not see them. The streetlight moon outside sent unreal shadows into the empty room. The light itself searched the darkness for her, living prey watched by walls and windows—

Her flashlight landed on a small object. She squinted and moved closer: sticks tied together with jute string, a crude bundle in the rough shape of a person.

She screamed and dropped it. She ran down the spine of the house, her body a shiver traveling over the staircase.

Cece messaged her aunt. *Did you smudge this place yet?*

Her aunt saw the message. The typing ellipses popped up. They disappeared. They popped up again. Cece waited, stomach in knots, for her aunt's response. They disappeared.

Nothing.

Fuck, she thought. She didn't have anything to smudge the place—or herself. The power wasn't on yet, either. It would just be her, her flashlights, and what was left of her phone and laptop batteries.

Cece's life had become a heap of boxes: clothes and miscellany in cardboard, to be delivered first thing in the morning. Renovictions were devouring the hungry city: stone facades and steel spines gentrified whole neighborhoods, creating towering fortifications against the increasing number of poor and unhoused people. It was her second time being uprooted in a year continuously marked by false starts and endings. In February, a miscarriage; a breakup in June. She crawled through the months in the detritus of her imagined future. *To desire is to mourn,* she'd written in her journal on a snowy morning, her handwriting foreign, girlishly big and shaky. She'd felt maudlin and grew red-cheeked even as the truth of both her desire and her mourning gnawed at her bones. The feeling—of emptiness, of ruin, of impossibility—stayed inside her, no matter what she did.

It had been sheer luck, or a turn of it, maybe, that she'd needed a place just as her auntie Deb was moving back to town; even luckier that Deb had found a whole house to rent at the edge of the city. The bus route ended just outside the small two-story home; black silhouettes of trees behind the property snarled up at the light pollution. Cece often thought about how her ancestors might have lived on the land before the city stretched and sprawled out over the coastline. The bones of those distant family members were, she knew, interred in the soil, some beneath the since-closed downtown library, smothered by its concrete. She tried to feel connected to them in each moment, learning the traditional calendar, noticing when sap poured from bark on the trees and the fireflies blinked their Morse code into backyards and the too-tall grass of abandoned lots. The connection felt good: a way to mitigate the alien chaos of the city, the place that screeched and menaced you with its strange machinery. It was nice, for once, to be at its edge instead of in its mouth.

A new life: so came this first night in the chrysalis of the empty house. Each room contained the ghosts of future memories. Aunt Deb would for sure put her cousin's photos up on the wall alongside kitschy Jesus artifacts and a patchwork quilt or two. Cece roamed from the empty living room to the kitchen, imagining their near future in the home. There would be dinner parties, board games, visits with friends. Maybe she could plant a garden. She knew better than to envision any further: the future was a room with a warp in the floor. It was a dangerous thing to think or speak into being, like a too-early pregnancy announcement.

"I don't mean any harm," she said to the house. "I just live here now. First-night jitters."

She laughed to herself and the air felt lighter. It was a roof over her head. It was the best she could do for now and that could be good enough.

———————

At the bottom of the stairs, a smell of blood: the wet metallic cling slapped her across the face, followed by a waft of rotten meat. Rustling sounded in the walls. Why had there been a doll? Her mind raced. A doll: apsute'gan.

"*Apsute'gan.*" *Her nukumij's soft fingers made the doll dance. Cece reached for the doll and her grandmother pulled it gently away, her eyes imploring and focused on hers. "In Mi'kmaw, tu's: apsute'gan."*

Cece repeated it and grasped the doll from her grandmother's hand. She made the doll dance, like her nukumij had. "Apsute'gan," she repeated once more in a singsong voice, and skipped out of the room.

The little doll, Rosie, had been her favorite: woven by one of her nukumij's friends. It was so unlike her other dolls, which were all white porcelain or brown plastic and wearing fussy dresses of shining satin and coarse lace. None of them quite looked like her, though she'd loved them all the same. She spent many afternoons healing their invented wounds and tried to be a nurturing mother, imitating the actions of care: invisible meals and pretend outings and real tea parties with luski on rose-lined plates.

This doll had been left behind by a child. Of course. She'd had a night terror that included the woman singing and it was juxtaposed with the doll that was left behind. A coincidence. Cece's knees shook as she closed her eyes and demanded that she accept it as the truth. Children made dolls all the time. She'd made her own, she'd made potions and strange concoctions and effigies in the woods her whole life. It was just for play, to imitate a mother, to feel less lonely as each friendless afternoon stretched before her. The doll was such an easy way to feel like she belonged to something, that something belonged to her.

She didn't know if she could get back to sleep. She sat on the floor of the living room, watching the streetlights make the trees, and their shadows, dance on the walls. Sleep found her again.

A singsong voice clamored into her thoughts. Fungi sprouted from the walls with many fingers, rustling like paper, an atonal music box tinkling: *Dead man's fingers break down the trees. Dead man's fingers crawl over me.*

Cece woke again, body tight with panic. Her eyes focused on the window once more. She tried to calm herself: Breath in. Hold. Breath out. *Watch how the lights outside make shadows on the floor.* It was just another nightmare.

She blinked back tears as she struggled to steady her breath. She didn't have enough money for a hotel. She didn't have a car to sleep in. She was stuck alone in the house with nothing until morning.

She stretched with a sharp ache in her side and tried to ignore the vomit curdling in her stomach, begging to be announced. The strange smells of blood and meat had vanished: they, too, may have been remnants from the edges of sleep.

She needed a distraction. She'd left her laptop upstairs. Dread beading sweat at her brow, Cece climbed, staring only at each stair as she went, unable to meet the gaze of the dark walls.

The top of the stair felt darker than before: the center of a collapsing star. A rustling was coming from the bedroom across the hall once again.

Cece ignored it and opened her bedroom door. She stepped inside. Nothing strange. Relief coursed through her. With a trembling hand she placed the lantern on the floor. She picked up her laptop and tried to turn it on.

Nothing. Cece placed it back down and grabbed her cell phone. Nothing. She groaned in aggravation.

A woman's voice started singing again: faint and growing louder. Cece dropped her phone and whirled around.

A woman stared through her with two voidblack eyes, screaming sockets howling emptiness and death.

Cece screamed. She couldn't resist her tears any longer. She ran for the door; it slammed shut. She pulled at the handle. The door would not move.

"Get out," the woman hissed.

"What is your problem, aqalasie'w? I'm trying to!" Cece yelled.

"My husband built this house." Each word hissed between the woman's stained and broken teeth. "This has always been my house." Her corpse-pale skin glowed dimly in the dark.

The woman blinked out of sight in an instant, and Cece began to sob. She tried again to open the bedroom door but the knob still would not move. She ran and tried to pull up the window but it was painted shut.

The house was breathing: the wallpaper shifted redpink in the soft light of her lantern. The curlicues on the pattern glistened and moved in a wet rhythm, becoming organs producing life, carrying blood and oxygen through the digestive system of the house.

The house is living. The house is watching. The house desires.

She pressed her hand against the wet wall, the slippery glisten of organs pushing back against her bare palm, sponge soft. She tried not to retch.

"Please," she screamed, "you want me to leave. I'll go. Please let me go. I'll never bother you again. I'll make sure my auntie doesn't move in, either."

Blood pooled in her mouth. The woman started singing as everything went black.

———

In the dark room the dollhouse burned jack-o'-lantern bright; its tiny bulbs cast orange shadows on its wooden walls. The house was her aunt's house: this new old place at the end of the line. A dollhouse the miniature of where she stood: a more comprehensible place, with walls that did not breathe and molder and change.

A rustling sound came from within its walls. Cece peered closer. In the bed a moth twitched and writhed. Its limbs kicked helplessly at the cold air, its wings thrashing with a dull thud against the tiny wooden bed frame.

"Don't worry," the woman cooed at Cece. Strands of her silver hair glinted in the lamplight. "We're going to make everything just right."

Head surging with pain and confusion, Cece turned to look in the direction of something she could feel looking at her. A little girl rocked silently on a chair, staring at Cece with wide doll eyes. Her dress had an unnatural satin gleam in the moonlight; her glassy eyelids blinked, rolled open, blinked, rolled open as she rocked back and forth on the chair.

"We told you to leave," the girl hissed. "But you didn't do it. Now you will become my doll."

Her snarling mouth stretched into a terrible distended smile.

"Yes. My little Indian doll."

Cece's gaze turned back to the dollhouse and to the small furniture in the room, getting smaller alongside her. All of it was warm and welcoming; it would be lovely once they were hers, wouldn't it? She could have that home of her own. Perfect tiny wooden oven, small Christmas light bulb buzzing, the whole house lit up pristine and warmbright as a happy memory, this new world of hers, this more inhabitable microcosm without floods and forest fires and collapsing bridges and late nights at work. Of course, she would need a poseable arm to get around and perhaps a bendable

knee. She tried to smile at the thought, but her face did not coop-
erate. Her body was becoming stiff, growing harder and thinner
and colder, more delicate, porcelain painted in a deep shade of
sienna, darker and more beautiful than she'd ever been, she realized, more perfect in the woman's image of her, more authentic,
more believably real—

The maggot singing rot dripped from the ceiling and onto the
floor. Flies buzzed at the windows, snails hatched and crawled
forth onto the floors, leaving trails of slime across her body, multi-
plying, and writhing in time to the mother and child's hymns and
nursery rhymes, tinkling music box lullabies—

She could be a perfect little doll. Pain thrummed between her
temples again. "Apsute'gan," Cece mumbled. The word resounded
in the dark.

Her grandmother's voice cut through the dark.

"Tu's."

Something shook her arm.

"Tu's."

Fear shot Cece onto uncertain legs: she was no longer able to
blink. Rage coursed whitehot in her stiff body as she shambled
forward, knocking the dollhouse to the ground. The woman and
child screeched in unison. A gust of wind knocked Cece backward
onto the floor. Her porcelain hand howled open and shattered and
she felt nothing, just the rage of becoming, the rage of undoing,
the promise, under it, of what she could build in its ruins.

She clambered over the maggots, feeling them writhe and smash
under her still-fleshed arms, crawling to the dollhouse. She threw
what was left of her weight on top of it, her shoulder breaking and
splintering the tiny furniture. In the sounds of music box melodies
were melting screams and shattering glass.

The floor began to shake as the house quivered its death rattle.

The writhing walls stopped breathing. The maggots and snails disappeared.

Cece opened her eyes—she hadn't realized they'd been closed. The room had returned to a comprehensible layout. She held her aching fingers to her face and smiled as they began to move. She sat up with a deep and grateful breath in her body, her home. Sunrise creaked through the window with the sound of birds.

Tiffany Morris is a Mi'kmaw writer of speculative fiction and poetry from Kjipuktuk (Halifax), Nova Scotia. Her work has appeared in *Nightmare* magazine, *Apex Magazine*, and *Uncanny* magazine, among others. Her full-length horror poetry collection is *Elegies of Rotting Stars*. Find her online at tiffmorris .com or on Twitter @tiffmorris.

BEHIND COLIN'S EYES

SHANE HAWK

Dad's still asleep, so I'm loading my gun all quietlike.

Everybody's snores drift down the hall to the living room couch where I sit with my favorite mongrel, Tiny, squeezing bullets into my Savage 99E's rotary mag. Maybe Mom, Grandma, and my sisters are dreaming about Dad and me bringing home Sergeant Rock, the all-powerful elk that always flees. I hope today will be the day.

My eyes want nothing but to close. Sacks of commod flour droop beneath them. I'm the protector of this house when Dad is off duty, and I haven't slept a wink from the noises outside.

The winter wind howls and the oak tree swipes at our roof with its giant branch-claws as if it wants in. The scratching never ends. Reminds me of the thumbnail coming loose on my left hand; I pick at it when I know I shouldn't. It separates from the nail bed a bit too far, and red-hot lightning shoots up my arm.

The back door creaks, rumbles, then slams.

My head and Tiny's whip toward the noise. (*Pretty sure I locked that door last night . . .*) I spring from the couch, and my protective little terrier hops to the carpet, following me to scope it out. As I tiptoe to the back of the house, rifle in hand, something murmurs from the dark corner where a couple of frozen pounds from our last victim lie. (*Did it whisper my name?*) We leave the covered porch's windows open to let in the freezing air: our make-do meat locker.

I name everything we kill and drag home. This one's Kolchak. Got his name from these new stories on the television, *Night Stalker*. I promise Kolchak that we won't waste any of him. We can't. But my nose picks up his dried blood despite the thick ice, and some stink coats my tongue, forcing a dry-throat swallow.

The blank windows catch my attention. Our closest neighbor is a few acres away and, like us, they don't keep night-lights on. The porch windows push out black—like I'm staring into Tiny's mutt eyes—and the dense trees block out the stars.

A whistle rings out like someone far away is calling their kids back inside. (*This late?*) Don't think there are any railroads around here either. I try to match the tune but can hold it only for a few seconds. The whistling stops abruptly after mine. It was probably just the harsh wind.

My retinas singe as I flip on the backyard light, so I scramble to turn it off and readjust my eyes.

(*Wait. What was that tall thing by the dog pen?*)

(*What were those red dots?*)

The flash image pulses in my vision as I tuck my rifle stock into my armpit. I flick the light switch again, leaving it on. Just the empty yard, crusted in snow. I ease my trigger finger. Swear something big was there. It was like a tree, or a man, or both. (*Am I dreaming?*) I pinch myself, and it hurts like hell. Nope, I'm just dog-tired.

Dad and I have a long day ahead of us, and I'm regretting not going to bed. We always leave before dawn, and he'll wake any minute now. It's my job to throw our gear into his pickup. That blue-and-white Chevy Cheyenne 10 is a beauty. Sometimes, on the way to Vernal, Dad lets me sit in his lap and pretend to drive. Vernal, Utah—where hunting's real good. There ain't much here in Tridell, or even Whiterocks, so we drive to our food.

We used to hunt with Uncle Chaytan, Dad's best friend, before his motorcycle accident. Uncle and Dad did a lot of stuff together down at his ranch near Fort Duchesne, stuff I wasn't allowed to know about—still not. They always answer my questions with a silent smile or a flat-out "no," leaving the curiosity monster in my belly forever hungry.

I return to the couch and reread my August issue of *Weird Western Tales: Jonah Hex* with a flashlight, Tiny curling up next to me. The first page is an advertisement for an authentic 1973 Daisy BB gun, and I giggle under my breath. I'm ten and three-quarters old, but I got two *real* guns myself. I can't hold in my laughter after I read a panel where a white cowboy yells, "Great Scott! Indians!" before an arrow ruptures his organs. Dad must have heard me because now he's stirring. I roll and tuck my comic book into the couch.

It's time.

We pull off the main road, sweat dripping down my back as the pickup's brakes squeal. The headlights brighten the ground, looking like when Mom puts that peroxide stuff on my wounds: a mixture of snow, mud, and pine needles.

My imagination runs wild, and I wonder how this area looked a hundred years ago. My school's textbooks mention nothing, not that this is Ute land, or that our tribes lived just north of here before a bunch of crinkly government paper pushed them elsewhere.

The velvet painting of Grandpa wearing a Hidatsa war bonnet enters my mind. It still hangs on the wall of a trading post in Denver. He journeyed when I was too young to remember. Old things deserve respect. Makes me feel bad whenever Dad and I do our job, clearing trees for the forestry service. All of them trees earned their rings, then *thwack*, gone.

"Colin, let's get a move on," Dad says, picking up Tiny and exiting the truck.

I stretch so good my body trembles underneath all the layers of my favorite blaze orange jacket. I love orange. It means grouse; it means deer; it means elk.

The slamming of the truck doors startles me. That backyard visitor, if it was real, still lingers in my brain.

I take turns narrowing and widening my eyes to see better as the frozen pine needles crunch beneath our boots. Fog hangs in the air, wrapping around us like a Beaver State blanket. The stars blink at me and Dad, reminding me of the sparkle of Grandma Gracey's jewelry, and a smile stretches my cheeks while the cold bites at my nose.

Dad and I sling our backpacks on and shoulder our rifles. We trade looks and nods and set off on our usual path. I sigh in my head, knowing there's nothing but shin-deep snow and darkness ahead of us. Tiny, she's in my arms and I get a little lost in those eyes again, like two black suns; she knows today is the day we secure Sergeant Rock.

After about a mile, an owl hoots, and though Dad is facing away, I know he's wincing with me. Boy, I don't think Dad's ever taught me to shudder around them, but I can't help myself. Might be in my blood. Those front-facing eyes give me the heebie-jeebies.

Tiny is making my left arm sore, so I switch. Making a fist, I loosen the flimsy bandage on my thumb. The nail bed has separated completely, but it's so cold out, I damn near don't feel its sting. I leave the bloodied wrap behind in the snow like a discarded soldier.

Dad says his rifle was his best friend during the War. It saved his life and never let him down. But he never discusses it. Two things Dad refuses to talk about: the War and the "school" they forced him into. But I lack the hide to question him like I'm some Indian Columbo. The last thing I want to do in the world is upset or disappoint him.

The wind picks up and wails against my ears. I ask Dad if we can take a break to sip water. He agrees right away. The cold must stiffen his joints. Shining our flashlights around, we find a few tree stumps to rest.

"No," Dad says in his stern voice, the one he uses whenever I make a mistake.

Biting my lip, I bring Tiny back up into my arms instead of setting her down.

"Dad, what are the stars made of?"

"They're our ancestors. They're always there, watching, making sure we are living the Indian way, doing the right thing."

(*The Indian way?*) Not sure if he's telling the truth or pulling my leg because he mimicked those Hollywood Indians with how he said it.

Tiny shifts her head with perked ears, so I listen hard.

A low whistle travels through the trees, ending in a higher pitch. My ears must be lying like earlier. Could be the wind again, or another nighttime bird. But Dad tenses, and we both peer into the blackness. (*Might be other hunters seeing if we're human before they fire. It don't sound like a cow whistle.*)

To prevent us from getting shot, I whistle back, but Dad lunges at me and covers my mouth before I can get a good one out.

There's a pause that feels like forever, with my blood pumping fast and thick through my palms and neck. Another whistle rings, this time unnaturally high. My spine is an icicle, my heart a raging engine.

As quietly as possible, Dad loads his bolt-action and readies it.

The crunching of snow, so subtle, almost undetectable, is nearby. About fifty yards out.

Fumbling to muzzle Tiny's snarling, my left thumb shouts in pain. She never snarls.

Holding it beneath his rifle, Dad clicks on his flashlight to illuminate the forest, though it's struggling to penetrate the dense fog, and it flickers. He whacks the flashlight to make the batteries connect better, exposing something up ahead. I squint to make out the vague outline of a figure walking between the trees.

The silhouette stops and turns our way, Dad's flashlight still picking up fuzzy detail.

Its eyeshine . . . blood red.

Before my mind can process, Dad is yanking me down our path, crushing my left hand in his grip. I want to scream my lungs out. We're booking it up the trail, the bitter wind forcing my eyes into slits. But I can navigate this path blindfolded. It's like we've done this before thousands of times, cutting through with ease. Our footfalls and Tiny's whimpers are all I hear.

We run for an eternity through the darkness. It's so complete it's like that Cygnus black hole they discovered not long ago.

Dad flashes his light to the right and says, "Over there." His words are drenched in exhaustion.

We stop behind a snow-covered pile of logs, catching our breath. My eyes burn as I wipe them with my frozen hands. Dad is panting but not dead-tired yet. He uses his boot heel to clear out a cut in the earth for us to huddle in. We take off our backpacks, and I set my rifle down. I crawl into his arms and sit in his lap with Tiny, our backs against the pile. Dad is alert, scanning the area with his rifle in hand. My protector, as always.

"What do you think it was?" I ask, knowing to keep my voice low.

Dad sighs through his nose. "Can't say. I—I don't know."

"It had red eyeshine like a bear. Do humans have red eyeshine?"

"Never seen a bear walk like that. And . . . humans don't got eyeshine, Colin."

My shoulders sink, and my mind races. I don't want to bug Dad, despite the storm of questions brewing in my head.

"Dad?"

"Yeah, Colin."

"I love you."

"Love you too, my boy," he says, squeezing and rubbing my burning shoulder.

Even though my heart is still thrashing against my rib cage, I bury myself deeper into Dad's chest, smiling. I'm drained. Could sleep right here in his arms, but I shouldn't. We've still got to be the hunter if we can avoid being the hunted.

Dawn is upon us.

Didn't mean to doze off, but my body needs the sleep, and my eyes had started to play tricks on me—had seen strange, floating orbs off in the distance before I last closed them. But now my vision is clear, and I take in Creator's work of art for a moment, how fiery oranges and pinks paint the sky, knowing it'll soon fade to a lifeless gray.

The air tastes metallic like my mouth is full of pennies. Hunched over in Dad's lap, I reach two fingers into my mouth. And as I pull them out, their new color glistens in the morning light, some shade of red I've never seen. Like ancient blood. I grimace and swallow the taste.

Then the pain hits.

It's like a blade is corkscrewing into my gums. I hold back a squeal, a hot tear melting its way down my frosty cheek. My curious tongue searches my mouth while the frigid air eats at my chattering teeth. It snakes its way between my top-left molar and the gum it's hanging onto by a thread. It comes loose with a weak snap, and my eyes go wide. I spit the tooth into my hand, and my tongue checks the others. My opposite molar on the top right is wobbly, too. After a few seconds, I'm holding two blood-caked teeth. My tongue can't help but play with the two new holes in my gums.

But I already lost my baby molars, and these are supposed to be my adult teeth. I scan the area for any sign of danger since Dad's off duty again. Bright colors peek through these wooden giants confining us. In a way, the close-packed trees are protectors, too.

Out of the corner of my eye, I detect movement in my right hand, so I bring it to my face. Small black veins sprout within each tooth. Like muddied, raging rivers after a rainstorm, the veins rush to cover the teeth. Suddenly I'm certain: something evil is in these woods. Then in a split second, all the blackness retreats, leaving the teeth salmon colored. When I nearly drop them out of fear, my eyes dart to my left hand.

All the nails are missing.

I start to—what I think is called—hyperventilate. (*Goddammit, what is happening to me?*) My right hand's still normal, just the left is all wrong, and I can feel my eyes twitch a bit too much, so I squint them shut—so hard the blackness goes all colorful, nothing but red through my closed eyelids. Forcing my brain to project a memory, it conjures up me and Dad at our favorite lake, me hooking a big, beautiful rainbow trout after hours of nothing. I shove my teeth into my breast pocket and push the worry away like I always do.

Dad wakes from his nap, and without hesitation, I grab some

snow to wash the old blood off. After wiping them on my pants, I plunge my hands into my pockets.

"Ready?" Dad whispers, prompting me to stand and stretch. His face says we won't talk about what we experienced hours ago, and inside my head, I wish we would. I open my mouth.

"Dad, what was the thing we ran from?"

Dad pinches the bridge of his nose. He reaches into his jacket pocket for one of his hand-rolled cigarettes and his matchbox. After lighting up and taking a few drags, Dad studies me for a moment, then waggles his eyebrows. "S'go then," he says with finality.

I swallow whatever anticipation is bubbling in my throat and offer Dad a hand to get up. We gather our things and continue our well-worn path, but it seems almost too worn. Since the hunting trail is packed down by a bajillion footprints, I set Tiny down to walk beside us. Sergeant Rock is nearby. I know it.

Tiny licks my fingers after I give her some pemmican. Well, not the real thing, but this jerky stuff is tasty enough. I couldn't last much longer without ripping, chewing, biting into something. My eyes are heavy, but at least my stomach ain't empty no more. Though, not having all my best chewing teeth is making this harder. I conceal my wincing from Dad, who's checking the area with his rifle scope. He's on his second day of fasting; no jerky for him.

"You ready to find our elk, Little Big Man?" Dad asks, shooting finger pistols at me with his signature half-mouth smirk.

He makes me giggle at this nickname. We watched that Chief Dan George movie at the drive-in a few years back with Chaytan. I stand at attention and mock a salute. "Sir, yes, sir!" For a moment, I forget Dad doesn't like me poking fun at military stuff. So much respect for the military, but never the government.

"Let's set up here. This is where they graze before passing through to the valley. Sergeant was here last time, so we must be patient. Now seal your food; they can smell for miles." Dad hands me his rifle while he kneels to join me on the ground with Tiny. His arthritic knees pop as he dusts his hands. Out of instinct, he reaches again for his cigarettes, but he follows his own advice and stops himself. No doubt Dad's sacred smokes wafting through the wintry breeze would tip off Sergeant.

There are few places I'd rather be than right here with Dad, waiting to meet the mighty Rock. Maybe fishing, but we're months away from warmth and running streams. Or summer: no school. I can put my new ten-speed to good use and get the next issues of *Turok* or *House of Secrets* off my favorite spinning rack, flip through those crispy pages by the riverbank. But then there's always Saturday morning cartoons with my sisters. We haven't watched in a while on account me and Dad have been busy with the forestry service.

As I sit here next to Dad, appreciation warms my blood. Grandma Gracey always reminds me to be grateful. I've learned a lot from her. And? I'm loving how determined Dad looks right now. He wants this as badly as I do. Yet, the thought of my plucked molars and nails gnaws at the base of my skull like some starving wolf whose hot breath and slobber signal that this is only the beginning.

A gust of wind swirls some browned pine needles toward us, carrying the scent of dead bark and chimney smoke. It's been a few hours since we settled in this downwind spot. The sun is making its way west, providing us with just enough warmth and light to lead us to where we need to be.

Something crunches the snow and snaps some twigs up ahead.

I gulp and control my breathing to make sure it ain't too loud.

Never know if these animals have Superman's hearing ability or not.

Dad gestures for me to get ready. Both our rifles are loaded, and Tiny's awareness is peaking as she watches the field.

There he is: Sergeant Rock, named after one of my favorite DC characters. He must weigh a ton. He alone can feed us for several months. And he's traveling in a herd of other wapiti, no longer rutting season. Looks like he's the lone bull walking among yearlings. I'm awestruck, admiring these beautiful creatures with their dark brown heads and legs, a light tan running across their torsos. The angle they're facing gives us a clear broadside shot, a lot less room for error.

Dad taps my shoulder, giving me the signal to bring up my iron sights. I don't have a neat scope like him, but it gets the job done. And Dad knows I want Sergeant Rock, so I aim for him and assume Dad will get a yearling. He counts down from three, then—

Birds break out of their nests and rage in the sky from the crack of our soft-nosed bullets and the yearlings bugle before stamped-ing away. Sergeant and one young elk remain like two fakes in a museum display. The yearling drops. But Sergeant . . . he staggers, shakes his head, and snorts out a plume of hot, angry breath. He doesn't drop. (*There's no way I missed.*)

Frantically cranking my lever-action and getting my sights set, I shoot him again in the same area behind his shoulder blade. Exactly like Dad taught me. It should mushroom inside him and mess up his innards.

Sergeant turns toward us, barks (*Holy moly! His eyes are glowing red*) and runs off in the opposite direction.

I shout, shouldering my gun and sprinting after my undead elk.

"Colin!" Dad follows, his boots pounding the ground behind me.

I'm running through a thicker part of the forest, no logging here, and there's more snow, about ankle-deep. Sergeant Rock is fading from view. I can barely see him. (*Is he now running on two legs?*) He's bleeding out, so I follow the red trail.

Dad and Tiny have caught up to me, and together we track the blood path. Tiny hops with ease through the snow. She's as hungry as I am.

The blood is getting spottier, and it's like Sergeant is now zigzagging through the trees. We veer left, then right, my eyes pinballing between the red dots in the snow and what's ahead of me. Like the beating drums at ceremony, my heart has found its rhythm, and it's burning and pounding against my lungs.

All three of us halt.

Before us lies a blood-soaked elk organ, melting the snow beneath it. Looks like a liver, or a lung. I'm still not too good at identifying. (*How'd it just fall out like—*)

The organ flops over.

It's squirming in the rounded pocket of snow. Tiny unleashes her fury by barking and snapping her jaw at it.

Dad and I back away, though something is tugging me toward the body part. My nailless hand actually swings forward before I instinctively recoil. Looks like a small animal is trapped inside the organ and thrashing to break out of it.

Then it levitates and explodes into red steam, raining fire ants and spiders onto us.

I scream and spring backward, my head slamming into something. Sharp pain rings through my skull and down my spine. Last thing my eyes take in before going black is Dad rushing my way, covered in bugs.

Soft light hits my eyes as I come to. The sky is noticeably different. Tiny licks my face, and I cringe in pain.

"Son." Dad towers over me, his icy hands rubbing my cheeks. "I was thinking I lost you. Hohou, Heisonoonin . . ." His eyes trail upward, and his chest huffs in relief.

The wriggling, exploding organ reenters my mind, and my breathing intensifies. Feels like I'm in my own weird western tale. "Where did all the bugs go?"

"Bugs?"

"Before I blacked out, that chunk of Sergeant burst into bugs. They were all over you."

Dad twists his face, checks his watch, then peers around us. "There weren't no bugs, my boy. Now, I know you're freaking out—I am too—but something's going on with your left hand."

I fake a confused face. To be fair, I forgot about my nails coming off in all the commotion. It hurts to lean over, but I get up anyway to inspect my hands, ready to put shock on display for Dad.

But there are nails, sort of. They're white and curved like mini elk horns.

"I seen nothing like this before, and I've seen my fair share of weird shit, Col."

In my head, I'm manic, but I try to keep a cool exterior, though I don't know how good that's holding up. My nerves are spent, like rats have been chewing on my body's wiring all day. My left eye is even twitching now, and my neck cords are being jerked sideways. "Let's go back to the yearling you downed, Dad. Load it up and get home. I'm tired."

Before nodding and helping me stand, Dad eyes me, inspects me like I'm some freak. But maybe I am. "How 'bout I carry Tiny? The temperature's dropping again, and you've got to take it easy, son."

I return the nod and shoulder my rifle. My body aches, my head hurts, and I'm due for a forever-nap. I give Dad a sideways hug as we march back to his kill.

While trying to whistle to the tune of my favorite Linda Ronstadt song, I discover I can't. I drum my fingers on my leg instead, but the elk horns tear my pants. (*Do I need to chop it off?*) I daydream about our record player, Mom's posole, and my warm bed—even if I have to share it with my sister Mary. I need out of this place.

"Well, let's get to it," Dad says, weariness seeping from each syllable.

We stand before the yearling, or what's left of it. The snow beneath it has melted away, revealing a bloodied patch of grass. The body is ripped in half, with its entrails completely scooped out. Its neck is sliced with some stringy muscle and cartilage pulled through the slit. The mouth gapes. Both eyeballs are missing, and all four hooves are ripped off. The sight makes my stomach queasy, enough to make me run to the side and spray the cold ground with hot stomach acid.

"Jesus H—What's gotten into you, Colin?" Dad asks.

But my vomit's all wrong, like I chugged black and red war paint and attempted Indian abstract art. Something else for the Smithsonian to steal. (*Is this blood? What's the black stuff? Who the hell mutilates a poor animal like this? Or was it that . . . thing from the backyard?*) Vomit makes Dad uneasy, so without looking I know he's averting his eyes.

To the left of what used to be beef jerky, there are two teeth. I check my jacket pocket for my top molars, but they're missing. My left hand yanks me forward, grabs the ivories, and shoves them, one by one, into my upper gums.

In an instant, my vision changes. There's no more color. (*Whatthehell? Whatthehell? Whatthehell?*) Everything is black with distinct white outlining. And I hear things . . . Things I shouldn't. I hear Dad's voice but look at him and his lips aren't moving. He's saying a prayer for me. He's worried about what's out here, what's happening to his only son.

The young elk convulses. Its head and legs thrash—even the detached hind legs—and a guttural bark escapes its throat.

My mouth opens but what comes out is foreign, like a hundred people's screams before their death, some deep, some high. (*What is pulling my strings? Will someone please . . . stop this?*)

"Oh, shit!" Dad stumbles to the ground, feverishly crab walking back toward Tiny, whose barking is lost in the uproar.

The yearling lets out a prolonged screech as if replying.

There's a commanding voice inside my head. It's telling me to "do it." (*Do what?*) My body constricts, forcing me to stretch and crack my back.

And in this cracking motion, my breathing is out of control, gasping. I'm behind my own eyes as if they're windows, and I'm paralyzed, watching Dad, Tiny, and the shrieking zombie elk. But the sound is muffled and echoey. With all my effort, I scream, but there's no sound. I can't move my limbs, and it feels like I'm lying on my back, strapped to a canoe floating above this dark abyss inside my brain.

From my eye-windows, I watch my hands grab my rifle, but I'm not moving them. The outside-me is stepping toward the screaming elk, finger on the trigger. I'm—or *it* is—placing the barrel to the elk's temple. It's cranking the lever to discard the previously spent cartridge.

Bam. Lever clicks.

Bam. Lever clicks.

Bam. I toss the gun (*or he/it does?*) and turn toward Dad.

His mouth is a vast tunnel, and his eyes are teary and confused. He's holding onto Tiny for dear life.

"Colin . . . hell's gotten into you?"

I try to force a fevered explanation out of my mouth, but I'm mute. The outside-me answers in my place.

"Whatever do you mean, Father?"

Dad raises an eyebrow, then looks left and right before asking Outside-Me for a hand up. I'm now bawling my eyes out, though I can't feel anything or hear myself. (*Why is this happening? I want my mom. My sisters.*)

"Father, let us take this animal's nutritional value and return to the family. I must meet—I greatly miss them. I present you with my hunting weapon to carve off the exterior."

[*Dad, no. It's not me! Please . . . Do something, Dad!*]

Some time passes, and I'm still in this two-window prison. I must have strained myself, leaving inside-me unconscious for a while. The outside-me is sitting passenger in Dad's Chevy, *my* seat, and is looking down at Tiny, *my* goddamn dog.

Dad has the truck's dome light on, and he's fiddling with the radio. The speakers spill out static and jumbled songs as he twists the knob toward the one hundred mark. Once the antenna catches the main Salt Lake City station, he turns the volume up. He knows this country-rock song is one of my favorites. Whenever it's on the radio, I whistle and tap my knee to the beat. But the outside-me is motionless, showing no knowledge of the music. It turns to Dad, and we both see him pursing his lips and nodding his head slowly.

"What is unsatisfactory?" Outside-Me asks.

"Oh, nothing. We're going to take a detour, son." Dad takes a drag of his new cigarette, cranking the window down to blow out the smoke.

The eye-windows reveal Tiny cuddling next to Dad's leg, the farthest she could be from me across the truck cab. "To where are we traveling, Father?"

"Chaytan's place. Need some good medicine for an ailment we've suffered before. Long ago."

His ranch, way out there where no one would hear a scream. Uncle Chaytan, with the dead eyes and crooked grin.

As the outside-me turns away, observing itself in the passenger mirror, I grow a crooked grin of my own.

Without warning, my vision darkens, and I can no longer see the mirror. Blackness coils around me like a vicious snake, like I'm even deeper in this hole. My own eyes invert back onto me.

Two menacing, alien gods loom overhead.

[[Your body is mine now, and this time, your family won't be able to kill me.]]

Shane Hawk (enrolled Cheyenne-Arapaho, Hidatsa descent) is a high school history teacher, writer, and editor. He entered the horror scene with his first publication, *Anoka: A Collection of Indigenous Horror*, in October 2020. You can find him in San Diego, wearing his *Support Indigenous Literature* hat, alongside his beautiful wife, Tori. Learn more by visiting shanehawk.com.

HEART-SHAPED CLOCK

KELLI JO FORD

I shouldn't have had one ounce of hurt left when I was led into the courtroom and saw Mom sitting behind the prosecution. Some days I swear I could feel her eyes burn through me like dry ice, not that I warranted any different. She and her sisters passed wadded-up Kleenex back and forth until the district attorney apologized for getting so specific about what could become of the human body. Then they got up and left one by one. After that, the only thing giving Mom any shape at all was the bench she sat on and the clothes she wore, still pressed neat as could be. There'd be no tearful embraces of the Hollywood sort, I knew. The heart is fucking gristle. The more you try to chew through it, the bigger it gets.

When the foreman rested his hands on the walnut rail and admitted they couldn't agree whether I was guilty of killing my baby brother, the courtroom grew tiny, quiet except for shuffling papers and the big clock ticking over my shoulder. The rest of the jury studied their knees. They crossed and uncrossed their arms. The foreman looked like he wanted to apologize to Mom, but the lady judge cut him off. She spoke to me directly, as if it were just me and her there. A woman wise as her ought to know that words after the fact have a way of piling up, maybe making pretty sounds but not changing the actions that brought them into being. So when she banged her gavel the last time, I took up my watch from the table, wound it, and put it on. Then I took the silence of those around me for what it was and followed the bailiff, keeping my eyes on the heavy, swinging doors.

I'd shown up outside Johnson City wearing my best boots, nothing to my name but a wallet full of pictures and a gym bag stuffed with a couple of shirts, a razor, and a bottle of cologne. My brother lived down the street from Mom, nearly thirty years old and sucked up on her tit like always. The way I saw it, he walked around like he was the good son because she'd raised him and left me in the Panhandle with Dad all those years ago.

Mom took me in. What could she do after I showed up like that? Day after day, I'd sit in the humidity out on her porch waiting for my brother to get home from his sign shop. He might raise a hand or he might just drive on by. Either way, I'd get up, feeling Buffalo Mountain lurking over me, and go knock on his door. He'd slide me a one-hitter to use on the porch, close the door, and go back to playing *Grand Theft Auto* or tussling with his boy. When I'd come in, his woman would get to smiling too hard, and I'd know they'd been talking about me—what I'd done and not done—and that when I left, they'd talk some more. I'd never done a thing in the world to him except long for Mom to treat me like a son and spend too much time feeling sorry I missed out on playing catch with him when we were kids.

I saw quick how Mom acted like the world never had seen a grandbaby, keeping my brother's son anytime he and his wife wanted to go out, spoiling the boy with whatever he wanted from her convenience store. Meanwhile, she sent ten-dollar bills folded into the flimsy cards to my boy back in Oklahoma, whose momma had made it clear she didn't want me around.

My mother signed for the car my brother's woman drove and probably bought him the house he slept in. She paid his way through college while I was scraping to get by. What she didn't do for him in the open, she did in secret so everybody would think he was a stand-up businessman. And yes, it's true I was fucking well tired of her and him acting like he was the only son. I started with good intentions. They just don't always get you far.

Granny Bess, Dad's mom who mothered me, died when I was in middle school. Dad did the best he could in his slowed-down ways. He painted his face maroon at the home games, helped me work on the old primer-patched farm truck so I could have something loud to drive around town. He never talked much, but he loved me as a man can, and he wasn't one to give up on somebody.

I played two sports in high school and kept it between the lines enough to walk with my classmates. I married a pretty girl and joined the Army soon after. Good things don't last, though. No matter what I tried, I ended shooting myself in the foot. The Army said I failed a piss test and my services were no longer needed. I'll just say I'd crossed some bridges you can't recross with my son's mother—and the boy, as far as she was concerned. Can't say I blame her. The judge divided me from the only things that mattered by three miles, more than twice the length of the city limits.

Once my counseling was up, Dad conspired with my mother to pay some of my fines, try to help me make a new start. About then, the mountains of Tennessee and a long-lost mother's bosom started sounding pretty good, I guess. Mom didn't bank on my moving east. If she did, she would have let me serve my time. Maybe that would have fixed everything.

As a boy, I kept an 8×10 in my room of my brother and me from before Mom took him and left me in the skinniest, dustiest, most godforsaken part of Oklahoma with Dad. Me and my brother aren't even a year apart, and in that picture we're dressed alike in these goddamn baseball outfits. Red socks up to our fat knees and full-size gloves almost as big as we are. We're laughing. My brother's got a slobber of drool on his chin, and I have snot running down my lip. I don't know if that was the only shot they could get of us smiling or if nobody cared to wipe our faces, but that's the one I found in a gold metal frame at Dad's.

Sounds stupid, but when my brother came to visit Dad's each June, I did my best to dress like him in ways he wouldn't notice. If he wore a red-striped shirt, I wore a red shirt. If he was wearing wristbands that summer, I wore a headband. I was the oldest, but I was always following him around, maybe imagining somebody still cared enough to buy us the same clothes and force them on us.

Mom and her sisters converged back home in the Cherokee Nation to see their mother each Fourth of July. Mom bought me and my brother a bus ticket east so she could pick him up and take him back to wherever they lived. Before the trip, Granny Bess would pack us thick-sliced baloney on store-bought bread, two bags of chips, and two candy bars each. She'd wrap sour pickles she'd put up and Dr Peppers in foil and stick it all in one big paper grocery sack to share. We'd have burping contests to piss off the old people around us and fight over the window seat to get the best view of the passing license plates to play the Alphabet Across America game I thought we'd made up. My brother always won. He was quick to point out the places he'd lived with Mom—California and New Mexico, Texas a little while before Tennessee. The ride was long, and getting off the bus, I always knew I'd be stepping back on it by myself.

Turns out, there's drugs to spend your money on in Johnson City just like the dusty Panhandle towns. They cost a fair bit more, but they're not hard to find. With no license, I sat around my mother's porch waiting on my brother, feeling like a stranger. Every now and then, a guy would pick me up to help him roof houses and pay me under the table.

The one time my brother's wife let him out of the house with me didn't turn out too good, though it started out all right. She was on a work trip, and their boy had a tee-ball game. Sitting there next to my brother cheering for his son seemed like the most natural thing. His son was the star out there, twice as fast as all the other kids, three times as strong. I was standing up yelling, swinging my hat over my head after he'd hit a triple, stomping my boots on the metal bleachers, and the boy looked over at us and grinned and gave a thumbs-up. He'd never met Dad, but he looked just like him, buck-toothed and goofy-faced.

I said as much, and my brother squinted up at me for a minute before saying, "He must take after his uncle. I couldn't hit a baseball for shit."

That's all it was. He looked back out at the field, shaking his head like there was something he was trying to figure out and couldn't. I kept on yelling. But he'd called me the boy's uncle. I heard it, and there was no taking it back.

After I convinced him to go out to the bars that night and leave his boy with Mom, I tapped his windshield at a California plate and said, "*C.* The Golden State."

He studied me again for a second, then said, "You know Dad beat the hell out of Mom."

I named another license plate.

"Why the hell do you think she finally left?"

"I thought she was looking for a man with a pot of fucking gold," I said, "and Dad was just a little too Okie."

My brother sped up to pass the California car.

"If he was so bad, what'd she leave me with him for?"

"You have any idea how many schools I went to?" he said. "Nobody had it perfect, Joe. Besides, the judge split us up."

That wasn't the story I'd heard. Regardless, our brotherly bonding should have ended there. He spent the rest of the drive on his cell phone, calling up his old fraternity buddies to come out. One of them had a real good time making fun of my accent, elbowing me so you could write it off as razzing. He even had something to say about the lizard-skin boots I had on, the ones I'd bought for my wedding. Usually the son of a bitch wouldn't have lasted two minutes, but I worked hard on my breathing, on not messing more things up. Not that my brother said anything to stop him. He just sat there smiling, spinning his stupid fucking wedding ring.

In the parking lot, I showed them I could drink, snort, or smoke as much as any of them and soon understood that it don't matter where you go. You're just fucking there, and you ain't nobody but who you were before you left.

When I was a boy on those trips to the Cherokee Nation, Mom and her sisters were a gang of loud-talking strangers who brought presents and swallowed me up in hugs and lipstick. My brother was ready to push them away and go throw rocks at the passing trains behind the house. Not me. I was always sitting too close or crying in the night for more water, staring after them like a starving dog on a doorstep. Mom and her sisters filled a room and dressed different from Granny Bess and the women I saw in the grocery store back home, a plain bunch who wore aprons for wiping water-wrinkled hands, cotton to keep them cool in the summer, and sturdy shoes, even in church.

Mom and her sisters were all beautiful Cherokee ladies, and Mom was the flashiest of them all. She kept her black hair dyed strawberry blonde and poofed it curly and big. She wore glittery makeup and perfume so flowery and sweet that it made me sick. She'd come back from the store and kick off her high heels with a groan, full of stories about schoolmates who'd got fat or men who'd talked sweet to her. The sisters would get to laughing, and all the sudden, my grandmother's little house was buzzing and alive with them. I know there was a time they all felt a little sorry for me, the way my mother gave me away. Maybe she just saw no good when she looked at me and knew that's all I'd ever be.

Now that I was in plain sight, Mom needed to keep up the show. She'd started buying me khaki pants to take the Panhandle out of the boy, giving me the keys to her car some nights, like we rolled back fifteen years and this is how it would have been all along. I've got to say, it felt pretty fucking good, but none of it added up could buy back time.

I was doing the harder stuff a good bit then, especially since I'd ditched the pricks my brother ran with and made my own connections. They were people who didn't get invited to his parties, but that was okay with me. I wasn't much on all those mousse-haired dickheads, anyway.

The beginning of the end was a minor dustup I had with Mom's driver-side door, which is to say I kicked the shit out of it after I got into it with a college boy and it was me who got hassled by the cops. In the name of "one more chance," Mom put me to work in her store and told me I could live in the little rent house next to it. She could have given me that job anytime she wanted, but now that it was her car repair I was in for, I reckon she figured she had to trust me to do right by her books and customers.

I wasn't going to ask for nothing I was afraid to take, but I was honest on the register. I can say that. I stocked the beer at the end of the night like I was supposed to and only took home a six-pack, a pack of Camel Wides, and a pizza.

I stood behind the counter like a rock, leaning on one hand and ringing people up with the other. Wasn't long, I was running up my tab, getting a loan on each check, paying my rent late in increments. But I came to work and did the job and, I reckon, became somebody she could count on to show. I'd already been told I'd better straighten up or ship out, all the way back to Oklahoma, like I was a boy again and she could just bundle me up and drop me off at the bus station.

I used my newfound friends for about the only thing they were good for—getting a couple of days' worth of crank at a time. There wasn't much I cared about in the world around me, and the thought of my boy a thousand miles away already growing up with a new dad, a goddamn foot doctor at that, just about killed whatever heart was left of me if I ever let myself linger. I'd start to consider ways of getting back home until the obstacles—my own stupidity, not least of all—became more than I could count. There was many a night when I thought of the store pistol, figuring the world and everybody in it would be better off.

I paced around the three rooms in Mom's musty, asbestos-siding rental all night. She called it "the cottage" and claimed it was furnished in her want-ads, when it just had whatever bare and broken thing the last guy left behind. Around and around I'd go, trailing my hand along the grooves in the wooden paneling, falling into bed just before sunrise and time to go back across the drive to the store. If I was on nights, I didn't sleep at all. Sometimes I'd work on a television or whatever piece of junk Mom didn't want to pay to get repaired. Only thing I did worthwhile was show up to work on time and keep a clean house. I don't know why, but the thought of a piss drop on the commode or a grease speck on the stove was enough to send me into fits.

I was heading across the parking lot after locking up one November evening when I saw a box sitting against the gas sign. Wasn't so unusual—on that stretch of road people throw shit out all the time—but the box was making little scuffling noises and kind of moving around. I walked over to see what the fuss was. There inside was the tiniest bunch of slick-black puppies I'd ever seen, scratching around in their own piss and shit, crawling over one another, whimpering and shivering.

I set down my sack of beer and cigarettes and tipped the box on its side. Out crawled this one puppy, the only one with opened eyes. Those pups were so tiny they couldn't even stand up yet, but this one with tan around his eyes and mouth inched his way out, sniffed the air, looked at me sideways with his half-blind gray eyes, and let out a bark twice as big as his scrawny body. Well, that was it. I couldn't leave them there. It was likely going to freeze that night, and I wasn't the man of the year by any means, but I didn't have the heart to walk away and have to toss their cold bodies in the dumpster the next day.

I went around behind the store to the dumpster and dug out a clean box that the dayshift hadn't broken down like they were supposed to. Then I pulled out my keys and went inside, helped myself to a bag of dog food, and headed to the back for some milk, using the glow from the coolers to see.

Once my arms were full of what I thought I might need, I headed back up front and saw a car idling in the parking lot with its lights off. I put everything on the counter, cursing because I hadn't locked the door behind me. I figured somebody was stopping for beer and they'd leave once they saw it was dark inside. But these two guys eased up to the door and looked around before one of them pulled on the handle. When it gave, they looked around again before stepping into the store, unaware I was standing right there, gripping the handle on the gallon of milk like it was a club.

Then I see they've pulled stocking caps over their faces. This is when my luck really kicks in. Two days back, I'd told Mom I would tinker with the tape-eating VCR but had barely gotten around to tearing the thing apart on my kitchen table. The cameras are just for show, and the pistol, tucked in a box on the other side of the counter, might as well be in Oklahoma.

I figure the element of surprise is all I've got going for me and that won't last, so I yell, "Hey!" At the same time, I step toward the biggest one and, with all my might, swing the gallon of milk into the side of his head. He goes down on one knee, stunned.

The other one spins toward me about the time my fist connects with his jaw. He takes a step back, then comes at me, and that's the last thing I know. Apparently he was holding something I hadn't seen, something solid. All it took was one thump to the back of my neck and I was out cold.

I listened to the big clock over the door tick for a while before I realized where I was: cheek stuck to the floor, surrounded by a puddle of milk in the still-dark store. I sat up and rubbed the back of my neck, feeling all the hours I hadn't slept weighing on me and a headache worse than any hangover I'd ever experienced. I wouldn't call it amnesia, but all I could think of was cleaning up the milk so I could get into bed.

After I'd wrung the mop and stepped out the door, I saw that goddamn box of puppies. And this is probably where you might begin to question my decision-making, wonder why I didn't call the cops or at the very least my mother. There's plenty of things I've got no good answer for. What I did was turn around and walk back inside to grab the dog food I'd left on the counter and another gallon of milk. Then I locked up, balanced that box of pups on my hip, and stumbled home.

By the time I got inside, those pups were whining and shivering to rattle the box so much I knew I wouldn't be able to do the one thing that seemed like the only matter in the world five minutes before: sleep. I heated milk on the stove and mixed it with the food and let it sit there to soften.

Those puppies made the biggest mess, crawling over one another, falling into the bowl, sucking milk off one another's tails. It was more stink and filth than I could bear, so I went back across the drive to get the clean box I'd left. My neck was so stiff I couldn't move without turning my whole body, but I couldn't help but feel the store staring out at me from underneath the orange streetlight.

I cleaned the puppies up the best I could with a shirt. Then I pushed them against the bed and sat there watching them nuzzle while I tried to eat cold pizza. After they settled into a big pile of milky sleep, I headed back across the parking lot. I needed some Advil, and as much as I dreaded it, I figured I better make that call.

I turned on all the lights, put on a pot of coffee, and locked the door behind me. I could hardly keep my eyes open dialing Mom's number. When I told her the store was robbed and I was hit in the back of the head, her first words, swear to God, were "What did they take? Did you call the cops?" I told her I wasn't sure yet and no, and she sat there for a minute to let the silence express the depth of her disappointment, I guess, and then she said she was on the way and hung up.

My lawyer says a severe concussion and repeated head trauma can cause you to act out of your mind, can cause rage and a lack of reason. I suppose years of pent-up yearning can do the same thing, but so can a bad man being who he is, so I can't say exactly what caused what happened next.

Mom and my brother's little boy showed up just before the cops, and when she came in, I was sitting up on the counter, holding a bag of ice to my neck, a Styrofoam cup of coffee steaming beside me.

"Are you okay?" she asked.

I shrugged my shoulders and slid off the counter, wishing right off the bat I hadn't, because the thudding pain went straight to my eyeballs.

She asked what happened, all the while opening the till to see if I'd taken out the night drop like I was supposed to. I had. The boy helped himself to a Push-Up Pop and sat at the booth in the corner with a coloring book. While my mom was darting around the office where the safe was, I felt sick, so I sat down and picked out colors for the boy. Sweet as they come, he offered me a lick of his ice cream. He was wearing his pajamas and had this crazy bedhead.

"Where's your daddy, Rooster?" I asked.

"Out with Momma," he said, still coloring.

Mom came in and stood in front of the register, clicking her nails on the countertop. I told her the best I could what happened. She couldn't get over why the glass door busted, or why there wasn't more of a mess—why the alarm hadn't gone off. No matter how many times I explained it, she kept saying, "So you were in here in the dark. With the door unlocked."

By now, the cops had got there, and we'd already determined all that was gone was the money bag that keeps the morning's cash, a ziplock bag filled with rolls of change she'd picked up from the bank and forgot to put in the safe, and some cartons of Camels. I went over the same thing again a few times with the cops, who seemed more interested in flirting with Mom than solving any crime.

Their gun belts squeaked as they looked from each other to Mom, taking their notes. I knew I wasn't looking good in this. They didn't outright say my wound was self-inflicted, but I figured they might as well. It didn't matter that one of them put on gloves and looked at the knot at the base of my neck, telling me I should be at the hospital.

It was getting daylight, so I told them they could see themselves out and started turning on stoves and prepping for breakfast. Mom followed them and stood at the cop car, curling strands of hair around her finger, shivering and nodding her head. Then one cop came back inside and asked me over to the counter to talk. Like the friendliest fellow in the world, he asked for a list of people who hang out at my house. I gave him a couple of made-up names, and he told me, "Take care of that neck!" and back out he went, where he stood drinking my coffee and hanging on Mom's every word.

When they were gone, Mom stood there in the parking lot with the sun peeking behind her. She was chewing on a fake thumbnail, and if not for the gas sign, it might've made a real pretty picture. She jumped a little when she saw me looking at her. Then she straightened her blouse and walked back inside.

————

Mom held me at arm's length by my shoulders so she could look into my eyes. I was tired again, head hurting. "I'm sorry, Mom," I said, and it was the honest truth. "I tried to stop them."

She sighed. She's a tall woman, has put on some weight. I'm wiry like Dad, so I didn't have to lean far when she pulled me onto her breast and stroked my head. My eyes started to water a little, and my nose got to running, and somehow I felt just a little better than I had in a long time.

"Are you sure you don't need to go to the hospital?" she asked, pressing the top of her cheek to my head.

I guess what got me so bad was I knew she meant it when she held me there. I could tell she loved me right then, and the world made even less sense than before.

"It's pretty funny, Joseph," she said, "that the VCR stopped working this week, isn't it? And that you said you'd fix it."

And she leaves it hanging there. This is all my fault. More than my fault for leaving the goddamn door unlocked. It's bigger than that. I'm nothing but a conniving thief, one she must love in little bursts but will always keep at arm's length in the ways it counts.

That's when I feel a white-hot flash move up through my chest and across my eyes. I pull away from her. She steps toward me with her head cocked, like she's sad and might want to go back to hugging. I push her hands off me. My brother's boy stands and drops his box of colors.

"Joseph," she says, and takes another step, and I feel myself ready to lose it, ready to knock my way out of this the way I've hit my way out of everything else I've come across, but I don't. I push her aside and run out the door. When I look back, she is on one knee, pulling herself up by the counter. The boy is crying. We make eye contact before I bolt across the drive.

―――――

Granny Bess had a barn cat she'd tamed up to keep around the house as a mouser. Wasn't long before the the cat would come up, purring for food, her tits hanging to the ground. She'd eat, then disappear again until she got hungry, and we knew she had a litter of kittens hid out somewhere. I never did see Granny Bess too big on animals, but when a gas truck plastered that momma cat to the road, I think she felt kind of responsible. She never was one to let an orphan starve, I reckon.

Me and her went out, her in her thin cottony dress and Granny Clampett boots, and dug around on our hands and knees until we found that litter of kittens. Then she stuck them in a box in the kitchen and got a baby-doll bottle with a rubber nipple from the toy box. She heated milk and put something she got from the feed store in it to keep them from getting the runs. Then she wound her alarm clock with the big bells on top as far as it would go, wrapped it in a baby blanket, and put it in there with those yowling kittens.

The box was so big, or I was so little, all I could do was stand on my tippy-toes and wrap my fingers and nose over the edge to look down on them. After they ate, they cuddled up together in one little fur pile on top of that clock. I remember feeling sort of happy-sad for those kittens, having one another but not having a momma. I imagine snot was running out of my nose, like it is in that picture in Dad's house.

"Look there," Granny Bess said, "they feel that ticking like it's their momma's heartbeat. Puts them babies right to sleep." Then she settled into a chair at the kitchen table and pulled me onto her lap, and I laid my head on her and watched the cats until I fell asleep.

My eyes were swimming. I was lying on the bed half-asleep and nauseous, trying to catch my breath when all that came back to me, something I hadn't thought of since it happened. The puppies started to cry and howl again, making all the noise their tiny bodies could muster. It was a terrible racket. I thought about putting them in the bed with me, but the thought of them shitting all over the place just about made me throw up. I wiped the fool tears from my face and focused real hard on slowing down my thinking.

I picked up the alarm clock from the milk crate beside the bed. I was wrapping it up in a sweatshirt when I heard a banging so hard it bowed the plywood door and shook dust from the curtains. I didn't know exactly who I was going to see, so I reached over and grabbed the dinged-up Louisville Slugger I kept beside the bed, took a deep breath, and unlocked the door.

My brother pushes in, red-faced and yelling. I remember thinking his eyeballs were going to pop right out of his face. "Go on, get out of here," I tell him. "I don't want to do this." But he's not making much sense, and I know this is when it all comes out, all those things he had said hushed behind my back. He's calling me a sorry son of a bitch, saying how I take and take and take. He says I never was any good, calls me crazy. As I'm hearing all this, as I take it in, I'm squeezing the bat that's dangling from my hand. He hasn't seen it. He's out of his mind.

The worst thing I ever have done, he says—and he yells "worst" real loud, catching me with his hot beer breath and spraying me with spit—is lay a hand on *his* mother in front of his son. At that, I take a step back and ease down into my kitchen chair, out of air and sure out of fight. I rest the bat on the concrete, lean my chin down onto its knob end, and close my eyes.

I'm a thousand miles away. The metal steps clink as I step into my trailer house. My wife is at the kitchen table slouching over a crossword like she used to. She looks up at me, startled. I'm sorry, I say, and my eyes well up. I hold up my arms and show her all the presents I've brought. My fingernails are ringed with grease from a good day's work, and she smiles like she always would eventually. I kiss her on the top of the head, and my boy runs out of his room. I hand him a red box with a bow on top. It's got holes cut in it, and as soon as he holds it up to his ear, he knows. He kneels down on the linoleum and unties the string, looking up at me one more time to make sure. I smooth his hair and open up the lid for him. Out crawls the black and tan pup, the spitfire. My boy yells, "Daddy!" and that pup is licking him in the face.

"Are you listening to me?" my brother screams, and when he does, I open my eyes and catch a wad of spit right above my lip. His eyes are so close they're like bloody mirrors. Before I can say anything, he pushes me full force in the center of my chest. I flip backward in my chair. My head slaps the concrete floor and busts open. Before I know it, I'm back up, and I've swung.

The hit was solid. I dropped the bat and vomit filled my mouth before my brother's body even had time to fall. I knew standing over him he wasn't going to be getting up for a long time, if he ever did. I sank to my knees, turned him onto his back, and pulled his hand to my mouth, smelling tobacco mixing with the metal from his ring and the blood dripping down my neck. I put his hand over his chest and cupped my hand over his caved-in ear, as if I could pull out the force the bat had put there. I bent over him, my forehead on his, calling out for him to wake up, for someone to please come and help me, but the room was empty.

I jumped when his eyelids fluttered and brushed my skin. "Sorry," I said, "I'm so sorry." He didn't answer, so I pulled him upright and twisted the weight of him over onto the bed, where I straightened his legs and pulled up his head for a pillow.

I sat there on the edge of the bed with my hands clasped for prayer that wouldn't come again, and I know I should have walked across the drive to call an ambulance. Should have brought my mother over. Taken some action to right this. But I couldn't take my eyes off my baby brother, a trickle of blood coming from his good ear staining my pillow. Beside him, buried inside a shirt, the clock kept ticking, marking my sin and my failure to act. I'd wound it tight.

I pulled the bundle tighter, closer against his chest, and leaned over to listen for his heart. Then I pulled off my shoes and stretched my body out alongside my brother on the little twin bed, nothing between us but a beating metal heart.

Kelli Jo Ford is a citizen of the Cherokee Nation. Her novel-in-stories debut, *Crooked Hallelujah*, was longlisted for the PEN/Hemingway Award for Debut Novel, the Story Prize, the Carnegie Medal for Excellence in Fiction, the Dublin Literary Award, and the Center for Fiction's First Novel Prize. She is the recipient of honors and awards such as an NEA Literature Fellowship, the *Paris Review*'s Plimpton Prize, a Creative Capital Award, and a Native Arts & Cultures Foundation Artist Fellowship. She teaches writing at the Institute of American Indian Arts.

SCARIEST. STORY. EVER.

RICHARD VAN CAMP

"Sugar Snow" they call it. It had been falling for hours. *Shit*, now I was going to have to do the church parking lot and then Ingrid's and then Frank Senior's. But I had to put the hours in. I had to continue to gain the trust of the Elders.

I needed their stories.

I was one of the three finalists for the Scariest Story Ever Award. The event was in Yellowknife tomorrow night; CBC was going to record it before a live audience. First prize was a thousand bucks and I had earned this. I'd done good. I recounted a story that I had heard a long time ago from Narcise, a trapper now long dead, about why horseshoes outside a home ward off the Devil. It got me a standing ovation. This was after I told the story of "How Cat Came to Be," as told by Irena Tobacco. I was lucky. CBC didn't record and broadcast and nobody had their cell phone out to record and upload to YouTube. There also wasn't a Tobacco family member in the room so I was good. My nomination to represent Fort Simmer in the annual territorial competition was official and I was feeling great. My only problem? I didn't have an even scarier story for the finals. To win I'd need to go to the source. I'd need to go to Mike in the part of town we call "Indian Village." Mike was Irena Tobacco's nephew and he, I suspected, was the keeper of the scariest story ever.

"Uncle Mike," as we called him, was going to be a grandpa at the end of the month. His small house was already filled with baby gear—a new car seat, a potty, three big boxes of Pampers were piled on the old freezer that had been humming here since the days of Aunty Irena. There was a blue hamper full of baby clothes already folded right beside it on a small shelf that showcased a bush radio that was turned off. There were pictures on the wall of family, friends: good times, cherished memories. And there were class photos of Junior, Mike's son: all the way up from kindergarten to grade twelve to Junior's graduation photos. You'd never guess that a kid who we all assumed was given the world would end up knowingly selling tainted drugs that took the life of a brand-new mother in Yellowknife. Junior was in custody and we'd learn soon what his sentence was, minus time already served. It was horrible, but I could use this to my advantage.

I loved how it smelled here: fresh brain-tanned moosehide on Mike's moccasins and mint tea steeping. But, like always—even decades later—the floor was cold. I should have brought my moccasins. It was going to be Halloween soon and it was, what, thirty-two degrees below out? Tons of snow. All of us were breathing a little easier knowing it wouldn't be a bad fire season next year.

I've always loved this house, despite the cold floor and the fact that all the stray dogs in Indian Village love to sit in the yard. I'd actually wanted to buy it after I graduated from college. It had a quiet furnace and a wrap-around design so the kitchen flows into the living room and there are three separate bedrooms around the corner. I took the tour when Irena's family held an open house. The family was going to sell it at a loss because Fort Smith was going through tough times. Mike was going to move to his cabin out of town. I put in an offer of ten thousand dollars less than it was listed. If I'd gotten it, my truck payments would have been more than my mortgage. But Mike changed his mind and decided not to sell. The house had a big yard on a pie lot that opened into a lush forest of spruce and pine. It always felt so cozy here—despite the floor—and I could see that Mike had hauled a big smoker for ribs and brisket on his porch right next to the barbeque.

I could see the newspaper on the table: *The Fort Simmer Chronicle*. The info for the final showdown for the North's Scariest Story was on page two. The story of Junior was on page one. Mike knew why I was there so I brought gifts and cash. I was hoping he'd make bannock. Mike's secret, I'd heard, was that he used warm water. He told a friend, "Just use warm water and everything falls into place."

"Mike," I said looking at the first box of food I'd brought him from the Northern: yogurt, strawberries, blueberry powder from Green Lake, Saskatchewan, moose dry meat from Bobby and Barb. "You know I'm representing Simmer in Yellowknife for that contest."

"Oh yeah," he said, putting a pot of fresh tea on one of his aunty's doilies. "That's tomorrow, hey? You're driving up?"

"They're flying me up." I nodded. "I need your help. Can you please tell me Irena's scariest story? I can pay."

He chuckled. He came back with two mugs: one for him, one for me. Then he shook his head.

Uh-oh. He shook his head again. I tried to laugh it off and said, "Come on. Don't be cheap. I got fifteen minutes before my dad picks me up."

Here I was in my forties and my dad was still picking me up when my truck was in the shop.

"All right," Mike said. "I'll tell you a story. A long time ago, I was seeing a—"

"I need Irena's story," I said firmly and reached into my pocket for cash. "Her scariest one."

Mike looked at me and he looked at the second box of food I'd brought him: blueberries, a big tin of Timmy's coffee, lard, butter, flour, raisins, a jumbo box of Raisin Bran, a no-name sack of one hundred tea bags, oranges, apples, bananas. "My oil tank is getting low," he said and looked to his moccasins.

I pulled out forty bucks and tapped it on the table twice. Mike had always had bad feet and he walked like a bear. He did his slow walk toward the cash and said, "Mahsi cho," before placing the money in his breast pocket.

I shrugged. "I know you're not supposed to pay for medicine, but you can always help a nephew out, eh?"

He smiled. "Oh yes, I can always help a nephew out. That first prize is a thousand bucks." He looked down at the two twenties hidden in his shirt. "I have a grandbaby on the way, and we're low on dog food, too." He pointed with his big Dene lips in the direction of the house where five big huskies and a few mongrel dogs all slept together out of the wind.

My cheeks burned as I reached into my pocket. I pulled out two one-hundred-dollar bills. "That's all I got."

He looked at me directly and grinned. "You sure you want Irena's scariest story?"

I smiled and sat up. If I had flippers, I'd start clapping them. "Oh yes. I'm ready."

"You're sure you're sure?" He peered at me and grinned wider.

I nodded and poured him tea before pouring mine. God, it smelled good. "Yes."

Mike took a big breath and stood tall. He put his hands in his pockets. He'd gotten bigger over the years. Not fatter. Just bigger. Here in our northern truck town of 2,500 people who are French, Bush Cree, Dene, English, and Métis, if you get a paunch the men will tease you and say, "Well, lookie here, you're getting a little roof over the toolshed." Most will blush, but it's a compliment because here in the north we tease those we adore. We tease who we feel safe with. We're also complimenting your life because if you've got a paunch, you're slowing down. You're enjoying Pimatsawin: a happy life, as the Bush Crees call it here.

"A long time ago," Mike began as he sat down on his recliner, "we would go camping and my parents would bring Aunty Irena with them. She had a cane and a bad cough, remember?" He motioned for me to sip my tea. I took off my jacket and placed it on the back of the chair I was sitting on.

Mike glanced up to the ceiling and stretched before looking at me and continuing. "Aunty would tell us scary stories and it would just wreck the whole summer because, after that, one of her stories would chase you." He smiled, shook his head, and looked out the window. He'd been getting shaky these past few months. I could see it in his hands. This was why he kept them in his pockets now. "Aunty never had kids that lived, and at night you could hear her in the kitchen tent going through things to steal for her own little tent. She'd set off mouse traps and you could hear her swearing in Cree and we'd all laugh, but she'd help herself to whatever she wanted, but we didn't say nothing. She was a good storyteller. But when we came back to town after camping, we'd all go to her house to hear more scary stories and we'd see what she stole right there on her counter: a box of spark plugs, a hatchet, packs of matches, earplugs, axe handles, food. Some things she needed. Other things she sold. Just like you."

What? I'm surprised by this: An insult? My cheeks flushed and burned.

He kept going. "Well, after some time now, Irena started to repeat herself and she kept telling us the same stories over and over and us kids, we started to figure this was on purpose.

"She was the one who told us the Dogrib or Tłı̨chǫ story about how Cat came to be," Mike said. I winced as this was the story I borrowed for the win the other night. Now I'd have to pretend I didn't know it.

He continued: "Irena said a long time ago when the world was new, there was a flood and all the people had to leave their homes and race to a small tiny place, an island, that wasn't underwater. There, the animals became friends and they could see that it was Cat who was the friendliest. Cat was the peacemaker. Cat was the romancer. Everyone was happier when Cat was around and it was Cat who stopped the wars between certain animals. It was a blessing, the animals agreed at night, that they had Cat to help bring light during such difficult times.

"Over time, the water started to leave and there was a land bridge back to the mainland and the people decided to travel together. But the Devil was waiting halfway. Some think the Devil is a handsome man in a suit but what they saw was a small boy with hay for hair and sticks for teeth. The child had no eyes. It grinned in their direction with its black stick teeth as the animals grew closer. Everyone got cold. People think Hell is a place of fire, but it's a growing hole of ice. Where the child would touch, there'd be a hiss of ice. The animals could smell Home through the wall of ice around the boy. They could almost see it.

" 'You can pass,' the child said as it twisted its head to hear where they were standing before clicking its stick teeth over and over as it sniffed the air. 'But you have to leave one of your own with me. You have to gift me a friend.'

"The animals knew that this had to be. The Devil had power. The child's hair ignited and they could see a small cold light in each of its eye sockets. It was waiting.

"The animals began to argue. No one wanted to stay behind. They panicked.

"As usual, Cat did not know what was happening because Cat was in the back visiting with everyone, wrapping his long slinking tail around the legs of those he visited. The lead animals knew this and realized at once that they could use it.

" 'Cat,' they called. 'Go to that boy on the bridge. He is pitiful and has no friends. Go find out who he is and come back and tell us.'

" 'Oh, I'd love to!' Cat smiled. 'No friends? Oh how sad. Let me help him. He must be cold standing there all alone.'

"Cat trotted forward and became the Devil's friend instantly. Cat wrapped his long feathery tail around the legs of the Devil and began to purr. The Devil smiled and purred back, like a huge lion. Cat loved this and climbed the body of the boy, who knelt down, and they began to talk as the animals watched.

"The Devil was happy. It moved out of the way and stood with its back to the people. They began to run past it quietly as it and Cat visited and laughed. There the animals discovered more water behind the child, stopping them from going home. They were hostage to the Devil until it was done with them. Water began to flood the animals and they had to stop and walk back toward Cat and the Devil.

" 'Look,' the Devil said to Cat and pointed directly at them. It had only been pretending to not see. It knew exactly where the animals stood. 'Look at your friends.'

"Cat looked and realized that he'd been left behind. 'I don't understand,' Cat said. 'This is my family.'

" 'Are they?' the Devil asked, stroking Cat's tail. 'They offered you to me so they could go home.'

" 'But I want to go home, too,' Cat said and looked pleadingly at all of his friends. 'I trusted them.'

" 'Yes, you did.' The Devil smiled as it turned and began choking Cat. It reached under his ribs and began pulling and twisting

Cat's heart. Cat choked and thrashed and cried out as the animals watched. Blood flew as Cat scratched and gouged the Devil's arm and the blood that splattered the ice bridge hissed and smoked. The Devil started to smile even harder, grinding its stick teeth, and then it started to laugh. Cat scratched and kicked and tried biting, but the Devil pulled his heart over and over with its fingers as it squeezed harder and harder on his throat. The people could hear the snapping of small bones in Cat's throat and his tongue bulged out. His eyes rolled back and his face was a grimace and the Devil then blew its breath into Cat and Cat became still. The animals who looked back were weeping. Some were wailing. Not one of them could look away.

"'Yes,' the Devil clicked. 'Yes. You belong to me now. From here, your teeth shall be sharp like mine.' He smiled. 'Your claws will be wicked and you will always remember that it was your friends who sacrificed you for your trust and kindness so now you will walk alone and be pitiful with this memory. You will always know you were given to me, the Devil—betrayed by your friends.'

"And just like that Cat hissed at the other animals when he wanted to talk and his teeth were sharp and his claws were wicked and the hair on his back raised in hatred for his friends. The water cleared and all of the animals were allowed to go home, but when they arrived they were heartsick for what they had done and now we know the story.

"That story is a great story maybe the first ten times you hear it but after the twentieth time over and over, she gets a little stale, hey?" Mike said. "It was like Irena was hitting the pause button on something even scarier. So finally, one day, Arlis, the oldest, spoke for all of us: 'Yes, Aunty. We heard that one already. We know how it ends.' We'd heard about a movie that was so scary that it had people fainting and running to churches. For some reason, we wanted to be that scared. All us little kids in Indian Village had a meeting and we said, 'Aunty, we want you to tell us the scariest Wheetago or Sasquatch or Aliens or Little People story you know. Tell us about demons. Scare us!' and Irena asked us, 'Why?' It was the way she asked it. It's like she set out a little snare braided with human hair, like she was showing it to us, shaking it a little, warning us.

" 'Because we're not little kids anymore and we know that it's all just pretend. There's no Wheetagos. There's no Sasquatch. There's no Devil. Aliens are just one big fib. Nothing you said is real,' Arlis said and we looked at one another. He said what we'd come there to say and now it felt dangerous.

" 'Are you sure you want to hear my scariest story?' she asked us.

"She looked sad for us. I should have paid attention.

"Arlis wrinkled his nose to steady his glasses back into place. He was the coolest babysitter. He'd let us do anything, even let us watch as much TV as we wanted, even until our eyes dried out and our vision blurred, so he could read more Stephen King. 'How 'bout, Aunty,' one of us said, 'we make a deal where you tell us your scariest story and we'll link arms. We'll even wear our jammies. We'll even bring our blankets. We'll all go pee before so we won't have accidents but if we link our arms together we'll be strong. Our medicine will be strong. We'll even get our Bibles and sweetgrass in front of us and we'll put rat root and sage behind us so nothing can sneak up on us. We'll be protected. Our courage will unite us. And if we do have to go pee in the middle of the night we'll all go together.'

"So my aunty said, 'Well if you want it. If you think you're ready, you have to do three things.' And we all looked at one another with wide eyes because this was now a possibility. We were all like 'What?'

" 'You have to do three things,' she repeated, and started to cough. We all looked at one another. Her cough was getting worse, deeper, cracklier. She turned and spat something into a Kleenex. She looked at what had come up for a while and shook her head before folding it and throwing it into the woodstove. We all looked at one another, winced and wrinkled our noses in disgust.

" 'So you kids really want to do this?' she asked as she sipped her tea. 'You really want the scariest story ever told?'

"We all cheered, 'Yeah!'

"And she looked at this one picture on her shelf of pictures. It was a frame you'd put a baby's photo in. It was facedown. She glanced at it before looking down and she shook her head, suddenly so sad.

" 'What's wrong, Aunty?' I asked her. Irena had been lonely these past few years. She used a cane now to walk and she was all hunched up. As her cough grew louder and her coughing fits lasted longer and longer, fewer and fewer people came to visit her. She was often the last on the list for food from the community hunt. With so little family left, she was starting to turn invisible.

" 'You only get to be kids once,' she said. 'After this story, you won't be kids anymore.'

"Everyone laughed but me. 'Yeah right,' they all said. 'As if. *Wah!*' But this was serious. I looked into the woodstove, and you could see that what was in the black waxy middle of the Kleenex still hadn't burned. It was so thick the fire couldn't grab it. Gross!

" 'Tell us!' Arlis said.

"It was a good thing he was bossy.

"I realized I was digging my heels into the carpet already," Mike told me, looking up suddenly, "because I'd never realized what we were all agreeing to. It's like we were all standing at the edge of a cliff no one told us about and what was waiting below was cold and starving.

" 'Okay, what?' the kids asked. 'What's the first thing?'

" 'All of you have to clean your rooms,' Irena said.

" 'Whaaa!' We were all crying, rolling around, yelling, 'Don't be like that. Don't be cheap! Don't make us. Come on. Anything but cleaning our rooms!'

"Irena said, 'No, you clean all your rooms. That's part one. You do that. Then you come back.'

"Well, we had to go house to house to help one another. It took a week for everyone to clean their rooms, eh? So finally we all came back, and we watched as she took her phone and she called all our parents and she said, 'Go in their rooms. If there's anything not perfectly right you call me.'

"The parents all called back or stopped by with food and said, 'Aunty, thank you. It's perfect. The bedrooms in our homes are spotless.' So all us kids started linking arms and some of us had little yellow ropes tied to one another in case today was the day and she was going to tell us her scariest story, and we said, 'All right you said there were three things we had to do. What's the second thing?'

"She said, 'You have to clean your yards—front and back—and mine: front and back.'

" 'Whaaa!' We all started crying. Even me. 'Oh hey! Come on now. That's enough now! We're just little kids.'

"She shook her head. 'Namoyah. A long time ago people had pride in their yards. I don't see that anymore. I miss that. Go clean your yards and then you come back.' Well, it took two weeks. We all teamed up and we got weed whackers, shovels, rakes, bags for leaves—good Lord, the dog poop! The dogs didn't like it: it was one disruption after another to their society meetings, I guess. We begged our parents and they helped clean up. There were chainsaws and axes for all the downed trees and there were bags of lawn clippings for the Town to pick up. And all those runs to the dump. I remember my dad making trip after trip with other men as garbage was placed on the side of the roads to be taken away. The people worked hard, together. We cleaned Aunty's yard—front and back—and you could see that it hadn't been cleaned in years. You know, I can still recall how good the air smelled after we cleaned everything up. You could smell the sap from all the trees we cleared and cut down. And the light was different. It reached us, you know?

"One by one the kids and their parents showed up with more food to thank her and she ate good. Aunty ate good. She filled her freezer, her fridge, her cupboards. All those berries and she kept asking for blueberry root, rat root, bear grease, goose grease—and she got it. I remember the tops of her cupboards had silver bowls filled with dry meat, dry fish, fat, pemmican—and she shared so when you visited now, boy, you ate good.

"So, finally now, after we all walked her around to show her all the work we did together, she said, 'I'm going to call the mayor, the chief, and the president of the Métis Association and they're going to do an inspection. Everyone always calls down Indian Village for being dirty and filled with Greedy Treaties and lazy Indians but they're going to see who we are now. We worked together and now we're the cleanest part of Fort Simmer.' And that's what they did. Holy cannoli, it even made the paper.

"Aunty said, 'You all live here as a family. We are all related in memory. It is a gift to live here, to come from here. The leaders, the police, the nurses, the church, everyone's trying their best. I like that new jungle gym elephant they put up for the kids at JBS with the slide for the nose.

"'When someone dies, who's the first to cook for you and shake your hand and sit with you? The people. That's who. You know, we have to reclaim our dignity and our pride. We're given these houses. We're given these yards. We're given these fences. They give us all this stuff and us, we forgot our part. But that's where pride lives: for when you work hard for what you have and share. I read the paper, me, and we're like wolves fighting for scraps. That's what the government wants, that we keep fighting, and that's why Hay River and Yellowknife keep getting better opportunities. It's time for us to work together again, like we used to.'

"So we cleaned Indian Village and even I remember how good it felt to get up and race around on my bike and see all the wood stacked from the fallen trees. Everyone was happy, giving one another the Fort Simmer Nod when you went by. All for a scary story. I still remember how everyone would go cruising through Indian Village at night in their trucks and say, 'Look at these beautiful homes. Look at all the yards, all clean.' And couples would hold hands and go for walks and kids would say hi on their bikes. We were happy and proud. To our surprise, the other sides of town started to clean up their own backyards: the Welfare Center, downtown, by Panty Point, the airport trailer court. Soon our town was sparkling!"

Mike took a long sip of his mint tea and so did I. This was frickin' boring. I already knew all this and it wasn't what I came for.

"So finally now at the end of summer," Mike continued, "Aunty did a little walk around the village with all of us kids one more time but this time it was for the Yellowknife paper and for the *Chronicle.* The reporters wanted to hear about how the promise of one story had cleaned up a larger part of Fort Simmer. She didn't need her cane this time and she said, 'Now this, this is how I remember Fort Simmer. This is how Simmer used to look and feel: proud.' And that was the summer and fall families started sitting on their porches with tea and coffee and bannock and the families started to visit once again.

"The mayor even said in the paper, 'I don't understand it. Fort Simmer has never looked cleaner. People from Hay River and Fort

Smith have been driving hours to look at our gorgeous town and they're even cleaning up their towns to compete with the beauty of ours. Good luck! And we hear that's sparked something similar with Fort Resolution and Fort Providence. My goodness! What a spectacle to behold. Hats off to everyone who volunteered their time to really show off the Garden Capital of the North. We are the Gateway to Wood Buffalo Park. We are the Pumpkin Capital of the north and our pelicans are going to be so happy when they soar back and they see their summer home looking so fresh and shiny.'

"Chief Danny got in there and squeezed in an interview. It was hilarious. 'Once again,' he said, 'when Columbus got lost we saved him, okay? The Indians saved him. Get that through your moon-yow face. When he saw how beautiful we, as Indians, were and continue to be. You know they say the prettiest women come from Fort Simmer and the handsomest men, too, ey? You know that, right? You didn't need to go to school to learn that, hey, Junior? You were born knowing that. I know they say the best don't adver-tise but come on now. I tell people when I'm in Ottawa where I'm from and as soon as I say, "Fort Simmer," they shake my hand and bow because Columbus called us "Indios." You know what that means? That means "With God." That's our heavenly natural light. Indios. Indians. We are the natural beauty where the divine earth meets the heavenly sky, Junior. We are Indios and now you know us as Dene, the original people. The First people of Denendeh. Land of the people.'"

Mike started laughing. "Holy cannoli, Chief Danny's statement went for pages and frankly no one can remember what the Métis president said because, well, you never want to take the stage after Chief Danny."

Mike shook his head again and chuckled. I shook my own head and smiled with him. He then looked at the clock: "Ahem, okay.

So that was the summer the Indians outshone everyone in Sim-mer and that started a chain effort where everyone competed with everyone to have the cleanest yard and most manicured part of town. And it is true: Hay River, Fort Res, Fort Smith, and Fort Providence cleaned themselves up, too, all because of Aunty Irena.

"And when all was said and done, Aunty's house was filled with kids from all parts of town: they all got together because they wanted to hear this scary story that had cleaned our town even though it hadn't been told yet. . . . We all felt a part of something huge. I remember that summer there were no break-ins anywhere. Lonny, the Dog Catcher and By Law Officer, went home every night because there was simply nowhere he needed to be because everyone was home helping out, doing chores, waiting for the night Aunty would tell her story. When she asked, 'All right, are you all ready for the last task?' we all cheered, 'Yeah!'

" 'Before I tell you the story,' she said, 'you have to bring your parents tonight at eight. Your parents need to hear the beginning. If they think you can handle it, I'll share it all.'

" 'Wait a minute,' Arlis said. 'You never said this was for parents, too. This is just for us kids.'

"But no one else said anything. I sat up and realized that maybe this would save us. If my parents got word of this, maybe they wouldn't let me attend.

" 'No parents,' Irena said, 'no story. If my boys had lived, I would never forgive anyone who took their happiness away.'

"We all looked at one another. Now *this* was spooky, but it actually felt good because Irena had given us an escape route. We all took off and grabbed our parents and begged them to come listen. Even me. I begged them to come, but they were drinking and Irena knew that. She let me come alone, like always.

"So at eight that night, Indian Village was packed with trucks.

Irena's house was filled with parents who'd brought gifts and food, but they weren't smiling. Something had changed. This was not fun anymore. This was real, they could see.

"Aunty met them at the door. Her fire was going in her wood-stove. She looked young again and she stood straight.

"'My goodness.' She smiled and looked at everyone. 'All of this for one scary story. Come in. Come in.'

"We could see a big pot of water simmering on her stove. The element was red hot underneath it. None of us were offered tea, coffee or water or juice. You could feel that we were all to sit and listen, so we all did. A big fan, one usually reserved for a long hot summer, was going, rotating slowly, probably to move the smoke and heat around.

"On her couch were two small somethings wrapped in two twisted black garbage bags covered with two blue baby blankets. Whatever was inside those blankets was small and every once in a while, when the rotating fan would pass by, the plastic around those two somethings would rustle. Like whatever these things were were unthawing and remembering that they were alive, kind of. Some parents pointed. Others grabbed their kids and left. 'No,' one mom said. 'We're going. That's enough. Aunty, why are you doing this?'

"'Because they asked,' she said and looked down. She was smiling, chuckling to herself.

"Other parents started to do the same. And when they left, more parents who were on the porch caught a glimpse of what was on the couch and they, too, took their kids.

"Whenever that plastic would rustle from the air of the fan fanning it, Irena would say in Cree, 'Namoyah. Awas. Awas. Not yet.' For 'No. Go away. Not yet.'

"As she spoke, I realized she was no longer sick. She wasn't using her cane. She'd grown. Could you draw power from the spirit of a story? I think so. She was living proof. Her house was now full of food and visitors and respect and gratitude. Our town was clean because of her. Families were visiting because of her. Now she just had to tell us the story.

" 'I'll keep my part,' Aunty said, looking at the few listeners who remained, but her voice had changed. She had a man's voice now. 'But I ask those of you who want your kids to stay kids, take them away before I start because once I start I can't stop. They'll get mad if I stop and we don't want them mad. We don't want to thaw them for nothing.' She looked at the two plastic somethings and, as the fan moved the air in the room, the plastic crinkled again. Did the bundles move? I swear they moved. It was like they twitched or were frozen and trying to stretch. Through the black garbage bags, I saw two little open mouths. You could see the outlines of whatever was inside those plastic bags when the air from the fan hit them and they looked like, well, I won't say it."

Mike looked down and then he looked at the gifts piled high for his grandbaby on the way. He started to have his tremors again so he sat up and continued.

"She then grabbed a mason jar and started to shake it. What was inside were black smooth rocks of all sizes.

" 'Oh, wait,' she said. 'They have a song for you. I'll teach you. They love this song as they wake up. It's a lullaby. It goes, "We need toes for our jar," ' she smiled and clicked her teeth, ' "and ribs for our soup. We need toes for our jar and ribs for our soup." '

"She looked mean chanting this, but we realized that it wasn't for her. It was for what or who was in those plastic bags that was making her say this: 'I need toes for my jar and ribs for my soup.' Each time she said this her voice got deeper and louder until she was shaking and chanting and as she moved the blankets moved until they started to jump. It was like they were altogether bound by the chant: 'I need toes for my jar and ribs for my soup!'

"*Sh sh sh,* the rocks raced around the jar, and when I looked closer I realized that they weren't rocks or pebbles. They were toes. Petrified toes.

" 'I need toes for my jar and ribs for my soup!'

"*Sh sh sh.*

"The dogs outside started to howl.

"When the pot started to boil over and we heard the hissing and spitting on the stove top, everyone stood and ran outside, racing to their trucks, holding the arms and hands of their children. And then Aunty Irena threw her head back and started laughing, started cackling.

"They say that that night the priest was awoken by begging families and a church service was demanded to bless the children and bless the parents. Some people smudged. Others went down to the rocks to pray and offer tobacco to the Creator and to their ancestors for protection."

"What did you do?" I asked.

He looked at me and then to his feet. "I stayed. I sat down. I served my aunty tea. I was the only one to stay and listen and hear the scariest story ever told, and I'm going to share it next week in Yellowknife."

"What?" I asked, surprised.

Mike looked at me for a long time. His features changed. They darkened. "You know what we lost, Simon? We lost the power of shame. Long time ago, in the seventies, if you came up here and you bothered a girl from Fort Smith? Holy cow, you'd get a frickin' lickin' from her brothers, her dad, her uncles, her grandpas, her exes. You got the shit kicked out of you in ways you'd never imagine. Then, if you still had the balls to stick around town, people would turn their backs to you. Treat you invisible. Even at the bank. Even at the Bay. Now we wave to the wife beaters, the pedophiles, the bootleggers." *The drug dealers,* I wanted to add. "We do this because we're scared. The courts take too long and those who are charged know who made the call and they are punished." Mike hung his head for a while. "I'm tired of all of this."

I hoped he was talking about his son. I prayed he was talking about his son.

"What happened to you?" he asked and looked at me.

Oh, shit. I sat up in my chair. "What?"

"You had my trust for a while, Nephew." His cheeks were red. Was he going to fight me?

My face started to burn. "What are you talking about?"

"This town wants to give you everything." He reached across the table and spread his massive hands, gripping the sides of the table. "I want to give you everything. But now I don't know."

I let my breath out and steadied myself. Shit. Here it came. I felt like I was on an elevator and the cord had snapped.

Mike held his hand up by his shoulder. "I remember when you were growing up, you had the sweetest smile. You were always helping people. It was good. We were happy whenever you were around. As you grew, you always respected the Elders. You were always serving tea at the meetings, always sitting with the storytellers, listening. But as you grew—and I don't know what happened. You never left. You never went for schoolin' down south. All your friends did and look at them now: happy, with kids, married. Making a living with purpose. What do you have that you haven't stolen?"

I could feel my jaw shift. I did this when I felt shame. I willed it back in place. "Mike," I said.

"Listen. I'm not done." His eyes were fierce when he looked directly at me and I felt his anger fill the room. "So you stayed and did little jobs. And then you started showing up with your tape recorder. You started recording the Elders and we were happy you were getting the stories down but you never brought them back like you said."

I raised my hands to talk.

"Listen," Mike said firmly. "You will listen because what I'm about to tell you a lot of Elders want to say, most of them are long gone now. But they left wondering why you stole our stories."

"Whoa, Mike," I said, embarrassed. "Take it easy."

"Listen," he said. "You're about to receive the biggest truth—and you've had this coming for a while. You came here tonight to steal a story, a story you don't have any right to. Why? It's to make money and steal what isn't yours. You came here with a pittance of what you wanted to make next week." He looked up at the ceiling. "But here's what we're going to do. You're going to stop."

"Stop?" I asked. I could not remember ever feeling so ashamed and scared. "What do you mean stop?"

He looked at me. "You're going to stop and you're going to listen. And you're going to go home and you're going to write out all those stories that you took and you're going to give them back: word for word. You're going to make copies of all those tapes from our loved ones, and give them to the families of those storytellers and those knowledge keepers. Their children and grandchildren are still here and they deserve their ancestors' stories. You're going to do what you said you were going to do a long time ago."

"Mike," I said. "That's, what, forty tapes."

He nodded. "Do this and you will be the hero you deserve to be for taking the time to do those things."

I thought about it. I had no money. I had my dad's cheap boom box that could duplicate tapes. This would take months to do. How could I type out hours of visiting and storytelling? How?

"Right now, you're calculating how long this will take you, right?"

I nodded.

"And right now you're feeling ashamed and embarrassed, right?"

I nodded and looked down. My face was burning.

"Nephew," he said and leaned forward. "This is your chance to make good on all that you promised. You do this and you will have the trust of the people. You'll have my trust and I will teach you everything I know. My own family, my own kids, they don't have time for my stories. They want to do this." He made a motion of playing video games. "I've got a cabin I haven't been to in over a year. Nobody wants to go there anymore. Nobody wants to hunt or trap or fish. They want it easy."

I nodded. He was talking about Junior.

"But you do all of this, Nephew. You keep your promises. You keep your word, maybe I'll give you my cabin and you will learn. You'll learn that a blue sky is dangerous and it's the gray overcast days when you haul your water, cut your wood, secure your camp. You'll learn how to read the land in the ways of our ancestors. I knew your mom, your dad, your grandparents. I remember what they knew. You could learn all of this through me, but no more bullshit, okay? No more ripping off people who believe in you."

I thought of Mike's cabin. He posted pics on Facebook. It was gorgeous. He had a tipi for smoking dry meat and dry fish, and he had access to the river. If I ever had a family of my own, I could take them there and we could be happy.

I had tears in my eyes.

"You deserve a family of your own. If you're not going to leave Simmer, you can learn from her, but you have to honor her with protocol and respect." To my surprise, he patted my hand tenderly. "And I will teach you how."

I looked at him. He was smiling, warmly.

"Remember when I told you what the three best lures for lynx are?"

I nodded. "Aqua Velva aftershave, rotten loach, and catnip mixed with peanut butter."

He nodded.

"Remember when I told you the three things you need to survive out in the bush?"

I nodded. "An axe, snowshoes, and a flint."

"Remember when I told you where to find the sweetest mint?"

"On top of a beaver lodge."

"That's right," he said and pointed to his temple. "That was—what—ten years ago I told you that. See? You've got it. You have the gift. You're a listener. Remember how I told you a long time ago that there is one listener in every family?"

I nodded. He had me. "Yeah."

"Well, you're it and I'll go even further. There's a treasured few in every town. I've been this one's for so long and I won't be here forever, so let's start over. No more bullshit. No more lies. I'm winning next week's scary story contest, Nephew. Call CBC and tell them you're giving up your seat to your uncle to represent Fort Simmer, and I'm giving you half the winnings."

I looked at him, surprised. "What?"

He nodded. "You're going to use that money to buy tapes, paper, whatever you need, and you're going to make good on everything we spoke about and then you will apprentice under me and I'll teach you what your grandfather knew: how to stop a windstorm with a willow and four rocks. I'll teach you everything I've become through stories and you will become this town through Spirit, stories, protocol, and memory."

I found myself smiling.

"Sound good?" He smiled.

"Yeah." My voice cracked. "Yes. Thank you, Mike." This is what I always wanted: to be held to something. To answer to someone. I heard a honk in the driveway and saw my dad's headlights shine in Mike's front window. The dogs outside barked and ran around the lights.

Mike waved out the window to my dad. "Watch my house

while I'm gone and I'll honor you with five hundred bucks for being my apprentice. Your life—your true and sincere life—begins now and I will help you. We—the Elders of this town who have no one to listen to them—will help you." He smiled. "Nephew."

I shook his hand and hugged him, really hugged him. "Thank you, Uncle."

"A long time ago . . ." Mike looked to me and winked. "I was on a similar path as you. Lucky for me, the right person at the right time set me straight."

I nodded.

"You can't bullshit a bullshitter, Nephew," Mike said and patted my shoulder. "Let our bullshitting days be done. Thank you for the food you brought me. Mahsi cho."

Richard Van Camp is a proud Tłįchǫ Dene from Fort Smith, NWT. He is the bestselling author of twenty-seven books these past twenty-seven years, and his novel, *The Lesser Blessed*, is now a feature film with First Generation Films. Van Camp is an internationally renowned storyteller whose passion is helping others reclaim their family medicines. You can visit with Richard on Facebook, Twitter, Instagram, SoundCloud, YouTube, and at his official site: richardvancamp.com.

HUMAN EATERS

ROYCE K. YOUNG WOLF

I remember the silence. Outside the circle, the land was pitch-black. Even with every constellation vibrating brilliantly above, pockets of space pulled every bit of light in, reflecting nothing. "They," the human eaters, move freely through the abyss. The other place most humans can no longer see.

There was no one to take the sight from me as a child. Or maybe the ones left that did have the medicine to do so chose to keep me this way. One of my own was born able to see, and one of his and his brother's, as well. If asked, I still help our family when one is born with the sight. Sometimes it's too much for their mind. Like my gah-guuhk, "grandma," before me, I'll do what I can to help my grandkids.

I whispered to them, "Just beyond the circle, past the reach of the fire, 'they' were there. Always present. Watching. Ready to eat away at you. Just like 'they' are now."

"Sick! Like, actually eat you? Cannibals?"

He's young. They're both young. Just thirteen. Hair still long, pulled back into single braids. The one with no filter, interrupting me, he still has baby fat and is short. The other boy, quiet, he's already a string bean, but strong. He keeps his little brother in line, says:

"If you keep interrupting, she's not gonna tell us anything at all!"

"That's right. No need to waste my breath on nuhn-guh-chees!" That means "no ears." My great grandma used to call her own grandkids that. I tell them, "If you have no ears you might as well just cut them off and toss them in the fire, if you don't want to listen."

Shocked, No Filter blurts out, "No, no. I'll stop. Tell us gah-guuhk. Who are 'they'?"

"String Bean, build that fire up more. It'll be dusk soon. No Filter, get the meat from the cooler so the food will be ready for when your folks get back. They're scouting out where they're gonna put you two out up top tomorrow. Best eat before it gets too dark."

No Filter: "We can't eat outside when it's nighttime."

I smile a little. "Sure you can. You just have to put a little food down over there away from you before you eat. Don't want your face to get twisted."

String Bean: "That's what happens when you look back at something at night, too. Right, gah-guuhk?"

"Huh? Depends. Always depends." This one, he listens more. Long memory. "You put some food down, even if you're one of those forty-niners out trying to snag, being dumb and young. Buh, dumb and old, too. Still trying to drink around."

No Filter: "Gross. They don't forty-nine anymore."

"Sure they do. They're just all old now."

No Filter: "Did you forty-nine?"

String Bean: "Geez, don't ask her that!"

These two make me laugh. No Filter, he always pulls the stories from me. So curious. If only they knew where we were camped right now. The stories this place has. The memories I have.

"Yeah, just no respect. No Filter at all! Here, String Bean, put the skillet on top of those two flat rocks. Move some more coals between the rocks."

String Bean works fast. The fire is going good now. Their folks should be here soon. The road up the mountain has shifted over the years. It'll take a few hours to reach the cliffs tomorrow. I used to drive those roads every summer. It's good to be back. The sky stretches on forever to the east. The clouds roll over the mountains to the west. The storms crash over the ridges like waves on sea cliffs. The sky is clear today, but up there on the cliffs, it'll hail and snow year-round. But when the lightning dances in the distance, you can glimpse the light shows once seen by our ancestors. What would they think of us now? So different, but our eyes the same.

The fire crackles, sending sparks floating up on the light breeze. I watch them drift along the horizon. Blue and gray watercolors paint the sky, framing the sagebrush-covered flats. Tiny lights from the town below shimmer.

"Oh-pah-zha-gitzs. It's getting dark."

No Filter: "Please, I'm sorry. Who are 'they'?"

"Something your father should have taught you about. But I guess I better tell you. I kinda like you. Don't want you to get eaten up there. Hand those steaks from the cooler to your brother. You know why you eat steak before you go out there? The meat will take longer to digest and the blood will help you as you fast."

No Filter: "What if I was a vegan?"

"You poor thing. Guess you'll just have to suffer more. Maybe just die all sad."

String Bean smiles while placing the two largest steaks in the skillet. They sizzle, and I smell the sweet aroma. I hear rustling just outside our camp circle. They've moved closer. Impatient. Hungry.

"Don't forget to go toss a few pieces outside the circle before you eat. It'll be dark by then."

String Bean: "So 'they' eat that instead of twisting our faces."

"They're not the ones that twist our faces. The dead are. It's a little trick, you see. The hungry spirits still wander around because they can't let go of what they've done wrong. Their sins, their wrong ways of living. They carry that and it keeps them here, bothering around. They come and go. Sometimes, with that food or drink you put down, they'll get pulled to that and eat on it a bit, instead of hovering around your face while you eat and drink."

No Filter: "Oh, sick!"

I chuckle a little. "That's why you don't eat outside at night and not put some down. Who knows what you're feeding from your own face. Putting food down away from you, we do this to draw those spirits to that food instead. The trick that I'm talking about is that 'they' also get drawn to those spirits. See, 'they' feed off the spirits just like 'they' fed off them before the person died. When they were human, they lived wrong, broke their prayers, vows, and were involved in bad doings. But there's a lot of different stuff that makes spooks. This is just a little bit of how my elders explained it to me."

String Bean flips the steaks and rotates the foil-wrapped potatoes and onions that have been cooking in the coals.

There is more rustling near the sagebrushes. The last bit of gray on the horizon is almost gone. Memories flood back to me. It was about this hour when my great grandma would be settling in to watch her evening shows on the mini TV in our living room/dining room/kitchen/guest bedroom. I'd ready my hands to adjust the bunny ears and make another foil masterpiece. The TV would come on with a high-pitched buzz and loud click. Static would cut in and out as I perfected each antenna on top of the little brown TV.

After the closing credits of *Silk Stalkings*, an old dirty detective show, ended, I'd turn the TV off and it'd be time for the real stories. I'd say something like, "Howah, them white people are sure crazy, Jojo!" She'd laugh and start in about how much she'd seen in her life. Some stories were about what she saw the nuns and priests doing at the boarding schools in the early 1900s. They were just like them crazy detective shows, except no one investigated what happened in the tunnels under the buildings or what happened in the chapels and nearly every room at those places.

One night, she told me about a man she saw who reminded her of the old stories. He was visiting the school, doing some repairs. She said he was tall. Taller than any Indian she ever saw. He was tall, like the human eaters that would carry baskets on their backs to steal us away in. A few of her classmates knew the stories and agreed he must be no good. His hands were huge, with long pointy fingers. He would stand in one spot, watching the children. Her and her friends would avoid his stare. She said his eyes were black, like pitch. Lifeless. Always watching. He had to be some kind of human eater. Just like the giants that wait in the dark back home.

Two of her classmates went missing around that same time. They never saw the man again. She'd say, "I still think about them some nights. Maybe if their parents had known about the human eaters, they could have told those kids and they could have known to stay away, too."

Now I tell my own family the stories. Maybe they'll live long and stay away from the bad ways, too.

"String Bean, move the veggies out of the coals and put your steaks on your plates. Go ahead, start cooking the ones for your folks. I'll tell you both who 'they' are, and you best keep quiet, so you remember."

String Bean gets to work. No Filter holds the plates on his lap. He glances over his shoulder and quickly turns back around.

"No Filter, what you've been hearing, that rustling behind you, that's 'them.'"

His eyes widen, and he tightens his grip on the plates. String Bean glances up at him and goes back to work.

"String Bean, your father told you about 'them' already when you were his runner this summer at the lodge, right?"

"Yeah. I keep clear of them now."

"We, well, we're not like most humans. Most humans don't have the sight anymore. Especially after all these white people and other ones who are backward without culture arrived here, our own relatives, other Natives, they lost their sight. Some, they don't want nothing to do with getting it back, either. But us few, we still know what is out there. We know the stories and why things happen that others can't explain. My elders told me stories about 'them,' and I'm doing my best to tell your folks and now you both, so you don't end up all gih-dih-shaz-zih, 'pitiful,' half-eaten and lost."

I look out beyond the light of the fire. The abyss is dense, even with the stars and the quarter moon already bright in the sky.

The sound of a pebble hits the brush inside the circle. No Filter flinches and goes to look behind him.

"Eh!" I say to him. "Don't be looking behind you. You need to remember this. When it's just you and String Bean up there, and you choose to look out past your circle tomorrow night, 'they'll' be there among the other things watching you. Waiting to see if you'll run and break your vows."

String Bean: "We won't run."

"You see, there is always a balance. Even the little people that change their faces and frighten so many people, some of them are here to help. Those boarding schools, they took our people's memories. They blocked many from being able to remember how to work with those things. I tell this now, so you'll know not to be afraid. They'll look into you both and they'll see our ancestors living in you. You both have the sight, but it fades if you let the fear get you. And it fades if you're stupid like a drunk, a druggie, or violent and cruel."

I look each of them up and down, and I close my eyes as more are gathering in the dark, just beyond the circle. I can hear their small feet running over the coarse dirt. In my mind, I see their faces changing. Some keep their eyes wide like owls, some squint them, looking far into the past and the future. Some looking straight through you. The little ones, many say they come from our mountains. This is what my great grandma told me, and what was told to her by her great grandma and all the ones that gathered under these same stars thousands of years ago.

I tell both boys again, "No, you don't be afraid. Those little ones, they know you. Just as they know me and all the ones who came before me. They'll be here long after we're gone. The same with the human eaters."

String Bean flips the other steaks.

I can see headlights glowing about three miles up the mountain road. Their folks will be here soon.

"Go ahead, rip a piece from your steaks and throw it out beyond the circle. Say in your mind, 'Go over there, stay away from me.' While you eat your steaks, I'll tell you about the human eaters."

Both look at each other and then do as they're told.

I move a larger log onto the fire with my stick. It sends more sparks into the sky. For a moment, the edges of the abyss are lit. A pair of large feet with skin pulled tight against the bones and tendons appears. I look at the long shadows dancing up thin shins that disappear into the pitch just below the knees. Again, the abyss is all that I see. I look up to the stars and remember when I was young, how determined I was to not show fear. The fire grows and crackles. The smell of water and willows wafts across the breeze.

The boys begin to tear pieces from their steaks.

"You see, 'they' are always there waiting to eat away at you. Long ago, our people could see them clear as day. Just like you two see me now. They were taught to stay clear of certain places at certain times of the year, just as I am trying to teach you and others the same. If you pay attention, you can still catch glimpses of 'them.' Human eaters would be seen down by the rivers among the willows. Tall as the trees, with huge woven baskets on their backs. When they'd catch a human, they'd cut their feet off so they couldn't run away. Sometimes they'd take their hands and eyes, too, before they'd put them in the baskets."

The crickets have stopped chirping. There is no breeze. The smoke from the fire flows straight to the stars.

"All things need to eat to survive. The human eaters, they eat those of us who are not living as we should. That's what board- ing schools did to our people. Colonization took our memories. Assimilation has us feeding our own eyes and ears to the fire. Some even feed their own young to it. Many of our people may have forgotten the old ways, but agreements were made that haven't ended just because our peoples choose to be blind and deaf. I tell you two this because the human eaters are standing behind you. Waiting silently in the dark."

String Bean shivers and straightens his back. No Filter hunches down in his chair and continues to chew on his steak.

"There was a lodge up in this area long ago. You can still smell what our ancestors could smell on that day in the lodge. The dirt holds the heat from the sun because of the sand mixed with the soil. When the breeze is just right, the scent of the hot ground and sagebrush mixes with the smell of the water and the willows. The sweet smell can drive anyone crazy on the last day in the lodge.

Two young boys ran that day. They broke through the circle, ran to the river, and broke their vow. By the time the older men caught up to them, the human eaters had already gone to work cutting flesh and bone, filling their baskets. The old men apologized to the tall creatures. The young boys were wrong to break their vows. They swore to take them back into the lodge. But it was too late. They could have only one back. His eyes removed.

"The women cried when they saw them bring the boy back. The older men told the people of the warning they were given by the human eaters. 'This world is changing. Soon, your kind will not be able to see us, like this boy. But we will be here. Always. And when you break your vows. When you live wrong. We will be there to eat away at you.' That's what they were told. Soon, only a few could catch glimpses of the human eaters moving among the willows by the rivers. Only a few could see them standing outside the lodges and outside the circles we make around our camps. When you live wrong and break your vows, the agreements that our ancestors made for our people to live right, 'they' eat away at you. Slowly, they cut away at your flesh and the flesh of your family. Sickness follows those ones around."

No Filter slowly finishes chewing and swallows the last piece of his steak. I look back to the abyss beyond the firelight. I hear small feet running just beyond the circle. A pebble lands between the boys, causing them to close their eyes. The fire crackles and sparks light up long legs, thin thighs. On each side hang long hands stretching into the points. Fingers twitching.

Headlights blind us. I can smell "them" mixed with the dust from the truck. Blood, musk, dirt, and water.

Royce K. Young Wolf is Hiraacá (Hidatsa), Nu'eta (Mandan), and Sosore (Eastern Shoshone) from the Wind River Reservation in Wyoming and the Fort Berthold Reservation in North Dakota. She is a member of the Ih-dhi-shu-gah (Wide Ridge) Clan and is a child of the Ah-puh-gah-whi-gah (Low Cap) Clan. She received her PhD in sociocultural and linguistic anthropology from the University of Oklahoma; her dissertation focuses on Native American and Indigenous language and culture acquisition and revitalization, Indigenous collaborative relationship (re)making, and visual anthropology. Young Wolf is currently a postdoctoral associate and lecturer in Native American art and curation in the Department of the History of Art and the Yale University Art Gallery and is a Presidential Visiting Fellow. Storytelling inspires all areas of her work. Storytelling is an art form she has been raised with.

THE LONGEST STREET IN THE WORLD

THEODORE G. VAN ALST JR.

Winter's hardest sun

      angled across Western Avenue

            leaving light without warmth in that way it did
            this far south in Chicago,

                    riding the same lonely slant of prairie it
                    had for at least a hundred years.

Its cruel flare lit the after-Christmas-before-Valentine's-Day deep January of bright and clear icy needles to the chest midafternoon on a frozen sidewalk out past 79th Street, where postwar brutalism mirrored the other end of this twenty-four-mile street, the longest in the world, or at least in the world that mattered, and a brooding young man in a heavy dark blue cardigan over white shirtsleeves and a thin, winesap tie sipped a scotch neat from a rose melamine cup and looked out a so-cold storefront window whose painted gold cursive letters announced JOHNNY LEE SR. AND SON, REALTORS, under a green-and-ivory-striped awning. Johnny Lee Junior cast his angry vision onto the avenue at street level through the thin, watery glass from inside a chilly fifty-eight-degree office where the sadness of living and never being known to anyone for anything of note, of any exterior accomplishment, was a thing unto itself. This specter with a fleeting value needing substantial translation and a bit of justification at minimum haunted the neighborhood, and right now it pressed down on the watcher at the window.

Johnny Junior stared through the wiggle glass, wondering if it would be his forever view whether he liked it or not, wanted it or not, and what his options might be. He was already feeling his soul slow-scream when a jagged-edged red brick sang through the heavy frosted air. Its scattered mica flecks flashed in the last of the sunlight, amber dying embers winking as they passed through the shade of the striped canopy and sailed into his face, shattering glass and orbital bone split seconds apart. White nasal laughter brayed out of the purplegray dusk, its source a fifteen-year-old '63 Ford Falcon wagon whose red brake lights never stuttered once to mark its passing south on into Beverly and out to Dixie Highway.

Chicago hitched ever so slightly but breathed the same as it ever did; in the normal course of things, that honky donkey carload would never tell their grandchildren what they'd done, even as they tilted out of their caskets into the long chute down to Hell while middle-aged Marys and Josephs ate wake-scented ham salad sandwiches and caught up on their kids' sad Little League triumphs and news of other white mediocrities. The city sighed along, settler sons and daughters telling its tale for a while, but not forever.

And sometimes not too long at all, because six weeks later, the last of his bandages down to a white one-inch square below his left eye, thankfully intact and working just fine, maybe even better than before, Johnny Lee Junior, closing up shop, went to hit the light switch by the front door and through the plate glass window watched that pale blue Falcon head his way again, this time northbound on Western Avenue. The dying sun flashed blood orange on the cream landau top and blazed its way along the chrome trim as the big, boxy Ford drifted by, neither its former driver nor any of her passengers currently possessed of their heads. Junior's breath drew up sharp and stopped as the Falcon pulled into an open triple parking spot across the street and up a piece.

An inky purpleblack long-haired and full-furred figure with a cauled white eye in one socket and a solid aquamarine orb in the other rolled out of the driver's seat and shot Junior a look. It popped the back of the wagon, lugged on something heavy in the cargo hold, and with a bit of effort yanked out a nylon mesh bag of severed white-boy and -girl heads it tossed over its shoulder, a nightscape dreadnought coach stomping into basketball practice. The heads' drying dead-chalk stares and carp-lipped, wondering mouths caught the last of the sun headed behind the building as the creature hauled them across the street.

Johnny Junior was glad Senior had gone home early. Man, he hated this kind of shit. Left Neshoba County as a young man looking to break with all that "country nonsense," he called it. When he got to the city, he learned Indian people mostly lived up north in Uptown, and though there was a good chunk of folks on the South Side, they lived way east of here, down in Hyde Park. The old man may have wanted to leave all that country mess behind, but his country ass still liked the peace and quiet at night. Junior did too, for the most part, so they lived a usually quiet life out here on the Southwest Side.

"Thought you might be looking for these," the creature said, giving Junior a chin-up nod under the jingling shopkeeper's bells as it pushed through the glass door, its trace of French accent living nicely within the Chicago dialect where no *h* appeared after a *t* in the spoken language and a soft, clipped, *d*-like *th* made t'ese and t'ose words sound a touch different. "Where do you want them?" it asked, the brass bells slowly tinkling to silence overhead.

"I don't," Junior said. "Take that shit right back outta here, Louis."

"Oh no, son. It don't work that way." Louis brought the bag of heads around in front of him.

"The hell it don't. I ain't asked you for that." Junior stuck out his chin, fished in his pants pocket for a Lucky Strike. He pulled a brass Zippo from his other one, lit up, blew out a big drag.

"Didn't have to ask *me*, but you asked, nonetheless," Louis said, dropping the bag with a thud next to the front door. "Or did you forget already how you took a brick to the face from these shits?" Louis looked over to Junior, lifted his face, gestured with his first two fingers up to his drooly gray lips, the universal sign for *gimme a smoke*.

Junior pulled out his pack, shook one up toward Louis, who took it, and said, of course, "Gotta light?"

To which Junior replied, "Want me to smoke it for you, too, Louis? Jeeezus Christ."

"Don't you blaspheme, Junior." Louis puffed away, slobbering around the cigarette with that dog mouth and big white teeth of his. His speech was fine for some reason, but eating, drinking, and smoking were something else to see.

"Seriously, Louis? You're an *abomination*, for Christ's sake. I don't think you get to judge, you know." Junior took a big drag off his Lucky, the smoke curling up, making him close an eye against it, leaving him looking more contemplative than he actually was as he regarded the bag of heads, eyes rolling and mouths moving, all trying to talk to one another, to him, to Louis, to anyone who could help understand what was happening to them.

Junior was unmoved, and since Louis was the cause of their disembodiment, he wasn't about to be any help to them at all.

"Goddamnit. This is a whole lot of white folks you've got here," he said.

"I know it."

"Then why the hell are you trying to drop them off on me?" Junior raised an eyebrow.

"'Cause you asked for them," Louis whined a bit.

"I did not, Louis." Junior looked at the ash growing on his smoke. He strolled to his desk, tapped the cigarette on the edge of an amber glass ashtray.

"Sure you, did, *Jonathan*," Louis shot back, going with the formal first name, "the moment you knew that brick was a half breath from smashing into your face." They both looked to the now repaired and repainted window, smoked bronze and reflected redgold light filling the framed glass as the sun headed down in earnest to the west behind them. No one had called him Jonathan since his mother, LaDonna, who had passed a few years back. Even the old man just used Junior.

"Okay, but now that I think about it, what kind of Indian time shit is this, anyway, man? I got bricked weeks ago. Why'd you take so long, Louis?"

"It takes as long as it takes sometimes. Like you said, it's a whole lot of white folks."

Louis and his brother Arnault, who was a bit slower but better natured, had followed folks up from Mississippi and Louisiana back in the day, hung around, got conjured up when needed and took care of things around the neighborhood that required taking care of. There wasn't anything traditional to the people about them;

they had just appeared one day and never left, became part of the community, and came when called. But you needed to be careful of what you asked for, because those two got bored easy and left a whole lot subject to interpretation. Also—good to know—you could joke around with Arnault, but Louis was serious. He *always* took things literally. And he was the one who usually showed up, like tonight. It could be hard to deal with, but they both had folks' best interests at heart, and you needed to remember that whenever they entered your life. Still, Junior wished Arnault was here instead.

The heads were starting to stink. And the croaky sounds they were making without their vocal cords were getting on Junior's nerves.

"Louis." He stared. "You gotta take these things outta here."

Louis took a last drag off his smoke, swung open the door, and flicked the butt out into the street. "I don't, Junior," he disagreed. He looked at him with his luminous aqua eye and said, "I'm gonna go now, okay?"

"No man. It's not okay," Junior said. "You can't leave those here. Take them—"

"Yeah. I can," Louis said. "Not my problem, man. Tell you what. I'm gonna go take a leak, me. You better figure this out by the time I get back. Do you mind?" he asked, heading to the restroom in the back behind the open office space consisting of Junior's and Senior's desks, along with a small reception area, decorated and normally occupied by Betty, who was a big fan of the color pink as well as her kids; their pictures competed with bows, ribbons, and thank-you cards from their customers and parents of the Gresham Howlers, the Little League team Johnny Lee Sr. and Son, Realtors, sponsored at the Chicago Park District. Lions, Rotary, and other fundraisers dotted the ledge in front of the desk.

"Guess not," Junior muttered to his broad, disappearing back.

"Thanks," Louis and his excellent hearing said to the dark hallway, shutting the bathroom door.

Junior sat in the near dark, his own smoke almost done. He hesitated to put it out knowing the smell from the heads would rush in to fill the void. They clacked their teeth and slow rolled their dried eyes at him. He stubbed his cigarette out in the ashtray and walked over to the front entrance. He grabbed the heavy coir WELCOME mat and covered them up, then started back to his desk.

The front door smashed into his left side, a blast of frigid air clearing out any trace of stink. Junior, thrown facedown on the floor, used his new vantage point to make a mental note reminding himself to talk to the cleaning service about getting the carpet shampooed.

"Don't fucking move! Give me all your cash!" shouted the would-be robber, barely hanging on to keep the door he'd just crashed open from slamming into the wall.

"I can't," Junior moaned, turning his head and rolling his eye back trying to get a look at him. "I think you broke my back."

"Bullshit. Get up." The masked intruder pulled the hammer back on a cheap revolver, waved it at Junior.

"I can't move man, I'm telling you. I think you—"

The toilet flushed down the hallway.

The robber whipped his head around but kept the gun pointed at Junior. "Who the fuck is that?"

Junior inched his hands up, said, "Can I turn around?"

"I don't know. Can you? Thought your back was broke."

Jesuschrist this man. "I wanna try, I just don't wanna get shot."

"Keep them hands up and go slow." The toilet finished its flushing, water trailing away, Louis's business headed out to Lake Michigan.

Junior edged up with his elbows, crooked his head around.

Holymoly. He knew this guy, even with his eyeholes-only ski mask. Their families went to old St. Monica's Parish closer to downtown, but still on the South Side, built back in 1915 they said, to "educate Blacks and Indians." The gunman was a scrawny five and barely half a foot tall, had on too-short blue school-uniform pants with white socks and black shoes, plus a navy Eisenhower jacket zipped all the way up to the edge of a pulled-down red knit ski mask that looked homemade. And get a load of that pistol. Must've been his grandpa's WWI souvenir at least, maybe even some buffalo soldier shit. He'd been terrifying and entertaining the neighborhood with attempted stickups and liquor store grabs for a few years.

Junior laughed. "Hey, you fuckin' dummy—didn't you see the 'no cash on premises' sign in the window?"

"Don't talk to me that way. I'm holding a piece on you. Now who the fuck is in the bathroom?"

Junior laughed some more. "Man, Rudy, why the fuck you still wearing them pants? You flunked out of school four years ago."

"Who's Rudy?" the little crook asked unconvincingly, gun on Junior, eyes on the hallway.

"Man, quit. There ain't no money here, but the devil himself is in the bathroom. You picked a bad day to decide to be a robber and not a burglar. You need to leave." Junior lay all the way back down on the floor. "Last chance."

"Get up. Open the safe. I ain't playing around." Rudy sounded sweaty already.

"There's no safe here. We don't handle cash. Hence the sign in the window. Hey. Mind if I smoke, Rudy?"

"Better give me one, too." Rudy rubbed at his mouth under his mask, flipped the edge up to right under his nose.

Junior rolled over, stood up gradually, hands out to his sides, eyes steady on Rudy. "I got no problem with that. Probably gonna be your last, anyway." He slow reached in for his pack, shook out two squares, lit one and handed the other to Rudy, who put it in his mouth and said, "Got a light?"

Jeeeezuschrist. Junior sparked the Zippo, handed it to Rudy.

The robber puffed his cigarette over the flame, then snapped the lighter shut and put it in his pocket.

Second mistake, Junior thought.

"You sell houses. You got plenty of cash." Rudy wafted a couple of lazy smoke rings over his head. "Stop bullshitting me and hand it over."

"You don't know how this works, man. It's all paperwork. There's no cash changing hands."

"There isn't?" He eased the trigger back into place.

"No, Rudy." Junior sighed. "It's signatures and stamps and shit. Unless you're a gangster. Then everything's in cash. But you don't know about that, 'cause you ain't a gangster. So, drop the gun and go home."

"He ain't going nowhere," Louis boomed from the hallway, his voice appearing before him.

And though he didn't want to, sure didn't mean to, Rudy dropped the gun right there, pissed himself a little.

"Glad to see you figured it out, Junior," Louis said, getting closer.

Rudy had sunk to both knees, the rusty revolver forgotten off to his side as all of Louis filled the frame of the doorway, came into the dusky last light of day.

"Jesus, Louis," Junior said, shuddered and snapped on his desk lamp. "Even I jumped. You're a spooky motherfucker. Don't do that."

Rudy and his big, big eyes looked at Junior, then Louis, then back again. His mouth was moving and not talking, just clacking and clucking. It reminded Junior of the heads in the bag.

Louis lunged out of the hallway and put a big foot on the gun, flicked it away.

Rudy flinched, Louis only a few inches or so from his face now, the cigarette burning forgotten in his hand.

"Better smoke that, son," Louis said, pulling Rudy's ski mask all the way up. He turned to Junior, asked, "Do you know this man?"

"I do," Junior said. "His name is Rudy."

Louis pulled the mask back down. "Think he'll be missed?"

"I don't know, Louis."

"I do," Rudy said. "I sure will be."

"Mmmmm, I don't see it," Louis said.

"I do!" Rudy hollered this time.

"Don't yell in my shop," Junior said.

"Lighten up, Junior. He's about to die. He has every right to get excited." Louis rubbed at his jaw, cricked his big, shaggy head on his neck back and forth.

"What?" Rudy asked.

"Yeah, what?" Junior echoed.

"Look, man. This is perfect," Louis said.

"How do you figure?" Junior threw his head back, looked over his nose, brows drawn close over skeptical eyes.

"Yeah, how?" Rudy said, no idea what he was talking about.

"You need to be quiet, Rudy," Louis said. "Move that rug."

"I ain't doing shit. I'm gonna—"

"*Move that fucking rug,*" Louis hissed with the voice of ten livid demons.

Junior, mid-drag, took a coughing fit, the plan catching up with him.

Louis caught Junior's eye with his own cauled orb. He flashed a red nictitating membrane across it and back again, laughed, and said, "Those things'll kill ya."

"*Now,*" Louis growled, turning back to Rudy.

The thief pulled the heavy rug off the pile.

The smell from the heads was overwhelming; their clacking teeth rounded out the tidal-pool-of-dying-crabs-in-the-midday-sun vibe. It quicklike got hot and cramped in the cold gray office.

Dry heaves erupted out of Rudy, doubled over, hands on his knees.

Junior laughed deep and stubbed out his smoke, squatted next to the desk, catching his breath.

Louis slapped Rudy in the back of the head. "Knock it off. I hate that shit, me! You gon' make me t'row up, too," his accent cranking up. "Arrêt!"

"Okay, Rudy." Junior stopped laughing, stood up, wiped his hands on his pants. "Time to go."

"Where we going?"

"Well, the only 'we' actually going anywhere is me and him, and we're moving this party elsewhere. You're at the end of the line, though, so it's kinda rhetorical. Sorry, man," Junior said.

"What does that mean?"

"Means Louis here is gonna kill you, then me and him are gonna leave."

"You can't do that. No way."

Louis smiled. "Oh yes, many ways, Rudy. I might even let you pick one."

"Well, ain't this some bullshit." Rudy seemed genuinely outraged.

"Not really, Rudy," Junior offered by way of condolence. "You decided to rob us. Man, we're part of the fabric of this neighborhood. Salt of the earth. Pillars of the community, all that bullshit."

"Conjurers of werewolves and whatnot, masters of some demon shit. Why'on't you put *that* on the back of them Little League jerseys?" Rudy took the last drag off his cigarette, flicked it onto the street through the broken door and shoved a hand in his jacket's side pocket.

"Wouldn't fit. Besides, nobody would believe it, anyway." Junior sat on the edge of his desk, not even worried about that hand in the pocket.

"It's how you motherfuckers get away with this shit."

"Get away with what, Rudy? Not getting robbed?"

"Man, you escalated it. Yeah, sure, maybe I shouldn't've been robbing you or whatever, but you're about to pin the murder of a whole ass white math club on me or something." He yanked off his red ski mask, threw it at the door.

"Yeah, about that. Poor timing, I guess. Sorry. Framing you would be a piece of cake, though, Rudy. It's why I've been thinking you're better off dead than going to trial. It'll be easier on your family, and if you choose wisely, it'll be way better than riding the lightning over at 26th and Cal," Junior said.

"Mmmmhmmm." Rudy pursed his lips, sank his right eyebrow.

"But still. I didn't ask you to kick in my front door." Junior raised his left.

"*My* front door?" Rudy said. "This is your daddy's place. You just work here."

"Name's on the glass, isn't it?" Junior glared at him.

"C'mon, Junior. Let's get a move on with this," Louis said. "I'm tired of listening to you two."

"See Rudy? Now you're making him mad."

"Sounds kinda mad at you, too, Junior."

"He ain't though, right, Louis?"

Louis shook his head quick from side to side, like a dog coming in out of the rain. He said, "I'm tired of both of y'all's bullshit. Rudy, you're about to die, so what do you want? To shoot yourself, or me to do it? You better pick quick, or I'm going to chew out your t'roat."

"Hold on, Louis," Junior said. "We have to make it look like a burglary or something."

"Do you even have anything of value in here?" Louis said.

"Well, yeah, wow. That's kind of a shitty thing to say," Junior snorted.

"No offense, Junior. What would you have in here, anyway? It's a real estate office." Louis shrugged.

"But yeah, it's our home away from home," Junior said.

"Okay, fine. What've you got?" Louis looked around.

"You know if you had a safe with a li'l money in it, well . . ." Rudy said.

"Shut up, Rudy," they both said.

"There's some silverware in the kitchen, and a radio that—"

"It's *flat*ware, Junior."

"Well Rudy's kinda dumb," Junior said. "Just throw everything in a bag."

"Including your supercool AM radio?" Rudy said. "Seriously, man? I'm gonna die for some butterknives and a plastic radio? Maybe I *should* go to trial. What the hell. What are you gonna do? Just leave me dead holding a bag of trash?"

The heads clacked furiously.

"Knock it off, Rudy. What if we—"

Bam.

Bam, bam, bam.

Louis shot Rudy with his own pistol four times, all in the face, said, "Seriously, Junior."

"What the hell, Louis?!"

"What?" He rolled that cauled eye at Junior, threw his hands up.

"We were talking." Junior shuddered.

"Yeah. Too much. For Christ's sake. You never shut up some-times," Louis said.

"That's great, Louis. But now we gotta make it make sense."

"What do you mean?"

"Well, why is this guy dead in my place of business with a bag full of white people heads, and another with some cheap spoons, and an AM radio?"

"Good question, Junior."

"How about a burglary that'll let me and the old man ask for some insurance money? Like we lost a bunch of cash."

"But your own sign, ya fuckin dummy. They ain't gonna buy it." Louis crossed his arms.

"Goddamnit." Junior ran a hand through his slicked-back hair.

"Blaspheming . . ."

"Sorry," Junior said.

"Mmmmhmmm." Louis tilted his head to one side, locked the big greenblue eye on Junior.

"We're gonna have to take this whole show out to the car," Junior said, looking at Rudy. "Stick him in the car with the heads and some loot."

"That could work. What about your door? Doesn't look like much of a break-in."

"I'll throw a brick through it. Grab the March of Dimes thing. Add it to the take. Turn out some of the drawers and grab the radio. Put everything in a bag like we talked about."

Louis laughed. "I suppose. Hahaha. But wait. Oh, no, Junior. Not the AM radio. How. Will. You. Ever. Replace. It?"

"Shut up, Louis. I'll get it back from evidence. Anyway, told you to take them heads out of here. And there you go. We're right back where we started."

"Hate a told you so." Louis's turquoise socket winked in the early night fast filling the office.

"Me too." Junior nodded. "Unless I'm the one doing it. Now get that shit outta here, Louis."

"Fine, den, Junior." He stomped his foot, stuck out his chin.

"Don't forget to stick the car keys in the ignition."

"Yup yup," Louis said.

"And adjust the seat for his tiny ass. Don't screw this up," Junior said.

"Relax, man. This the shit I know how to do."

It was dark now, the sun all the way behind the rows of modest houses stretching west to the suburbs. It was quiet out this way in the evening. Not much happened in the neighborhood, at least on the other side of Western. Lately, nighthawks and foxes, badgers, and a coyote every now and again would show their face in the alleys between the streets, behind garages and garbage cans; spring was on the way no matter what the air said tonight. They had no worries first taking the bags out to the Falcon, then Rudy by the wrists and ankles. It was Junior, Louis, and a wind so cold you could watch it trace watery blue under the streetlight. Not a single car disturbed their work.

"What's next, Louis?" Junior asked, pulling out a cigarette, peeking in the back of the wagon, admiring his packing skills, wondering what the cops would make of this.

"What do you mean, man?" Louis twisted up his first two fingers and Junior passed him a smoke.

"Where do you go after this? What do you do?"

"Hadn't really thought about it. Me and Arnault, we just show up when we're called," Louis said, rolling the square between his spider-long clawed fingers.

"But what about when you're not on call, or whatever? Like, in between?" Junior asked, tapping the cigarette on the back of his hand.

"I don't know. We just wait, I guess." Louis snorted through his nose, raised the cigarette to his mouth. "Give me a light," he growled, annoyed.

Junior reached for his lighter. Not finding it in its usual spot, he patted his pockets, then cursed under his breath as he popped the wagon open, waved hello at dead Rudy and pulled his missing Zippo out of the would-be thief's pants. He lit his smoke, kept the flame going and brought it over to Louis, who slobbered and puffed away with his cigarette, the occasional drag hitting home, flame finally jumping to a cherry end.

"Where do you go? When you're waiting?" Junior couldn't leave it alone. He snapped the lighter shut; naphtha fumes lingered.

"I told you, man. I don't know." Louis blew out a huge cloud of smoke.

Junior's eyes got big as he thought, *Dang. Did you even inhale, Louis?* Then, quickly, "How can you not?" Junior pestered.

"I don't *know* that either," Louis said again, his own eyes bigger, the seafoam beryl flashing, milky clouds roiling across the caul.

"What *do* you know, then?" Junior squinted at him, pulled his face back ever so slightly.

They smoked in silence for a bit. Nothing came down the street except occasional breezes and the random smells of folks getting supper going. They could hear snatches of the neighborhood settling down for the night. Car doors slammed. TVs snapped on. Dogs barked, and gates screeched shut. Evening bloomed, its temperature dropping with the last of the light.

"I don't know about too much at all, like you keep saying without saying. But what I do know about is this." His gray lips and too-long teeth mistreated the cigarette he was trying to hold in his mouth while he held his thick ropey arms wide at his sides.

"Killing motherfuckers or smoking cigarettes?"

"Neither. I'm talking about helping, man. It's what we do. The neighborhood, the people." Louis rubbed away at some smoke that got in his eye.

Junior waited on him to finally quit. Louis relaxed.

"Okay, Louis. But in between the helping. What happens?"

"Nothing, I guess." He shrugged his massive shoulders, voice tired.

"How can that be? How is it nothing?" Junior stared at his cigarette, smoke pouring up in waves, tracing tiny gusts of air.

"It's not really nothing, but it ain't exactly anything." Louis thought for a bit, said, "We don't really exist, I guess, unless you call us, believe in us. It's all about the ask, Junior."

That tracks, doesn't it? Do any of us exist, after all, unless or until we're called to do so? Are we really alive if someone isn't dreaming us into existence? We're all of us one dimension removed, one silent plane away from someone else's reality, waiting to be conjured up. Who sends prayers your way? Who calls you in? Who's remembering you exist? Is it down to just you? How do you reach them, remind them to think of you even as you pull apart, fade and twist under the blackness of space, drifting beyond sound? Past the void's silence, the in-between's pieces of quiet, when

no

one

will

listen

to

you

scream.

Theodore C. Van Alst Jr. (enrolled Mackinac Bands of Chippewa and Ottawa Indians) is the author of mosaic novels *Sacred Smokes* and *Sacred City* as well as the editor of *The Faster Redder Road: The Best*

UnAmerican Stories of Stephen Graham Jones. He is an Active HWA member whose work has been published in *Southwest Review*, *The Rumpus*, *Chicago Review*, the *Journal of Working-Class Studies*, *Apex Magazine*, Electric Literature, *Indian Country Today*, and *The Massachusetts Review*, among others.

DEAD OWLS

MONA SUSAN POWER

Every summer, my parents put me on a Greyhound bus from Chicago to Bismarck, North Dakota, so I can stay with Aunt Phyllis for two weeks. Mama clambers on the bus to get me settled, trying to find a nice Amish person to look out for me. There's always one who agrees to be my guardian, at least through Minnesota. Mama says she would like to go, too, but we need a break from each other. I agree silently in my head. Agreeing out loud would be disrespectful. In my world older folks can say any damn thing that takes you apart, but a kid has to swallow the truth until you grow up.

Aunt Phyllis and I get along easy. She can be stern in the way of her job as a school nurse for United Tribes Technical College—dispensing aspirin for headaches, VapoRub for a chest cold. But with me she smiles and listens, goes along with my modest proposals—a dip in the school swimming pool, catching a movie at the new Kirkwood Mall. (Well, it's been there for at least ten years now, but locals are still excited enough to call it "new.")

Aunt Phyllis even agrees to take me to see *The Shining* with

Jack Nicholson, which is just out, though she doesn't like horror.
I like anything spooky and have read all of Stephen King's books.
I already know what'll happen in *The Shining*, but don't care. I
want to *see* it.

It's ninety degrees here today, so I don't understand why Aunt
Phyllis brings a blanket into the theater. We've got our hands
full with popcorn and Coke, and now this heavy green blanket.
Embarrassed, I look around at people in other seats to catch if
they've noticed. I'm what Mama calls a "super sensitive preteen," at
that age where you think you're the center of attention, with everyone monitoring your every move like they care. Which Mama
says they don't. She could be right, but I sneak glances around us
anyway. No one seems to notice. I like that the audience is over-
whelmingly Native—probably mostly my own tribe, Dakota, or
members of the Three Affiliated Tribes. In Chicago, we're always
outnumbered, like a million to one. When the lights go down and
Coming Attractions begin to roll, Aunt Phyllis spreads the blanket
across her shoulders. She tells me I can have a wing if I get cold. I
shake my head, no.

I have to let go of the book version to like the movie; there's
a lot of changes. But creepy is creepy, and Jack Nicholson does
"crazy" really well. I'm gonna be popping out at folks with my
"Heeeeere's Johnny!" imitation for days. At the movie's end when
the camera does a close-up of Jack's dead face, frozen like an ice
man, I realize Aunt Phyllis is shivering. She clutches the blanket in
a death grip like it's field dressing to keep her innards from falling
out. I put my hand on her arm and she looks at me. Her eyes are
big with terror; they take a second to focus. When she recognizes
me, she smiles. "I'm okay, Amy," she says. "That was *too* much!"

I've noticed that when you see a good horror film, your senses
open up like you're a bug with a thousand feelers. You hear more
noises, sense every breeze. That night when I'm settled into my

aunt's apartment on the United Tribes campus, a creaky old building that's been here since the place was a military fort, I can't shake the feeling someone's watching me. I'm reading one of Phyllis's fat romance novels where the bad guy becomes the good guy though *I* don't forgive him for an early rape the way the heroine does, but I'm distracted by the chilling sensation of an observer studying my every move. I keep looking from my makeshift bed on the couch to the living room's grand staircase, which is chopped halfway up, a wall built over it to make the second floor into another apartment. I swear there's an invisible man hunkered down on the useless steps, not just watching me, but absorbing. Taking something away. When I get tired enough, I fall asleep, though I'm glad I have Phyllis's green blanket across me now.

I wake up to the stares of owls. Phyllis lives with what she calls "a plague of owls." Someone gave her an owl clock for her birthday, then a friend made her a macramé plant hanger featuring an owl, and now she's got a menagerie but is too tenderhearted to give them away. Most mornings they look like they're grinning, but it's raining today, so every stinking owl, whether ceramic or painted or woven of string, glares at me like I'm stealing something. I stick out my tongue at them and make the bed.

I ask Aunt Phyllis about ghosts, if she thinks there might be another presence in the building. I know United Tribes used to be Fort Lincoln, an internment camp for "enemy aliens" during World War II. Hell, *we* were considered "enemy aliens" in our own territory not long ago, so I have some sympathy for the ones locked up here back in the day. Maybe a few of them are still angry, wandering around nursing grudges?

It's like Aunt Phyllis doesn't hear me; she asks if I want waffles for breakfast. But once we're eating that golden food sweet with syrup, Phyllis launches into a story about her first love.

"This is back when I was a nursing student, serious, no time for something floofy, like romance." Phyllis has a dark moon face that features a sensible mole at the side of her mouth. It's large as a chocolate chip and seems to affirm everything she says. Somehow, I can't imagine it allowing any kissing. "At least, that's how I was until I met Hiro."

Phyllis and the mole keep talking. "From my looks, he thought I was one of his people, and I figured he'd be disappointed to learn I was Dakota. But that made him even more excited, and he jumped around in that horrible imitation of how we *never* really danced, hitting his mouth with his hand. Woo woo woo . . ."

Ugh! I roll my eyes, and Hiro has definitely lost some appeal at this point.

"I was volunteering here all those years ago, getting on-the-job training looking after German seamen we'd hauled from their ships, and later fellow Americans of Japanese descent that white people thought might be spies."

Yeah, what *is* it about white folks? I think. So paranoid about anyone who looks different. Phyllis tells me that Hiro was from California, didn't even speak Japanese much, though he could understand it when his grandparents were talking. They were dragged out of their American lives because Japan attacked Pearl Harbor. He talked to Phyllis whenever he could, told her she was beautiful, made her tiny cranes out of paper scraps he said were meant to bring abundance. He asked if she'd consider dating him when the war was over.

Phyllis's moon face goes sad. "I never gave him a straight answer, though I *did* dream of dating him. No one *ever* gave me attention like that before. I was always 'Buffalo Woman' to everyone, even as a girl. Which I realize now is an honorable Dakota name, but when I was young just made me feel like Old Reliable."

She tells me Hiro was handsome, his black hair falling in a wave over one eye. "Like a sweet rogue," she says. The mole looks astonished.

"I should've gotten over my shyness," Phyllis scolds. "We don't remember that others can't read our minds, that what we think must be obvious *isn't* always clear to them. The rest of his family were in an Arizona camp. Not sure why they were separated. He was alone here. I could've made the difference instead of sopping up all his compliments and love, taking all his luck one crane at a time."

I know where this is headed. The only question is, how bad? Turns out, pretty bad. Phyllis's moon face is crying when she tells me Hiro hanged himself in one of the dorms. She gestures with her hand, pointing up, when of course what happened to him was an awful dropping down. I wonder if this apartment is one of those dorms. I know enough not to ask. Aunt Phyllis never does say whether she thinks United Tribes is haunted. Her story is her answer. Tragic things happened here.

A week into my visit, I wake up shivering. My teeth are chattering. The green blanket is up around my shoulders but can't make a dent in the cold. The owls look wary, even though bright sunlight streams through the windows and across their wings. I'm shaking so hard I lose coordination, can't stand up. "Auntie!" I bellow, and she comes running in her bathrobe, which I notice for the first time is a silk kimono—the jazziest item she's ever worn.

Aunt Phyllis rubs warmth into my skin, hugs me close until her heart pumps life into my core.

"Why's it so cold in here?" she asks, opening the windows. Warm air smelling of cut grass floats through the window, cheering both me and the owls. The clutch of ice is gone. Still, she makes me drink warm cocoa with an extra Vitamin C tablet, just in case. Takes my temperature.

"Normal," she says, then laughs, as if it's ridiculous to attach that word to *anyone* in our family. I laugh, too, and cross my eyes at her, stick out my tongue. For Aunt Phyllis, I'll be a kid again instead of a near grown-up, poised to be thirteen.

Every night now I feel watched, though I can't see anyone else in the living room except the owls. I'm reading a more high-quality romance novel, set in the times of Arthur and Merlin, wishing I had magic in my hands right about now, or at least a sword. I'd make visible whatever is stalking me, run it through. I wonder why *this* visit is different—why of all the times I've stayed here it's *this* year that feels haunted, like I can't be alone with myself? The useless stairs always gave me the creeps at night, but not to where I felt studied, judged. Is it my fault, this spookiness? Did I bring something that isn't appreciated? All I'm doing most nights is reading. Aunt Phyllis goes to bed early and her television doesn't get good reception.

Mama phones me the next morning like she can read my thoughts. We don't talk for very long—it's so expensive—but when Aunt Phyllis pops in the shower, I ask Mama about ghosts at United Tribes.

"Don't you remember?" She sounds irritated. According to Mama, I'm at that age where everything I'm told goes in one ear and out the other, and items worth remembering are displaced by utter nonsense she doesn't know *where* I pick up! "We saw one on the campus road that time," she says.

A prickle of cold runs across my scalp. I'm staring at my aunt's owl calendar pinned to the wall beside the kitchen phone, where a Great Horned Owl, dignified as Merlin, watches me back like he can see beyond tooth and brain into my very soul. I close my eyes. "Tell me again," I say to Mama. My voice sounds young and pleading.

"Well, I guess you were little," Mama concedes. She has

gentled—something you can never count on, but when it happens, you're grateful. "You must've just been out of kindergarten." As Mama talks, I can envision the penny loafers I wore back then with such pride, what I thought of as my first grown-up shoes. Mama tells me how we stayed with Aunt Phyllis but drove down to Cannon Ball one day to visit her brother. Didn't return until after supper. "It was twilight when we reached the entrance to United Tribes and as soon as we crossed over to the main trail, we saw the man in the blanket."

Yes, I can see him now; he was shuffling by the side of the road, a gray blanket pulled close around him, covering his head and body. The way he walked made him look old. Mama reached across me to roll down the window, prepared to ask if he needed a ride. I remember her gasp, how she rolled the window shut faster than I thought was possible, and then the car leapt forward. Mama was never one to shelter me, so when I asked her what was wrong, she'd said: "That thing isn't a man. He doesn't have any legs or feet. He's floating, not walking."

"An unhappy ghost," I'd chirped, mimicking something I'd heard. Always wanting to sound so smart. And Mama just said: "Is there any other kind?"

Now she says she hasn't a clue what kind of ghost he was. A Mandan warrior, his entire village wiped out by smallpox? A camp internee, missing his relatives? "There are layers of loss in most places," Mama says cheerfully, probably mollified by having my complete attention for once. I thank her, and we get off the phone.

I have only two nights left here in North Dakota. I'm already missing Aunt Phyllis and maybe even her owls. I stay up late to savor the last drop of this visit and fall asleep reading the book about King Arthur. Someone wakes me by shaking me rudely—so hard I'm nearly knocked off the couch. But there is no couch, only tall grass and the Missouri River only a half mile in the distance, sunrise painting it a sludgy red that looks like blood. At first, I think I'm alone, sitting on the ground with my legs poked out in front of me as if I'm a wooden doll. But I hear a polite clearing of the throat on my left and note a young woman collapsed onto the grass in a puff of old-fashioned dress. She's pretty, though. Her eyes are cold gray, like the blade of a steel knife. The part in her hair is severe, so perfectly straight I again think of sharpness, of slices and cutting. The rest of her hair is wound up in a fancy swirl of braids—it must take some time to craft that particular look. I can tell she doesn't like me from the way she holds her mouth. *Her lips are tight as a trap,* is what I'm thinking, which doesn't even make sense, but I trust the thought like a warning. I look down at myself, still wearing the pajamas I wore to bed. Maybe she doesn't like me because of how messy I am—my long hair in tangles down my back, my pajamas rumpled. *No, she doesn't like you because you're Dakota,* that savvy voice in me says, the one that feels like it can read minds. I want to get away, to find the trapdoor that leads back into United Tribes and Aunt Phyllis's owl-infested apartment, but the cold knives of the woman's glare keep me in place. I can't move beyond wiggling my toes.

Like a bird flying up from a hidden nest, she rises suddenly in the most graceful motion. She reaches down and grabs my arm with icy fingers, yanks me to my feet. She's impossibly strong even though we're the same height. She keeps hold of my arm and drags me a little behind her, so I stumble through the grass as we march toward the river. *A forced march* echoes in my head. She takes me to higher ground so we can look across the river in the direction of Mandan. Though nothing appears the way it should. The streets and highway are gone, and there's a fort in the distance. She gives me a shake with her cold little hand, and that snap adjusts my vision; it's like I'm looking through binoculars or a fancy tele-scope, though it's only my eyes blinking in morning light. I see the fort up close, see a column of men on horseback, their guidons whipped by prairie winds. The woman points, has me follow her finger, which singles out a figure I immediately recognize, someone I even wrote a paper about in fourth grade: General George Armstrong Custer. In my paper, he was a reckless egomaniac, an ignorant fool hungry for gold and glory—nothing more than a vanquished enemy, a squashed bug. But here I am facing Libby, his widow, which complicates everything.

I can't believe I didn't figure out sooner who she was. I'm a little afraid of the next thought: *What's she want with me?* The obvious answer follows straight away: *It can't be anything good.* Libby looks capable of strangling me with her dainty white hands. I think she suspects that if I'd had ringside seats at the General's final battle, I wouldn't exactly be cheering him on, rather helping my people dispatch the crazy soldier and his men.

I want *out* of this dream. It's a small comfort to realize I must be asleep, wandering through tall grass with the dead widow of a General my people ended. I've never dreamed something so real before. I can feel the cool earth beneath my toes, feel snapping winds, smell grass and the light floral scent of Libby's perfume. I take a step backward, away from Libby and the view of her husband leading his men on their last campaign. Then another step. Libby doesn't notice. She's too busy watching the Seventh Cavalry head out for Montana Territory, their final destination. I turn to run and that's when Libby realizes she's losing her hostage. She jumps on my back, knocks me down. I'm embarrassed by how weak I am compared to her, but she has the strength of death. She lifts my head only to smash it on the ground, pounding it against a flat rock. My face is warm with blood. My thoughts no longer have anything intelligent to say. I'm on the lip of a vast darkness, about to lose consciousness, when I hear a screech.

Libby's weight is off my back. Gentle hands reach for me and set me upright. Libby is gone, as is the view. I'm standing alone on a useless set of stairs that leads to a blank wall and never the second floor. There's blood dripping on my toes. But I was wrong; I'm not alone. A young man is beside me, his arm around my waist like he's afraid I'll crumple if he lets me go. Which I just might. It's hard to see past the blood in my eyes, but I notice the young man's thick black hair, how it covers one eye in a rogue wave.

When I wake in the morning, poor Aunt Phyllis discovers me mysteriously battered, my blood spattering the couch and floor. Her menagerie of owls has been destroyed—the ceramics broken, the macramé hanger slashed to pieces. We should be frightened and sad, but there's an air of sweetness in the room that covers the mess. Aunt Phyllis gently leads me into the bathroom where she washes me, inspects my injuries. She insists we check for concussion since I have a nasty lump above one eye. She doesn't ask for explanations yet. Sometimes it's convenient being Native—we've got a pretty high tolerance for weirdness.

Aunt Phyllis is checking me over again before we have breakfast. She asks me questions about the month and date, my address. She moves her finger around for me to follow, which reminds me of Libby, pointing out her lost General. Phyllis notices my right hand, how it's still balled up in a fist like I expect a fight. She covers it with her own hand, squeezing gently as if to say, it's okay, you're safe, you can let down your guard. So I allow my hand to open. Aunt Phyllis notices what's hidden there before I do. I can tell because she gasps and covers her heart. The paper is pretty well squashed, but as it sits on my open palm, it begins to unwrinkle itself and once more takes the shape of an origami crane.

Aunt Phyllis is crying. Big wet tears that skirt her sensible mole. She reaches for the crane, then hesitates.

"It's okay," I tell her, and I lift the bird higher as if encouraging it to fly from my hand to hers. "I was in danger and he saved me."

Mona Susan Power is an enrolled member of the Standing Rock Sioux Nation. She is the author of four books of fiction: *The Grass Dancer* (winner of the 1995 PEN/Hemingway award), *Roofwalker*, *Sacred Wilderness*, and the novel *A Council of Dolls*. Her fellowships include an Iowa Arts Fellowship, a James Michener Fellowship, a Radcliffe Bunting Institute Fellowship, a Princeton Hodder Fellowship, a USA Artists Fellowship, a McKnight Fellowship, and a Native Arts and Cultures Foundation Fellowship. Her short stories and essays have been widely published in journals, magazines, and anthologies. She lives in Saint Paul, where she is currently working on a new novel titled *The Year of Fury*.

THE PREPPER

MORGAN TALTY

"Mahčawi-áwassis" is how Mom starts her letters. Unusual child, she began to call me when I was sentenced. "Kosemol"—I love you—was always part of the letters, but it was never the last thing she wrote. She ended each letter with "Aməssanínakʷat." *It is a disgrace.* I never knew, and still don't, what she meant by "it." Maybe if I hadn't done what I did to my grandfather (he was dying, for Christsakes, and he made me believe), if he hadn't been part of my crimes, her letters would end only with kosemol.

I was more sick in the head back then. And if I were eligible for parole, that's exactly what I'd tell the Maine board.

I don't know when it started, my illness, my not feeling right. As a child? A young adult? In middle school on the rez, I took a vow of silence after a white teacher told me to stop answering so many questions in history class. Almost two years I didn't talk. I mean I did, alone and sometimes with my grandfather, who I know relayed my words to my worried mother—my mother who perhaps relayed them on long-distance calls to my father, who couldn't care less about me—but I never spoke to anyone else. I

broke my silence not even on my behalf. I spoke without thinking. I was walking the rez roads down to a social (I wanted ribs
from the BBQ) when I realized a truck carrying dirt was about to
hit a small girl and I yelled—screamed, really, with all that I had
held in for two years—for her to move. She did. It just came out
of me—I'd had no control. I felt so bad I'd broken my vow that
that night I kneeled in front of the open woodstove, flames licking
at my face, and thought about sticking my head into the fire as
punishment. But my grandfather was there, he was always there,
always always, and he said to me, "Why would you want to do
that, gwus? You saved a life."

Why did I want to do it? Maybe I've always had something
wrong with me.

Aside from these feelings, these acts and others like pinching
my skin until I bled or hitting myself, it wasn't until I was twenty-
three when I started to get really sick. It was spring 2012. I was
working full-time at a bakery off the reservation, making sure that
if the machine making cream horns fucked up I was there to tell
someone about it. My father, who was white (Irish and something else) and with whom I had no relationship (he loved my
mother for one night only), had died from a massive heart attack
the year prior, and had left behind a lawsuit against Social Security,
which in death he won and in life I inherited. Just under forty
thousand—enough, when the time came, to allow me to do what
I thought needed to be done, to act against what was coming or
to act against what had always been here.

When I got sick, I still lived at home on the reservation, the
Island. Same house, same room. All the houses on Sand Beach
Road looked the same: built with federal monies, all shaped like
rectangles in different colors. Our house was beige, fawn colored.
Mom worked as a CNA in Overtown, wiping shitty asses, and
so what I brought in from the bakery helped with rent and food

and utilities and cell bills and TV and internet. Growing up, we struggled, and before my grandfather got sick he helped out when he could, with whatever was leftover from his low-paying job as a janitor. And my living at home was also good: I was there to help with my grandfather, who was dying that summer, slowly and not yet so painfully of stage four mesothelioma (the coming months is when he got bad sick). The asbestos the BIA used when building some homes on the reservation had something to do with it, but they deny it. Or maybe it was because he smoked three packs of Marlboro Reds a day. Either way, he had tumors pressing on his organs. Our house had only two rooms, and he slept in my bed. I took the floor.

Again, it came on so slowly, my not feeling good. One morning I woke up so dizzy, so faint, and my heart racing. I counted, and my pulse dashed at 127 bpm. The feeling went away, but then that night on the floor I woke up every hour, my chest chilled like dry ice. It hurt to swallow, and the pain never went away, and each night was the same. It was real even though it wasn't. Google suggested I had esophageal cancer, and I convinced myself I would die along with my grandfather who lay in bed; thought, maybe, I'd die before him. I saw the only doctor on the rez, this white guy we all called Doctor Tim and whose eyes were as wide as half-dollars. (I wonder if he retired specifically because of what I did to him?) Doctor Tim had me see an ENT whose scope hooked my nose like the gill of a fish as he looked down into my throat. "All looked fine," he said. I then did a barium swallow—"just to be sure"—and I lay in all sorts of positions while I drank a liquid as thick and as white as paint and watched it on a monitor as it traveled down the center of my skeleton.

Nothing. Everything was fine except everything was not fine.

So they gave me meds. An antidepressant at first. Lexapro, and some Ativan for the period of time it took for the Lexapro to

kick in, which never did kick in. So they changed it up at what
felt like random, a Bingo cage rolling and instead of numbered
balls out poured Prozac and Klonopin. But that didn't work,
and I continued to wake each night, on the cold floor, at every
hour, with the same chilled knowingness that I was dying. I got
so skinny but bloodwork all came back good. Ten months had
passed, my grandfather still alive but the pain really there, and
I had lost my job. But my dead father's money arrived, to us, to
the living, yet I didn't care about it until months later, when I
was taken off the Lexapro, taken off the Prozac (the Klonopin
remained), and they put me on Seroquel, and over time Doctor
Tim increased the dose until I got fat and they settled at a mil-
ligram almost fifty below the number I was ultimately sentenced
to prison for without parole: five hundred years. What a number!
Mom wrote once that if Columbus had a sentence like mine, he'd
just be getting out. She ended that letter like she ended all of her
letters: Aməssanínakᵂat. It is a disgrace.

My grandfather had two children: a son and a daughter. Mom
was first. I'll tell the story even though it fills me with rage. His
son, an uncle I never met, was born with Down syndrome. His
name was Nelson, but they called him Nelly. The whole rez called
him Nelly. (I would have called him Uncle Nelly.) My grandfather, who told me everything in the world, never spoke of him to
me, and so it was Mom who said Uncle Nelly was hard to raise.
This was in the '60s, and at the time our tribe's health facilities,
Mom said, were falling apart like waterlogged paper cups ("those
ceilings were always leaking and damp," she'd said). Everyone on
the rez loved Uncle Nelly, especially a medicine man who is now
dead. (He thought Nelly's condition gave him a gift no one else
had.) Nelly was given the same opportunities as everyone else:

he went to school on the rez, and then went to high school in Overtown. Mom once said that it was hard enough being ski-cin, pɑnawάhpskek, at a white school, but add on a disability and things get tougher.

Nelly loved two things: yelling "bullshit!" and holding shiny objects. Things that sparkled and caught light like heaven. The wenooches at that school knew that, and one day when the bell rang, they used promises of a palmful of sparkly sequins to lure Uncle Nelly to one of their trucks whose back fender had a dozen ropes tied to it and on the ends dragging the ground were a dozen shiny cans covered in those sequins.

They made him chase after the cans. They drove slow. Drove fast. Never let him get one. It was a game, a terrible game, and it went on for some time. No one really knows what happened. Maybe he got hold of one and the driver gassed it and pulled Nelly forward, but what is known is that he fell and bashed his head so hard he ultimately died of his injuries.

I wish I knew my grandmother. She died not too long after Uncle Nelly. My grandfather said it was diabetes that did it, but Mom told me the truth. If the men responsible had gone to jail, if some form of justice had prevailed, maybe that darkness wouldn't have taken my grandmother. But that's not how it worked.

I said my grandfather always seemed to be near me when I needed him. I tell Nelly's story because I am my grandfather's Nelly. The one he missed out on. Growing up, he taught me every-thing Uncle Nelly couldn't learn. At his camp, cigarette hanging from his mouth or dip in his lower lip when we needed to be scent free, he taught me how to defend (these were the most fervent les-sons). He taught me to hunt. Taught me how to track, to assess the edges of animal prints in mud or snow. Taught me to be quiet (Uncle Nelly didn't know what quiet meant). To set snares and where to set them. He showed me how to handle guns—rifles and pistols—and how to clean them, how to care for them. How to aim and to fire. How not to miss even though at first I wanted to. I had no desire to kill a deer or a moose or a rabbit. It wasn't like I was brainwashed by all those colorful Disney cartoons I watched—like *Bambi*—and ultimately looked at these animals as something human. No. They looked so foreign, like stars, so pristine in real life that to kill them felt like a grave sin. The way a doe's eyes blinked, the way its tail flapped. But my grandfather insisted, and with a shaky aim I managed to shoot and kill my first deer, was able to untangle the rabbit's limp neck from the snare. My grandfather showed me how to pray, how to thank the animal for its life. He showed me how to butcher the animal, to make use of every inch of its gifted body. "Don't waste," he said. He showed me how much salt and pepper to put on a readied steak, showed me when to take the steak out of the skillet to let it rest and bleed out. Before we ate—those fresh steaks were so tough to chew, like belief and faith—he showed me how to set the first plate not for us but for the spirits we were giving thanks to and giving back to, but I still wonder if we did give anything back.

There are some things I wish I could take back. Notélətamən, I add often in my letters to Mom. *I'm sorry about it.* But she never acknowledges it. She can't. Or maybe, like myself, she doesn't know what "it" is, can't pinpoint exactly what we were or still are in conflict with.

When I was sick, those eleven months later, when I was on those antipsychotics, I should have told Doctor Tim about the delusions. I should have. But I felt fine even though I was not fine. I felt welcome in my mental state (I no longer thought I was dying). With my father's money, and with no job, I bought a PlayStation 4 and *Dying Light*, a zombie game. This was a bit before Christmas and the rez was covered in snow. My mother didn't care too much that I wasn't working—she liked having me home with my grandfather. At night, when she was home, we all listened to my grandfather's favorite music—he loved James Taylor and Carole King—while we played board games. Scrabble, Monopoly, and Life, which my grandfather thought was too unrealistic. "Where's the 'your family member died' card?" or "'You've run out of smokes'?" As sick as he was, he asked often for a cigarette, and one time I got him one but at the very moment he put the lit smoke to his mouth I took it from him and he called me a fucking shithead.

During the board games, we always laughed at what he said. I liked these times while they lasted, sure, but I preferred when my mother was at work, when the music wasn't playing (I could listen to "Fire and Rain" only so many times). In our small room my grandfather watched me play video games, and, when he felt well enough to make sound, each time I sliced through a zombie he'd let out a "Ho!" or a "Get him!" like it was a sport he was proud I played. I would go all night, almost all day too—I barely slept, barely ate (but was still getting fat from the meds). I got hooked. Or I was hooked by something that met my illness and made sense. When I beat the game, I spent hours on the web, lost in forums reading people discuss the end they said was coming December 21. I read an article in which Boston university Professor Dr. Steven Schlozman said an outbreak would be very, very unlikely, which I believed for a brief moment until all I'd absorbed took over my brain like a virus. I ate up all the movies: *Night of the Living Dead*, *The Last Man on Earth*, *I Am Legend*, *28 Days Later*, and both *Dawn of the Dead*s. I even tried watching *Shaun of the Dead* but I detested it because I thought they were making a joke of something that I knew was coming, that I knew wasn't unlikely but very, very likely. The signs were all there.

My grandfather watched the films with me occasionally, when he felt well enough, which became rarer and rarer. Mom worried about all the gruesome images, asked my grandfather if this was okay, and he said it was. "I like it, doosis," he said. "It's comforting that they suffer more than me." A laugh. His laugh. When she had gone to work, I asked if that were true, and he said "Yes." I wondered if the movies gave him nightmares. They gave me nightmares, but I loved them. They felt like training simulations.

One dark night, we were watching *The Walking Dead* (I'd bought the first season) and after the third episode, I asked my grandfather if there was a word for zombie in our language, in our culture.

"No," he said. "Nothing like that exists for us."

"There's gotta be a word," I said.

He thought. "If there is, I don't know it."

"Really?"

He thought again. Or maybe he was just trying to catch his breath. "Nàka, maybe."

"Nàka?" I repeated. "What's that?"

"The former living."

"So it means zombie?"

"No, not in that sense."

I went to ask more but my grandfather's face scrunched up in pain and he grit his teeth so I let him be.

Nàka. A word can mean anything if you make it, and I made it out to be just that. The Nàka were coming. I don't need to say it again, don't need to say what I would tell the parole board.

I began to take notes. I rewatched every Nàka film and TV show, pausing them at what I thought were important moments, lessons to be learned. Thought and considered the ways people weren't prepared and thought about how if they were what their futures would have looked like. How different it would have been for them. My annotations were immaculate, precise, and specific. It was my study, which is what my lawyer argued later to contest the prosecutors' argument that this material, which included maps and secret locations of stashed goods, was indication that it was all planned, all premeditated.

I took these notes when my grandfather was sleeping. I think it was the one thing I never wanted him to know about, afraid he wouldn't get it. But once, when I thought he was out cold, he was awake.

"What are you doing, gwus?" he asked. The TV was paused and glowed the quiet room a soft blue.

I didn't want to tell him, but I told him, because I always told him everything.

"I'm scared," I said.

"Of what?"

"When the day comes."

"That day's not coming," he told me. "You're worrying about nothing."

That he didn't see it, or couldn't see it, angered me. It was the second time I was ever angry at him, the first being when I was nine and he took my .22 rifle away because I wasn't paying attention and shot too close to him near the bottles I was aiming at, the bottles he was setting up for me. Looking back now, of course I shouldn't have been angry with him. He was right. Nothing was coming. But I couldn't see that. Couldn't agree with what he thought. When Mom was gone during the day (or night, when she worked nights), I began to move the TV and PlayStation out to the living room, took notes and studied out there. When Mom was home, I stayed away from the room. My grandfather started to make loud pained noises, and sometimes, when he was feeling his absolute worst, I'd hear him say to Mom, hear him plead with her, "Let me go," wanting Mom to make his end come sooner, something he never said to me because when Mom was gone, I left my grandfather alone in the dark. It was my punishment for him. I felt no remorse at the time, but now, now I feel it. The deep shame. But back then? I didn't care. I had to prepare for the day. I had to be able to save us from what was coming.

My neglecting him lasted almost two weeks. It hurts me to say this, but he was the one who brought me back to him, the one who apologized. Now *that's* something I should have been sentenced to jail for. I went to his bedside to give him his meds. "I've done some thinking," he said, using everything in him to speak. "And there is a story in our culture of the dead rising."

The story was not true, I later realized. But I was after information, anything that could help me and my mother survive. My grandfather, I knew, would not make it to live in the new, fallen world that was coming.

"What is it?" I asked, eager. I sat down on the bed.

I remember he had to remind me, by pointing, to give him his medication. And I apologized two, three times, hurried to give him it, waited for him to swallow it, which he did with difficulty.

"What's the story?" I asked.

"I only ever heard it in panawáhpskek," he said.

"But you can translate it?"

He could, and he did. At the time, I did not realize he was telling me the story of ésahsit, the flaming skeleton. Long ago, he said, two skicins went hunting, and when they unloaded their canoes on a place they thought was good they set up camp. In the middle of the night, while one slept, the other saw the Nàka peeking at them, coming at them through the trees. The way my grandfather described it was something out of a movie. So stereotypical. How did I not see it, I can ask, but I know how. I was so lost.

The one skicin who was up and saw the Nàka walking all slow and drooped and growling tried to wake his friend, yelled at him, but he slept so hard. "He's coming to eat us," he told his friend, but his friend did not wake up. And so, he stood and aimed and shot one, two, three, four arrows at the Nàka, but the Nàka kept getting closer. There was nothing he could do, so he decided to leave his friend. He had no choice. He got in his canoe and hurried back to his people, to whom he then told the story, my grandfather said, and the next day a search party went out. But all they found was blood and some organs, no bodies, and they followed after the tracks, which led to Mount Katahdin, where it is said the Stone People live, first beings with hearts of ice. Our ancestors searched, but all they found were tracks. Bloody tracks. They never found the first Nàka, and they never found, my grandfather said, either one of the dead as they walked among the living.

Deep down I think I knew he was lying, because why would I have asked, then, "You're telling the truth?"

"Gwus," he said. "Cross my heart and hope to die."

And that was it. Whatever doubt I had about that story was gone like most of the human race would be soon. I refused to accept that the story he told was about the ésahsit, was about the flaming skeleton. It was about the Nàka. Later, when lying in the back of an ambulance with several bullets in my arm and a hole through my leg, my bloody hand cuffed to a gurney, I would realize he lied. And I would realize why he lied, what he wanted: me. He wanted me back, so that perhaps I could do what my mother would not. But right then, at his bedside and holding his hand, the story over, I felt I was not alone in what I saw coming: The End.

I stopped researching in the living room and brought everything back to the bedroom. My grandfather, whose pain was getting worse, asked questions when he could. "Do you have plans?" "How are you preparing?" "Will you think of me?" Looking back on it, the questions were all ambiguous. They were never specific, never asked in the context of the great Nàka rising I saw coming, so perhaps he was asking me about after he was gone, was trying to see my future that he would not live to see because he would be dead. He had such terrible chest pain, could barely breathe. Could barely swallow. The tumors pressed hard against his organs. Mom started to stay home more to be with him, to be with us. I was glad she stayed home, because I had preparations to make. My leaving infuriated Mom at first. "He's your grandfather," she said. "And he needs you here." But when the problems of his chest and breathing cleared like a cloudy sky, my grandfather said, "He's preparing to miss me. Let him be."

If only he had any idea what I was preparing, I don't think he would have defended my decision to leave when Mom stayed home.

"He's preparing," my grandfather said again, to which my mother finally said to me, "Go on then."

In a way I was preparing. Preparing to miss him. Miss him in a world I thought was going to be taken over by the Nàka. Preparing to survive and be alive to miss him and remember him and to give thanks to the spirits whom among my grandfather would walk.

Late April he was at his worst. The snow was gone and the earth was soft. I started buying, making purchases. In my research I had a long list of things to buy. ("It wasn't premeditated!" my lawyer yelled.) The first gun I bought was a Glock. Then I bought another one. A third and fourth and fifth. Then I bought two concealed pistols and ankle holsters (I strapped one to me at all times). I bought knives. Long knives. Short knifes. And like the pistol on my ankle, I kept one on me every day, and I even slept with it. Then I bought a crossbow, a powerful one (400 feet per second). Then rifles. Lots of rifles. Semiautomatic ones. Automatic ones. And shotguns. A lot of pump action. I bought so much ammo. There were a dozen gun sellers in the area, and I went to all of them, buying and buying and buying. The last three weeks my grandfather remained alive, I spent close to thirty thousand dollars on guns and ammunition and flashlights and food rations and first-aid kits as red as the canisters I filled to the brim with gas; bought tactical gear and bulletproof vests and clothes I reworked with duct tape to be bite proof (my mother kept asking me where her clothes were going); bought tents and solar-powered generators and backpacks stuffed full of necessities and high-calorie foods and three canoes and water purifiers and iodine tablets. I fortified my grandfather's camp—it was off reservation, only a few miles upriver by canoe or boat—by boarding the windows and circling the camp with fish line that held makeshift chimes to alert us of intruders, of the Nàka, and I stocked my grandfather's camp with more supplies and more guns and ammo to last, enough to get by until . . . until what? I don't know now and I didn't know then. I was concerned only with the immediacy of the threat.

While my grandfather lay in bed, while my mother remained at his side, I prepped. I stayed away. I scouted the Island, the reservation. I looked over my notes, my annotations. I studied the maps I'd drawn, walked treaded and untreaded trails to the river. Ways out. I had several intricate paths noted that led to escape by water, each with a canoe and supplies hidden nearby. I had plans of escaping, and then ideas of returning, when the time was right, to reclaim the Island in the aftermath of the Nàka to rebuild a truly sovereign nation from the ashes of the fallen world that had told us we were free. "Bullshit!" Uncle Nelly echoed in my ear as I worked and thought about all of this, as I prepped.

I've heard it told that before we were forced onto the reservation, we used the Island as a burial ground for our dead, and among those resting in the earth I buried gun after gun after gun all over the reservation, all throughout my escape routes, so for whichever scenario I found myself in I would not be without a weapon at my disposal. I also buried supplies. Backpacks filled with necessities. Buried it all, all of it, all over this graveyard of a home given to us in a treaty. I wonder now if I had dug deep enough if I would have woken the Nàka. But I buried just below the surface so I could easily get at the weapons should I have needed them.

When I finished, when the final gun was buried (a bolt-action rifle, I remember, because it was fawn colored, like our house), I returned home covered in mud for the last time. It was actually the last time I'd ever set foot in that house. Mom never asked what I was doing when I came home covered in mud. It was a Friday, and my grandfather was crying to my mother. I could hear him. He was asking her, pleading with her when he had the breath. "Please," he said. "Do it." I stood in the doorway and he looked at me, sweating, shaking, barely breathing. My mother came to me and said, in passing, "He'll be gone soon. Don't go. The clinic's not answering, and so I'm going down there to get the doctor to come up." Doctor Tim. I wonder if he knows I'm sorry.

If she hadn't left, perhaps I wouldn't be where I am today. I don't know. But she did leave. And I am where I am.

"Turn the heat down," my grandfather said, barely audible.

I did.

"Bin," he said, meaning "abin," sit, but two syllables were too much for him at that moment.

I sat next to him.

The back door slammed shut and I heard Mom's car start, heard the engine revving the way it did, and then it got quiet.

He was trying to talk to me. Trying to clear his chest and throat like, again, a cloudy sky trying to part. When he could finally say something, my grandfather said, "Are you prepared?"

Yes, I told him.

"I don't want to come back as one of them," he said.

"A Nàka?" I asked. "Is it happening? Is it now?"

All he would say is: "Are you prepared?"

Yes, I told him again, and then, into his ear, so close to his face I felt the sharp prickle of his stubble, I spoke: "I'll make sure you don't come back." I held his small, frail body. "Kosemol," I said, and he tried to say it back, I think, but all I got was hot breath on my face.

I knew what he wanted. Or I thought I knew what he wanted. Maybe he wanted it; maybe he didn't. But I did know the repercussions of it. According to my notes, the way to end a Nàka is to kill the brain. Mom would come home with the doctor and they would see the scar, the mark, the blood, the death. But he would not come back and we would be safe. The End was here.

My grandfather never said my name—he always called me gwus—and so I was shocked when he said it. "Nelly," he said. "Death is coming, and I will not return." Again, looking back, he said this in general and not about the Nàka. He said it about himself. His death was coming. Not the dead. But I took it that way, the way I think he both meant it and did not mean it. He wanted this so badly. The pain he suffered made it easy, but was it right?

It's not what they make it out to be in the shows. Sticking a blade through a skull, I mean. It's like trying to pierce a rock. But I managed to do it—how he sighed!—and in doing it I cut myself so my blood mixed with his blood, and we both spilled red on the bed and nightstand and floor. I don't know whose blood was on my shirt and pants. It must have been both of ours.

He lay there, dead, not coming back, not suffering, and I felt no sadness. Only relief. Happiness even. And then that happiness turned to fright, not at what I had done but what I thought was now coming. When Mom returns, I thought, I have to take her. It'll be time to go.

I changed my clothes, washed the cut on my hand, bandaged it, and waited for my mother to return. When she did, Doctor Tim was with her. I met them in the kitchen. I was shaking. Mom said, "What's the matter?" and I told her he was gone, and as Doctor Tim passed by me and walked down the hall Mom's mouth turned upside down and her lips quivered. She hugged me, and I said, "We need to go. Now."

She let go, eyes wet. "What do you mean?"

"They are coming," I said. I gripped her shoulders. "We need to go."

Mom looked past me down the hall, where Doctor Tim yelled, "Oh, my God!"

I shook Mom back to looking at me. "Now!"

"What did you do?" Doctor Tim asked, hurrying down the hall. He had his cell out and dialed what I thought were three digits.

Mom started to say "What are you talk—" but I spun and knelt down and unholstered the pistol on my ankle and with such a loud bang I shot the doctor in the thigh, grazed him on purpose, and I went to him and with the heel of my foot I crushed his phone. Mom had her hands on her ears.

"We will need you in this new world," I said, standing over him, and I went to Mom, whose hands covered her ears, and I peeled them off and said, "Fix him up and then meet me at the trail near the lumberyard, the one that cuts west. We will escape that way."

"What did you do?" the doc was saying, groaning, holding his leg. "Are you off your meds? What is wrong with you?"

Mom jittered and stared not directly at me but just barely past me at Doctor Tim, her line of vision grazing me. I shook her hard.

"Do you understand!" I yelled.

"Yes, yes," she said, as terrified as I was but for different reasons.

I left the house. Neighbors were at the end of the driveway, asking me what was going on, what that bang was, and I screamed to them all, while running, that it's over, that the Nàka are coming, and that you best get your things and go if you want to live. I started to think of the dead buried all over the reservation. It was only a matter of time, I thought, before they dug themselves free and were after us, our own people but not our own people because they were infected with a disease that in the movies seemed to always begin with white people.

I hurried, sprinted down to the woods and cut through trees whose limbs scratched me and whose ticks let go and crawled on me. On my way to the trail near the lumberyard I came across four young boys in the woods smoking cigarettes and I ran right through their little circle, yelled to them to get home, that it's ending, that it's coming, the Nàka. And when they didn't run I stopped running and turned around. They are your people, I heard myself saying.

"You have to go," I told them. "Now!"

They laughed hysterically.

"It's not funny," I said, and I pulled out the pistol, which quieted them. "This is serious. Go. Get out of here before it's too late."

They wouldn't have run if I hadn't shot at their feet.

The trail I told Mom to meet me at, the one that would bring us to a canoe, was shaded. The sun was setting behind thick pines. I thought to sit but then I heard sirens. It was starting. The chaos. I had to move, and I wasted no time: I unearthed every gun I buried on that path, took them from the small or oversize duffel bags that held them and made sure they were loaded and ready for anything that might come and get in the way of our leaving. I packed the canoe with some guns and ammo and food and some backpacks with supplies. And then I went back down the path, to the start of it, and sat against a tree and in a bulletproof vest I waited for Mom and Doctor Tim while holding tight a Century VSKA AK-47, thirty rounds with one in the chamber, and I thought, as I waited for Mom and Doctor Tim, of the order of the guns I had unearthed and readied: another AK, two 1911s, a Smith

& Wesson M&P 15, and two Mossberg 500s in case what came was too much to fight off and we got caught in close combat. As I was thinking through this lineup, I remembered I had buried another gun and forgot to unearth it: a pump-action .22, similar to the one my grandfather let me use and eventually took away from me. I stood and turned to go dig it up, but at the calling of my name I spun right back around and crouched and aimed the Century in the direction of the sound.

They said my name again.

It was almost dark; their flashlights searched and shined and sparkled while the sun set red behind thick green pines at my back.

"Where's my mother?" I asked. "And the doctor?"

"Just come out," a voice said. "Let's talk."

"We're not here to hurt you," another said.

I gripped the Century tighter.

"You have ten seconds to tell me where my mother is," I said, and I started counting. But I made it to only four when their light found me and one of them yelled, "Gun!" and so I had no choice but to open fire. I sprayed as many bullets as I could without losing control of the Century. Voices yelped—I'd hit them, one or two or all of them. Some fired back at me but I hid behind a tree. When the shots stopped, I opened fire again, and when my clip was empty I tossed the gun and grabbed my small ankle pistol and unloaded the last three shots in their direction while I made my way to my other Century and aimed it in their direction.

"Bring me my mother," I said. Forget the doctor, I thought. But nobody responded. The lights—headlights?—were still shining and so I shot them out. In the dark, I waited, aiming the Century in the blackness at those who sought to take what we had so they could survive. We've been here before, I thought. Things don't change. I began to worry that they had taken my mother. Raped her. Killed her. Raped her again. I thought of them eating her—not the Nàka but those who were after us, those who would become cannibals when the world lacked food.

"Where is she!" I yelled, and then lights so bright blinded me and I squinted but before I could shoot I was hit in the arm once, twice, three times, and then one knocked me back—it had hit my chest, the vest. I dropped the Century and crawled away from the bright light and to the two 1911s and fired them with no regard for anything and emptied the clip in one hand and then dropped it and then emptied the other. I stood up and not thinking, I ran past the Smith & Wesson M&P 15 and was out of the light, and right before I got to the two Mossberg 500s the light found me and a bullet tore through my thigh and I dropped. I crawled, bleeding hot, hoping that my mother would come, maybe even with the doctor, because I needed him now, and we'd get in the canoe and let the current take us, Doctor Tim fixing me up while my mother held off those on the shore who wanted what we had: things that were not theirs.

At the edge of the water, I was on my back, my fingers dipped in the flow of the river behind me. I waited and watched upside down the orange red of the sun hit just a sliver of the river before it disappeared like a lit room's door closing shut. Mom did not arrive. The doctor did not arrive. It was four men who arrived. Four men in full tactical gear, their rifles aimed at me from above and their lights obscuring the stars in the sky, and one of whom yelled, "He's down and unarmed!" while another said, "You killed nine of my brothers and sisters." And I said, the last thing I remember saying before waking in the ambulance, cuffed to that gurney and feeling myself on fire while a paramedic said, "What do you have to say for yourself?" like he was my fucking judge, realizing the story my grandfather told me was about the ésahsit and not the Nàka, I said to the four men: "Make sure it's in my head. I don't want to come back to this bright place as one of them."

I don't miss the world I'll never see again. It's clear what I'd tell the parole board if I were eligible: I was more sick in the head back then. But I would also tell them, trying to stand on my bum leg that's stuck straight like a two-by-four, that the world, your world, the one they want to protect, is too sick for me, is too sick for all of us. We are not miracles gone wrong but instead we are miracles going wrong. But will people see this? I'm not sure. All I know is that Uncle Nelly was right. "Bullshit!" That's all everything is right now. Bullshit for the dead like him, bullshit for the dead all over the world, and bullshit for the dead to come.

Morgan Talty, a citizen of the Penobscot Indian Nation, is the author of the national bestselling and critically acclaimed story collection *Night of the Living Rez*, which won the New England Book Award, was a finalist for the Story Prize, and was a finalist for the Barnes & Noble Discover Great New Writers and the 2023 Andrew Carnegie Medal for Excellence in Fiction. His writing has appeared in *Granta*, *The Georgia Review*, *Shenandoah*, *TriQuarterly*, *Narrative* magazine, Literary Hub, and elsewhere. A winner of the 2021 Narrative Prize, Talty's work has been supported by the Elizabeth George Foundation and National Endowment for the Arts (2022). Talty is an assistant professor of English in creative writing and Native American and contemporary literature at the University of Maine, Orono, and he is on the faculty at the Stonecoast MFA in creative writing as well as the Institute of American Indian Arts. Talty is also a prose editor at *The Massachusetts Review*. He lives in Levant, Maine.

UNCLE ROBERT RIDES THE LIGHTNING

KATE HART

Uncle Robert rode the lightning and survived.

If Robert had said he grabbed the live wire on purpose, many would have believed him, but it was both an accident and a miracle. The charge threw him clear across the construction site, sending a shock wave around the chain-link fence that fused the whole damn thing together before it returned to restart his heart.

Robert did not live to be an old man, to tell his grandchildren how the steel in his safety boots melted his toes into oblivion, or to show them the scar where his belt buckle branded itself into his stomach. But how invincible he must have felt for that remaining year, walking gingerly on newly fried feet, permanently branded a Marlboro Man or rodeo king or whatever prize he habitually wore at the waist. After all, long before he rode the lightning, he'd spent six months of his childhood in a full-body cast. A football tackle crushed his hip and back, stunting his growth forever, but bones are stronger where they've healed, so most of Robert's small skeleton had been ready for a fight since middle school. And with that much luck, how could he turn down any challenge that came his way?

Robert's best friend Gregory was technically his nephew and one year older. Another stroke of luck: growing up an only child with his big sister in her own house nearby. She was raising a pack of might-as-well-be-siblings for Robert to play with when bored and leave behind when bored with them.

But he never left Gregory behind. A lanky blond-haired Chickasaw who never got his tribal card, Greg grew up tall and wiry, a lean mean fighting machine who always looked out for Robert. He was a fisherman and a rock climber, made art pieces from glass, and always got on the floor to play with little kids and kittens alike. Everywhere he walked, he found arrowheads and crystals, snakes and snails, scanning constantly and missing nothing. He smoked like a chimney. He smiled a lot but hated photos, and in the few that were taken he's just the top of a bowed head.

One year he dragged every Christmas tree in his childhood neighborhood off the curb to make a giant pine fort in the family carport. As an adult, he delighted his nieces by sculpting a snow truck bursting through their fence. On vacation in Santa Fe, he thought they were lost in the desert and set off on foot to find them, getting a cactus through his boot before discovering that the girls were far less rebellious than their uncle: being told not to walk to Lone Butte, they'd just stayed on the property. At least he got to gross them out with the blood.

But if they'd been lost, he would have found them, because Gregory could find anything he looked for—except peace. He surely found the White Dog's Road, if it didn't find him first, because even if he didn't know to look for it, he didn't need a tribal card to make his way home. The ancestors know the real ones. Even the blond ones.

Gregory's paternal family had been in Indian Territory since the Trail of Tears, but his father had gone on to Vegas when Greg was two, only to abandon his new family and come back to his first wife when the kids were fully grown. Robert's paternal family came from New York, and though his father was a good and loving man, he'd been sent to the Sooner State in disgrace after drinking the family business into the ground. Both boys were born and raised in Oklahoma, but their shared maternal side had arrived from Texas around statehood, and it was back to Texas that the young men went when they decided to give up on high school.

They got jobs in the Dallas area, and on the weekend of Robert's twenty-first birthday, a year or so after the electrocution, they went to a party that wasn't for him. It may have been a biker party, or just a party that bikers attended, but details are few and there's no one to ask now. They drank beer and gambled and probably smoked some reefer, because long before McConaughey was dazed and confused, those boys were l-i-v-i-n'.

But at some point, Greg and Robert got separated. A few hours or maybe a few days elapsed, and on Tuesday, June 15, 1982, Robert's body was found floating in Grapevine Lake at six forty in the morning. His death certificate says "asphyxiation," a result of an accidental drowning.

It's possible he stumbled over the edge and fell in, though that lake is mostly beaches with a shallow approach and calm water. But Robert did not die with his boots on. And Robert always had his boots on. The steel that had melted his toes in the last pair now protected what was left in the new ones. Maybe they filled with water and sank, but everybody knows what a bitch boots are to take off. Gambling with bikers can be a dicey business, and if Robert was winning . . . who knows. The bikers might have been Hell's Angels, though in Texas, more likely Bandidos, but even if they were just a bunch of good ole boys, the cops would not have been eager to investigate further. Robert was just a working-class kid from Oklahoma. The case was closed, as was the casket.

There's a resort there now, on Grapevine Lake, with a cantina and a marina and a stage called the Glass Cactus. But Robert doesn't haunt the Texas Gaylord Marriott.

Robert rides the lightning.

When Robert died, it killed Gregory too, though it took another decade to do it.

After Grapevine, he lived with his sister's family in Tulsa, in a rent house at Forty-First and Yale. His sister collected antique tins and lined them up on shelves in the kitchen. One day she came home and heard those cans rattling. She told the girls to stay in the car and went in the garage, shouting that she had a gun, though it was just a hairbrush. His sister was smaller than Robert and hadn't broken many bones, but she'd been broken in other ways, and finally this was someone she could fight.

But the burglars shoved the fridge against the door and ran out the back, taking some jewelry and some other small things with them. A few weeks later, a man strolled by, wearing the brand-new leather jacket that they'd stolen from Greg's closet. Gregory was working roofing, and his sister called, demanding he round up his biggest friends. But there was no ass-kicking, no matter how well deserved. He already knew what was worth looking for, and what he could afford to lose.

His brother-in-law got promoted and the family moved to St. Louis, so Gregory went back to Dallas, to be closer to his remarried parents. But he never visited his sister's new house, not even when her family moved back home. After the family trip to Santa Fe, they never saw him again.

He moved to Florida and married a woman but invited no one to the wedding. He told no one when they divorced, and he told no one he wanted to die. His family got the news late at night in '93, the week the Branch Davidians burned in Waco, a decade before that town was caught in a shootout between the Bandidos and another biker gang. His body was sent to Oklahoma, his sister chose a wildflower arrangement for the service, and his brother-in-law gave a short but heartfelt eulogy. A friend put climbing ropes in his coffin. His ex-wife did not attend. He was buried next to Robert.

Everything in this story has been true so far.

Robert crosses the Red River on a Harley every night. He brings the thunder of Oklahoma across the Texas line, roaring into roadhouses and whooping up a storm. He's so much bigger in the afterlife, new boots and buckle and no pain, strutting across the sawdust floors with a confidence he never felt before. The girls at the bars line up to two-step; the boys buy him shots and inquire about his ride. Robert lets the fiddles wail and guitars scream while he line dances, or he hits the old jukebox and finds a song from what should have been his glory days. Rock and roll had been dying in the early '80s but the Stones were still around; he liked a little Van Halen and when Willie sang "Always on My Mind." The devil went down to Georgia a few years prior, but he did not take Robert with him.

Robert prefers the lightning.

Every night he hunts the man who's wearing his boots, and when he finds him, he'll take a seat. Pull up a barstool. Pull his bike alongside. The man will wonder if he's seen this guy before, and his friends will say maybe it's time to go. But Robert will invite them to have another drink, then he'll pour lakes of liquor into their gaping mouths. He'll bet and beat them with two pairs, then two fists; he'll beat their bikes, trip them with live wires, and keep rolling right on by. He'll let them surface, then push them back under, give them a knife wound that the coroner ignores. He'll give their best friends shotguns and watch them bite the bullet. Their sisters and nieces will flinch every time the phone rings forever and hear sobbing down the hallway late at night.

He'll mark their deaths an accident. Asphyxiation. Lightning strike.

The White Dog's Road is made of stars, and at its end are the ancestors. To join them, you must cross a slippery log, or else languish in the west as a ghost.

It makes as much sense as anything.

But Gregory's still following Robert. Moving on foot and missing nothing, he watches thunderheads build on the horizon. They spread like a mushroom cloud, nine miles high, radiating, a warning before the explosion instead of after.

But by the time he gets there, he's too late. Robert's gone.

Sometimes Greg beats Robert south and sits outside the roadhouse. He nods at girls as they pass by. They only see the top of his head. He watches beetles scuttle, hears the semis whining by; if he sees the man in his jacket, he figures no harm, no foul. The lean mean fighting machine was always a gentle giant, and if he could just catch Robert, maybe they could both be moving on.

But Robert's always there and gone like lightning.

Gregory's mother dies in Mississippi and is buried beside him in Oklahoma. His sisters and their children attend the funeral, fully grown or damn near to it, and one of his nieces has a baby. She's given it his middle name and followed it with Robert. Her second son's a climber, just like Gregory.

He never meant to be an ancestor, but it's the only thing more unavoidable than taxes.

The family lines he shares with Robert go back to jolly old England, and some of the ones in his father's line go back to Scotland and Wales. They had their own ways there, and then the Romans came, and then the Christians and the Anglicans, all before they set sail for America. So Gregory has his pick of journeys home, but he still can't leave Robert.

But Greg is patient. And there's lots to explore. There are no arrowheads, except for Sagittarius, but he comes across lost souls and helps them find their way to Heaven, or Valhalla, or back to Earth. Wherever they're supposed to go. He is a ferryman on a river of stars, a fisherman again catching light.

Gregory could always find anything, and he finds peace in searching, so he lets his uncle-brother have his way. Someone has to be the god of thunder. He and Robert occupy the nighttime sky, and someday their paths will cross again. Maybe Robert will find the man wearing his boots. Maybe he'll find them at the bottom of the lake.

But for now, Gregory waits to take Robert home safely. Uncle Robert rides the lightning and survives.

Kate Hart (Chickasaw citizen/Choctaw) is the author of the young adult novel *After the Fall* and a contributor to several anthologies. After earning degrees in history and Spanish, she taught young people their ABCs and wrote grants for grown-ups with disabilities, then founded Natural State Treehouses with her spouse. Born in Oklahoma and raised in Arkansas, Hart lives on a mountainside in the Ozarks, where she enjoys woodworking, fiber arts, and hiking with her family.

SUNDAYS

DAVID HESKA WANBLI WEIDEN

"No, please, I don't want to," I said. "Please, don't—"

The priest grabbed my shoulders and turned me around, then pushed me against his desk. He pulled down my pants and underwear. I squirmed and tried to move away, but he was too strong.

"Please, it's not my day! It's not Sunday!" I said, and started sobbing.

He released his trousers and pressed up against me, his hands moving frantically and his bulk pinning me down. I began screaming as he found what he was looking for, the sound of my cries filling up the room. I tried to focus on the small scissors on the desk, the word *REX* stamped on one of the blades. I grabbed them and held them like a dagger. I could cut him, or I could stab myself. Either way, this would be over. I raised my arm—

I woke up with a start and tried to orient myself. I stared at my dresser, nightstand, and lamp but felt like I was still at the Holy Reward boarding school, my nine-year-old self being raped by the pedophile priest. Another goddamn nightmare, the latest in a series over the past month. For fifty years, I'd been able to forget about what happened to me, but the memories had recently returned with a vengeance. And I was sick of it. I couldn't sleep more than a few hours a night and was barely functioning at work. I was a short-haul truck driver, and had been surviving on Death Wish coffee, Monster energy drinks, and NoDoz pills, sometimes all at once.

Even worse, the lack of sleep was causing my nightmares to bleed over into my waking life. I was seeing stuff out of the corner of my eye that wasn't there, and sometimes I'd hear faint voices when no one was around. That's when I realized I was really losing my shit.

I knew what my wife, Connie, would tell me. She'd say, *Thomas, you need to see a therapist.* But Connie was dead. Pancreatic cancer. It happened so fast I barely had time to say goodbye. The week after her funeral, I took a bottle of Dilaudid pain pills left over from her final days and opened it. I took out a few tablets and held them. They were triangular and looked like a shield. Then I put them back in the bottle.

I wasn't stupid. I knew that Connie's death had triggered some type of PTSD, or whatever they were calling shell shock these days. I'd served in the Army in the '80s for a six-year hitch, and I'd seen plenty of soldiers with mental health issues. But I never thought I'd be one of them, especially for something that happened when I was just a kid.

I'd been sent to the Holy Reward Mission residential school when I was nine years old. My father had passed away and my mother couldn't take care of all my brothers and sisters. There were no jobs on the Rosebud Reservation and money was scarce. My mother grew increasingly desperate, and she finally made the decision to send my two older sisters and me to the school, a hundred miles away. The day we left, my mother sobbed and promised that she'd bring us home soon. She didn't know she'd be unable to keep that promise, as she passed over to the spirit world herself just four years later.

It wasn't so bad at the boarding school at first. Yeah, I was forced to cut my hair and wear a uniform, but I was getting regular meals and my own cot. The worst part was the loneliness, but I made a few friends and was able to see my sisters on Sundays after mass. All in all, life at the school was hard but not as bad as I'd feared. Until I met Father Raubvogel.

None of us could pronounce his name correctly, so we called him Father R. He asked me to stay after choir one Sunday afternoon. I immediately assumed that I'd ruined the songs because I couldn't remember the words. He asked me what my name was, and I told him, Thomas Bear Nose. He smiled and said my name was perfect, that my nose looked like a bear cub. He said I had a beautiful singing voice. I was surprised but flattered. No one had ever given me a compliment like that before.

I began staying late after Sunday services. We'd practice the hymns and songs, and I'd help out with various chores—picking up trash, putting the hymn books back in the racks, sweeping the floor. He'd give me a big hug when I left and thank me for helping him. After a while, the hugs became more frequent. And then his embraces became something else, something I didn't want and didn't understand. He told me he loved me and that God loved me, but the only thing I felt was despair. I was ashamed and humiliated, and I prayed daily that it would stop.

I wish I could say that I finally rebelled against Father R, but the truth is that he lost interest in me. He brought in another boy to help him on Sundays, a third grader named Johnnie Two Bulls. I was freed. I know I should have reported Father R to the school superintendent, but that was beyond my young self. And who would have believed me? Indians were considered to be ignorant savages by the school's administration. We were warned every day that our salvation could be gained only by rejecting our heathenish culture. So, I stayed quiet and tried to forget. That worked until I heard that Johnnie Two Bulls had died. He'd hanged himself in the laundry room.

I shook off the lingering images from my nightmare and went to the kitchen to make coffee. After it finished brewing, I poured some java in my last clean mug, the one with a photo of my wife and me and the inscription, *Happy 30th Anniversary, Tom and Connie!* I took a sip of the bitter coffee and stared at her picture.

I wondered if I should head over to the Rapid City VA clinic and see a counselor. They were trained to help veterans with PTSD and other issues. But I'd have to tell the therapist about Father R and relive the whole goddamn thing. I picked up my coffee mug and started swirling the remaining brew around. I didn't stop until it spilled out onto the table.

The hell with it. I had to do this my own way. No therapists, no counselors. I'd start by finding out how much Holy Reward Mission School knew about their pedophile priest.

I picked up the phone and dialed my old friend Harold. The phone rang a few times, then I heard his voice.

"Tom! How you doing?"

"Hanging in there," I said. "How about you?"

"Same old, same old. Counting the days until retirement, then I get to do some real fishing."

Harold was a tribal cop. He worked days and nights chasing after assholes on the rez, a thankless job. But he was smart as hell and liked by everyone. Back when we were kids, I'd never have guessed he'd end up in law enforcement, but he seemed to love it, and I doubted he'd ever actually retire.

"You interested in grabbing some beers tonight?" I asked. "On me."

"A'ho, it's a Native miracle! Might be the first time you ever bought me a drink. Where you wanna go? The Derby? I get off work at seven, could head over around eight."

"Sounds good," I said. "See you then."

Later that night, I drove to the Derby, the only Indian bar in the area. Harold was already there, drinking a Bud Light. He was out of uniform, wearing a black Sinte Gleska University T-shirt and an old blue hoodie. I sat down next to him.

"Started without me, huh?"

"Early bird gets the beer." He raised his bottle and took a drink. "What are you drinking? You still like that Coors crap?"

"Pure Rocky Mountain spring water," I said, and signaled for a beer.

"So, how you holding up?" he asked.

I wondered how much to tell him. He'd been my lifeline during Connie's illness, driving her to the doctor if I was at work, making sure we had groceries, and sitting with me at the hospital. Later, he helped to arrange her funeral and memorial service.

"I don't know," I said. "Some good days, some bad days. Worst part is nights. Having a hell of a time sleeping."

"Yeah, I thought you looked a little run-down. You taking any of that—what's it called—mela-something?"

I shook my head. "Doc gave me some Ambien, but I didn't like it. Gotta tell you, this no-sleep crap is messing with my head. I'm seeing and hearing weird shit, even when I'm awake."

He took another swig of his Bud. "I hear you. I had a spell of bad insomnia back in the day. You remember that time with the car wreck and the kid?"

I nodded. There'd been a gruesome car wreck on the reservation that killed a mother and her baby, and Harold had been the first one on the scene.

"That was rough. I just kept thinking about it, man. Kept seeing that wreck in my mind, over and over. Couldn't sleep; started to feel like I was going crazy."

"How long it take you to get back to normal?" I asked.

He stared out the Derby's front window. "Ah, jeez, must have been a couple of months. Finally got it out of my head." He took another drink. "Sounds like you're having a tough time with, ah, you know. Connie. But you'll make it."

I paused. "Not gonna lie, the past six months have been hard." I stared at my Coors. "But I think I got it figured out now."

"Yeah? Tell me."

I stopped and gathered my thoughts. "Don't know if you remember this, but my mother sent me to a boarding school in fourth grade. Holy Reward, out by Yankton? I came back four years later."

"That makes sense," he said. "We knew each other in first grade but started hanging out in high school, right?"

"Yup. Anyway, my time at the boarding school—it was, ah, sort of . . ." I'd never spoken of this to anyone besides Connie. I didn't know if I could even say the words out loud.

"So," I said, "there was this priest at the school, and he—" I tried to speak, but my throat closed up, and I couldn't breathe for a moment. "This priest, he . . . messed with me."

Harold nodded. He didn't look away from me, as I'd feared he might. "I figured that's where you were going with this," he said. "How old were you?"

"Nine. Freaking nine years old."

He scowled. "That's goddamn sick. Sorry, man."

"Yeah, it was. What's worse, I figure the school had to know what was going on. I been thinking that I'll call a lawyer, take 'em to court. Get some justice or maybe just—"

"You said Holy Reward, right? That's the school where this happened?"

I nodded.

"I read something about that place, a while back," he said. "Give me a minute, okay?"

I looked around the bar while Harold scrolled on his phone. The bartender, Sharlene, was busy wiping some old bottles of liquor on the back bar, trying to remove the dust and grime that had built up on them. She saw me looking at her and smiled.

"Here it is," Harold said. "Saw this in the Rapid City paper. You weren't the only one. Bunch of students filed a lawsuit against Holy Reward a few years ago. Guess they had the same thought as you."

"Really? I never heard about that. What happened?"

"Hate to tell you, but it says here the case got thrown out. Court said they'd waited too long to file it. Damn shame. The school should pay."

He handed me his phone, and I read the article. It was true. Three teachers had been accused of abuse and the victims filed a suit against the school. But the South Dakota legislature had passed a law back in 2010 that required a lawsuit to be filed within three years after the abuse happened. What's more, no victim over the age of forty could bring a lawsuit against a boarding school, even if the administrators knew about the attacks. The students' lawsuit had been tossed out, and no criminal charges had been filed against anyone.

I took a second to let all of that sink in.

"Well, damn. Guess I can't sue the school." I drained the last of my beer and pushed it away. "But I don't understand the part about criminal charges. Why didn't they arrest anybody for, ah, assault?"

Harold set his beer down. "We're talking about an incident that happened fifty years ago, right?"

I nodded.

"Hate to be the bearer of shitty news again, but this is something I know," he said. "In South Dakota, an abuse victim has seven years to file charges after the crime is committed."

I didn't understand this. "You're saying a kid only has seven years to press charges? But what if they, you know, block it out of their mind? Doesn't that count?"

"Afraid not. Man, I wish I had better news. The statute of limitations is pretty short for these cases. There might be an exception for what's called a Class C felony, but that wouldn't apply for a crime that happened so long ago." He squeezed my shoulder. "Sorry, Tom. The whole thing stinks."

My plan to get justice was over before it started. I couldn't sue the school and couldn't file criminal charges against the priest, assuming he was even alive. I needed a moment alone, so I walked to the men's room.

Inside the bathroom, I stared at the graffiti on the walls, some of which looked to be decades old. JUSTICE FOR LEONARD; A705 FOR-EVER; WILD BOYS. Above the door frame, TI WICAKTE. In English, *he kills their home*. It meant that a murderer not only kills a person but also destroys the victim's family and friends. Staring at those words, I realized that, in a way, Father R had killed my home, not to mention poor little Johnnie Two Bulls and probably many others.

I walked back to the bar and sat down. "You want another?"

"No, I better be getting back," Harold said. "Got an early one tomorrow."

"Hey, one last thing." I turned toward Harold. "What if I wanted to find that priest and talk to him? Do you cops have a way to find out where people live? Some kind of—"

"Hold up, Tom." He raised his hand. "You can't go and confront some old priest. I mean, he's probably dead, but even if—"

"But what if he's not dead? Could you find him?"

"Depends. If it's a common name, probably not. If it's a—"

"It's not common," I said. "Father Raubvogel."

"Rah-what? Spell it for me."

I spelled it out.

"What's his first name?"

"No idea, we just called him Father R."

Harold took the last swig of his beer. "That seals it. You need a full name. Look, you could get on the internet and try to find out more. Go to the school's website. But this guy's got to be, what, maybe eighty years old? He's most likely dead or in some nursing home. My advice is that you move on. You got a shitty deal, for sure. But the past—man, you got to let it go."

Let the past go. Somebody once told me that the past is never over. At the time, I thought that was ridiculous, the sort of thing a person says to sound smart. But now I understood—no matter how hard we try to create our own reality, we're bound by the web of our ancestors, our family, ourselves. The decisions we make and the choices of others.

"Go home, okay?" Harold said. "Get some sleep."

I shook his hand and left. I realized I was starving, so I drove to the casino and ate at the buffet, happy to be alone with my thoughts. After dinner, I played a few slots, hoping my luck would change, but nothing hit. Thirty dollars later, I decided to go home, where I'd put on the TV for a while and then try to rest.

I watched the local news and an hour of CNN, then I powered up my old computer to check on basketball scores. I saw I had a few email messages, including one from Harold. This was strange, as he preferred to talk on the phone rather than communicate on the computer. I clicked on his email, and saw these words:

WALTER RAUBVOGEL 1879 West Hampton Place, Sioux Falls

It took me a second to understand, then I realized what Harold had done for me. The son of a bitch priest was still alive, and living only a few hundred miles away. I stared at the computer screen until the letters blurred into nothingness.

The next day, I woke up refreshed, having thankfully been spared any nightmares during the night. I went to the kitchen, and then I remembered.

Sioux Falls. The priest.

I sat down and pondered my options. Harold had advised me to forget about what had happened and get on with my life. I'd tried that, but it hadn't worked. The past had come for me, unbidden, and stolen whatever comfort I had left in this life.

It was time.

It was a four-hour drive from the reservation to the city, so I grabbed some beef jerky and Cokes and stuck them in my gym bag, along with my jacket, gloves, and a photo of Connie. I didn't think I'd need it, but I went back to my bedroom and took my handgun, an old Springfield Armory XD.

I hopped in my Ford F-250 and pulled onto Highway 18. It was Sunday, so the traffic was light. I tried to listen to the radio, but turned it off after a few minutes. Instead of music and news, images of long-forgotten classmates from the boarding school came into my head. We'd studied and played, ate and drank together, our paths crossing for a few years and then diverging. I wondered what had happened to them, and if they remembered our time at the school.

And then other memories came to me—the weekly attacks by Father R, the days I prayed for an escape. As painful as it was, I forced myself to recall the details of the assaults. The words he'd spoken, the way he'd groomed me. And I thought about little Johnnie Two Bulls, who didn't deserve any of it.

The drive seemed to take almost no time at all, and before long I saw that I was on the outskirts of Sioux Falls. I took a right off the highway onto Valley View Road, drove for a few more miles until I saw a faded sign that proclaimed HAMPTON GLEN MANUFACTURED HOME COMMUNITY.

The homes were small but nicely maintained, with pocket-size yards and a handful of forlorn trees. After a few more turns, I pulled in front of the little house. The address that Harold had given me. The place where Father R lived. It was painted a jaunty yellow, except for the window frames, which had originally been white but were now gray and rotting.

I took a deep breath and tried to steady myself. For a moment, I considered turning around and going home. What could I accomplish by speaking to the old priest? What if he had dementia or Alzheimer's? Maybe Harold was right, and I should just move on with my life.

No. I'd come too far, and I needed to see this through. Not just for me, but also for the other students who'd lived through Sundays with Father R.

I grabbed my gym bag, marched up to the front door, and rang the bell.

No answer. I waited a minute and rang one more time.

"Yes?" The door opened, and an old man peered at me from inside. He had white hair and eyebrows, deep furrows on his face, and gray-blue bags under his eyes. He was dressed in a faded green polo shirt and tan pants. I couldn't see any resemblance to the man who'd tormented me. It had been fifty years, but this person was completely different. It appeared that Harold had sent me to the wrong address.

"Sorry," I said. "I'm not from around here—was looking for an old teacher of mine. Didn't mean to disturb you." I turned away.

"Wait, please," the man said. "Who are you trying to find?"

I turned back. "A teacher I had many years ago. At a school near Yankton. Sorry to—"

"Holy Reward? Holy Reward Mission School?"

"Yes," I said. "That's it."

The old man smiled. "I taught there for fifteen years. My first assignment. I'm Walter Raubvogel."

I tried to mask my surprise. "Father R? That's what we—I mean, you were called—"

"Yes, I remember," he said, and chuckled. "No one could say it correctly. And who are you?"

"Me? I'm, ah, Tom. I was a student there a long, long time ago. I happened to be in Sioux Falls, and thought, maybe, I could say hello."

He didn't say anything.

"I'm sorry to bother you," I said. "I don't get to this part of the state very often, so—"

"All right," he said, and opened the door. "Come in, but I must warn you that it's a little bit of a mess. I can't bend over to sweep and dust the way I once could."

I stepped inside. To the left, there was a small kitchen area, with a little sink and an avocado-green refrigerator. A kitchen table and chairs. An old-fashioned corn broom propped up against the wall. In the living room, there was a beige couch, an upholstered chair with a floral pattern, and a coffee table. There was a painting of a horse hanging above the couch, a crucifix on the other wall.

I glanced over at the man again. This time, I saw the resemblance. It was him, without a doubt. I felt dizzy, almost faint, and shifted my gaze back to the horse.

He saw me looking at the painting. "One of my early attempts. Not very good, I think, but it fits the space. Please, have a seat." He gestured toward the couch. "Can I bring you some hot tea?"

"No, thank you. I'm fine."

"Well, I'll get myself some. Let me know if you change your mind."

I put my bag on the floor and sat down. To hide my nervousness, I folded my hands together and tried to smile. After a minute, he returned from the kitchen and sat down in the chair across from me, a small cup in his hand.

"So, Holy Reward," he said. "As I mentioned, that was my first assignment. After I left, I was in ministry for a few years, then I moved to the Cannon Ball School in North Dakota. Nearly twenty years teaching there! When I received emeritus priest status, I decided to return to South Dakota to live. And now I'm back in ministry, part-time."

I wasn't sure what to say. "Cannon Ball—is that an Indian school?"

"Yes, indeed. The Standing Rock Sioux tribe. Such delightful children, eager to learn and wonderfully obedient."

I gave a slight nod. *Obedient?*

"You must tell me more about your time at the school," he said. "When were you at Holy Reward?"

I guess he didn't remember me, which wasn't surprising, given that I'd been just a kid then. "Way back in the early seventies," I said. "Started there in fourth grade, left after seventh and went back home."

He stirred his tea. "It seems so long ago, doesn't it? And sometimes it seems like just yesterday."

I didn't say anything.

"You mentioned you went back home. Where is that?" he asked.

"Rosebud. My mother died and I had to go back to take care of my little brother and sister."

"Oh, my. I'm sorry. I hope she found peace with the Lord before she passed."

I flashed back to my beautiful mother—the beadwork she created and tried to sell for a few extra dollars, the times she went without food so that her kids could eat. It seemed obscene that he would mention her memory.

"It was hard," I said. "I was only thirteen—still a kid. Way too young for my mother to die. Way too young for a lot of things."

He set his tea down and looked closely at me. "The Lord never gives us more than we can handle. I'm sure you've heard that before, but it's true."

"Yeah, I saw that on a bumper sticker once."

He raised his snow-white eyebrows. "It's no cheap slogan, I assure you. But, please, tell me more about you. Did you enroll at the Jesuit school at Rosebud when you went home? That school, I believe its name is, ah—"

"Saint Francis. No, I didn't go there. I went to Todd County, the public school. It was different than Holy Reward, for sure. No religion classes, no praying. No choir practice."

I looked over to see if there was any reaction, but he stayed silent, so I went on. "My grades were okay, nothing great. After graduating, I worked in construction, roofing, that sort of thing. All in Rapid City. Did that for a while, then I joined the Army."

The priest looked surprised. "The Army! Were you in a war?"

I shook my head. "No. I was a motor transport operator. Move cargo and personnel, make sure everything gets where it's supposed to be."

"That sounds like important work." He took a drink of his tea and smiled. "We all play a role in God's plan."

I gave a half smile in return, but I'd had enough small talk. It was time to get started.

"I remember you drinking tea back when I was a student," I said. "In your office, after choir practice."

"Yes?" he said. "That doesn't ring a bell."

"You had a little electric teapot that you kept on the table behind your desk. Do you remember that?"

He shifted in his seat. "You were in choir at Holy Reward?"

"Oh, yes. You told me I was a wonderful singer."

He paused. "I'm afraid I don't recall that. You must understand, I taught thousands of students at Holy Reward and Cannon Ball. There's simply no way to remember all of them. Much as I would love to. Tell me your name again?"

"Thomas. Thomas Bear Nose."

He shook his head. "I'm sorry, no recollection."

Could he be telling the truth? Had he molested so many students that he couldn't remember them all? Or was he trying to con me?

"I think I would take a cup of hot tea," I said. "If it's not a bother."

"No, of course not," he said. He got up, very slowly, and walked over to the kitchen. "Let me pour you a little, and then I do have an errand I must attend to."

He poured some tea into a small cup, removed a saucer from a cabinet, then set them down on the coffee table in front of me. I saw that the teacup was embossed with an elaborate image of a dragon. I nodded my thanks and took a drink. The tea was strong and tasted almost floral, with an edge of citrus flavor.

"The tea—it's called Silver Tips Imperial. It's harvested only when there's a full moon. I'll pour myself what's left here." He refilled his cup and sat down again. "So good, it's positively sinful."

"Very nice," I said, "but I don't think it's a sin to drink it."

"Just a figure of speech! I wouldn't say drinking a cup of tea is a mortal sin."

"What is a mortal sin, exactly?"

He took another sip and closed his eyes as he swallowed. "Well, that's a sin of a very grave matter, committed with full knowledge of the sinner. But even a mortal sin can be forgiven."

"How does that work?"

He flashed a thin smile. "All people fall short of the glory of God, but if we make a full confession, God forgives us."

I nodded. "Are there any sins that can't be forgiven? Something so terrible even Jesus would condemn it?"

"Only blasphemy," he said. "All other sins can be forgiven, so long as the sinner has confessed and repented."

"Sounds like a good deal for the sinner," I said. "Does he have to confess to the authorities, like the police? Or just to another priest?"

"My goodness!" he said. "I can see that Holy Reward did a wonderful job sparking an interest in scripture with you." He glanced over at the digital clock on the oven. "I really do have to attend to my errands, sad to say. But I'd be happy to continue this at a later time. I assist with the rite of Holy Communion at Saint Benedict's, if you'd like to attend."

He picked up my nearly empty teacup and walked to the kitchen.

"Just one more question, if you don't mind," I said.

He turned and faced me. "Yes?"

"Did you confess to raping students at Holy Reward?"

"I'm sorry?" His mouth dropped open, then he collected himself.

"It's a simple question," I said. "Did you ever repent for molesting your students?"

"You have me confused with someone else, sir. I believe it's time for you to leave." He pointed to the door.

I reached inside my gym bag, took out my handgun, and aimed it at him. "Sit down."

He didn't move for several seconds, then slowly he walked back into the living room and sat down. His left eyelid was twitching violently. "There's no need for that. You don't—"

"Shut up," I said, "and answer my question. Did you ever confess to hurting those kids?"

He held the palm of his hand out, and I saw it was quivering. "I never touched a child, and I'm offended by your accusation. Your memory is flawed."

"My memory is fine. Do you remember Johnnie Two Bulls? That ring a bell?"

He flinched, and I saw I'd struck a nerve.

"A terrible tragedy," he said. "That child came from a damaged background. As I recall, the parents were alcoholics."

My anger was now fully ablaze. "That may be true, but Johnnie was a sweet kid, and he killed himself because of you. You murdered him."

"He took his life because he refused to accept the Lord! He's in eternal damnation now."

I moved a foot closer and trained my gun directly at his forehead. "If anyone's going to hell, it's you. You started raping me when I was just nine years old. Every Sunday afternoon! You remember now?"

"You are mentally ill, sir!" His voice was shaky, but he kept going. "I've never seen you before, now or at Holy Reward. I recommend you seek immediate—"

I took the gun and pistol-whipped him on his right temple. The force of the blow knocked him out of his chair and onto the floor, and he instinctively raised his hands to protect himself from another. I heard a chorus of angels singing in my head.

"Look at me!" I said.

He dropped his hands and stared at me, hatred in his eyes.

"You remember me now?" I raised the gun.

He leered at me, a look of contempt on his face. "Yes, of course I remember you. Your hair used to stick straight up—I called you the Indian porcupine." He rubbed his head where I'd hit him.

"So, you admit it," I said. "You knew it was me all along."

He got up and sat back down in the chair. "Not at first. But then I recognized you." He smoothed his hair back. "I thought this day might come. But I've made my peace with the Lord. Do what you have to do."

"Oh, hell no," I said. "It's not gonna be that easy. I want to know—why did you do it? We were just kids!"

He looked annoyed. "Do what? I gave you love and attention, which you'd never had before. You were abandoned by your mother and I helped you."

I raised my arm to strike him again, but something stopped me. I lowered my hand.

"What do you know about love?" I said. "Hurting a kid ain't love, that's for sure."

"We gave you the gift of Christ and saved you from your heathen ways. That is true love, whether you accept it or not."

Unbelievable. He was using his faith to justify harming children.

"You tell yourself whatever you want," I said. "But you did it because you wanted to. Because you're sick."

He didn't say anything, just looked up at me with a superior expression on his face.

I had an idea. "You said any sin can be forgiven if the sinner confesses and repents, right?"

He looked at me warily. "That's correct."

I pointed the gun at his head again. "Well, it's your lucky day. You get to confess—to me. Tell me how many kids you hurt. If you throw in some repenting, you might get to live the rest of your shitty life."

He shook his head. "The only confession I'll make is to God. You can't bully me."

"You'd rather die than confess your sins?"

"I have nothing to confess. The Indian children—they were little savages when they came to me and I reformed them. That's why they loved me so much. Every single one of them. Even you." He looked at me with a victorious smile. "It was a blessing."

"You really believe that? The kids loved you and what you did to them?"

He just smiled.

I was dumbfounded. This old pedophile apparently believed that he *helped* us with his attacks and that we'd *liked* what he'd done to us. How could he not know the pain—mental and physical—that he'd caused us?

The clock on his oven beeped, and I looked over, startled. Then I saw it.

The broom.

"Don't move," I said, and walked over to the kitchen and picked it up. It was one of the old-fashioned kinds, with corn bristles and a long wooden handle.

"Get up," I said.

He looked at me but stayed sitting.

I raised the gun. He stood up.

"Come over here," I said, and pointed to the kitchen table.

He moved closer but kept his eyes on my handgun. I put the broom down and pulled a chair out of the way.

"Turn around," I said.

"What? Turn where?"

I pointed in front of me. "Face the wall."

He did it.

"Now pull down your pants."

He turned back around. "I certainly will not—"

I pistol-whipped him again but took some heat off my swing. I wanted him to stay conscious. It was getting easier to hit him the more I did it.

He bent over, his hands on his knees, and started whimpering.

"Get up and pull down your pants and underwear! Face that wall, now!"

He stood up and turned his back to me, then undid his belt and his pants, which fell down comically. I saw he was wearing tighty-whitey briefs, although they were closer to gray in color. He put his hands on his underwear and stopped.

"Those, too." I motioned with the gun.

He began to sniffle, but he pulled the underwear down around his ankles. "Please," he said, "you've made your point. Please, just—"

"Shut up and bend over. Lean on the table." I tried not to look at his wrinkly white ass, which resembled a deflated soccer ball. I picked up the broom and moved directly behind him. "Put your hands on top, where I can see 'em." He bent over and grabbed the sides of the table. Now he was weeping more loudly.

I put the gun in my pocket, picked up the broom, and tried to figure out the angle. I turned the broom backward, so the bristles were behind me and the handle faced forward.

"All right, now you get to see what it's like. You move off this table, and I'll put a bullet in your head."

I took the broom handle and thrust it toward his ass. He began to move from side to side, trying to avoid it.

He shouted, "Stop! Don't do it!"

"Shut up," I said. I was going to show this old pedophile what it felt like to be abused and injured, to lose your dignity and humanity.

This was the moment I'd been waiting for my whole life. The chance to get justice for all of the kids Raubvogel had harmed. The children—like me—who'd carried around the trauma for decades, forever haunted by the specter of their abuser. And for those who hadn't made it out, like little Johnnie Two Bulls. This was our moment.

I adjusted my grip on the broom handle. The old priest began to sob again, his body quivering.

As I braced myself, an image of Connie flashed into my head—my final moments with her at the hospice. She was worn down to almost nothing, and it was difficult for her to speak. I'd sat at her side, barely able to contain my grief, and told her I'd be with her soon. She shook her head and motioned for me to come closer. She told me she loved me, and I held her hand. She said there were three spirits standing by her bed, and they needed her to join them. A man was dying in bad pain and they had to help him find some peace. She paused and said one last word to me: "Wokintunze." She closed her eyes and then she was gone.

The next day, I looked up the meaning of wokintunze in Lakota and discovered that it meant *forgiveness in the presence of the Creator*. I'd wondered what she meant by that word. At first, I thought she meant that I should forgive her for dying and leaving me. But I realized she was telling me I needed to let go of my anger and shame. The feelings of worthlessness and self-loathing I'd carried for so long. I didn't know if I could forgive Father Raubvogel, but perhaps I could forgive myself.

I stared down at him, the broom handle poised to exact my vengeance. His body was trembling and shaking, pulsating with fear. He wasn't crying anymore, he was keening—an eerie wail like an animal in its death throes. The sound echoed off the walls of his little house, ringing and resonating in my ears. I paused and looked out of the small kitchen window and into the backyard, where I saw the wind blowing, a tree gently swaying.

I pulled the broom back and set it on the ground. I stayed behind him, waiting to see if he would get up, but he remained facedown on the table, now sobbing quietly. After a few minutes, I got my gym bag and went to the front door. Before I left, I glanced back at the old priest, still spread out on the kitchen table, motionless. He looked like a broken rag doll.

On the drive back to Rosebud, I watched the chaos of the city and the suburbs slowly fade away as the native grasses and flowers began to appear by the side of the road. Connie always loved the wildflowers, especially the irises and the mariposa lilies. I saw a mule deer and a jackrabbit and spotted an eagle flying in the distance. The sky was shining and radiant, and I had a clear view of the road ahead, the horizon opening up before me.

David Heska Wanbli Weiden, an enrolled citizen of the Sicangu Lakota Nation, is the author of *Winter Counts*, which was nominated for an Edgar Award for Best First Novel. The book was the winner of the Anthony, Thriller, Lefty, Barry, Macavity, Spur, High Plains, Electa Quinney, Tillie Olsen, CrimeFest (UK), Crime Fiction Lover (UK) awards and was long-listed for the Hammett Prize, the Shamus Award, a Colorado Book Award, a Reading the West Award, and the VCU Cabell First Novel Award. The novel was a *New York Times* Editors' Choice, an Indie Next pick, a main selection of the Book of the Month Club, and named a Best Book of the year by NPR, Amazon, *Publishers Weekly*, *Library Journal*, the *Guardian*, and other magazines.

EULOGY FOR A BROTHER, RESURRECTED

CARSON FAUST

Helek'shene tvhvsh' means, most literally, *breath of life*, which is what our brother lacks. The wife of one of Callum's many lovers drained it from his belly with her husband's bullet a few weeks back. Mid-September, Callum bled out real slow by Pump 3 at Carter's Fast Stop. Ambulances don't hurry out to places like Ridgeville, South Carolina. And why would they? We're just a bunch of mixed-up Indian cousin-fuckers, aren't we? Even if they tried to hurry, it probably would've taken them too long to get here anyhow. There was no saving him. Callum would've likely died in a hospital bed. Least this way, he didn't leave us with a bill. That said, it ended up costing us plenty to take care of Callum after Angela Ford gunned him down.

I can tell you the price of my brother's body.

Cummings Chapel charged us $885 to burn our brother down to nearly nothing. We paid $79.99 for the dark blue urn we poured him into once the chapel returned him to us in crinkled plastic that reminded me of a cereal bag. Holding all that was left of him in my hands, Callum couldn't have weighed more than a few pounds. As we poured him into the urn, I tried not to spill a single wisp of him. Though he was so much less now, I wanted to make sure he was whole.

Before the fire whittled him down, the cops went through everything they found on his person at the time of his death. They were exact, so I will be too:

In his pocket, a dime bag of weed. In his right ear, a diamond stud—fake, but beautiful if the sun hit it right. A faux-leather jacket thrifted from some shop in Charleston. His keys, hung around his neck by a faded teal lanyard, and a keychain—a rabbit's foot, once white, now painted red. It made me wonder about all the blood he lost. How much of it left him before everything blurred and faded to black?

On the slab, Callum weighed one hundred and fifty-eight pounds. His skin, his jeans, his jacket, his shoes. Heart, lungs, brain, bowels, teeth—it all came to one hundred and fifty-eight pounds. All the blood left in him came to that. So how much would he have weighed if he hadn't lost any to the ground, to the cracks in the blacktop? Either way, most of all that rose up as smoke, and now we're left with the four pounds of him that remain.

In a place like Ridgeville, what happened to Callum isn't all that surprising. He insisted on loving men out loud, which is more than most folks like him could boast in this town. Any queer folks around here are quiet about it. Even more of them silent. Being the way he was had been dangerous enough in a town as small and Bible'd up as this one.

I always figured the earthly price for Callum's goings-on would be heftier than the unearthly one. I ended up being right, though I never wanted to be.

Helek'shene tvhvsh' can also mean *God*, which Callum also lacked. Church was a chore. To him, the man upstairs was just an imaginary friend certain folks never grew out of. The Bible was at least interesting. Snakes spoke. Fire came down from the sky. Water turned to blood. Water turned into wine. Wine became blood. You drink.

In the Good Book, sons also came back from the dead. This makes me believe that not even death is permanent. But Callum believed in what he could hear, see, touch. He believed in only what his body would allow him.

When we were little, when he heard our parents scream at each other, he believed they might tear each other apart. A shove into the cabinet, a slap across the face, a fist wrapped around a neck. He believed they might tear us apart along with them. So we held each other together. If everything else was falling away, Callum made sure we had each other. So, if our parents were hollering, we tucked our small selves under my bed and counted paper flowers on the wall.

By the time he was ten and I was eight, we could count high enough to know that there were eighty-two daisies on the north- and south-facing walls and seventy-eight daisies on the east- and west-facing walls. We counted them each time. We kept counting until the day our father left. We kept counting when the house was finally silent. Eighty-two, seventy-eight. Eighty-two. Seventy-eight.

I have to assume that all those times we'd count the flowers on our wallpaper felt like prayer to Callum. Or, at least, the way I think of prayer. Even when you know the answer, even when you know what you need is right there, the praying helps. Though he knew those numbers wouldn't change, he repeated the counting each time. Just the same as me knowing that God is there, watching, listening. Though I know He's there, it helps to talk to Him. These rituals are just a way of reminding yourself where you are. Trouble is, now I don't know where Callum is. I know I should know. I know I should believe he's somewhere good. Somewhere better. But I don't.

All I know is: what's left of my brother weighs about four pounds.

Callum's body has been burned down to the dregs. This means, of course, that we need to build him a new body from scratch if we want to bring him back.

Esv means *hands* in the tongue that was first meant for us. In the language that our auntie Ina must feed me in pieces if we are to bring Callum back right. With ours, we pull muck from the Edisto River. Once the sun sets, my half brother, Kemly, and I go to the shallowest parts of the river and bring night-dark mud to the shore, collect it on an old blue tarp that we pulled off the top of Kemly's old trailers. *No shovels, no gloves, no nothing,* Auntie Ina told us. *Nothing but flesh can harvest the earth you plan to make the flesh out of.*

It is Auntie Ina who guides us. We borrow her knowledge. Her knowing is what makes the difference between Callum being alive or staying dead. So, handful by handful, we gather the earth that would become Callum's flesh.

Kemly and I share a father—a man known to spread himself around. Spread himself thin. That may be why our father gave Callum his own name—he could see that this son would share both his wandering and his lust—though our father would probably turn over in his grave if he knew his son lusted for other folks' sons.

Callum and I share both mother and father, but it was Kemly who got the first call when Callum bled out—when his body went cold under the hot sun. Much as I don't want to admit, it hurt that Kemly knew first. Because I can't even be sure the knowledge hurt Kemly. I don't think it did. It was like he'd expected the call. Not in the same way I had. For me, *expect* wasn't the right word. For me, it was *dread*. For Kemly, to *expect* meant to *prepare*.

I was not prepared.

I fell apart. I lost my job. Clay Mound Elementary offers two personal days a year to all teachers. I burned through those, hardly noticing them pass. The administration figured it was easier to replace me. *You let us know if next year is more suitable. You just need to get better,* they said.

Nothing got better. Losing Callum gutted me. For weeks, I couldn't eat. All those dead-brother casseroles. All the dead-brother fresh-baked bread. Cobblers and pies and puddings. But in those weeks after, hunger never came. My body just kept eating itself, and I was glad to be disappearing.

I might have vanished altogether had Kemly not found me curled up on the kitchen floor of my apartment, passed out. He told me I'd fainted, and I wondered how long ago that had happened. After I refused food, he forced me to drink a red, sun-warm Gatorade from the back seat of his pickup. *You can't keep on like this, Della,* he said.

In that moment, I was amazed by how much clearer my head was. The hunger I couldn't feel and the faintness that protected me from all that grief had kept the world foggy. All that sugar rushing to my blood burned the fog away. And the grief, fresh as ever, replaced the haze. I knew the fog would swallow me up. But the grief would swallow me up, too.

He's not supposed to be dead, I said.

Kemly stayed quiet for a while, afraid his next words would break me open. He said them anyway: *There's nothing we can do.*

But I knew he was wrong. I feared I was wrong, too, but in a different way. Not that what I wanted to do was impossible, but that it might be unforgivable.

Kemly, Callum, and I all have Auntie Ina in common—our father's eldest sister. Earlier that week, after I begged him, Kemly agreed to drive me to her. *Only because you're in no shape to drive,* he said. *Can't let your next fainting spell be at the wheel.* What I think he meant was that he cared about me. He meant he hadn't prepared to lose me, and he was afraid that he might.

That's the only reason he'd agree to this. In our family, we're afraid of Auntie Ina. We'd always been told to be. Our mothers told us it was smart to fear her. And our father's avoidance of his own sister told us it was smart to listen to our mothers. *She's estranged because she's exactly that, Della—strange,* was all my mother would say.

Of all of us, Callum was closest to our auntie. You could even say that he was drawn to her. He used to go around our mother and invite Auntie Ina to family functions: our birthdays, high school graduations, even some of the Christmases when he was feeling brave. Not that she was partial to any of these gatherings. I always thought she came just to push buttons. Smoking Camel Reds on the porch as presents were being opened. Grinning smugly at our mother from across the room as folks filled their paper plates with beans, pulled pork, and potato salad.

The tension between our mother and Auntie Ina was no ordinary kind of familial disdain. It was a disdain that echoes through a lot of folks. All us Edistos here in Colleton County knew Ina was a conjure woman. A rootworker. Folks from other tribes might call a woman like her a medicine woman, but not here. Here, you either get God in your heart, or you don't. Those who sought her gifts might call her a fortune teller. Those who wished her dead called her a witch.

Auntie Ina lives about thirty minutes out from Ridgeville in a town called Cottageville. Took Kemly about forty minutes to get us there though, since he was driving all nervous. *You doing okay?* I asked. He usually drives like a madman. The fact that I feel safe as his passenger is strange. I asked, point blank, if he was afraid. *Nothing wrong with being wary 'round a woman who can pull your mind out through your nose.* Can't fault him on that logic. Based on what we were about to ask her to do, there was no reason she couldn't.

As we pulled up to Auntie Ina's house, I could see Kemly's hands trembling, despite his best efforts to hide it. We had never been here, though we've known Auntie Ina's address for the past twenty-some years of our lives. Callum found it in a pile of old envelopes when he was twelve or thirteen, and, like all forbidden knowledge does when you're small, the address stuck: 2833 Burr Hill Road.

We knocked, but Auntie Ina didn't come to the door. She beckoned us in with a holler, expecting us. We entered. And should I be ashamed to say I was surprised that the inside just looked like a home? No animal bones hanging from the ceiling. No feathers resting on the windowsills. No dolls dressed like us with needles poking out of the limbs. Just dark-paneled walls, a floral-print sofa, a coffee table covered by a white doily, and a small dining room table covered by a red cloth, surrounded by three empty chairs.

In the front room, there are bookshelves filled, not with books, but with pictures of family. Save for a few mirrors, the walls were full of family photos as well. There are several of Callum, Kemly, and me together, through various ages—toddlers, kids, teenage years. Even a couple of years' worth of my school pictures as Ms. Davis—my earlier years of teaching. Callum must've been sending

Auntie Ina these pictures over the years. I'd never known. Kemly looked just as surprised as I was, even if his surprise was a bit more subdued.

We went through the front room, back toward her kitchen, which doubles as the little shop she runs. Canned peas and jams and beans—the berries and beans and roots all grown by her, prepared by her—filled entire walls' worth of shelves. At a small table by a window, crouched on a stool, Auntie Ina sat, painting her nails a bright cornflower blue.

Auntie Ina looked up from her nails, cocking her eyebrow. *Can't say I expected to have any visitors after Callum's passing,* she scoffed. *But it's good to finally see you kids.*

I'm sorry, I said. And I meant it. *That we never reached out after.*

Never reached out much, even before. You sorry for that, too? Auntie Ina asked.

We're not here to start shit, Ina, Kemly said, still on edge.

I know exactly why you're here, Auntie Ina said, focusing back on her nails. *Same reason you never came around before. And the reason you're scared shitless, Kemly. You can't start shit if you're shitless in the first place.*

Ma was right about you. Right to keep you at arm's length if this is how you act, Kemly growled through gritted teeth. I wanted to swat him upside the head. He'd ruin everything.

I speak my mind is all. Auntie Ina clicked her tongue. *That's why some folks around here don't like me.* She paused for a moment and added: *Sometimes I speak other people's minds, too. Yet another reason folks stay clear.*

Fuck this, Kemly said, beginning to turn back toward the front door. But I grabbed him by the shoulder. I felt him tense beneath my grip.

Fuck nothing, Kemly, I whispered, even though the whispering wouldn't mean that Auntie Ina couldn't hear every word, maybe even every thought. *This is all I have. The one shot I have to bring Callum back.* I felt Kemly relax a little, but I needed to make sure he stayed. I needed my next words to hurt. To nail his feet to the floor. *He could be alive if you picked up your damn phone.*

You and I both know he wouldn't've lived, Dell.

Then this is the only way we have, I said. *We owe him that. We both failed.*

We both knew that, as blood poured from our brother's belly, he called us.

Both of us.

Twice, he called me. Three times, he called Kemly. The only two people Callum could think of calling as his insides poured out, making little rivers in the cracked blacktop.

I think it's still true that the ambulance would have been too slow. I think it's still true that Callum would have died, regardless. But I can't help but think that if Kemly tossed our dying brother in the back of his pickup, he could have gotten him to the nearest hospital fast enough that he might have lived. Even if he would have died anyway, he might not've had to die alone. If we had picked up, he would have known we cared. He would have known how much we wanted him to live. He died slow, and the whole time had no one.

Now there's only one way of letting him know how much we want him to live.

It took weeks to convince Auntie Ina to bring Callum back. Kemly didn't stick to visiting her with me as we waited for her response. I came by her place every few days with flowers or family photos or anything I thought Callum might've brought her over the years. She seemed to chew on my request like a piece of cud, as if to make sure everything went down right. I knew it would take time and patience, but I also knew, deep down, that she wanted our brother back as much as we did. I knew that, like us, Auntie Ina felt Callum's absence deep in her chest. She told me as much, after October rolled around, when she finally agreed.

Callum was one of the few who came to me without needing anything. No curses, no cures. Just plain old company. She smiled, looking out toward her garden. *He'd tell me about you, mostly. Some of Kemly. He was proud of y'all. Sad often, too, for himself. But he was here. And, you're right, he still should be. But I need you to know that this ain't for you or Kemly, or even for me. It's bigger than that—than us,* Auntie Ina said, her smile fading. *And it ain't me this is going to take a piece of. That will be you.*

Unable to help myself, I asked her why she was agreeing to this, and what it would take. Auntie Ina took Callum's ashes from me, and then she told me. This was what she was getting ready to tell me all this time. This was what she'd been chewing on. *Callum's the one who needs to carry the roots after I'm gone,* Auntie Ina said. *Was always supposed to be him.* But it seemed I would do in a pinch.

She took me to the kitchen, where she unlocked a cabinet in her shop I hadn't noticed before. This was where she kept the things she grew that weren't for eating. These plants were grown for spellwork.

Kemly will help us, too. He'll come back, I said, but Auntie Ina shrugged the words off, not all that concerned either way. She looked at me, content. As if, in me, she had everything she needs.

I can tell you the cost of my brother's body.

First, it takes time. Days to prepare. There is much I have to learn from Auntie Ina in order to be of any help. But I am a teacher, after all, which makes me a good student. Our language has never come easy to me, though. My folks never spoke it, could never give it to me, but there are pieces of it I must learn, and

Auntie Ina knows it all well. *Because the roots work best when you talk to them right.* And so, while Kemly works at the truck yard in the days, I learn Auntie Ina's ways as best I can, as quickly as I can. When Kemly gets off, we all do a different kind of work together. It takes a lot of bodies to build up a new body.

After we collect the muck, the roots, and after we knead most of Callum's ashes in, we shape his body next to Auntie Ina's garden. With us, we have the ashes, a coffee mug, and bottles of water.

We begin, and October stretches.

As I follow Auntie Ina's instructions, it's easy to forget what's being built. That this mound of earth will become Callum's skull. This muck will be his chest, his belly. The black water from the Edisto that's soaked into this muck will soon run through Callum like blood. It's so easy to forget. But that isn't the case for our brother. By week's end, Kemly is shaken. He does not look down and see what will soon be a body. He sees something completely inhuman. He sees something that will never be human.

We can't be doing this, Kemly says. But he's wrong.

We can. And nothing has ever felt more right. I am lighter than I've been in years. I think back to how my body fell away from me in those weeks after Callum first bled out. How hunger never came. How I began to disappear. My body feels far away now, but it is not despair that has pushed hunger away this time. It is not that I am losing myself. I am pouring myself into something better. It is not fog that blinds me. It is light.

I'll have no part in this, Kemly says, as if that changes anything. *This isn't holy.*

I say nothing as he leaves us. Let the crickets and the frogs sing him out. I have never felt holier.

But that is part of the cost—my brother's body has cost me a brother.

It doesn't matter for long, because I build a new one. Callum's new form is shaped. As Auntie Ina and I form the river muck, as we knead Callum's ashes into it, it firms up. It feels like clay, and becomes easy to shape, as if the earth knows how our hands want to guide it.

Vpel', his shoulders.

Vhvl', his arms.

Vpu'yv ekwel, skull.

Ehe'yv, mouth.

Kwvt, neck.

E'mv, body—the whole of it, complete.

Brother, kokenee'shv.

This body we build does not yet look like Callum, but at Auntie Ina's instruction, we sculpt the mouth wide open. Like a man dying of thirst, waiting for rain to fall from the sky. *But it is you who will drink,* Auntie Ina says, because she can hear inside my head. As we build Callum up, as we get closer to completion, it seems easier and easier for her to step into my head. As the walls of Callum's self grow stronger, mine seem to weaken, but I don't care.

As we continue in Auntie Ina's garden, I watch as she sifts what's left of Callum's ashes into a coffee mug, pours water over them, and stirs it into a gray paste with her long pointer finger, her chipped, blue fingernail. She adds more water to thin it out and hands the mug to me. *Drink* is all she says, looking irritated that she had to repeat herself. I feel sick. Not sick to my stomach, exactly. More like a queasiness bubbling up in my throat. She probably doesn't need to step into my head to know what I'm thinking this time, so Auntie Ina just shakes the mug at me impatiently.

I drink it down.

It burns. As if the ashes are still scorching.

I heave, and hot blood rushes from my mouth. What else could it be but blood? What else could be so red? And it falls onto the clay chest. *Think back to the rain, girl,* I hear Auntie Ina say, and she grabs a fistful of my hair at the back of my head, steering me to the mouth of the clay head. Blood and ash drain from my mouth and into the sculpted face. I heave so completely that it feels like my ribs are shifting, breaking beneath my skin. I want to scream. Nothing comes but the taste of ash. The taste of copper. I hear a scream, but it isn't mine.

It's Callum's.

And as Callum screams, I think of the way babies scream when they're first pulled from their mamas. They scream because this is the first time they see light. They scream because it is the first time air touches them. They cry to rid their bodies of the world they left behind. I try to imagine that Callum's screams are shedding whatever came after he died. Imagine if all that came after was *nothing*. Just the same black that came before birth.

I don't have to imagine all that black falling away. I am feeling it fall away. Hearing Callum's scream, I know the sound is not mine. But it is mine. Because I made it. I gave my own breath for it. I hear it as if it's coming from my lips. As if it came from my lips like all that ash. But that's not all that rushes in. In the screams, I hear the howl of the bullet that killed. Feel the blood rush from my belly, from my mouth. Feel my lungs lag and then stop. This is how it felt when the black crept in. Blur and then shadow and then cold from the inside out.

The screaming stops because I will it to. Everything will be fine now. Be silent. Be here.

I look down at a body that, moments ago, was not a body. And Callum looks just like himself. He stands. He looks just like me.

We share blood. We share breath.

We look at our auntie. We look so alike, she and we.

———

We are not a trinity. Nor are we holy, my brother and I. Though we are the father—for I am a creator, and this body that holds him was made by my hands. We are the son—for though I am a daughter, Callum and I are one now. We are Della, and a brother standing beside her, within her. The important thing is that we are not without. We are the blood in our veins and the ash in our mouths. We know what it is to be alive and dead—sometimes all at once. We know what it is to be apart and together, all at once.

Our auntie has given us a garden, which is more than we have been given before. Among her crinum lilies, the lantana, the marigolds and hollyhocks, we build what comes after both life and death. Our bodies are both earth and flesh. We are buried and we are alive. We nourish the roots that burrow into us. And when those we love fade away, fall to the earth, get swallowed up, we will take them in. We will soak up their skin, pull it up with the roots of the plants that wind through us, and they will be with us. We will not be trinity. We will be more.

Carson Faust is two-spirit and an enrolled member of the Edisto Natchez-Kusso Tribe of South Carolina. His debut novel, *When the Living Haunt the Dead*, is forthcoming.

NIGHT MOVES

ANDREA L. ROGERS

Germany, Spring 1968

In a dark corner of the Das Geschlachtete Lamm tavern, Walter Rock stared at the painting of a snarling beast cornering a lamb while he thought about the letters he'd stopped getting from Janie King, a girl he'd met just before he shipped out. Across the room, three other servicemen were at the bar. Beer steins clunked loudly on tables and the various conversations, all in German, were white noise to Walt. He had come into town with three other soldiers: JohnBoy and Christ were both white boys, their Christian names forgotten the way a nickname will remake a man, and Carl was a Black man from Chicago, born to a German mother, a war bride. Somehow, after stationing Carl in Germany, the Army had forgotten Carl spoke German. Now, it was a closely kept secret between Walt and Carl.

Walt was reaching for the pencil and small notebook he kept in his pocket when Carl interrupted, hissing, "Los geht's, Chief."

JohnBoy had been told to leave, but a knot of people had

formed around him at the front door. Christ was nowhere in sight. Being arrested would cause all kinds of problems back on base for the four servicemen, all kinds of problems the two undrunk men weren't interested in. A large black-haired man had JohnBoy by the sleeve, his finger bouncing off his chest like a sewing machine. JohnBoy spoke no German, unless he was drunk, but even sober and speaking English, JohnBoy managed to make more enemies than friends.

Carl was trying to make peace between the angry, dark-haired German and the drunk farm boy. He handed Walt some money. "Go buy some beers for our hosts," Carl said loudly. JohnBoy had finally shut up, and the German had gone back to stand with his friends. He was still angry, but quietly so. When the barmaid delivered the steins of beer to the men, they only glared at the servicemen. Not so much as a "danke," let alone a "danke schoen."

Beers gifted, Walt followed Carl's lead and helped hustle John-Boy out the door.

Christ was waiting for them at the train station. There was no train in sight.

"The trains run on time in Germany, boys."

"Looks like we're using the Fuß-mobile," Carl said.

An older, bearded German sat on a bench in the waiting area. His eyes appraised them skeptically as they left the station platform. The road stretched into the dark before them, curving away from the lights of the station, a light gray rip in the darkness. As the men reached the curve of the road that would hide the station from them, the German man stood and yelled, "Vorsicht vor dem Wolf, Jungs!"

The hairs under Walt's collar prickled, but only Carl stopped for a moment. The Germans rarely taunted the American soldiers, but it happened enough that the men had learned to ignore it. When Carl turned back to Walt, he looked perplexed.

It was a five-mile walk back to base. Having missed the last train, the men's next best chance of getting some sleep before daylight was a farmer driving home into the valley and offering them a ride in the back of his truck. Stranger things had happened. Overhead, clouds heavy with rain hid the moon as they walked into the wind. Occasionally, lightning brightened the distant sky beyond the clouds.

Walt dropped behind the other three, ignoring their conversation, his adrenaline still up from the encounter in the tavern. Carl fell back next to him when Christ and JohnBoy loped ahead, drunk fools gambling on a drunken race. Like Walt, Carl had enlisted to avoid Vietnam.

"What did that guy say?" Walt asked.

Carl shrugged. "Beware the wolf."

"They have wolves here?"

"Supposed to have been hunted out. There are stories, though."

"Yeah. In Oklahoma, too."

The darkness the men were walking into was deeper than the blackness around them. The army base sat in a valley covered with old-growth forests. It was different from the woods in Northeastern Oklahoma. Taller, darker, covered with thick beds of moss that sucked at your boots. Walt wondered if the girl back home, whose letters he'd been missing, had applied to Haskell Indian School like she'd told him. Was he just a boy she met in a diner? Had Janie King only given him her address so he'd get up and leave her a decent tip after four hours of coffee and pie and conversation? A girl like that probably had better things to think about than Walt, plans that didn't include a boy whose best life choice was enlisting in the army to avoid being forced to fight in Vietnam. His older brother had died in the Tet Offensive. Most of his older friends had been drafted as soon as they got out of high school. Walt wasn't going to college and voluntarily enlisting gave him the best chance of not getting killed in a war started by France's colonization.

Carl gestured toward a dark ruin off the road ahead of them and patted the pack of cigarettes in his pocket. He hollered at Christ and JohnBoy, who were still racing each other, too drunk to be concerned that they were going to be worn out by the time they reached home, possibly because one of them had a blue bottle of sweet German wine.

The ruin they took shelter in was a house that had no roof to speak of, but it provided a decent windbreak. Carl handed Walt a cigarette and a lighter. The clouds parted. For a moment the men who were just barely men saw the unbroken circle of the full moon.

"Did you ever see that Lon Chaney movie? *The Werewolf*?"

Walt felt as if spiders were crawling up the back of his neck, the raw and recently shaved area at the base of his skull. He hunched his shoulders up to make the feeling go away.

"You mean *The Wolf Man*?"

"Yeah. Isn't this kind of like that?"

"Carl, man, you need to cut that out."

Carl laughed.

Back on the road, there was the sound of an approaching motor, a truck leaving the village and driving down into the valley. They saw it stop where Christ and JohnBoy were standing at the edge of the road. Walt took one last long drag on his cigarette, then put it out. Carl reached out to stop him from walking up to the road, listening to raised voices. He pulled Walt back behind the wall of the ruins when he heard the passenger side door screech open.

"I don't think this is a ride we want to take, my friend," Carl said.

Christ had already turned and was running toward the woods when they heard the wine bottle smashing into the side of the truck. JohnBoy was wielding it and backing toward the edge of the road, keeping the large German from the bar from swinging at him as he backed away. Carl and Walt ducked low and watched from the safety of the ruined house until, of course, JohnBoy made a beeline to them.

When he reached them, he was out of breath, still carrying the jagged neck of the blue wine bottle. They watched the driver of the truck step out and stand at the edge of the road with the black-haired man. The two German men argued briefly, then the driver returned to the truck. From the road's edge, the dark-haired man yelled, "Hütet euch vor dem Wolf, Jungs!" Both men laughed, and the dark-haired man returned to the idling truck. They sat there for several minutes before driving slowly down into the valley.

"Looks like we're going for a walk in the woods," Carl suggested. He and Walt walked together ahead of JohnBoy.

"Again with the wolf warning?" Walt asked quietly.

"Yes. This time it was to protect yourself from the wolf."

"Great," Walt said.

Behind them, they heard JohnBoy holler.

"At least we got an Indian chief to lead us."

Walt stopped.

"He's drunk, man. He won't even remember this tomorrow," Carl said.

Walt waited for JohnBoy, anyway. If someone asked him why Carl could call him Chief, but a drunken white farm boy couldn't, Walt couldn't have explained it. When Carl said it, it was filled with an admiration for the American Indian that he had learned from his German mother and Walt could forgive that. When JohnBoy said it, it was full of the mockery of a man whose family had stolen your land.

And Walt had told JohnBoy the last time he'd said it that there better not be a next one. There were some things a man had to keep his word on. JohnBoy was still carrying the broken neck from the wine bottle, though. From his pocket, Walt pulled out a knife he'd bought in a German market, a bone-handled silver Indian head knife about three inches long. He opened it and stepped into JohnBoy's path.

"What was that?"

JohnBoy stepped back, surprised. His face was confused, a reflection of the drunken blackout brain he was probably experiencing. He looked as if he had no idea what he'd done or said.

"What the hell, man?" JohnBoy managed, before he stepped back drunkenly, then suddenly clutching at his belly vomited on his own boots. From the edge of the woods, Christ watched them and shook his head. Walt pressed the silver blade back into the bone handle, the small silver circle embossed with a Plains-style warrior profile complete with headdress, reflecting the full moon's light. He slipped it back into his pocket. He and Carl didn't wait for their sick companion. They left the stink of sweet wine and stomach acid behind them.

JohnBoy's puking shifted into dry heaves, a sound like a miserable animal rolling across the grassy field, barely audible once they were in the trees. Once JohnBoy stopped, he whined for a few minutes about being left behind. The guys didn't slow down, and he didn't speed up. He was still in the field when they heard the wolf howl.

Those prickly spiders under Walt's collar were back and the three men quickly turned toward a crashing behind them.

"Run!" JohnBoy screamed as he came loping toward them, dropping the broken bottle. He had almost reached them when a large, dark creature hit him from behind and knocked him off his feet.

"Scheiße!" yelled Carl.

"What the hell is that?" screamed Christ.

The snarl was doglike, *big* dog–like. Walt had seen packs of dogs take down cattle in a similar fashion back home. It was hard to get away when there were two-inch teeth sunk in the back of your neck. If there were a pack of these big dogs, they were goners.

Carl ran back and picked up the blue bottle JohnBoy had dropped. Walt took his knife back out of his pocket. Christ turned and ran away in the direction of the road. The creature had torn into JohnBoy's thick neck, remaking his screams into bubbly gurgles. JohnBoy's limbs thrashed. Carl ran and kicked the creature from behind and it turned and snarled at him, teeth snapping. Walt grabbed JohnBoy's legs and tried to pull him away from the beast. The giant dog swiveled on Walt. It lunged and sank its teeth into Walt's right shoulder, knocking him backward. Before Walt could thrust his elbow between his face and the muzzle of the wolf, the wolf's teeth came down biting into the bridge of Walt's nose. Walt rammed his left elbow into the wolf's right ear and the creature turned his teeth into the blocking arm. Blood filled Walt's eyes, the saltiness burning. Walt's right hand swung the still-open blade wildly while Carl kicked the wolf. As the wolf growled and turned to snap at Carl, Walt found purchase in the creature's throat and he plunged in deep. When he felt the point hit, he twisted and shoved harder, not stopping until he felt the creature collapse.

Walt's face and arms throbbed. He struggled to keep his eyes open. Carl ordered him to sit still as he rushed to tend to JohnBoy. Walt was kneeling, but struggling to stay upright, terrified as he felt the skin around his eyes swelling, making it hard to see. Still, he was in better shape than JohnBoy, who had stopped crying. Now the only sounds coming from his torn throat were wheezing. The ground beneath the men had turned to mud from the blood and the struggle. It stank of old death and new sacrifice, the viscera of a man whose insides knew he was a goner before he was gone.

JohnBoy was dead before they heard the car's horn from the road, long and mournful. Too late, Christ had waved down a late-night driver, but the man wouldn't step out of the car.

Carl turned his attention to Walt, tightly wrapping the worst gash in Walt's arm. He worked quickly and efficiently in the dark. Walt felt weak and somewhat nauseated. He wondered if he might get to go home now and marry Janie before he lost her to some college boy who wouldn't be drafted or even have to enlist. Janie would run her soft hands over his scars and braid his hair when he grew it out, maybe. They'd have kids who'd go to college just like their mom and not die in some foreign country playing warrior.

For a moment, the moon came out from behind the clouds again. The steady rain drops washed the blood from Walt's eyes, allowing him to see a little as it washed away the briny blood. Carl handed him a torn piece of cloth to use as a rag, to wipe his damaged face, to stanch the blood rapidly flowing from his punctured nose. His arms and shoulder stung in the cold rain, and he began to shake.

He turned to look at the body of the creature in the moonlight as a flash of lightning threw the world into contrast, like a black-and-white film. Walt stumbled to his feet, aghast at what he saw in the lightning's flash. Thunder rolled across the fields and through him. Where the rain should have been falling on a wolf, it instead washed blood off the naked body of the dark-haired German.

What they had killed had morphed into a man, the first man they had ever killed. They had trained for that, stabbed, fought, and shot sawdust dummies, but this man was real. No, he was a real man now. But he had definitely been all hair and teeth and blood moments earlier, a wolf that had bitten deep into Walt's flesh. You never forget your first kill, they say. Walt knew then that his first kill would curse the rest of his life.

Andrea L. Rogers (Cherokee) is a writer from Tulsa, Oklahoma, currently living in Fayetteville, Arkansas. She graduated from the Institute of American Indian and Alaskan Arts with an MFA in creative writing. Her book *Mary and the Trail of Tears: A Cherokee Removal Survival Story* was named an NPR Best Book of 2020 by both NPR and American Indians in Children's Literature. Her book *Man Made Monsters* won the 2023 Teen Walter Award.

CAPGRAS

TOMMY ORANGE

As the plane took off, I reached two fingers back to knead the area above my shoulder blade, where there was a knot as hard as a knuckle. I pushed the balled meat back and forth, to dissipate the sharpness of the pain. When I touched what seemed to be the heart of the knot, I heard dirt being dug up with a shovel. I looked down the aisle behind me, where there was of course nothing near resembling what might have caused me to hear the sound, and yet there it was. *Clink. Clink. Clink.*

I kept rereading the same page of my book with the vague suspicion it was slightly different each time. Leaving Oakland, the night sky was moon bright with clouds scattered evenly across the view from my window, half opened like an eyelid. The book I kept failing to read was about a man who suffers from a rare psychiatric disorder called Capgras delusion, which makes you think imposters have replaced your loved ones.

My French publisher had paid first class for the long flight to Paris from San Francisco, but my wife and son were in economy, all the way back in a part of the plane that felt unreachable from first class.

I had another go at the same page, but my eyes moved pointlessly over the words on the page as if over clouds—and with as much meaning gained.

When the Italian herb chicken I'd preordered was served, I wasn't hungry yet but made myself eat. I've never known how to say no to free food, and I was eager to try this meal, having heard somewhere that the difference between economy and first class was the difference between a horsefly and a horse. It did not taste like chicken, but what they'd have chicken taste like if they didn't have access to real chickens to gauge the likeness.

"It's good, if you can stick with it long enough," a young man across the aisle said to me. I looked down at my chicken, wondering if I could stick with it long enough.

"We had to read it for school," the young man said.

"Oh," I said, through a mouthful. "The book, ha! Thank you," I said, laughing a little and lifting my fork his way in a toast. I didn't know what the fork lift meant, nor to what my thanks referred. The young man didn't seem to know either. He put his headphones back on and returned to what he was watching on the back of the seat in front of him. I went at the chicken with a little too much force and my fork scraped my plate; then in a flash I saw what I thought was a face that turned into the gold handle of a chest. It was just a moment before dirt fell on top of the chest, so I didn't know, and wondered if it was a memory, but then what memory could it be? Not a dream I could remember. So a movie I'd seen recently? But what movie?

Putting my headphones on, I navigated the available airline movies. At first to see how bad it could be, I chose a family comedy led by a dog. I hated myself for finding it so hilarious, and laughed out loud when one of the flight attendants walked past. I ordered a drink and then two more after that one, and cried when at the end of the movie the lead dog gets reunited with her puppies.

I ordered a drink every time a flight attendant came by after that. They were free, and hypothetically bottomless. I remember nothing else from the flight after a certain point.

When I opened my eyes, it felt as if I'd been turned upside down and shaken. The plane was landing, and they made announcements in French about the weather, or the landing—I guess it could have been about anything. The knot had worsened, and besides stumbling out of my seat from drunkenness, when I walked down the aisle, I felt a little hunched over—weighed down by the knot. I reached back and felt a physical lump there, a rising between my shoulder and neck. Between my staggering and hunching, I must have left the plane looking like Dr. Frankenstein's assistant, Fritz, so often mistakenly thought of as Igor. In grad school, I almost wrote my dissertation on the parallels between Mary Shelley's *Frankenstein* and the United States government creating Native people as wards of the state. Coincidentally, Mary Shelley references Native people, and has her monster weeping over what happened to Native people in America.

The lump felt bigger by the time I was off the plane and in the terminal. The messenger bag I carried my laptop and books in weighed my opposite shoulder down, making the lump seem more pronounced.

When I reached back to knead the thing, the clinking returned, that digging sound. I didn't turn around to look for it this time.

"Tom," I heard my wife say from a distance. I don't think I'll ever get used to anyone else besides my wife and my immediate family calling me Tom. The name Tom was for stiffs, people already dead walking around in suits. But I'd outgrown Tommy and had chosen the more serious *Thomas*. When my wife said *Tom* again, it was with some mix of urgency and annoyance. I thought of the Capgras delusion when I saw her and my son, Alix, at baggage claim. There was something about seeing them in a foreign country that made them seem not themselves. I was tired and there was some drag from the half dreams I had had on the plane, some blur to the lines of what was what, in the way my wife and son were holding hands and sort of swaying—but no, it was me who must have been swaying.

"What's wrong with you?" asked Anne.

"Sorry, just didn't sleep. Or slept too much," I said. I was still doing my best not to sway and to stand up straight—avoid hunching.

"You don't know which?" she asked.

"Yeah, Dada. How do you not know which one?" my son said, laughing, one of his front teeth gone and the other on the way out, just sort of indefinitely dangling there in the soon to be double-wide window in his mouth. Later, Alix ended up losing the tooth, then found out the French tooth fairy was a little mouse—*la petite souris*—and decided he preferred a fairy.

"Well, I tried to sleep, and then I think I either dreamed I tried to sleep but couldn't, or I really couldn't and just had my eyes closed while thinking about it all really hard."

"How do you think *hard*? And can you think soft?" Alix asked.

"That's *exactly* what Daddy's doing, Alix. The soft kind. You haven't even told us about first class yet. How was it? Tell us everything," Anne said.

"It wasn't much. The plates they served the food on were fancier than the actual food, and you can turn your chair into a bed. Oh, and you get as many free drinks as you want."

"Is that why your breath smells so *hard*?" Alix asked. I squinted at the flight numbers on the baggage display to make sure we were at the right one.

"Tom, your son asked you a question," Anne said.

"They give you hot towels and warm nuts," I said.

"Hot towels and warm nuts?" Alix asked. "What for?" His questions came fast, and urgent, like he needed to know the answers to things faster than he knew they could come, and that the only way to ensure he could get the answers as fast as possible was to ask them with a kind of electricity.

"Are you sure you're not underselling it because you think we'll be jealous?" Anne asked.

"I mean, it was way nicer than coach, or economy, or what do they call it now?"

"What do *they* call it now? So you already consider yourself separate from us peasants?" Anne asked.

"Peasants," Alix repeated and laughed. He'd been calling us peasants when asking for snacks, or to do something for him around the house. He picked it up from the internet somewhere, and though I didn't think he knew what it meant, or anything about its history, he knew exactly how to use it.

"What is a peasant?" Alix asked, as if listening in on what I was thinking.

"It's what your dad thinks we are now, Alix," Anne said, and that's the last thing I remember, though we must have gotten in line for a cab, or been picked up by the publisher who would have been holding a sign with the last name *Blaine*, but I don't remember any of it, and was too embarrassed to ask later, and had long since stopped asking for parts I didn't remember, and had even harbored suspicions my wife was making things up when she knew I was in blackout territory, rewriting recent history for reasons I hadn't ascertained yet.

"And . . . we're here!" the driver said to us, then moments later, with an almost violent swiftness, the cab driver slid the van door open, saying a little too excitedly the word, "Voilà!"

All the interviews they'd set up with local journalists about the translated publication of my book took place on the top floor of my publisher's office in a meeting room with no windows, and bright white walls with no paintings or decorations on them. There was a sizable flat-screen TV on the wall. It was quiet up there on the top floor in a way that seemed to match the blankness of the walls. The first interview was with a journalist from what my French editor called France's *Wall Street Journal.*

"As opposed to France's *New York Times?*" I asked my editor, trying for a joke.

"The French *New York Times* one is at half past fourteen," my editor said.

I was not used to how the rest of the world functioned on what Americans considered military time, but to most was simply the way they kept track of time: after twelve o'clock came thirteen, and on to twenty-four, and then zero for the new day. I found that I liked the twenty-four-hour way of keeping time, how it eliminated mix-ups around a.m. and p.m. Hours starting again at one after twelve—that made less sense.

The first interviewer, the one from the French *Wall Street Journal*, wore all black and came in wearing a beret, but had taken it off immediately and put it in the corner with his carrier bag and cane. I wasn't sure if it was a functional cane or one for style. The journalist's name was Pierre, and he had a thin mustache. I believed momentarily that I was on a French candid camera–type show where they would catch me looking flabbergasted at a French parody of itself acting as if it wasn't—the thing to finally make me crack would be a baguette produced suddenly with maybe a glass of red wine and one of these now so characteristic voilàs I kept hearing with increased frequency. There seemed to be almost no occasion necessary for these increasingly ubiquitous voilàs.

Before the interview I went back to my tabs about the Capgras delusion, and found another delusion named after *The Truman Show*, which caused people who suffered from it to believe their life was an elaborate film set and everyone around them a part of the film about them. It was, of course, not a candid-camera show trying to catch me shocked at a ridiculous French parody of itself but was actually a ridiculous French parody of itself by accident.

"So, your book, this is fantastic. Now tell me, how long did it take you to write?"

"I guess it was about four years, give or take."

"Which would you do if you had to, give or take, as you say?"

"If I *had* to?"

"I just love the way they come away from this crash, this accident, the way they must reckon with the sins of their lives, of that day before the crash, and how they all come to terms with their sins, and the blood, oh your descriptions of the blood spill were sublime!"

"I don't know that I would agree that they all come to reckon with sin. That's not at all what I intended, what I wrote. And regarding the blood, what does 'sublime' mean here for you?"

"Please tell me, does this Native American social worker you have, who drinks too much, and is maybe at fault for the whole accident in the first place, for the wreck and the wreckage—does this character most resemble you?"

"No. I mean, none of the characters are *me*, or resemble me in any significant way, or, I guess they're *all* me, as any fictional characters are kinds of stand-ins, imposters of their authors. Have you heard of this delusion? It has French origins, the Capgras—no, sorry. Never mind, no, none of the characters are me because I didn't write a memoir, I wrote a novel."

"Short-story collection, no?"

"Well, linked stories—"

"I was wondering about your ideas about the correlation between car crashes and sex?"

"I don't know what you mean."

"Haven't you seen the Cronenberg film?"

"The what?"

"Can you talk a little about reconciliation and the Native American experience? For example, would you describe yourself or your characters as bitter and looking for some kind of reconciliation?"

"Bitter? Reconciliation?"

"*Le Calcul* is, of course, a terrific book, and, by the way, we're going to write an excellent review of it. This is very impressive for a debut."

"Thank you, but this is my fourth book."

"Well, your first French translation, so a debut here in France. Debut, one of those French words you pronounce the French way in English, like cliché and chef and menu, and well, I suppose there are so many, but debut, it just means first appearance, and this is your first appearance in the French language, so . . ."

"Faux, as well."

"Excuse me?"

"Faux, as in *faux pas*. We say the same in English as in French."

"Ah, yes, faux pas."

"No, but also just faux, too—I mean just faux. We use this to mean fake with other things."

"With other things?"

"Like faux hawk for a certain mohawk, or . . ."

"Faux hawk like a fake Mohawk person, like a fake Indian?"

"No, no, no, the hairstyle. I mean a different version of a mohawk, the hairstyle."

"Oh, I see," Pierre said. And there was a pause filled with a tension I didn't know how to diffuse. So I left it there to look around the room as if to find something new there. I wished there was a clock to look at. Pierre was texting or taking down notes on his phone. I felt the lump behind me throb. Just once. And I reached back, which then I found I couldn't, so I tried with my other hand and couldn't. It throbbed again, and I shifted the way I was sitting to accommodate the thing.

"Are you okay?" Pierre asked.

"Fine. Can we go back to what you were saying about sin earlier?" I asked.

"I think we have all we need. It's okay, it's perfectly fine what we have," Pierre said.

"We?"

"It will be good. I think it will be a good article," Pierre said, and gathered his things.

Me and my wife and son rented electric scooters and rode them through the Paris streets in bike lanes and on sidewalks toward the Eiffel Tower. We rode the scooters along the Seine. Alix rode with me, standing in front of me on my scooter, squeezing the accelerator—with me in charge of the brakes and steering. Young people were riding electric scooters everywhere now, in America and Europe. It was like a vision of the future in the present no one had recognized fully as the future yet, and maybe never would. The future itself was constantly being replaced by the ever-present present, which never looked enough like the future to *be* the future—plus there was always more future to be had, and the past could loom too, always threatening to come back. But something about the effortlessness, the standing position, the speed and wind through your hair, its soundlessness, all made the electric scooter experience feel futuristic. I didn't feel the lump as I rode, not even as a knot or kink. I could move freely and felt like lifting my arms in the air, but knew it would have embarrassed Alix. Actually, I would have been embarrassed myself by how much I loved to ride along the Seine on an electric scooter, but Alix loved it as much as I'd ever seen my son love anything—and this love of anything my son loved transcended all embarrassments. Even Anne was smiling and laughing at the thrill of the ride, the absurdity of seeing the ancient-feeling city, which was two thousand years old, so as old as Jesus and modern time. So, ancient enough, anyway, most especially because we were standing and basically flying on a platform run by electric current—this with the City of Lights just coming to life as the sun set.

The interviews on the second day were very much the same as the first: in the same room and with seemingly the same misinterpretations of my book, only even more strained because nearly all the journalists on the second day required a translator.

The last interviewer was from Switzerland. I hadn't realized they spoke French in Switzerland. I wondered if there was a Swiss language and looked it up while the Swiss journalist settled in and set up her phone to record. There was no Swiss language and yet somehow there was a famous knife named after a Swiss army in an almost infamously neutral country? Nothing makes sense the more you look into it. The Swiss journalist cleared her throat.

"Sorry," I said, then bowed my head in apology. The woman had orange hair and freckles like my mom. I had freckles too, though they've faded somewhat with time. My freckles were my loudest reminder that I would never look Native American enough, would

never be able to walk into a Native space and be accepted as anything other than an unwanted complication.

"I see you have freckles," the Swiss journalist said. "You don't
see many Indians with freckles."

"How many Indians *have* you seen?" Here I knew I was losing
my patience, that the last day of interviews had worn me out.
The Swiss journalist turned red at my question about how many
Indians she'd seen.

"I've been to the States many times. I know people in South
Dakota," she said defensively. Of course, it was South Dakota.

"I'm sorry. It's been a long day. I'm sure you've seen your share
of Indians."

"My share?"

"The freckles are from my mom's side. Scotch-Irish. She looks
a little like you."

"And do other Indian people think you're white?"

"I haven't asked them."

"I mean, do they treat you like you're . . . one of them?"

"One of them," I said, and breathed a big breath in. "Can we
get back to the book? I don't see how this is relevant."

"There's an argument to be made that it *is* relevant, but I won't
make it. Let's talk about the end of your book. How the Indian has
his moment with God, about his sins, how he saves the people he
almost killed awash with blood, how he dies in saving them. There
seem to be some nods to Jesus, and I know many Indian people are
Christians now. Can you comment on this possible Indian Jesus
figure, and do you think there's a correlation between Jesus's story
and the Native American experience? Also, is there some sense of
resurrection we're supposed to derive from the sacrifice he made
to save them, and the ghosts that appear thereafter?"

The Swiss journalist will never know why I stood up and

walked out of the office, out of the building. She'll never know that I understood fully in that moment how wrong they'd done the translation, how the only way for me to know just how wrong they got it would be to learn French and learn it well enough to read my book. This would never happen. My perspective on the French translation of my book was related to my new paranoia about somehow developing, then progressing further into Capgras delusion, purely based on knowing about the Capgras delusion. The Swiss journalist wouldn't know that I would drink way too much alone at a bar next to the bookstore, then go to my reading and read from the Bible the whole time as a response to the overly Christian interpretation/translation of my book. She wouldn't know that people would end up walking out of my reading in frustration, because it was supposed to be an on-stage interview with a prominent French intellectual, but I would read and read until every person had walked out, including the French intellectual and my French editor, until the French police were called and they escorted me out of the bookstore, with only my wife and son there to console me, near tears on the street, the crossed arms and shaking heads of so many French people around us. The Swiss journalist would never know how happy I was to have them there, how completely my family accepted my tears, my Native American freckles, even if they didn't know why I'd done what I'd done with the Bible. As we walked away from the mess at the bookstore, I felt the weight of the lump return, and felt it throb. Alix noticed as I succumbed to its weight.

"What's wrong, Quasimodo? Wish we were going to your precious Notre Dame?" Alix said with a French accent that wasn't half bad.

"Yes, master," I said, and hobbled along. Alix laughed, so I played it up even more. Felt the throb: the lump maybe growing, but I became the character, and listened to my son laugh at me being stupid, my wife rolling her eyes and getting out her phone to figure out dinner.

My French editor had promised to take us to an authentic French restaurant after the reading, but seeing as he'd fled the scene, we were left to figure it out on our own with the help of Yelp. I got the tripe sausage—so, intestine sausage. The flavor and smell of the sausage haunted me for weeks. Over dinner, I told my wife about the interpretation and translation of my book. About the Swiss journalist and the Indian freckles. I hadn't told her before the reading. She'd been baffled at my insistence to read from the Bible, but mostly, during my reading, she and Alix had wandered the bookstore, having heard me read in bookstores across the United States when the book was first published the year before way too many times to care anymore.

"Let's, why don't we . . . we can change how this ends," Anne said.

"It's too late," I said.

"Why'd everyone leave Dada's reading?" Alix asked.

"It's not too late to save the ending of our trip, I mean," Anne said.

I was to leave first for a speaking gig in Portland. Anne and Alix would stay to enjoy Paris for a few more days.

"Let's get scooters again," Alix said.

And soon none of it mattered: as we accessed our scooters with our phones, and rode along the Seine, dust behind us, we were all more ready than we knew to quietly fly like that, around tourists and Parisians with the lights on the Eiffel Tower just blinking on, and the stars, the few of which could be seen, doing the same. We smiled wide and wanted to yell something out into the Parisian night, against the Seine, ashamed and proud at once of being American and not American and something else, from a future once dreamed of, a hoverboard-robot eighties dream we don't even remember anymore. We wanted to yell because we knew the future might not come; or this might be the closest humanity, in its current iteration or incarnation, gets to the future. So we rode our electric scooters along the Seine, happy because nothing makes sense, with enough sense made within ourselves, our trio, to feel that, if even just for the moment, we were riding into the opening light of the Parisian night with purpose; even if we were not thinking of happiness, it was happening. We'd all end up knowing later, maybe when it was too late, or maybe when we were old enough to want to remember better times, having lost hope in a future that more and more seemed wouldn't come, or, if it came, meant only the end of time.

I touched my forehead to the back of my son's head, and he reached an arm back to hold my big head. I looked back at Anne, who was looking up at the now fully lit Eiffel Tower. There was nothing up until then, nor would there ever be any better moment in my whole life than that one.

Still, the lump throbbed.

The morning I was to leave for the airport, I got a text from my editor.

> *Come to the office now to meet your translator. There*
> *should be time before your flight.*

The text had come in late the night before, but I was just now getting it, having woken up early after passing out early. I was suspicious about the meeting. My editor had left the reading and

ditched out on dinner. So then why would he lure me into the
office? To punish me somehow? Publicly demean me? And hadn't
all the confusion been related to problems with the translation?

B rt there, I texted back.

"I'm going to my publisher's office to meet the translator before
my flight, so I'm gonna say bye *now*, okay," I whispered to my still-
sleeping wife, trying not to wake Alix.

"Okay," she woke up enough to say. "We love you." She was
being brief in order to not be awake so long as to not be able to go
back to sleep. I kissed her cheek and rubbed her arm.

On the walk to the publisher's office I felt heavy with dread,
but also heavy from the lump becoming a hump, and sore, and
like it would be cancer, that this was how it would end for me, a
drunk Indian humpback, like Kokopelli, playing Indian tropes in
my books like the expected flute songs. I also felt like I was going
to a job and my boss was waiting to give me a talking-to. Being a
writer could feel like you had many bosses and none. I didn't know
what I'd say to the translator.

"Hello!" my French editor said, giving me a hug and two kisses.
"Are you okay?" he asked, which I took to be related to the reading,
what I'd done with the Bible.

"I'm so happy this is working out. That I get to meet the translator," I said.

"He's been out of town, and I wasn't sure if he'd make it back
in time, but he's here. I have him up on the top floor where you
did your interviews."

This seemed innocuous enough, but strange. Meeting up there
had made sense for the interviews. But not for this.

"I'm sorry, but why are we meeting up there?" I asked.

"Come, you have little time," my French editor said.

"Is everything . . . okay?" I asked on the way up.

"Everything's fine. What do you mean? What could be wrong?"

"It's just that, my reading. You left and—"

"Oh, I'm so sorry. I thought I told you my daughter went into labor. I left well before you even started."

I believed him. I did. But I didn't believe anything. Not all the way.

"Hello, so nice to meet you," the translator said with a smile.

"You too, and thank you. Let me just say thank you so much for all the work you put into the book," I said.

"I'll leave you two to it then," my French editor said.

"It's my job," the translator said.

"Yes, sure, but surely there is passion with this kind of work, and it's not just any job. I imagine it's difficult, no?" I noticed this ending of my sentence with "no" was something people who speak English as a second or third language did. It wasn't on purpose. It just happened. Was my syntax itself being replaced with an imposter?

"It's nothing, really. You did all the heavy lifting." The translator smiled and reached out his hand for a shake. I wondered, but wasn't sure, if we'd already done this. "Arnaud," he said.

"Speaking of the, er . . . lifting, what you did," I said, and didn't want to rush into questioning the translation, but had a plane to catch. "There's something I noticed about it, something the interviewers brought up having to do with . . . with sin."

"Sin?"

"Yes, like from Christianity."

"I'm sure there's been a misunderstanding."

"Misunderstanding? Several journalists commented on sin and redemption."

"I'm only doing my job, sir."

"And why did that include making my book about Jesus?"

"I'm so sorry."

"No, no, I'm sorry. Here I am falling apart in front of you, and we've just met. And I'm sorry about accusing you of a poor translation."

"There's something I have to tell you."

"What's that?"

"I'm not your translator."

"What?"

"It's not me, I'm so sorry."

"What are you talking about?"

"I'm just a copyeditor here. Your editor asked me to pretend to be your translator, that it'd make you happy and be over quickly. He said it was important to you, and I didn't think we'd really get into it. I'm so sorry. My name is Vincent," he said, and reached his hand out to me to shake again.

"Enough!" I said. "Enough with the handshakes. What is going on here? You're telling me you're a fake? You're pretending to be my translator? What is this, some kind of joke? I don't believe you. This is sick!"

"No, no. I promise you we'll get Francis in here and he'll explain everything. He wanted you to have this moment before leaving. I'll go get him. Everything's fine. Your real translator's out of town."

"I don't believe you. You're trying to get out of what you've done to my book!" I stood, not knowing why. This scared the man, and for a moment scared me too, as I caught my reflection in the TV, and watched the lump, which seemed to be growing, and pulsing. Vincent stood up and ran out of the room.

I looked back at my reflection in the TV. My eyes were too wide-open. My hair was disheveled. My face was puffy and getting puffier. Then the thing growing in my back burst. The Kokopelli broke through. Blood sprayed the TV. Flute music played from somewhere behind me, or from beneath my skin, which was now sloughing off. The Kokopelli was becoming me, or getting rid of the egg I had been to make way for it. I was becoming this stupid southwestern, pan-Indian stereotype, but I'd already been one. A drunk Indian. The sound of blood dripping turned into a clinking sound, the digging, and when I looked at my reflection again it was just me again in the dark gray staring back. And there in that stare, my face, came a memory of looking at myself in the reflection of my car window after something had happened. Something I'd been pushing away. How long ago? Was I already too deep into something I wouldn't be able to dig my way out of? And there was that image again. Of me digging holes on our property back home. Multiple holes or multiple tries at one hole. There was nothing else from the memory left to make sense of it, and it just as easily might have been a dream. That look in my eyes, though. There had been a body. Slung over my shoulder. The hump, its weight. A body. But what body? I reached back and pushed down on the thing as hard as I could and it came, in a flash, a new memory. It was of me swaying. My wife digging, burying a body. She kept looking at me to see what I was seeing, how much I was comprehending. In another flash, I was in bed asking her about what she'd been digging for, and she told me it must have been a dream, that she'd never dug a hole in her life. I let go of the lump and looked back into the TV. I called my wife, but it just rang and rang. Approaching the flat screen, I put my ear to it. *Clink, clink.* The digging. I tasted metal in my mouth.

I reached back for the lump and pressed on it again and saw nothing with my eyes open but swirling colors, then a kind of hole opening, and there, there, the hole became a steering wheel, my hands, the road home, a local tweaker dashing across the road like a deer. I let go of the memory like it was too hot to hold.

I walked out of the conference room, out of my publisher's office, off to find a bar, or a store that sold liquor, to treat the thing eating me, or to dig deeper the hole I'd been digging for more years than I could remember. But no. I would not drink. I would wander. Find God in the Notre Dame. Or that hunchback. I would find that the body I'd been carrying, and the one that I'd buried was mine. I would go to the bell tower, unring the bell that had been rung in me long before I knew there were names for God or songs sung on flutes by Indian Gods worn out by time and stereotype. I would stop drinking and return home to the body inside my body, the one that I had abandoned and made myself carry. Or the Kokopelli would become me. And I would lose my name and body on the streets of Paris.

I walked to the Seine and looked into its black-green flow. Knew nothing that I thought should happen, would happen, just like it'd always been.

Tommy Orange is a graduate of the MFA program at the Institute of American Indian Arts. An enrolled member of the Cheyenne and Arapaho Tribes of Oklahoma, he was born and raised in Oakland, California.

THE SCIENTIST'S HORROR STORY

DARCIE LITTLE BADGER

Bets had known Dr. Anders Lilley since they were postdocs, long enough to interpret his many smiles. Anders grinned through nearly every emotion: amusement, joy, melancholy, anxiety, annoyance, fury. Currently, his smile telegraphed a subtle playfulness. He'd speak soon. Anders was a skilled entertainer, an especially useful trait in the sciences, where half the work was communication. With anticipation, Bets watched his face.

At thirty-seven years old, Anders had thin lips parenthesized between well-defined smile lines; his brown hair was fastened in a high, messy bun. "Look at us," he said. "Like three friends sitting around a campfire."

"Are you calling that a campfire?" Dr. Harmoni Coelho teased, pointing at the tea light on their table. Anders, Harmoni, and Bets were dining at a courtyard restaurant near the convention center. They were participants in the annual Oceanographic, Environmental, and Planetary Sciences Conference, a machine fueled by overlapping presentations, intense networking, and ten thousand over-caffeinated scientists.

"Use your imagination," Anders encouraged. He popped a beignet into his mouth, delicately wiping his sugar-dusted fingertips on a cloth napkin. To wind down the night, they were sharing a dessert plate and sipping on beer (Anders; he insisted that beer was the official drink of geologists), wine (Harmoni; red wine, never white), and Shirley Temples (Bets; she really had to learn the name of a different nonalcoholic mixed drink 'cause ginger ale and grenadine got old fast).

"As a boy," Anders mused, "I spent every summer at Diamond Lake with my brothers. We'd go swimming and tell ghost stories around the fire till our brains were so full of make-believe monsters, there wasn't room for anything else."

"Distraction from fear with fear," Bets said, swirling her Shirley Temple. "Cool."

"Isn't escapism the reason everyone enjoys horror?" Anders asked.

Bets shrugged, smiling faintly. "Personally—"

"It's why I do," Harmoni interrupted, failing to hear Bets, who usually spoke softly, rationing her volume to maximize its impact. "But being a grown-up horror fan is rough. I can't suspend disbelief anymore. It's too easy to sniff out fiction."

Anders's laugh lines deepening so subtly, the change might have been a trick of shadows and candlelight. "Adults are a tougher audience than kids," he agreed. "However, our stories can be scarier, too."

"Prove it, Rock Man," Harmoni challenged. "Tell us a ghost story."

"My pleasure." Anders raised his beer can as if toasting the challenge. "Tonight, ladies, you won't need to suspend any disbelief, 'cause my story really happened."

"Suuuuure."

"Cross my heart," said Anders. "In fact, *I* dare *you* to prove otherwise."

In response, Harmoni placed her mini composition notebook on the table; she flipped to a clean page and labeled it *PLOT HOLES*. "Ready."

Bets scooted to the edge of her seat, listening, observing. "Last year," Anders began, his smile fading, "I received a direct message from Mike Waterloo. In high school, we were friends. Good friends, even, but it's been almost two decades since then. The first DM was nothing extraordinary. Mike asked me if I was still a geologist. Yes. Well, Mike was a nurse at Saint Mary's Hospital, New Mexico, and he had an urgent public health question. What do you think my old friend asked, Bets?"

Classic Anders. During conversations, he ran a mental tally of all voices, pinpointed the quietest person in the group, and questioned them until the tally evened out. Bets assumed it was a professor thing, a method to encourage equal class participation. When Anders wasn't studying sea-level indicators, he taught at Arizona State.

"The hospital was sinking," she guessed, "and Mike needed a bedrock expert to check its foundation."

"Then you discovered something shocking," Harmoni jumped in. "There were ancient catacombs under the building, a burial ground predating humankind itself. Are we close?"

"No." Anders smiled in approval of their creativity. A-plus work, Bets thought, pleased. "Actually, Mike asked me whether the ground could emit radiation. I explained that there are natural background sources of radiation all around us, including underfoot. But terrestrial radiation is usually very low, harmless. Nothing likely to cause a health crisis. He pressed the issue. Was an extreme situation possible? Say, a lethal dose? Enough to damage the chromosomes in every cell? That freaked me out. I asked, 'Are you treating acute radiation poisoning? Should folks in New Mexico be concerned?' He wasn't sure. Since April, five people between the ages of eighteen and twenty-seven—three men and two women—had died of unknown causes in the ICU. Now, two teenagers were hospitalized, their health deteriorating rapidly. All of them demonstrated similar, horrific symptoms, and recent tests on the teens indicated they no longer had functional DNA. The only link between the patients, as far as Mike could tell, was a ghost town named Pinot, which was abandoned in the mid-twentieth century. All the patients visited it shortly before getting sick. Specifically, they'd explored the town's stables."

"*Specifically*, what were their horrific symptoms?" Harmoni asked.

"Testing me already?" Anders grinned.

Harmoni tapped a capped pen against the table, drumming out a soft, steady beat. Bets had observed this behavior before, knew that Harmoni tapped when she was anxious. Fingernails, pens, forks—she'd use anything handy as a drumstick. Recently, the drumming had been more common, which made Bets worry. She'd known Harmoni only two years. The young professor was mysterious in myriad ways, since she rarely discussed her personal life, instead preferring abstract subjects, current events, and work-related talk. Would Harmoni ever feel comfortable enough to confide in Bets?

"Mike spared me the details," Anders said, "but I know what happens when all your DNA's destroyed, thanks to an essay I wrote for a high-school philosophy class. I had to answer the classic 'Ship of Theseus' question: If the components of a ship are replaced over time, when—if ever—does it become a new ship? To get points for creativity, I tackled the question from a biological point of view. There's an old claim that the human body replaces itself every seven years, cell by cell. Obviously, the reality is more complex. Some cells last decades, others days. I did a little research and learned that the average turnover time is:

"a few months for red blood cells,

"a few weeks for skin cells,

"and a few days for the gut lining,

"with billions of cells replaced every day."

Anders clasped his hands and leaned forward.

"You need DNA for cell division, protein creation, important stuff. Essentially, if your DNA stops working, you fall apart piece by piece. Am I close, Harmoni?"

Harmoni wasn't a geneticist or doctor, but she did study the human impacts of environmental disasters. Slow, cumulative suffering. Long, complex deaths. Her providence was lead in water, heavy metals in crops, mining runoff, factory waste. She spoke to the ill, to the dying, and to grieving families. For a moment, Bets worried that Anders's story had raised a sore subject, because Harmoni diverted her gaze to the space over his shoulder and idly picked at a hangnail on her thumb. Her fingers were always picked ragged.

"Yes," she finally said, and then her focus snapped back to Anders. "Infections probably killed Mike's patients early in the process. What happened next?"

Anders cleared his throat. Then, in earnest, the geologist told his story.

The day after Mike contacted me, I borrowed a clean suit, a Geiger counter, and a respirator from the university. My younger cousin Archie lives near Saint Mary's Hospital, and I was worried for him, for his neighbors. Was there a bioweapon in Pinot Ghost Town? A contaminant? Could it be neutralized? Would it spread? We had to understand the danger to prevent more deaths.

It was dark when I reached Archie's place. In fact, I drove past his driveway twice before noticing the narrow dirt road leading to his home. Archie built his house in front of a plateau. At night, the grand formation resembles a wall of solid shadow, but the sun brings out layers of red and orange sandstone; its western face glows at sunset. Since it was two a.m., and Archie gets grumpy if you disturb his beauty sleep, I parked, notched back the driver's seat, and tried to doze in the car. However, the sunroof made me feel exposed, vulnerable. I couldn't nod off. We know so little about the universe, and that scares me. There's danger, no danger, and the unknown, which can be either. And which—in the case of Pinot Ghost Town—can kill.

In the morning, aching and exhausted, I joined Archie for breakfast. As he cooked eggs and Spam in an iron skillet, I asked him about the ghost town.

"That dump?" he asked. "It's just a couple of boarded-up shacks and condemned stables. Ghost towns are boring. Why do you care?"

That's when I showed him Mike's earlier messages. "There may be a source of radioactivity in the stables," I explained. "I'm here to find out."

"Absolutely not," he said. "You're a bow tie–wearing academic. Leave dangerous investigations to the pros."

I explained that the pros were failing to protect people. Plus, I had a Geiger counter. Even so, Archie invited himself along to protect me. If I tried anything hardheaded—his words, not mine— he'd grab me by the Doc Martens and drag me outta town.

After breakfast, we climbed into his pickup truck and headed to Pinot Ghost Town, so named for the wine-red stripe in the nearby cliffs. Archie was wrong about one thing: ghost towns aren't boring. There's a thrill to exploring contemporary ruins, hence the booming genre of urban exploration videos. As a geologist, I get the appeal.

Every geology student learns about stratigraphy. You can study layers of rock and reconstruct the history of the Earth going back hundreds of millions of years. Strata tell stories about the world that existed before the first human breath, and we use those teach-

ings to understand our place here, now, and to predict futures beyond the last human breath.

Similarly, ruins are extensions of the people who built and lived within their walls. And they show us what we'll all become: the stories of everything and everyone we leave behind.

At our destination, Archie parked a quarter mile away from the town. He sat in the truck as I trudged up Pinot Road; during the drive, I'd convinced him to stay behind, since I had only one respirator. My tech didn't detect any worrisome levels of radiation, even when I neared the buildings. They were all dried-out husks of graffiti-embellished wood. The two shacks, which were positioned side by side and nearly identical in shape, size, and wear, had neither doors nor windows, just busted-out rectangular holes. In the distance, the abandoned stables were larger than both shacks combined. I also noticed a rustic windmill with just two remaining blades.

I stopped about thirty feet away from the nearest shack, hesitating, remembering my promise to give the buildings space. According to the Geiger counter, I was safe. The dangerous source of radiation, if one existed, must be farther into the desert. Sadly, my full-body getup wasn't appropriate for a hike. Must've been ninety degrees. I was already sweating buckets, huffing and puffing through the respirator. So, in lieu of more walking, I surveyed the area with a preposterously tiny pair of field binoculars.

Didn't notice any UFOs or suspicious barrels of waste, but the graffiti was nice. The shacks were tagged with names and cartoon scribbles—Bart Simpson wearing turquoise; a turtle on a skateboard; two bluebirds with long, shapely human legs; the phrase there is no tomorrow written over and over and over again in a tornado of words. The stables, with their wider walls, had the best selection of spray-painted art. A flock of one hundred or more stencil-precise crows spiraled around a jagged, plank-size hole in *the side wall, as if they were being sucked into the darkness. And a girl with short pink hair—a bob, very cyberpunk—was painted on one side of the stables, her back flush with the edge of the wall. The girl's lips quirked in a slight smile, and her brown eyes watched the crows. There was a cloudlike thought bubble over her head, but her thoughts were illegible, since somebody had defaced them with wild, formless scribbles of dripping black ink. Somebody, maybe the same person, had drawn a skull-and-crossbones symbol on her chest, over her heart.*

Reception gets spotty in the desert, so Mike's warning didn't arrive until then, as I stepped into an unpredictable bubble of connectivity at the end of the road. My cell phone dinged, and a three-word message popped onto the screen: It's not radiation.

He'd sent more messages, but when my phone is locked, it displays only one at a time. There was no way to respond or scroll through my message history. Unfortunately, I couldn't use face recognition to unlock the phone, and my gloved hands were useless on the touch screen.

In a panic, I started running back to the truck, but I quickly got woozy, steaming in my personal sauna, my goggles foggy and my eyes stinging. Thankfully, Archie's truck was driving toward me up Pinot Road, followed by a white SUV.

The vehicles both parked on the road. Archie hopped out of his truck, and a grizzled, forty-something man in a cowboy hat and a holster stepped from the SUV. I insisted, "We need to go," but the stranger made no attempt to move his vehicle, which was blocking our escape.

With the energy of an old-west lawman, the stranger patted his holster, which contained a taser and pepper spray. He barked out, "Why are you dressed like a spaceman?" Before I could explain that it was a hazmat suit, Archie said, "None of your business." There must have been an earlier clash between them, 'cause Archie rarely jumps straight to anger. I should've feared the stranger—and I did, on some level—but the unknown scared me more. If radiation hadn't killed those people, my Geiger counter couldn't protect us.

I explained, "I'm a geologist, and this town is dangerous. Please, let's go."

In response, the man hollered, "You aren't going anywhere, Walter White." Then, he said, "Hey, Siri, call the police. Nonemergency number."

A couple of seconds later, his smartphone's AI chirped, "Sorry, I'm having trouble with the connection." There was no coverage. In a snap, visible tension replaced the man's swagger, like we'd backed him into a corner instead of the other way around. I said, "It's okay. Maybe mine works." Then I tore off my gloves, unlocked my phone, and read all of Mike's recent DMs. Unfortunately, his messages only made the situation more confusing.

Anders rubbed his chin, which had been clean-shaven at the beginning of the conference but was now rough with a three-day-old beard; he forgot his razor at home, Bets hypothesized. He'd been absentminded lately, missing lunch meetings and locking himself out of his lab after-hours. Perhaps it was his schedule; this semester, to pay off extensive dental bills, Anders was teaching four classes, instead of his usual two. "Ladies," he said, "do you know of anything that can rapidly and stealthily replace all the DNA in an adult human body with a single repeating sequence: TAAGATAAGATAAGATAA—"

"No," Harmoni said, cutting him off before he could repeat "TAAGA" a fourth time. "Radiation definitely wouldn't do that."

"Well, according to Mike, the victims' genomes were trans-

formed into a nonsensical pattern of nucleotides. There's still no
official explanation. Probably never will be." Anders leaned forward. "However, I have a hypothesis."

"Do you?" Bets murmured.

"Oh, yes."

*As Archie argued with the stranger, I glanced back at the stables.
They were now many yards away, but even without my binoculars,
I could see that the pink-haired girl—the painting—was looking
at me.*

She hadn't been doing that earlier.

*I shoved Archie toward the truck, shouting, "It's not safe here!
Go, go, go!" Must have sounded nearly delirious with fear because
this time, everyone listened. In the pickup, Archie did a U-turn,
driving off-road to pass the SUV, and I rambled about Mike's messages and the moving painting. Archie didn't believe my claims
about the painting; Mike's messages, though, those freaked him out.
Archie kept mumbling, "It has to be a bioweapon."*

*Then, as if it had just occurred to him, he tapped the rearview
mirror and asked, "Do you think that guy's involved?" The SUV
was tailing our truck.*

*I had no clue. He was unpredictable, though, so I suggested we
drive somewhere public, a place with cameras, in case he made
more unfounded accusations or tried to start a fight.*

*Ultimately, we parked at a four-pump gas station. Hoping to
diffuse the situation, I ditched the clean suit and found a copy of
my business card. We didn't owe the man our IDs, but there was
no time to fight with an armed, high-strung fan of Clint Eastwood.*

*Thankfully, the business card convinced him I was a geologist.
My plain clothes probably helped, too, since I was wearing a pocket
protector.*

———

"You were wearing what?" Harmoni interrupted.

"A pocket protector. Don't be a hater."

She held up her hands in a placating manner. "No judgment! I just didn't realize anyone still used them."

"They'll come back in style," he insisted. "Anyway, in exchange for my card, the man gave me this."

Anders flipped open his leather wallet and rifled through its pockets. Then, he slapped a business card face-up on the tabletop. White text on black cardstock read:

SAMUEL BART RODGERS
PRIVATE INVESTIGATION

"Your story has props," Harmoni said. "I admit: that's persuasive."

Curious, Bets plucked up the card and studied it front to back. The edges were crisp, the material expensive. According to his business address, Samuel Bart Rodgers was based in Arizona, not New Mexico, but PIs could travel. That said, there were a thousand other reasons Anders might carry the card. It neither confirmed nor debunked his story.

He continued speaking.

Samuel suggested an exchange of information. We bought soda from the gas station convenience store and reconvened on a metal bench behind the building. It must have been where the attendants had smoke breaks, 'cause there were half-gone cigarettes around our feet.

Without getting into details—Mike technically wasn't supposed to share the DNA results with outsiders, but he trusted me—I explained that several adults and teens got fatally ill after visiting the abandoned buildings. Specifically, the stables.

That interested Samuel, since he was looking for a teenage girl named Aggie who went missing in Pinot Ghost Town. "Her parents hired me after the police investigation hit a wall," he explained. He'd been watching the area, secretively observing the people who visited the ghost town. My weird outfit set off his alarms; initially, he thought we were cooking drugs or retrieving a body.

Then Samuel showed me a selfie of the missing girl. I'd seen her before.

Sort of.

She had pink hair.

I pointed at the picture and said, "Her portrait is on the stables!" I thought I'd made a major break in the case, but Samuel just side-eyed me like I'd enthusiastically declared that the sky was blue. He explained, "Aggie's friends painted that mural during a vigil after she went missing."

Suddenly, Archie recalled, "Oh, yeah! I remember this girl. She was big news, once. My friend even helped with the search efforts. They checked every building and combed the desert, too. It was a while ago. That's why I forgot."

I asked, "How long, specifically?" He explained Aggie vanished over a year prior. She and her friends had used the abandoned buildings as a hangout zone, their own little clubhouse city.

After he was hired, Samuel conducted his own search. When he started, Aggie had been missing ten months. According to Mike's timeline, shortly after that, in Saint Mary's Hospital, a twenty-two-year-old was admitted with symptoms resembling acute radiation poisoning. He'd be the first victim of Pinot Ghost Town.

"Around then, I observed a young man at the stables," Samuel confirmed. "He was just a graffiti artist, though, so I didn't confront him."

I asked, "What did he paint?"

"Nothing impressive," Samuel replied. "He doodled in the thought bubble over Aggie's portrait. Her favorite poem used to be there, as well as her name and birthday."

I asked, "Are there other buildings in the area around the ghost town, and if so, did you check them?" Samuel said no: aside from the two shacks and stables, nothing remained but scattered lumber, stone foundations, and rusted tin cans.

"What about the wells?" I asked.

"There are none," he said.

Surprised, I insisted, "Are you sure?"

Samuel asked, "Why would there be wells?"

The answer, of course, was "because of the windmill." The old, two-bladed wreck by the stables was probably built to pump water from an underground aquifer. If I was correct, other people could have tapped into that resource. Aggie might've discovered a hidden well, fallen inside, and died alone in the dark.

Because it was too dangerous to return to the ghost town, I strongly advised Samuel to give the area a wide berth. However, he could survey the area with a drone and look for rings of stone. He neither agreed nor disagreed, never admitted that our information had been useful. Just grunted, finished his cola, and left with a dismissive "Stay out of trouble, boys."

I think he followed my suggestion, though, because a few days after my amateur investigation, Aggie's body was recovered. Her body was—as I'd feared—in a dry well, which had been hidden by a bush and further concealed under a flat slab of wood. Aggie's recovered phone contained two ominous final pictures. One showed her hand lifting the wooden slab. The other showed the pit; her flash couldn't dispel the deepest shadows. It's believed that Aggie had leaned into the well to take a better picture. Some-how, she lost her balance, fell headfirst, and died on impact. Her *friends, who'd been in the stables when she vanished, hadn't heard a thing.*

There have been no more deaths related to Pinot Ghost Town, and to this day, the cause of the DNA damage is officially unknown. However, I hypothesize the mutagen was Aggie herself.

Aggie was just a nickname. Her true name was Agata.

A moment of confused silence passed before Harmoni clapped. "The repeating DNA sequence. A-G-A-T-A . . ."

"Got it in one," Anders praised. "It all started after a vandal defaced her portrait, erasing her poem and name. This seemingly harmless act laid a curse upon the stables. Until her body was recovered, Agata haunted her victims at a molecular level."

At that, he sat back, clasped his hands, and waited for input.

"Why did she lash out at everyone?" Bets wondered.

"Perhaps for Aggie it wasn't just the vandalism that enraged her," Anders guessed. "It was . . . being forgotten."

Yes, Bets decided, that's a very reasonable answer.

"Well?" Anders asked. "What did you think of my ghost story? Was it convincing?"

The women exchanged glances.

"I enjoyed every word," Bets said, "but it never happened, Anders."

He gasped in mock outrage. "Excuse me?"

"She's right on both accounts," Harmoni agreed, holding up her notebook. Bold, underlined text read: _PLOT HOLES = WE'D ALL KNOW ABOUT THE PINOT GHOST TOWN INCIDENT._ A list beneath the major plot hole included questions like *PI shared case deets with random men???*, *Could police track Aggie's phone?*, and *Who covered well after Aggie fell?*

"If multiple people died because their DNA went haywire, the news would be everywhere. Television, medical journals, Reddit. It's weird enough to gain traction." Harmoni hesitated. "There were also a few . . . issues with the crisis response and scientific details. That's okay, though! I don't enjoy horror for its scientific accuracy."

"Plus," Bets added, "in the story, your behavior was all wrong. You know the importance of safety protocol, and you'd never put a family member like Archie at risk."

Anders's expression shifted from a mildly frustrated smile to an amused, crow's-feet-revealing grin. "Fine." He looked away, as if chastised. "You're both right. I invented the whole thing."

"Where'd the PI's business card come from?" Bets wondered.

He returned it to his wallet, winking. "It's my secret identity."

"Stop pulling my leg," Harmoni groaned.

"Okay, okay. Samuel's my brother-in-law." Anders finished his beer and flagged down a waiter to order another. Then, he said, "Either of you have a story? I want to be scared, too. And after all the criticism I got, it better be so realistic, it passes peer review."

"May I?" Bets asked, and her friends both looked surprised, in their own way. Harmoni's eyes fixed on Bets, unblinking, and Anders flashed a quick, genuine smile. "Should we be worried?" he joked. "There's something about you, Bets. A vibe. Like you were the creepiest kid at summer camp."

"I never went to summer camp," she said, smiling back at him, "but growing up, whenever possible, I watched scary movies on TV. Sci-Fi Channel originals (before they rebranded as S-Y-F-Y), classic slashers, found footage. Everything and anything."

"Cheers to that," Harmoni said, raising her half-empty glass of wine.

Bets nodded in agreement. "Over time, my habit blossomed into a love of B-horror movies. The cheesier, the better. Give me the self-aware and unashamed: perfectly terrible dialogue, over-the-top acting, and gallons of corn syrup blood; thirty-year-old teenagers falling into the mouths of Halloween-store monsters; the passion of an actor's full-chested scream. Give me horror without fangs. Yes. I used to love that stuff."

"Used to?" Harmoni asked. "What happened?"

Bets sighed.

One day, the edges between the movies and my life . . . blurred.

I'd been working on a grant to study the effects of flooding and hurricanes on the homeland of an unrecognized coastal tribe. Y'all know how most disaster prevention and mitigation efforts completely overlook small Indigenous communities. We're rarely tallied in the "greater good."

And honestly, my research would've benefited everyone. Why should humanity make concessions to destruction? There will always be more demands, and its hunger only grows.

Twelve hours before I learned the fate of our grant, my anxiety demanded a movie, and Fun House of Wax V *was streaming on Netflix. I hadn't seen* Fun House of Wax III *or* IV *but figured that continuity wasn't too important.*

The plot usually goes: On Halloween night, the titular fun house opens its doors to a new group of archetypical college kids. Inside, there are games, curio cabinets, a maze of mirrors, and rooms full of wax monsters. But at midnight, the monsters grow skin, fur, and scales. Hunted, tormented, the teenagers must escape the fun house or survive until dawn.

Even though the movie was filmed in the late 2010s, it didn't use CGI, and the practical effects were excellent, considering the shoestring budget. All in all, the Fun House*–verse represents an enjoyable franchise, with one caveat.*

B-movie characters rarely make the wisest choices, but the char-

acters in **Fun House** *movies are next-level terrible at staying alive. In one scene of* V, *the jock sticks his head in a werelion's mouth just to prove that it's harmless. You can imagine how that scene ends.*

Before long, I was shouting at the television. "Don't split up in the maze! Don't hide in that oven! Don't try to run in four-inch pumps! Don't turn your back on the murderclown; he's not actually dead!" I know, I know. It's a movie. But how could I resist? The plot was just. So. Frustrating. All the hapless teens could have survived the night if they'd made the right choices. The very obviously right choices. No question. It's like their self-preservation skills were . . . flipped.

Inevitably, just the final girl remained. She stood outside the fun house, her dress tattered and splattered with blood. In my world, it was midnight, but in the movie, it was dawn. Monsters screeched and roared as they turned back to wax. And then, convinced that all her friends were dead, she lit a match and threw it on the wooden porch.

The final shot revealed her boyfriend had survived and was hiding in the fun house maze. I remember shouting at the final girl, "You could have saved him!" and then, "You killed him!" I was still shouting when the screen faded to black.

As the credits rolled, I felt uneasy. Like somebody had slipped into my house during the movie and was now hiding, waiting. Before bed, I checked the windows, locked all the doors, and peeked in my bedroom closet. Everything was fine. So I told myself: The movie scared you. Relax.

However, that made zero sense. How did **Fun House of Wax V**, with its over-the-top acting, hilariously excessive death scenes, and predictable outcome, scare me?

I didn't sleep well, awaking groggy and confused by the tail end of a half-remembered dream. The day deteriorated from there. Our department's parking lot was full, so I had to park across campus. We were in a record heat wave. Temperatures breached one hun-

dred that morning, and there was no shade on my walk to work.
Campus needs more trees. It's a goddamn concrete heat island. Gets
worse every year.

By the time I reached the air-conditioned building, my shirt was
drenched with sweat, which left off-color splotches under my arms
and down my back. I had to wear a stiff old blazer to hide the mess.
Despite all that, some part of me was optimistic that the grant news
would turn my shitty day around. They'd approve it.

Our grant was denied.

"What?" Anders groaned. "Why?"

With a bitter smile, Bets explained.

According to feedback, we'd "failed to meet the relevance thresh-
old." It was a high bar, they explained. Many important projects
had competed for the funding. Therefore, we were invited to resub-
mit in one year with revisions. They encouraged us to shift our
focus to "issues affecting larger populations." Essentially, they were
reluctant to fund the research benefiting our small group of Natives
who were clinging to the remnants of their homeland, as if they had
a future. As if we've ever had a future.

Well, I rallied my team's postdocs and grad students, and we
brainstormed justifications for our project. Of course we'd resub-
mit. We'd convince them that our original goal was relevant. We'd
find the words to do that.

As I scribbled ideas on a dry-erase board, it struck: an overwhelm-
ing sense of déjà vu. My whole profession, passion, existence . . .

. . . reduced to the single, futile act of shouting at a movie. Hop-
ing that this time, somebody will listen.

Bets paused to study Anders and Harmoni, observing a familiar dread in her friends' eyes.

"Hence the reason I don't watch B-horror movies anymore," Bets said. "That feeling of helplessness—it's seductive, but it isn't true. We can be heard. We can make change. We have a future. Our children have futures. Right?"

Uninvited, a memory played across her mind's eye: crestfallen, walking back to her car, her shirt partially unbuttoned, her wool blazer folded over one arm. The asphalt shimmers with heat; the low air bakes her legs; the sun burns her face. Sweat trickles from her pores like melted wax.

The writing on the wall promises: there is no tomorrow.

It's lying.

"Right?"

Her friends didn't respond, instead choosing to drink.

Unsure of what else to do, Bets leaned across the table and blew out the candle.

Darcie Little Badger is a Lipan Apache writer with a PhD in oceanography. Her critically acclaimed debut novel, *Elatsoe*, was featured in *Time* magazine as one of the best hundred fantasy books of all time. *Elatsoe* also won the Locus Award for Best First Novel and is a Nebula, Ignyte, and Lodestar finalist. Her second fantasy novel, *A Snake Falls to Earth*, received a Nebula Award, an Ignyte Award, and a Newbery Honor and is on the National Book Awards Longlist. Little Badger is married to a veterinarian named Taran.

COLLECTIONS

AMBER BLAESER-WARDZALA

Death being mounted on walls was nothing new to me. Deer heads and fish bodies had adorned the walls of my relatives' homes. Trophies. I had never questioned their presence there. I had even listened to the stories—because there was always a story.

"That fucker fought so hard that I thought I had hooked Mishibizhii himself," my favorite uncle had told me once, motioning to the northern directly above his couch. "Bent my rod, he did. He was so set on escape, on not being caught. But I lived through Indian Boarding Schools. Ain't no fucker more strong-willed than me. I got him in the boat eventually. Weighed thirty pounds, the old bastard did. Can you believe it?"

With each telling, the fish weighed more.

I liked those stories. Liked the way my relatives' faces lit up as they retold the capture of their prize. And I grew used to the glassy eyes that watched my every move. Death lived in those houses like an old friend, like she was one of us, a member of the Cloud family.

In Anishinaabe tradition, hunting was not just a way to pass time. It was part of the cycle; it was a way to survive. Those animals gave their lives so that we might continue ours.

But when I walked into Professor Smith's suburban house for a party to celebrate the end of the semester and our class together, I was more than taken aback by the heads on her walls.

I was the last to arrive, having come from my job at the restaurant. I had recently been promoted from hostess to server. Or they told me it was a promotion. I suppose they thought making tips on top of my hourly pay was enough to persuade me that having to see to someone's every need was a good job, was better than organizing and arranging the seating. But I hated it, was bad at it. I left every night near tears, swearing I would never go back. That I had had it. That I would start looking for a new job the very next day.

I never did. I always went back.

That night was no different. In fact, that night was worse. I'd dropped a tray of food in the middle of the restaurant, pieces of the ceramic plates flying everywhere. I'd stood there frozen, everyone staring at me. My boss, without saying a word, handed me a dustpan and a broom. Instinct kicked in and I began to clean, my hands trembling. My coworkers didn't offer to help and instead walked around my mess, giving one another knowing looks.

After I had finished cleaning, my boss screamed at me in the kitchen for five whole minutes, loud enough that the whole restaurant could hear. I knew they heard because one of my customers, an older white man, patted my back when I came to ask him and his wife if they wanted dessert. He looked at me with pity in his eyes and said, "Don't worry, sweetheart. No boss can stay mad at a girl as pretty as you."

The last thing I wanted to do after work was go to a party, but I needed a letter of recommendation from Professor Smith for an internship so I wouldn't have to spend the summer at the restaurant. So I had to go, had to be gracious, had to make small talk and make sure she liked me. Make sure I ended the night with her thinking to herself, "Huh, that girl has a lot of promise."

But as I let myself into the house and saw the glassy eyes on her walls, I knew coming had been a mistake.

I stood there, frozen, one arm out of my coat, trying to believe what I was seeing, trying to conflate it with the image of the seemingly sweet professor I had known for the past semester. Sure, she was one of those straight, white, ally women who centered themselves in topics of race and sexuality, but most were well-meaning, in the end. At least, I had thought they were until I found myself staring into the dark eyes of a bodiless human.

"Meg! We've been waiting for you!" I heard Professor Smith say.

In my numbness, I didn't realize she was talking to me, because she used the stupid nickname a different professor had given me in my freshman year because my real name, Megis, even with the Americanized spelling, was too hard for him to pronounce. Everyone at the university called me Meg now.

I realized she was speaking to me when she took off my puffy coat, hung it on an acorn hook on the wall, looped her arm with mine, and led me into the living room where the other students had gathered. I didn't even fight it, my body not remembering how to make choices of its own. My brain stuck on the male head with the deep-set, dark eyes, like my brain was a DVD with a scratch on it.

Her living room was large and imposing with a giant marble chess set near the arched windows, a stone hearth (the mantel of which was covered in tourist souvenirs from holidays abroad), a Persian-style rug, and vintage-looking sofas and chairs that didn't seem at all comfortable. And there were heads. Heads of every shape, every color, every hairstyle. Male heads, female heads, nonbinary heads. It looked like every college pamphlet sent to prospective students, to show the "diversity" of their institution.

But even more noticeable than the heads was the empty space above that fireplace. There was no break in the watching eyes except for this one location, the only white wall. It felt naked and incomplete, and I couldn't look at that vacant space without feeling a sense of shame, like Professor Smith had come to the party without any pants and I was gawking at her bare legs and underwear.

"Look, everyone! Meg's here. We're all together at last," my professor said.

The other students, thirteen total, smiled and waved at me, said various greetings and then returned to whatever conversation they were currently involved in. One of my classmates, the only other BIPOC student, was missing. Where was she? We didn't know each other that well, but I could at least count on her to have my back.

I was not close with anyone else at the party. I was a Native scholarship student who spent all her free time working or doing homework. They were all white students born into privilege. None of them was rude or racist or anything like that, but any time I spoke to them, we were both uncomfortable, trying to find things we had in common besides classes and our majors. They always wanted to talk about pop culture or classic white, American writers. I knew little pop culture and had only read Emerson and Melville and Fitzgerald when it was a course assignment. And they had never read Silko or King or Momaday, had only heard of Erdrich but never read her, and knew one or two Harjo poems. Our conversations would move to the weather within the first five minutes.

Professor Smith looked at me, eyebrows raised, her lips still set in that perfect little smile. She was waiting for something from me. What did she want? My brain moved slowly, processing, trying to move past that initial shock. But I still could not remember how normal conversations were supposed to go, what she could possibly be expecting me to say when her home was a diversity graveyard. My eyes flitted away from her and back to the fireplace and that empty wall.

"You must be in high demand," Professor Smith prompted me, squeezing my arm tighter in hers. "I'm so glad you were finally able to grace us with your presence."

An apology. The most basic of human interactions. That's what she wanted.

"So sorry for being late, Professor," I said. I could barely even feel the words forming on my robotic lips. My eyes were locked on the head to the left of the fireplace. A Black woman with a full afro. Her eyes were wide, unnaturally wide, as if in terror, but someone had smoothed the rest of the expression off her face, tried to make her look serene. Only her eyes revealed the truth. "I had a shift tonight."

"Ah, that's right! Apart from being an excellent student and writer, you're also a dedicated member of the working class! How are you liking your job, dear?"

She walked over to the built-in bar and poured a drink.

"Fine, yeah. Just got promoted to waitress," I said. I couldn't move my gaze from the Black woman, as if we were in a staring contest.

Professor Smith walked back over to me, two drinks in hand. "Well, that's excellent news, dear! Congratulations. At what establishment do you work again?"

She pressed a glass of white wine into my grip. She didn't ask if I was of age. And I wasn't. But still, on instinct, I brought the glass to my lips. It was so full and my hands so shaky that I nearly spilled it on me.

"Alfonso's on Main and Milwaukee," I said.

"Oh, Alfonso's! I haven't been there in years. My husband and

I will have to go there again sometime soon. Maybe we'll even get you as our server. What days do you work?"

My gaze moved to the head only a few feet from the Black woman's. A smiling woman with tons of freckles. By smiling, I mean the lips were, showing off her perfectly straight teeth. The smile had no effect on her empty eyes.

"Almost every night, really," I said. I was surprised, surprised how ingrained small talk was in me. My mind still broken, still reeling, but my words able to act almost normal.

"Well, I applaud you, my dear," my professor said.

At that moment, a middle-aged man came over, wrapping his arm around her waist and murmuring something in her ear. She said something back and then turned to me and said, "Do excuse me, Meg. My husband needs my help with the hors d'oeuvres, but I'll be back in one moment so we can continue our chat."

I nodded, not saying anything. I was too busy silently counting the number of heads on her walls: twenty-three in total—that I could see, of course. Who knew how many lay behind closed doors or up the stairs. Was there one directly across from her bed, watching over her and her husband as they slept, like some demented crucifix you would find in Catholic bedrooms? I took a long, deep drink of my wine.

I should leave. This was my chance to escape, to run. I looked at the other students clustered in the living room, trying to see if anyone else was going to make a break for it too. They were all laughing and smiling. No one was looking at the heads. No one seemed bothered or on edge. All of them acted like they did in class. Was it in my imagination? Why was no one else upset? Did they know something I didn't? Had Professor Smith explained the heads before I got there? Maybe they were leftover Halloween decorations—even though we were well into December. She was a busy woman. I'm sure her husband was busy too. Maybe they just never got around to taking them down. They looked too real to be decorations, but I guess if they lived in a house like this, she could splurge on Halloween décor.

One of my classmates, a boy named Trevor, filled the space next to me that Professor Smith had vacated. Trevor and I were both sophomores with the same major—English. We had all the same classes, and he always sat next to me. I was starting to suspect that Trevor saw me as more than just a friend and classmate. He was a nice enough guy and pretty smart too, but I wasn't looking for a relationship. And even if I were, Trevor wasn't the one I would go for. How to put this nicely . . . while handsome in a conventional way, Trevor lacked original thought. He could quote any scholar and almost every novel ever written, but the moment you asked him to think something or say something that hadn't been handed to him, Trevor looked like he was going to have an aneurysm, his entire face bone white and his eyes flicking back and forth rapidly.

"Hey, Meg, how's it going? Great house, right?" he said now.

"Yeah, sure," I said, then leaned closer so no one could overhear and dropped my voice. "Um hey, don't you think some of the decorations are a bit . . . odd?"

He looked around the living room, his bushy brows raised. "What are you talking about?"

"The heads, Trevor, the heads."

"Oh, those. One of a kind, aren't they? Some of the seniors told me about them at that English major party. I guess you weren't there, were you? You never hang out with us, but I bet you're pretty busy with work and all. Well, apparently, she's been collecting them ever since she started teaching. Crazy, right? I was never good at collecting. Do you remember those collect all fifty state quarter things from when we were kids? I would get like ten, and then I would end up spending them on candy or something. It's amazing she's been able to keep this up for like what—twenty-five, thirty years? I could never."

What else had I expected from Trevor? It was a good thing he hadn't been born in Nazi Germany.

I looked around at my other classmates, sure one of them had to be more reasonable than Trevor, had to realize that we had all just stepped into the den of a serial killer and probably were not leaving here alive. But there was still no sign of mounting panic in their eyes. All of them were laughing, chatting, seeming to be having the time of their lives. What the fuck was the matter with them?

"Trevor," I said, "you're a . . . sensible guy, right? Doesn't it concern you where she got the heads?"

He gave me a look that clearly said that he thought *I* was the crazy one. "Why would it? Sam said—you know Sam, right? Junior, lots of curly red hair? Well, Sam said Professor Smith loves telling the story of each and every one of the heads. There are even little plaques under them that tell a bit about how Professor Smith knew them and acquired them. It's really fascinating stuff."

I set my wineglass down with a bang on an end table. Two of my classmates glanced over. Some of the white wine splashed onto the carpet, and for a brief moment, I was happy it was white and not red. Then I remembered that I was currently at risk of being murdered and there were more pressing things than me staining the carpet of my professor's white-picket-fenced home.

"Holy shit, Trevor! Did you not just hear yourself? 'Knew them?' 'Acquired them?' Trevor, she murdered them!" I hissed.

He laughed. That was it. It was the last straw. I couldn't stay here. While everyone else might think this was normal or cool or whatever, I did not want to stand around talking about writers as dead people watched over us.

"No, she didn't, Meg," Trevor said. "You're starting to sound just like Tracee. She wasn't here more than five minutes before she dipped. The heads freaked her the fuck out."

So that's where Tracee was. At least I knew it wasn't just me. I wish I had had the sense to get the fuck out right when I got there. But it wasn't too late. I could ask Professor Smith for a recommendation another day—or I could ask a different professor who didn't have the body parts of humans on their walls. That was probably the better option.

"I feel bad for Tracee," Trevor continued. "Professor Smith really took her leaving personally. She's definitely going to be harder on Tracee's paper than she would have been had Tracee just stayed. There's really nothing to be freaked out about. There were contracts signed. It was all above board."

I had been staring at the front door, trying to think of a nice way to end my conversation with Trevor. My head whipped back toward him.

"Wait, she hasn't submitted our grades yet?" I asked.

Trevor didn't seem to hear me. "Really, you should learn about all this from Professor Smith. Oh, there she is. Hey, Professor Smith! Can you come over here a second?"

Professor Smith had just returned to the living room, carrying a tray of hors d'oeuvres. She set them down on the bar. Trevor waved at her, motioning her to come over to us. I smacked his hand out of the air, holding it down at his side. "Trevor, don't!" I said.

But it was too late. She was already walking in our direction and blocking the way to the front door.

"Yes, Trevor?" she asked.

"Yeah, Meg was wondering about the heads. Some of the seniors told me about it, but you know Meg. Always so many questions," Trevor said, pushing me toward our professor. "I thought it might be best if you told her all about it."

I gave her a tight smile, trying to look normal and calm, but I knew I looked more constipated than anything. "No, no, I'm fine. I don't know what Trevor is talking about. I was just saying you have a beautiful home and a . . . unique sense of décor, that's all. Nothing else."

Professor Smith smiled widely at me, her gray eyes glistening with excitement. She grabbed my forearm and pulled me to her, her wedding ring digging into my skin. "Oh, Meg, I'm so glad you asked! Yes, I would be happy to tell you all about my collection. Let's start from the first head, shall we?"

"No, no, it's fine," I said. "I'm sure you have more important things to do."

She laughed. "Don't get me started on that. I'm so behind on my grading, but that's not important right now. Nothing would make me happier than spending some time with you."

She started pulling me toward a pair of swinging double doors. I sent Trevor a terrified, pleading look, but he had already joined a conversation with two other sophomore English majors and wasn't paying attention to me anymore. For weeks now, I had been catching him staring at me, and the one time I wanted him to be looking he wasn't. I tried to make eye contact with some of the other students, but as usual, I couldn't get their notice. It was like I didn't even exist to them.

On the other side of the swinging double doors was a giant, completely white kitchen. Not a stain to be seen on the counters or the white tiled floors. The only color was the head directly above the table in the breakfast nook.

"That," Professor Smith said, pointing at the head, "is Ji-Yoo Baek. He's the first student I ever helped. He was an international student from South Korea. An excellent writer. Wrote some of the best stories I've ever read. His parents wanted him to pick a major that could help him make money—what parent ever wants their child to major in English? However, through my encouragement and assistance, he chose to get his degree in Creative Writing, and before he had even graduated, I helped him sign with an agent."

I felt sick. I stared at the oak table instead of looking at the head. Knowing the story, knowing the man's promise made this worse. Made it harder to look into his dead eyes.

"He published two excellent collections before he ended up here. I have a few extra signed copies in my library, I believe, if you would like one," she said.

"No, I'm good," I said.

"Nonsense, I'll get you some copies before you leave. Such an excellent boy, he was. Shame he couldn't have produced more. But sometimes dying early helps. Gives your notoriety an extra boost."

At least he had accomplished something before he died. At least he had a legacy. That was better than dying as a no-name server. I squeezed my eyes, tried to force that horrible thought from my mind. I was no better than Professor Smith.

We stood there, her hand gripping my arm, for a few more minutes. She stared at the man's head, and I looked anywhere but at him. There was a suffocating blanket of silence pressing down around us like we were in a church. There was a soft, nearly loving look on her face—almost like how mothers look at their children. Almost. But the motherly look had fused with something warped and rapacious. Like Scrooge McDuck when he sees a pile of money. Or like a wiindigoo from my tribe's stories. And like the cannibals from our tales, she had grown a taste for taking human lives, and she wanted more. Hungered for it. Never to be satisfied.

After the prayerlike moment was done and that greedy look started to melt from her eyes—just a little bit—she took me back out into the living room where the rest of the students had gathered around to watch Trevor and another boy play a game of chess.

Only among a group of academics would a stupid game of chess get that much attention.

Professor Smith didn't pause by the students, didn't let me go to them. Instead, she pulled me from head to head, telling me their names and what it was she had done that led to her accessorizing her home with them—introductions, encouragements, mentoring, letters of rec, loans. There was nothing she hadn't done. And all of it ended the same way.

I could have made a break for it. Yanked my arm out of her grasp and ran, left all my stuff behind. I definitely could have outrun her in my black no-slip shoes. It probably would have been the smart thing to do. But I couldn't just leave. This wasn't about a maybe-internship anymore. She hadn't filed our grades yet. One bad grade could sink my GPA, could lose me my scholarship and place at the university, and then I would be stuck working at Alfonso's until I made one mistake too many, and they let me go. And then what would I do? Get a job at McDonald's? At Walmart? No, no, no. I couldn't do that. I was the first person in my family to go to college, and I was the only Native at the school. If I failed, if I screwed up, it would be like saying my people didn't belong in that environment, didn't deserve education and better jobs. So I couldn't leave. Instead, I had to stand there, plaster on a smile, and listen to her stories. My shaking right leg my only giveaway.

It was when she was telling me about the tenth head that I realized she never told me how they died. Never said who did it or how it was done. In my mind, I imagined them walking across a stage in cap and gown and kneeling down, resting their head in a guillotine. Professor Smith stood above them smiling, holding the guillotine's rope delicately in her dainty hands. I couldn't bring myself to imagine the rest.

When she had told me the story of each and every one of the twenty-three heads in her living room, all of them similar in age, she led me to those uncomfortable looking sofas. The other students were still gathered around the chess board, chatting to one another as they watched Trevor come closer and closer to victory.

Professor Smith sat down, pulling me with her, since her hand still gripped my arm. Seated, she let go of me at last, and she leaned back. She sighed, a little smile playing across her lips. I perched on the edge of the sofa, my right leg jiggling up and down.

"Each and every one of these people was my protégé," she concluded. "I helped them in their careers. And in return, they kindly donated their heads. A museum of my goodwill, really. Do you know that I have a head of all the major religions? That girl there? The smiling one with the freckles? Jewish. That boy in the far left corner? Muslim. The Christian I have shoved away in the guest bathroom upstairs, because we see those all the time. In my entryway, I keep the Buddhist. The Hindu and the Sikh are right over there by the bar. I have all the sexualities too: gay, lesbian, bisexual, transgender, queer, asexual, straight. You know, all the mainstream ones. I also have almost all the races. Just missing one. I have a spot picked out for that lucky person."

She looked to the empty space above the mantel.

"A prime location," she said. "For my great white whale. Figure of speech, of course. The Christian upstairs is white. Plus a few others down here. I don't need any more of those."

Across the room, Trevor moved his queen, taking the other boy's only remaining bishop. Professor Smith was staring at me, waiting for me to ask what her great white whale was. She was trying to draw me closer, for me to take the bait, but I wouldn't be like my uncle's northern. I wasn't going to be pulled into her boat.

"Aren't you curious what I'm missing?" she asked.

"It's late," I said, standing up. "I should be going."

There was nothing wrong with making a polite exit. She couldn't downgrade me for that. I had stayed, listened to her stories, been a good enough guest. She would have to understand that I was exhausted—work all day and then a party after? Anyone could see why I didn't want to stay.

But she stood with me, reaching out and resting a hand on my shoulder. "Nonsense, Meg. You only just got here forty minutes ago, and you haven't even had something to eat yet."

It couldn't have been only forty minutes. It felt like so much longer.

"Thank you for a lovely evening, but I'm exhausted. And not hungry," I said and tried to move toward the front door.

"I insist you eat," she replied, staring directly into my eyes. I looked away, down to her pointed-toe heels. "Charles!"

Her husband appeared at my side with a small plate covered in various hors d'oeuvres. He was standing between me and the exit, and his wife was standing between me and the windows. He smiled at me, that same sort of hungry look in his eyes that his wife had, and pushed the plate into my hands.

"Eat, eat," Professor Smith said and shoved me back down onto the sofa. The force of it caused me to spill several deviled eggs. "You must be famished, all that hard work at the restaurant. On your feet all day. It must be exhausting. A girl as intelligent as you, as talented as you, shouldn't have to do all that manual labor. You should be doing something more productive, more suited to your talents."

She sat down next to me again but much closer this time. Her knee pressing into my thigh. The armrest of the sofa shoved into my back. I felt like a leaf in fall, collected and pressed between pages to preserve it. Keeping it from continuing the life cycle: breaking down and fertilizing the soil so something new can grow from it.

"A girl like you," she said, her voice barely above a whisper, "is rare, Meg. So hard to find. There's only one like you in the entire university. Did you know, in my thirty years at this institute, I've seen only one other? They slipped right through my grasp then. I won't make that mistake again. This time it will be different. For us."

She looked back up, to that blank white space above the mantel. "Did you know my collection actually inspired some of my colleagues to start their own? Dr. Ludwig, you know him, correct? Well, he has an absolutely wonderful collection, but he has the full, stuffed bodies. You really get a good sense of who they were before when you have the whole body. Especially since Dr. Ludwig made sure the taxidermy modeled their poses off photos of them from when they were alive. Really excellent work. They feel almost like people."

She reached over and took a salmon puff off my plate. She rolled it between her fingers, still staring at the white space. Across the way, Trevor knocked over the other boy's king. The other students laughed and clapped, slapping Trevor on the back. Trevor beamed.

"He has all the races, Meg. Every single one. Bagged himself that great white whale."

Professor Smith looked at me with those gray eyes. A wiindigoo stared out.

"But enough about me and my ambitions. Let's talk about you, dear. You're such an amazing writer. With the right person on your side, I could see your name being among the greats. Can't you?"

My lips were pursed with another excuse, something about family visiting, about having to meet them at the airport. My body straining, squirming to escape the pin of her legs. I went still, and the half-formed excuse fizzled away as her words sunk in. I pictured it for a moment: Erdrich, Orange, Cloud. Megis Cloud, one of the three Native fiction writers that nearly anyone, even non-Natives, could name off the top of their heads. There was nothing more that I wanted in the world. I hadn't even realized I wanted it until that moment, until she dared me to dream. Now I couldn't stop picturing it. I leaned back and bit into a tartlet.

"I know how difficult university life can be," she said, "for someone from a . . . diverse background. Is there anything I can do to help? So hard to get anywhere on your own these days. Life is always easier with a friend, isn't it?"

She popped that salmon puff into her mouth, chewed, and then smiled at me.

Amber Blaeser-Wardzala is an Anishinaabe writer, beader, fencer, and Jingle Dress Dancer from White Earth Nation in Minnesota. A current MFA candidate in fiction at Arizona State University, her writing is published or forthcoming from *The Iowa Review*, *Passages North*, *Tahoma Literary Review*, *CRAFT*, and others. Blaeser-Wardzala is a 2022 Tin House fellow and a 2021 fellow for the inaugural Women's National Book Association Authentic Voices Program. In 2022, her novel in progress was shortlisted for the Granum Foundation Prize. She is the current nonfiction editor for *Hayden's Ferry Review*. Find her on Twitter and Instagram @amber2dawn.

LIMBS

WAUBGESHIG RICE

A mid-autumn gust rustled the last browning leaves from the trees as evening approached. The branches swayed gently, animating the landscape around the two men traversing the rugged terrain that one called Anishinaabe Aki and the other called Ontario. Makwa stepped carefully over the deadfall and rocks that appeared to blend in the dull gray of the deepening dusk. A few steps behind him, Carter's feet clumsily snapped twigs and rustled fallen leaves, amplifying their procession to the otherwise silent forest.

At any other time of day, Makwa would have tried to temper the other man's gait in case of nearby game, but with the sun now below the horizon, they were winding down a long day of scouting. Fatigue kept them on a hushed path back to the cabin, much to Makwa's relief. The man he led talked too much when he wasn't tired.

"It should be just over that ridge." Carter broke the silence, reassuring himself of the way that Makwa already knew. The big fur trading company built the log cabin decades earlier and abandoned it shortly after traders went farther west. Here in the late-nineteenth century, land encroachment by settlers was empowered and encouraged by the newly confederated country called Canada, at the expense of people like Makwa, his community, and the land they called home.

Makwa looked from the darkening ground up to the line of bare trees on the incline ahead of them. The last of the faint white daylight in the west silhouetted the cragged, empty branches of the season. He watched the plume of his breath soften the dark lines of the trees, and he wiggled his fingers to push warmth into his hands.

The two men crested the hill and sauntered down the other side to the cabin. Makwa and his family sometimes used it for shelter from storms on their hunting excursions. The one-room structure was nestled among pine trees on a small plateau, and they could make out only the subtle pitch and the logs of the outside walls in the dusk. Carter stepped in front of Makwa to lead the way up the few steps of the porch and through the front door. He pulled the wooden portal open and stomped inside, while Makwa eased his feet onto the planks of the entrance.

Before he could set down his rifle, he heard the pop of a match and watched Carter guide the flame into an oil lamp on the table at the far end of the room. He cupped the dwindling flame in his calloused hand, illuminating the light brown, scruffy beard on his jaw, and walked across the room to light another lamp on a low shelf. A faint orange glow washed the room, and each man took off his hefty wool jacket and bent to untie black boots, which constricted swollen feet after a long day of walking the rocky shoreline and rugged inland around the big lake. Carter was surveying the land for a company down south that wanted to build an all-purpose outpost for logging, fishing, fur trading, and potential mining, and Makwa had been hired as his local Anishinaabe guide.

Both stripped down to the long-sleeved undershirts and suspenders that held up their heavy pants. Makwa brushed his long black hair from his eyes and crouched by the woodstove to start a fire. Carter ran a hand through his shaggy brown hair and dropped a notebook on the scratched and dented wooden table. He turned to grab a tall bottle of whiskey from the shelf behind him and tapped it twice on the table beside the journal, as if to summon his counterpart. He nodded at Makwa as he pulled out his chair, which creaked along the wooden floor.

A language barrier kept conversations between the two men brief. Makwa knew enough English to guide and advise the visitor, but Carter didn't know Anishinaabemowin, the language spoken on this land since well before the Europeans arrived just a few short centuries prior. He made no attempt to learn and inquired only about the surrounding resources. Given that, the men bonded over very little, and found few opportunities to speak affably. Carter was often impatient and commanding, while even-tempered Makwa carried himself mindfully.

Satisfied with the growing blaze in the black stove, Makwa closed the iron door, and his wool socks shuffled along the boards to join Carter at the table.

"Good walk today," Carter proclaimed.

"Hmmmm," Makwa responded.

"Don't think this is the spot, though."

Makwa shrugged, and Carter opened his notebook to glance at his scribbled observations. He flipped back through a few pages of notes from their excursions over the two previous days in other directions. Carter let out a frustrated sigh and assertively shut the tattered cover. He reached for the bottle and pulled off the cap as he leaned back in his chair. He tipped the brown liquid into his mouth for three solid gulps and slammed it back onto the table.

Makwa looked unflinchingly into his blue eyes, and Carter nodded and urged the bottle over to him.

Makwa watched a tiny bead of the liquor travel down the side of the bare bottle. The familiar scent burned into his nostrils. The wind outside picked up and pushed against the door. "Drink up, Mikey," Carter commanded. "We gotta talk."

"My name is Makwa," he corrected his counterpart in a stern monotone.

"I'll call ya what I'll call ya. That Indian name won't do ya no good outside this bush, anyway. Drink up."

Carter's eyes were glossy already, after just a few swigs. The wear of the day's trek had tired them both. They had eaten a robust shore supper of whitefish and fried potatoes on a smaller lake to the south, but their stomachs were once again sparse this late into the evening, and the alcohol moved quickly.

Makwa gently wrapped his tanned fingers around the bottle and hoisted it to his mouth. The burn plunged from his throat down to his gut. He noticed again the black rot between Carter's teeth as a smirk opened at the side of his mouth. It was the same unnerving grin he bore earlier when bludgeoning the fish they pulled from the lake for their meal. His lips seem to pull tighter with each strike of the stone in his hand into the small skull. Makwa carefully slid the bottle back across the table to him.

They repeated the back and forth in silence until the bottle neared its halfway point. Each man sat back more loosely in his chair. Carter cleared his throat after another swig. "We been out here three days," he said. "You ain't shown me much."

"There's fish in all these lakes," Makwa rebutted. "You'd see the moose if you weren't too loud walking around."

"I told ya, the company don't give a shit about moose. They only wanna set up here if they can dig gold outta the ground or turn these trees into money. And they don't look that big around here."

"If you cut them all down, you won't see moose no more."

"That won't be my problem."

Makwa's dark eyes scowled at Carter, and his face contorted in response. They both swayed slightly in their seats, their posture softened by the booze.

"You got some mouth on you, boy," the visitor uttered.

Branches scratched against the log walls as the wind began to howl.

"You got no respect for this place," the host replied. "You only want to make money here."

"You're goddamn right I do!"

Makwa clenched his jaw before sweeping the whiskey bottle off the table in a fit of anger. It bounced across the floor and landed on its side, spilling the pungent liquor across the scratched planks and into the cracks. Carter dove from his chair to salvage what was left, tipping the bottle upright. He stumbled forward, trying to get back to his feet, and grunted as he fell into the opposite wall. The metal tools that hung on pegs clanged together in a sobering cacophony. Makwa turned in his chair to square up with him, anticipating Carter's rage.

Carter rose, and in the faint lamplight, Makwa noticed the bulging whites of his eyes before a fist hooked into his jaw with a crack. The blow knocked Makwa to the floor, and in a drunken daze, he struggled to get to his hands and knees. Carter cocked back his leg and drove his foot into Makwa's side, knocking the air out of his lungs and seizing his diaphragm. He writhed on the floor, struggling for air, and just as he was able to suck a panicked breath into his windpipe, another kick to the face knocked him out cold.

When Makwa opened his eyes, his sagging head was pounding. He struggled to straighten his neck and blink his vision into focus. He was back in the chair, but couldn't move his arms. Twine chafed at his wrists, tied behind the wooden spindle. He jerked his shoulders outward to free his hands, but his numb fingers suggested that was futile. He looked ahead to see that now-familiar rotten smirk leering back at him.

The wooden legs creaked on the floor as Carter pushed his chair back to stand. He stepped around the table to approach Makwa, placing his palm on the tabletop, and leaned in. He kept his other hand behind his back.

"That's my last bottle," he said. "Good thing I'm getting the fuck outta here tomorrow. I can get more."

Makwa gagged at the scavenger's pungent alcohol breath and the close sight of his weathered face, pocked and lined with scars that the wiry beard couldn't fully conceal.

"You wasted my time here," Carter continued. "I dunno what you're trying to hold on to. But it's useless. We're coming no matter what. There ain't shit you can do about it."

Makwa swallowed hard to prepare to speak, but his swollen tongue in his dry mouth held him back. He could feel the wood grain on his bare soles as he shuffled his feet. Makwa craned his neck down to see if Carter had stripped him of more than his socks, but his wool pants were intact. His gaze rose until it met Carter's vile grin.

"That's right, you look at me when I'm talking to you," he said. "We're gonna get rid of all of you before too long. Just gettin' in our way."

Carter nodded and turned to grab the bottle with the last of the booze he'd managed to save. He concealed something in his other hand.

Makwa coughed to rumble his voice louder. "What do you want

from me?" he uttered hoarsely. He watched the settler's greasy brown hair dangle as Carter threw his head back to down more of the whiskey.

Carter slammed the bottle on the table, then twisted his torso to face Makwa, allowing his hidden hand to fall in front of his hip. The orange flame in the lamp on the other side of the room reflected off a polished dagger in his grip, curved to a menacing point. He pivoted his feet and raised the blade, stepping slowly to the captive.

"Bekaa!" Makwa shouted. Carter towered over him with a steely gaze under his furrowed brow. "Bekaa!" repeated Makwa. He shut his mouth once he felt the blade gently press against his cheek. Makwa locked his eyes straight ahead, careful not to budge. Carter lowered himself slowly to the floor in front of the chair, keeping a menacing stare on his captive. He looked down and grabbed Makwa's foot, pinning it to the floor with a strenuous grip.

"Gegwa! Gegwa!" shrieked Makwa, kicking both of his feet to free them of Carter's grasp and forcing him to drop the knife. Calmly, Carter wrapped one hand around Makwa's shin, lifted the heel with his other hand and twisted it to the outside. A loud pop came from Makwa's knee and he yelped in pain. His lower leg hung limp, immobilized by torn ligaments.

Carter methodically gripped the other leg in the same way and contorted the heel to cripple Makwa's other knee. Tears peaked on his cheekbones and streamed down to his jaw as his howls grew. Carter picked up the dagger and moved his hands back to the first foot. He pinned it firmly to the floor, and Makwa was unable to free it this time. His knees burnt in pain. The blade sliced through the flesh and bone of his big toe, and blood pumped in short spurts onto the floor as Carter pulled it away. He stood and dropped the bleeding appendage onto the table.

Makwa wailed and sobbed, squirming in his seat. He squeezed

his eyes shut and gritted his teeth. Carter watched him writhe for a moment, and without sound or expression, descended once again to remove the rest of the toes. One by one, he chopped the smaller digits from the limb, as Makwa's pitch elevated into a steady distressing resonance that Carter seemed to ignore entirely. The bones of the supporting toes snipped off more easily and bled less, but Makwa's pain and fear only escalated.

"Please," he began to petition his attacker, "please stop. What do you want? We'll leave. We'll go north from here and never bother you again."

Carter wiped his bloody palm on the outside of his thigh. He looked down at the stained blade and flipped it back and forth in the light.

"Please!" Makwa shouted now, but Carter just shook his head. He avoided eye contact with Makwa and knelt in the blood as the bound man began screaming in his language again for the torture to stop.

The sharp blade dug into the wooden floor as the big toe on the other crippled foot fell away. Makwa only gasped now, struggling to bring air into his body. He gagged on his swollen tongue, choking on his terror as his eyes scrambled around the room for anything to focus on, to distract him from this mutilation. But his eyes blurred and went dark, and he could no longer make sense of his surroundings or distinguish the features of the man he had guided through his homelands.

Carter placed the severed toes from the second foot onto the table. He dropped the knife beside them, and the hollow clunk of the wooden handle snapped Makwa's thrashing head to attention. He looked at his attacker standing before him, who appeared bigger as the walls of the room seemed to close in on them both. He stared Makwa right in the eyes, and extended a fist in his direction. He turned it up, and uncurled his fingers to reveal the last baby toe in his palm. It looked pale in the orange light, drained of its blood that stained the cracks of Carter's hand.

Makwa's eyes bulged again. The burning agony in his limbs flared together in constant torment. His blood trickled from the stumps where his toes were cut onto the floorboards, staining them a deep purple that would remain for as long as this torture chamber stood. Carter rolled the last toe over in his palm with his thumb. He bounced it lightly as he scanned it, then looked up to find Makwa's eyes. The colonizer's dark pupils squeezed out the blue of his irises in the dim light. He brought his palm up slowly and then popped the toe into his mouth. Makwa heaved and gagged as Carter chewed slowly on the flesh and bone.

He caught his breath, but couldn't control the rapid panic in his lungs. Carter kept his gaze on him until he swallowed, stoic yet threatening. He stepped around the chair to the wall with the tools that he had crashed into when he stumbled to save the bottle. Makwa's eyes followed him. Carter pulled a handsaw from the wall and pulled it close to his face to inspect it. The lamplight beaded on the sharp edges of the saw's teeth. Satisfied, he walked back around the other side of the table and seated himself in the chair he'd taken earlier.

"Here's what I'm gonna do." Carter broke his silence as he placed the saw in front of him. "I'm gonna take your limbs. Bit by bit. Gonna start with your feet. Then the rest of your legs. Then I might need your fingers. Somewhere in there, I'm gonna take your eyes."

Makwa felt the sweat running down his sides. He looked down at his drenched clothes and saw for the first time that he had pissed himself. After screaming relentlessly, he no longer had a voice to protest or negotiate. His bottom lip trembled and his head shook frantically.

"And if you ain't dead yet, I'm gonna take your heart, and probably your lungs, and whatever other guts I can take. I'm gonna take you apart piece by piece. You think this is slow? Wait till you really get to know me.

"But that won't be the last of me. The rest of your family will get to know me, too. And so will their kids. And their kids' kids. I'm gonna pick you all apart. Starting with them limbs and then . . ."

A heavy thud at the door distracted him. He looked up, and the knock sounded again, twice. Makwa remained still, not wanting to draw his attacker's attention back to him. They heard the noise again, which sounded like a branch knocking against the door in the wind, but in a steady rhythm.

Carter looked back at Makwa. "Don't try anything," he commanded, and then stood to inspect the source of the strange noise. The floor creaked under his steps. He threw the door open to reveal only the darkness of night. Nothing was visible from the threshold.

Carter stepped out onto the small porch to look around. A strong gust blew across, broaching the enclave of evergreen trees that surrounded the cabin. It was the last sound Carter heard before a thick, broken branch fell from one of the taller pines above and struck him on the head. He fell forward, unconscious, and rolled down the slight slope, coming to a halt on the flat ground between the trees.

His senseless body lay there only a moment before a root shot up from the glade and wrapped around his leg. Another snaked around his torso, while more still bound him to the surface of the Earth. The roots constricted his body with tremendous force, and Carter awoke to this trap and screamed.

But the terror-stricken scream was short-lived, as another root impaled the back of Carter's head, shooting out his mouth on the other side. Another thrust upward through his chest before curving back around his torso. As quickly as the trees' roots confined him, they pulled him into the ground to reclaim his matter for the land itself. The hole that opened to devour the body closed, and the ground covered itself back over to erase the settler's presence.

The wind rattled the door. The trees eased their movement, and the rustle of the gusts eventually died down. A calm fell. Makwa's heartbeat softened, and he carefully wriggled his wrists from the drunkenly tied twine, loosened in the struggle. The wooden chair creaked as he turned to look outside, glimpsing only serene darkness through the gaping portal. He tightened his lips and nodded.

He tipped the chair to collapse to the ground, bracing for the impact that paled compared to the burning pain in his legs. His palms caressed the grains of the boards as he dragged himself to the bed to pull off a wool blanket, which he draped around his legs. His brother would come looking for him at dawn. He drew in a long breath and waited for sunrise.

Waubgeshig Rice (Anishinaabe) grew up in a Wasauksing First Nation on Georgian Bay. His experiences there inspired his first short story collection, *Midnight Sweatlodge*, which won an Independent Publishers Book Award in 2012. His debut novel, *Legacy*, followed in 2014. A French translation was published in 2017. His latest novel, *Moon of the Crusted Snow*, was released in October 2018 and became a national bestseller. Its sequel, *Moon of the Turning Leaves*, is forthcoming in 2023. He lives in Sudbury, Ontario, with his wife and three sons.

ACKNOWLEDGMENTS

We want to thank all the supporters on Twitter and elsewhere who got the ball rolling and have cheered us on for years now. This project also couldn't have happened if all the established writers told us "no"—they all said yes, and were gracious with their support during the whole journey. Truly grateful as well to our open-call readers, David Tromblay and Bear Lee. There were a lot of stories, and we appreciated them all. The process had its stressful nights, and without some key people, we could have lost it. We need to thank our agent, Rachel Letofsky, right up front as well as our agency and all the fine folks at CookeMcDermid. Thanks for all your support and introducing us to Anna Kaufman and the wonderful crew at Penguin Random House on both sides of the border; up north/ over east folks needing our thanks are our McClelland & Stewart and Random House Canada teams Stephanie Sinclair, Jared Bland, Joe Lee, Sue Kuruvilla, Sarah Jackson, and Deirdre Molina; and down south at Vintage, our thanks to Kayla Overbey, Nancy B. Tan, Karen Thompson, Robin Witkin, Christopher Zucker, Perry De La Vega, Julie Ertl, Abby Endler, and Sophie Normil.

It's truly special to see this book with a simultaneous release across colonial borders.

Hard and not hard to believe this all came from a single tweet, but that's community.

From Shane: I'm beyond grateful to be at the forefront of a project like this that will hopefully spark many more to come. Ted's become my literary best bud, and I couldn't ask for a more solid coeditor for this undertaking. Thanks to my dad for reading countless drafts of my own story and helping bring family lore to the page, and thanks to my mom and grandma for pushing me to keep going and supporting my every move. Finally, a thank-you to my wife, Tori, who was by my side throughout the entirety of the thing, giving me advice, pep talks, and love.

From Ted: Shane, man, no way we could've done this without your heavy lifting. So cool to become literary best buds and hang out. To Poe, Barker, and King, and everyone filling those footsteps along with our dreams and nightmares. To Quasimodo and Frankenstein's monster, my early movie heroes who taught me that humans trying to create monsters become ones themselves. And to all those late-night sessions around the fire and in bars and hotel lobbies after *those* people have gone off to bed, and we can tell our stories that scare each other and make us laugh like no one else on earth. It's something else to be a monster-made man in a world of man-made monsters.

PERMISSIONS ACKNOWLEDGMENTS